The Witch from the Sea

A Novel

by

LISA JENSEN

Reno, Nevada

The Witch from the Sea

Beagle Bay Books,
a division of Beagle Bay, Inc.
Reno, Nevada
info@beaglebay.com

An earlier version of this book was published in German as *Die heimliche Piratin* (List, Munich; 1998).

Visit us at our website: http://www.beaglebay.com

Library of Congress Card Number: 2001089482

ISBN: 0-9679591-5-2

First American Edition

Printed in the United States of America

For the memory of my father, Art Jensen
the old salt
who always loved a good yarn

For my mother, Barbara Jensen,
who always knew I could do it

And for Jim,
who keeps me surprised

Acknowledgments

Thanks to my publishers, Jacqueline Church Simonds and Robin Simonds, for believing in this book, and to my editor, Vicki Hessel Werkley, for so skillfully midwifing it into existence. Thanks also to my brothers, Mike Jensen and Steve Jensen, my first and most constant readers, and to Vicki Bolam and Christine Borkowski, my most intrepid readers, for their stamina and good suggestions; to Jeanne Houston, for her early and endless encouragement; to cyber wizard Alan Luckow, whose generosity of time and labor guided me into the computer age; to "Mac Medic" Kevin Lewis for all those house calls and neverending tech and moral support; to Nancy Raney, for her eternally sympathetic ear; and to Lia Matera, whose professionalism, sound advice, undaunted good humor and hilarious emails inspire me every day.

The Witch
from the Sea

PROLOGUE

Boston, 1823

My first taste of freedom was almost my last. I very nearly balked at the blackness of the February night out beyond the iron gate and at the icy wind shrieking its warning in my ears. *Go back, foolish girl. There is no place for you out here.* But there was no place for me anywhere in Boston. Certainly not at the Worthen Female Academy; its forbidding stone face loomed in the dark behind me like the prison, the tomb it was. My only chance at freedom lay beyond the gate, and my passion for freedom was stronger than my fear; it only needed to be slapped and coaxed and bullied into life, like any infant thing.

A night-soil cart rumbled over the cobbles in the next street, the hollow clop of hooves echoing like the footsteps of ghosts. I was haunted by so many ghosts, everyone I had lost. Mama, dead in her childbed. Papa, lost to his rage. My half-brothers, both gone away. The iron froze to my bare hand as I gripped a bar, raised the latch, and nudged open the gate. I would go too, and I mustered the courage to push the heavy gate shut behind me and abandon myself to the night.

It was easier to move quietly without my usual armor of pantalettes and cumbersome skirts. I'd stolen this outfit of woollen trousers and greatcoat and coarse linen shirt from the servants' castoff clothing put by for the poor. I was tall for a girl of sixteen and possessed of no great delicacy of form or feature, as had been brought to my attention on many occasions. But those defects would help me, now. I ought to have cut my hair short as well, but my long, dark hair was all I had left of my mother; I would be like Samson without it—weakened, helpless, lost. So I had plaited it back and stuffed it under my collar. Stray Indians with long, plaited hair were not uncommon along the waterfront.

It was heretical to pose as a male, I knew—a crime against God, never mind the crime of theft. Yet more sins, more black marks against me in God's accounting book, beginning with the sin of my mother's tainted blood, that crippling defect for which there was no remedy. But I cared not. If goodness were to be forever denied me, I would embrace sin, and gladly. Five long years at Worthen had failed to improve me. My time there had been like a suffocating nightmare from which I was only now waking.

I heard again my Aunt Fiona's prim voice ringing all round the vast and polished rooms of her Boston townhouse as I cowered before her, alone and miserable. "I have no place to keep a child, here, Victoria," she told me. But I knew she had sheltered my fair-skinned brothers, my father's sons, when their mother died. Before he removed them to the country to start a new life on the farm with his new bride. His heathen bride. My mother. Had she only lived, had my Papa only kept his reason, I should not have been an orphan begging for my Aunt Fiona's charity.

"My brother has been sadly negligent in his paternal duties," Aunt Fiona went on. "But you will receive a proper Christian education at the Worthen Academy. When you learn some manners and accomplishments, in time . . . the other won't matter as much." I could see her appraising my dark hair and eyes. My otherness. "Remember, you are my niece. And your Papa was a good and respected man in this town, once. There is no shame in being your father's daughter."

Or my mother's. And I lifted my head and met my aunt's gaze. I was done with begging.

The memory of my aunt dissolved in the black night, replaced by the pink face, golden ringlets and vicious blue eyes of the prettiest, most well-bred young lady among my new classmates, accosting me in the stairwell. "Your mama was a heathen red-Indian witch who turned your papa crazy!"

I heard again the satisfying smack of my hand across her pale face. "My mama was better than all the simpering white women in Boston!" Which outburst landed me in the private study of a most furious Miss Jane Worthen to demand an apology I could in no way provide, not even to save my eternal soul.

"Do not imagine that because you are young and ignorant that you can escape the wrath of Almighty God," Miss Jane seethed. "Children are born in sin and depravity. Only Divine Grace can redeem you, and that is no easy goal to achieve. Passion is the work of the devil. Pride and anger must be rooted out, for they lead to wickedness. Piety and obedience lead to God's favor, yet these things alone cannot save you. Good works alone cannot save you. Nothing can save you from the fires of eternal damnation as long as there is depravity and wickedness in your heart."

How could it be wicked to defend the memory of my mother? Stony silence was my only response.

"You are in very grave danger, indeed, Miss MacKenzie," my captor warned. "You have more to repent than most, given the un-Christian circumstance of your birth. Purifying grace is a gift from God, through His Son, Jesus Christ. Only those who honestly repent their sins and renounce pride, passion and anger may receive it. I shall not punish you now; that is in God's hands. But remember, God sees everything you do. And He keeps excellent accounts."

Now, another ghost wavered into being before me in the black night: Bet, the upstairs chambermaid, my only friend. She'd been dismissed for her wanton passion for life, her wilful humor, her brazen disobedience. "Oh, Tory, don't you see what will happen?" she chided me on the day they sent her away. "They'll keep you here forever until you're just like them—a dried-up old maid without even the memory of a life to keep you warm!"

Of all the terrible things ever said to me at Worthen, that was the worst. Bet's words gnawed at me like a curse until I knew I would risk any punishment, any fate, to be free.

The wind gusted in the street as I hurried on, dead leaves and debris pattering along the cobblestones, whispering in the dark. When fierce winds blew, Mama said it was a giant imprisoned in the House of Winds, twisting and turning to be free. When blue lightning tore open the black sky, Mama said it was only Grandfather Thunderer frightening off the demons before he bestowed the gift of rain on the people of the earth. In Mama's stories, the gods were kind and loving—Turtle, who carried the world on his back, Sky Woman, who gave birth to Creator, who made all the creatures of the earth.

Now, the winking stars in the moonless black sky spied down on me like the thousand eyes of the God of Wrath. But I was done with repenting. They had never been able to drive the wickedness out of me. They could never make me ashamed of my mother.

I had lost so much—my family, my childhood, everyone who had ever loved me. But not myself, not yet. Anger, disobedience, passion—these were the only tools left me with which to fashion a life. If I still could. If there was still time. I would go far away from civilized Boston, somewhere the God of Wrath could never find me. There were ships leaving every day from the harbor: merchant ships and whaling ships, their decks crammed with every sort of sailor bound for every sort of place. One of my brothers had run away to sea on such a ship to make his fortune, as any boy may do. I didn't know starboard from larboard, but I knew only a ship would take me as far away from Boston as it was possible to go.

I hurried past the eerie rise of old Fort Hill and toward the pungent odor of brine and fish on the freshening breeze off India Wharf. It was the scent of freedom. Along the way, I committed the last sin of my civilized life. A small murder. Victoria MacKenzie died that night. But I was born.

BOOK I

TORY

Take a good heart and conterfeit to be a man.

As You Like It, Act IV, Scene iii.

CHAPTER 1

Blessed Providence

Perhaps I ought to have given the civilized world one more chance. But it was too late, now. What had been a dark bruise on the water far astern had now swollen into the ominous shape of a black schooner flying a black flag emblazoned with a white death's head and a blood red heart. Even I had been at sea long enough to know what that meant.

Our lading was too heavy to outrun the black ship. And as she came nearer, we could see all too plainly the wild man looming in her bows. His square brown face glared out from under a riotous tangle of black hair and silvershot beard; his burly frame was barely covered by tattered clothing fastened with a red sash. He gripped the forestay with one hand while the other pointed a long-barreled pistol into our midst, ready to fire on anyone foolish enough to resist. Other men every inch as dark and menacing lined the schooner's low rail as she came alongside our merchant brig, the *New Hope*, her cannons trained on our broadside.

"*Buenos dias, norteamericano,*" thundered the dark apparition in the bows, surveying us with a grimace of contempt. In careful, accented English, he added, "Heave to, *amigos*, or die." Diabolito.

Who had not heard of the notorious pirates of Cuba? Napoleon was gone, and with fewer warships on patrol, the Indies had become infested with these savage brethren calling themselves Diabolito or El Malo and known to murder at a whim and maim for sport. Even I had heard of them in far-off Boston, although like every other scrap of useful information learned at the Worthen Female Academy, I'd had to pick it up from the gossip of servants.

I'd known the *New Hope* was an unlucky berth from the moment the mate found me cringing and wretchedly seasick in the ship's boat—from my first sight of Captain Calhoun, her strutting little coxcomb of a master, who enforced his every whim with his trusty knotted cat. We'd already had three floggings, and we were not yet two weeks out of Boston, scarcely halfway to Barbados.

At least the men were too concerned with watching their own backs to pay much attention to me. Still, the effort it took to maintain my disguise was exhausting—binding my bosom under the loose, checkered merchant seaman's shirt sold to me on account from the slops chest, greasing back my hair, griming my face. Even in the relative privacy of the steerage— where I'd been banished to learn my duties from the steward— it required cunning to keep and use a bucket for a chamber pot when the steward was away or scavenge rags for my monthly bleeding.

The only place I felt at ease was aloft in the rigging. When I was first ordered to "lay aloft," I was terrified. All I perceived as the deck fell away below me was a roar in my head and the ecstatic urge to abandon myself to fate, to let go and fly. But I grew to relish my duties aloft as a kind of refuge—stowing, reefing and furling the sails, and tarring the lines, up where the wind was fresh and wild, and I could feel the life of the ship humming in the sticky lines. But back on deck, my dream of freedom could scarcely flourish in so bitter and dispirited a company. And now this. God would have his little joke.

The schooner's two raked-back masts were rigged fore-and-aft with two square topsails on her foremast for speed. Her decks were nearly flat, uninterrupted by coaches or quarter-deck but for a low cabin top astern; she was as light and sleek as a harrier, built for cunning. Her men were baying and hooting at the rail as their grappling hooks pulled our two ships close together. Their pistols, cutlasses and swords were at the ready, but we could offer little resistance; we were too bone-weary from the morning's battle with a squall that blew us far off course for Barbados and too near the Windward Passage and the Cuban coast.

The brawny black-haired demon with the red sash kept to his foredeck, calling out orders to the others in a rapidly cadenced tongue I took for Spanish. At his signal, the pirates swarmed aboard the *New Hope* like black ants engulfing a lump of sugar. Relieved of what few pitiful firearms the men could muster, our crew was lined up amidships.

When at last even Captain Calhoun ceased his useless blustering and adopted a picturesque attitude of defiance, the fierce pirate on the foredeck called down the length of his own ship.

"*Listo, Capitan!*"

"*Bueno.* Thank you, Mr. Nada." A man of middle height and solid build appeared on the low cabin top of the pirate ship and stood there, surveying the scene aboard the *New Hope.* There was not much to distinguish him from the others, but the fine scarlet waistcoat he wore over his open shirt and trousers. But the other pirates left off their talk and swung their attention to him. Even the black devil on the fore-deck, the one called Nada, appeared to wait for instruction.

"I leave you in command," the fellow addressed Nada. He caught hold of a taut line, leaped across to the rail of the *New Hope* and swung himself down to our deck.

I tried to shrink even deeper into the feeble shelter of my clothing, wedged into the line next to Mr. Adderly, the scowling mate. No doubt, he was trying to think of some way to blame the pirates on me. Yet, I could not help but steal a look at the buccaneer leader as he passed by, his complexion burned brown by the sun, his eyes as black and shiny as wet stone beneath thick, ragged brows. His brown hair was thinning on top and there were traces of silver in his shaggy side-whiskers, short pigtail and the long mustachios drooping down on either side of his clean-shaven chin. But his movements were quick and agile, his expression keen.

"Gentlemen," he announced, "I am Captain Hart of the *Blessed Providence,* and by now, I think, you can guess my business."

Not only was Captain Hart not Cuban, there was a trace of lyrical Scots burr in his speech that reminded me, fleetingly, of my father.

"It will go much better if you tell me now where your valuables are hidden," Captain Hart went on, affably, as if inviting us all for a drink at the tavern. "I'll have 'em in any event and resistance would be ill-advised."

"Valuables?" spat out Captain Calhoun. "We're a trading ship out of Boston for Barbados. Our only cargo is grain. There be no valuables."

The pirate captain turned to grin at Calhoun.

"Ah! But you see, Captain—you are the captain, are ye not?—I see a plain little merchantman out of Boston at this time of year, and I see a riddle. Why brave the cold of a waning Atlantic winter for grain? Where's the profit in it? It's early yet for the sugar season. What's the hurry? What have ye got to bargain with that won't keep 'til spring? Can ye solve this riddle?"

Calhoun was silent. The pirate captain strolled toward him, still smiling.

"Someone on this ship can answer my riddle, Captain, even if you cannot. My men are perfectly willing to cut out tongues until we find the one that talks. Or any other likely appendage."

At a glance from Hart, two pirates sprang upon Calhoun, one to hold him fast while the other yanked his right arm taut and flourished a cutlass above it.

"Your flogging hand, no doubt, Captain. Wouldn't want to lose that."

Jem, the cabin boy, squeaked beside him, and Calhoun growled, "Grain! Carving me up for mincemeat won't change that."

"Nor will it net me my prize," Hart agreed. "In my experience, threatening the captain is hardly the way to loosen the tongue of a common seaman. But there be other ways."

Captain Hart turned to Jem. "Come here, boy," he said, kindly, but Jem shrank back. The pirate captain stepped toward him and gently took the boy's chin in his hand, turning the small head slowly to one side. "Pity," he sighed. "One of these perfect ears must be defective . . . ."

His knife was out in the blink of an eye, teasing the crease behind Jem's ear while his hand slid down to grasp Jem's throat. Calhoun was still held in check by two pirates, but I saw in his iron-hard eyes that he had no intention of interfering. Whatever happened to his favorite boy, his greed was more compelling than his affection. The others looked merely dumbfounded. How could they answer the pirate's question when they didn't know, themselves? Only I knew.

Jem was like all the insufferable Boston girls I'd known at Worthen—fair-haired, petty and mean. But I had no wish to see him whittled down to gore before our eyes. And for what? To protect a few barrels of specie that were meant to purchase human slaves? Hardly a cause to die for.

"Captain Hart! Sir!" My voice was husky with apprehension as I struggled to keep it from wavering. All eyes swung toward me, and I felt Calhoun's like burning darts. "Captain, I know a riddle too, sir."

Hart dropped Jem and came to stand before me. "I love a good riddle, boy," he beamed, dark eyes sparkling. As keen as they were, they had not yet penetrated my disguise. I might yet bargain for another few minutes of life if I did not lose my nerve. Fortune must have had a reason to show me what I'd stumbled upon in the hold yesterday.

"There's some say a barrel of flour in the ship's lading is worth its weight in silver."

"That's a riddle?" Hart frowned. "Where's the joke?"

"No joke, sir. I've seen 'em."

Mr. Adderly's lean, wiry arm tensed against mine. It had been his order sent me into the hold yesterday, hoping to interrupt the captain and his boy; the mate was never content unless he was stirring up strife among the others. I dared not look into his face, but when I dropped my eyes, I saw his hand clench into a fist. The blue snake tattooed behind his knuckles bulged with fury.

"Flour," Captain Hart repeated.

I nodded. "In the lading."

The pirate captain barked a laugh and tossed off orders in Spanish to his men. A group of them went below, and it wasn't long before their cries of triumph echoing back up the hatchway told their captain they'd discovered his prize.

It took a while for the pirates to identify the flour barrels that contained hidden silver and haul them all up over to their compatriots on the black schooner. They helped themselves to the rest of the cargo, as well, and foraging teams went off to ransack the pantry and the galley—where they found little worth having—and Captain Calhoun's cabin, where they made off with bed linens, writing and charting equipment and several bottles of quality port.

Our crew was allowed to loiter amidships under the watchful eyes of an armed guard. I stayed clear of Captain Calhoun, who was still fuming and cursing and had not ceased to glare at me since I'd first opened my mouth. I knew it was his life savings I'd betrayed to the pirates, transferred into silver for the voyage to the Indies—where coin earned twice its weight among the cash-poor planters. I had overheard him explaining the scheme to Jem in the hold: to purchase slaves on his own account at auction in Barbados to barter for the highest grade of sugar when the crop came in. Beyond what the cargo of flour earned for the company, the profit would be all his. But that plan was dashed to pieces now, thanks to me, and the others made a great show of avoiding me, afraid to attract any overflow of the captain's wrath.

I wished I could shrink down to the merest atom adrift on the wind, free, with only the sea for company. I was reaching behind me for the support of the rail when my hand closed on damp cloth with hard muscle inside. Across the deck, Calhoun let fly another burst of invective, drawing the attention of the pirate guard, as my arm was twisted behind my back and the leathery elbow of Mr. Adderly snaked round my throat from behind.

"Never once thought old Pat Calhoun might have a partner in his venture, did you, boy?" the mate hissed in my ear. "Well, it's part my stake as you've just handed over to this Cuban scum. My years of work and toil you've thrown away. And I'm damned if I'll lose it all without some satisfaction for my money."

I could feel the rage coursing through Adderly's wiry frame, more potent than any weapon. I flailed back with my free arm, but struck only air. I kicked behind me, but I was off-balance as he dragged me toward the rail, and I couldn't put any weight behind the kick. His arm cinched ever tighter around my throat, and my mouth opened wide for air that would not come. My head was forced back and my eyes drank in the blue sky, going black around the edges like burning paper as the life was forced out of me, the final page of a life that had scarcely begun. In my suffocating frenzy, the blackness was forming into a face, calm and quizzical, surely the angel of Death. Then Adderly gurgled behind me, and I was shaken free to throw myself on the rail, gasping for air. Behind me, an enormous bald-headed, bare-chested African had Adderly by the throat with both hands. The mate's face was purple, but he had breath enough to dance in a rage, his feet scarcely touching the deck, writhing like a puppet in the black pirate's grasp.

"Hector, what in damnation . . . !" roared Captain Hart

as he came racing across the deck.

"Him be devilin' this boy." My savior shrugged.

"Are ye all right, lad?"

I managed a nod.

"Oh, aye, but you'll pay for this, Jones!" wheezed Adderly, "You rat-faced—"

"T'was you sent me into the hold in the first place!" I rasped back. "I'd never've seen the damn specie, otherwise!" With no little satisfaction, I saw Captain Calhoun's acid glare shift from me to Adderly, who blanched under its heat as Hector, the African, hauled him back to his fellows.

"Gentlemen, you disappoint me." The pirate captain glowered at them all. "I might have traded you your sorry lives in return for the bounty Blessed Providence has disclosed to me this day. But now—"

"*Muerte!*" Nada shouted from the foredeck.

Hart's glance swivelled to me. "What d'ye think, lad? Burn 'em all to perdition?"

They were all staring at me, now, and I confess I felt a thrill of power, of consequence, such as I had never experienced before. But did I want to see them all dead, our ship burned to ashes? What would happen to my freedom, then? I shook my head.

"Quite right. Let Providence deal with 'em," Hart agreed briskly. "We'll waste no more of our time." He turned to address Calhoun. "It won't be a luxurious voyage, but you'll make some port before long, barring another squall. But take my advice and steer well clear of Cuba. I'll not be so forgiving next time we meet."

Then Captain Hart glanced back at me, still clinging to the rail. "Coming, lad?"

He was right, of course. Staying aboard the *New Hope* now would be the end of me. In my experience, the murder of a vagabond Indian was considered rather less heinous a crime than his birth. And this in Boston, the very cradle of demo-cratic justice. I could expect justice to be much more rough and swift out here on the open sea. But . . . pirates. The very word

was a charm to terrify children into obedience. Seagoing mur-
derers who plundered for sport and tortured for fun. In a seafaring community like Boston, pirates were thought to be devils incarnate.

But so were Indians.

At least I had heard the pirates laugh.

"Idlers will be tossed to the sharks, but an honest sailor
is always welcome aboard my ship." Hart beamed at me.

I could only nod, again, afraid to speak, lest the pirates
discover just how dishonest a sailor I really was. Captain Hart
inclined his head toward his own ship, and I edged across the
deck, past Adderly's choleric face and Calhoun's murderous
eyes, truly my last link to the civilized world. And all I could
feel was relief.

CHAPTER 2

The Charioteer

I scuttled across the two ships' rails and dropped down to the deck of the *Blessed Providence* as Captain Hart ordered his men to lock my former shipmates into their hold.

"*Muerte?*" Nada suggested, helpfully, as Captain Hart came over the rail after me.

"Not worth the trouble, *hombre*. Just see they're quick about it."

"*Si, Capitan.*"

"Stand fast there—what do they call you? Jones?" Tom Jones was the first name I'd been able to think of when Adderly found me stowed away in the gig. Worthen had not been good for much, but I had unearthed some interesting volumes beneath the religious tracts and pamphlets in the neglected library. "There'll be work aplenty in a moment."

"Aye, Sir."

As the captain and his men swept across the deck to confer with the helmsman stationed far astern, I studied the pirate crew. There were no uniforms of any kind and many pirates went shirtless, with sashes or leather straps tossed across their weathered shoulders for holding their weapons. They displayed little of the grand finery of the pirates in the broadsheet ballads Bet used to smuggle into Worthen with such glee. Here or there, I glimpsed a random wisp of costly lace or headscarves dyed in vibrant colors, but more common were homespun cotton and battered trousers worn with hard use. The fine embroidery on Captain Hart's scarlet waistcoat was by far the bravest display, although I noticed that many of the pirates wore some article in that same blood-red hue—a sash, a kerchief, a pair of grime-encrusted scarlet leather boots.

When they were all back aboard the black schooner, I was put to work with the others making fast a towline between the two ships. I did not need to know Spanish to perceive that Nada was arguing strenuously for destruction of the *New Hope* and her crew. But Captain Hart ordered her dismasted with a cannon shot and towed back into the current that would carry her north by west above the Cuban coast. By the time her crew freed itself, she would have drifted up into the Bahamas or been wrecked along the way.

When the towing commenced, I went forward, out of the way of the men working the huge gaff mainsail, and eased myself down on a coil of cordage stowed beneath the foremast shrouds. It was the first moment I'd had to reflect since the morning's squall, and as anxious as I was over all that had happened, I felt exhaustion stealing upon me. I realized just how long the day had been when I saw the twilight already creeping out of the east. But glancing aft, I saw something even more astonishing, someone I'd not seen before. He might have been a trick of the light, or my own weary eyes, he was so different from the others. Indeed, he was like nothing I had ever beheld in all my life.

He was a young man, well-built and fair-haired, perched on the cabin top holding to the starboard shrouds. A breathtaking glimpse of broad, sunbronzed chest was visible beneath his split-open shirt. Thick, coppery-golden hair fell loose to his shoulders, a beacon of brightness among the dark heads of his mates, and a light fuzz of golden beard softened the clean angle of the jaw underneath. The red sun sinking into the sea behind him glistened in his golden hair; he looked spun from gold in a halo of red fire.

It wasn't cold, but a convulsion of shivers erupted from somewhere deep in the pit of my belly. And something more— a tremor of recognition. As if I knew, had always known, that this beautiful, godlike youth was meant for me. And the convulsions began again. An instant before, I'd been too exhausted to move; now I felt I could dive over the side with the rope in my teeth and tow the *New Hope* to perdition all by myself. I wished with all my pounding heart that someone would give me that order; sitting still here, now, was suddenly intolerable.

Who was he? Had he been below all this time? He was too much at ease among the others to be a hostage, although there was something of the noble young lord about him. I stole yet another surreptitious glance, afraid he might vanish with the shifting light, and I noticed the bandages binding up his arm inside his shirt. Flesh and blood, then. And I found myself rising, as if mesmerized, to move aft toward this apparition as Captain Hart strode up to him across the cabin top.

"And how fares our new cargo, Master Greenwood? Safely stowed away?" There was something farcical, but affectionate, in the captain's tone, and the fair youth bore it with an easy shrug.

"Aye, Captain. Although I never thought to see the day I'd be reduced to ship's accountant."

"You'll not board any more prizes until your arm heals, Matty," Hart declared. "I'll not have you tripping over the side and feeding the sharks out of heedlessness. Besides"—and here, the captain grinned—"your father paid handsomely for your education. T'would be a crime not to use it."

"Hellfire, Captain, a rat in the hold could be educated to tally up a treasure!"

I could appreciate just how expensive his education had been at some fine New England school, for if I still knew day from night, I knew his voice to be pure American Yankee.

"Calm yourself, laddie," the captain chuckled. "There was no sport in those Boston sluggards. Rest ye up for bigger and better prizes yet to come."

The captain ordered the towline to the *New Hope* severed and gave further orders to make for the open sea, avoiding the reefy Cuban coast in the gathering dark. Then his eye fell on me.

"Stand by there, Jones," he called to me. The golden pirate he called Matty followed the captain's gaze and glanced directly into my face. Immobilized by eyes as clear and vivid a blue as the tropical sky, I was made keenly aware of my own matted hair, dirt-begrimed face, and tired, awkward frame in my shapeless clothes. I felt like some big, clumsy rustic before this sleek young god. But for the insistent throbbing in my loins, it was difficult to remember that I had ever been a girl.

Then the captain gently prodded the golden pirate in the elbow and nodded. The youth sprang off the cabin top to the deck before me and lowered himself down the hatch. I watched the bright beacon of his hair disappear into the gloom.

"All hands below!" Captain Hart shouted. "Time for the sharing out."

The men were already coming in from their stations and clattering down the hatches. I saw Nada go aft and take the wheel from the gray-bearded helmsman, who followed the others below. I had never heard a command to "share out" aboard the *New Hope* and must have looked bewildered; after the captain jumped down to the deck to follow the men, he paused to motion me toward the hatch.

"Below with ye, Jones. I reckon ye've earned a share."

I followed him past the lower deck and down into the murky hold. By what little sun was still slanting in through the skylight, I could make out several barrels from the *New Hope*. Their tops were prised off and a dusting of white flour coated everything. Some planks had been set up for a tabletop between two crates, and the golden pirate sat on a stool behind them with a pen, scratching at an open leather-bound book. Next to him on the surface of the planks were stacks and stacks of silver coins sorted into equal amounts. I noticed a few things scavenged from the *New Hope* piled up beside the makeshift table, including a red quilt I'd once spied on Captain Calhoun's bunk. I realized this must be his silver, as well. His and Adderly's.

The men were all crowding round the table in a mood of happy expectation. Two bottles of Calhoun's port were already being passed around as Hart took up a position behind the pirate, Matty. The captain spoke to them all in Spanish and swept his arm toward the *New Hope* goods, and there was mumbling and nodding all around.

Someone nudged my elbow. I looked up to see the African, Hector, smiling down at me, and wondered how pathetic I must look in my ignorance.

"*Capitan,* him keep the stores for the *Providence,*" Hector explained.

"And the silver?" I asked.

"Why, that be ours, boy. According to our shares."

He had his knife out, peeling the greenish skin off a large island fruit. He handed me a wedge of orange flesh. It was a sweet, lush sunburst in my mouth and I devoured it with greedy abandon; we'd had little to eat but hard biscuit aboard the *New Hope.* Chewing industriously, I watched the pirates present themselves one by one at the accounting table. Captain Hart slid a stack of coins to each man as Matty made notations in his book. When most of the others had gone back above, their pockets and pouches jingling with silver, Hart spied me in the shadows and motioned me forward.

"Saw no action to speak of," the captain said, in English. "But ye gave us some useful information, and that's worth a share." Matty made a note in his book, and the captain nudged a little stack of coins in my direction.

A stern voice in my head left over from my long years at Worthen warned that I would seal my bargain with the devil if I accepted such ill-gotten plunder. But it had been a long, long time since I had been worth anything to anybody. I scooped up the coins.

"And a full share for yourself, Mateo," Hart said to the young pirate, nodding toward the last stack of coins.

"But Captain, I didn't even board."

"You know the Articles. Besides, ye'll make it up to me, lad." The captain grinned across the gloom at me. "Ye both will. Now, Jones, find yourself a berth for tonight. Short of a typhoon, we'll not need ye before daybreak. We'll take your mettle in the morning."

He called out in Spanish to some men still loitering nearby. A tall, dark pirate detached himself from this group and loped a few steps toward me, taking me in from top to toe with a single flicker of his eye.

"*Vámonos, muchacho*," he drawled. He plucked up the red quilt from the *New Hope* stores and led me up the ladder to the lower deck. I trailed behind him, stuffing my coins into my shirt, as he kicked aside some damp debris and bent to pluck up a tangle of hammock netting blocking his path. In the fading light, I saw piles of soiled canvas and netting shoved aside between crates and cordage. Pirates must make their berths wherever they happened to fall.

The dark fellow spoke to me in Spanish, and I turned to face him again. But his voice fell away as he peered at me more closely. My heart almost stopped under this sudden scrutiny, but he turned abruptly away and motioned me to follow him deeper into the shadows. It was gloomier back here, with no more daylight coming down the hatchways, but no other pirate nests were about. He led me far back into a dim corner between two bulkheads and stopped to gesture with the quilt into the shadows.

"Gets chilly at night, even in the tropics." He spoke in perfect English tinged with British irony. "You might appreciate this. Boy."

I was too stricken to respond, so he pressed the quilt into my hand. "Don't worry, I'll shape my silence to your wit. What else may hap to time I will commit."

Then he ambled away toward the hatch without a backward glance, leaving me in utter confusion. Between the surprise of his English—had he spoken poetry to me?—and the sarcasm with which he had pronounced the word "boy," I knew that, exhausted as I was, there would be little sleep for me this night.

And yet I must have slept, the way the golden pirate, Matty, haunted my dreams. I felt connected to him by something deeper and older than memory, more potent than longing. And my dreams told me why.

A dim room stinking of sweat and poverty, a few mean sticks of furniture. A middle-aged woman at a small table, dripping colored beads and threadbare shawls, a blue turban wrapped round her head adorned with a single peacock feather. I sat opposite her with Bet at my side. Bet, my mentor, who persuaded me to slip away from the dancing master and come out into the teeming streets of Boston to taste of life. I had seen him for the first time in that dim room, the golden spirit of all I longed for.

"You must ask a question," Bet prompted.

And I asked the only one that mattered, the one I asked myself every day, a foolish, female question. "Who will love me?"

Fortune spoke to me, that day, through the wrinkled hands and weary voice of Madame Romano, through the cards she laid out in a pattern on the table. The Star, a young woman at the water's edge beneath a canopy of stars, the card of looking forward, the stars of hope. My card. And then, the sorrowful cards for everything I had lost. My elder brother, Josh, tall and sandy-haired, killed in the sacking of Washington City. Mama, lifeless in her childbed, her stories ended, her laughing black eyes closed forever. My father, glaring at me from the prison of his grief, no longer able to distinguish the daughter who lived from the infant who killed my mother. My second brother—Andy, my last ally—run off to sea, lost to me forever. Fortune knew it all and showed me in the cards.

And then he was there on the table before me, like a sun on the horizon. The card of the Chariot—a golden youth in a halo of fire driving a chariot drawn by lions. "The card of what will be," Madame Romano declared, "The hope of the stars fulfilled." My Charioteer.

I was too dazzled to notice the other cards. Only the Knight of Coins stood in opposition, a dark, somber man astride a bull. But Madame Romano quickly dismissed him as lethargy, idleness. My stagnant life in Boston, the hopeless life I must escape. The other cards, she confirmed, pointed to a happy resolution.

"With your dashing Charioteer!" crowed Bet.

In nearly five years, I'd never dared to nurture hope. I had been alone and unloved for so long. But Fortune was ready to spirit me onward, and the Charioteer was the emblem of Fortune's favor. Somewhere in the great world, he was waiting for me, my gift from Fortune for all I had lost. If only I could free myself to find him.

I awoke suddenly in the damp blackness belowdecks, to snoring and muted grumbling in foreign tongues. Or was it the babble of my own ghosts? I had abandoned everything I knew for this life with these strangers on the open sea. But this must be where freedom lived. And the Charioteer would be my reward.

CHAPTER 3

A Woman of Virtue

I roused myself well before dawn, the knots in my stomach a much more efficient alarm than any ship's bells. Not that anything as regular as bells were to be found aboard the *Blessed Providence*. When I went above, a fresh breeze blew the acrid odor of stale wine into my face. Piles of sodden, colorful rags littering the deck turned out to be pirates snoring in their cups. I had to step lively to avoid a well-drained port bottle careening about the deck with the roll of the ship.

Still, the schooner appeared to be competently manned. Hart and Nada were at the binnacle in conversation with the grizzled helmsman. Others were keeping watch in the bows and clawing along in the rigging. I could not see the golden pirate anywhere and was almost ready to believe I'd only dreamed him. As for the English pirate who spoke in riddles— well, all the dark-eyed Spanish-speaking pirates looked so alike.

I'd be hard-pressed to pick him out of a crowd.

"Ah, Jones!" the captain called out as he strode across the cabin top. "Attend me, boy. We've no regulations here like what you're used to, but we do abide by certain laws."

I took a step aft, and it leaped out at me, a glint of steel in the sun. When I saw it was a rapier wielded in the good right hand of the golden pirate, Matty, I lost the wit to jump away.

"First law—no merchant sailors' rig here!" he cried, slicing the point of his blade so swiftly down through the open yoke of my loose, checkered shirtfront that the frayed fabric gave way under its force, parting almost to my waist. I could only stare into Matty's widening blue eyes, scarcely aware of the icy kiss of the rapier point snicking lightly over my shoulder, peeling back my shirt like a banana skin. As the fabric fell away, the shape of my cursed breasts was unmistakable under the filthy rag that bound them.

There was a moment of absolute, perplexed silence. I tried to cross my arms over my breasts, but the remains of the shirt still dragging at my elbows rendered the effort useless. And it was already too late.

Matty recovered himself first, and cried out in a voice mixed with equal parts horror and delight, "Captain! We've a female aboard!"

"Nonsense!" roared Captain Hart, from the cabin top.

"B'God, Captain, I've not been at sea so long I fail to recognize a woman!"

The pirates on deck circled warily round me, but not too close, as if mine were a malady that might be catching.

"Jones!" barked Hart. "What is the meaning of this . . . costume? Are Yankee merchantmen so desperate for hands they must sign on . . . girls?" He pronounced the word as if he didn't care for the way it tasted in his mouth.

"I never signed on, sir." My guilty secret had been a burden for so long, it was almost a relief to have it discovered at last. "I was a stowaway aboard the *New Hope*, and not a man among 'em ever discovered me."

"That lot couldn't discover salt water in the sea!" Hart

retorted. "Jones . . . but I suppose your name is as false as your tongue."

"My tongue is not as false as yours, Captain, for you said any honest sailor was welcome, and I joined this crew in good faith!" My own anger surprised me, but what more could I lose, now?

"Have you an honest name, then?"

"Lightfoot," I responded. "Tory Lightfoot."

"What manner of name is that?

"*Indio*," muttered Nada at Hart's elbow, watching me intently.

"Aye, it's . . . a family name." My mother once told me of a Mohawk ancestor called Cat Foot.

"And what port d'ye hail from, Tory Lightfoot?"

"None, sir. I fly no nation's colors."

"What, and no master to board you when you put into safe harbor?" cried Matty, to a chorus of ribald chuckles.

Odd, that while few of these pirates chose to speak English among themselves, they seemed to have no trouble understanding it.

"And what trade d'ye know that might be useful aboard a ship, Tory Lightfoot?" quizzed the captain.

"I sailed two weeks on the *New Hope*. I'm a good sailor, sir."

"Sailors I have aplenty. And belay that 'sir' business! I'm not some merchant captain to be fawned over. What I meant was, have ye no special talents?"

"I'm strong. I can learn anything. I can cook . . . ." What had I ever learned at Worthen that could be of any use to me now? "I can mend . . . a little." I glanced up hopelessly at the sails.

"Oh, bother the girl!" fumed Hart, his eyes narrowed in menace. "T'was a time when death was the punishment for a female disguised in a sailor's rig. And death to the man who smuggled her aboard." His tone implied that he was sorry this sensible custom had ever been abandoned and that it might, in fact, be ripe for revival.

"In that case, Captain, you'd have to stretch your own neck. She'd never have had the wit to come aboard without your urging."

I recognized the accent of the tall English pirate, who had come down from the rigging.

"Oh, aye. But damn it, Jack, what am I to do with a lass?"

"*Capitan,* there must be some way for a strong *señorita* to earn her passage, eh?"

Rude guffaws accompanied this suggestion. But Captain Hart quelled them with a single, sweeping stare.

"She'd be more use to us as a hostage than as a diversion for this lot," the Englishman suggested.

"Perhaps," Hart considered. "No rich relations, by the look of her, but we might sell her. She might pass for mulatta at the flesh markets of Barbados and decorate some planter's bed, eh?"

"Well," the English pirate observed in a voice that was not loud, but carried wonderfully across the deck, "if all she can do is cook and mend, she won't fetch much of a profit in Barbados."

This was greeted by another chorus of bawdy hilarity from the pirates, the most raucous coming from Matty Greenwood. And I could not will away a vague surge of shame that burned my cheeks, shame for the very virtue the Worthen sisters had taken such pains to drill into me. What could I say in my defense? I could only stand there, absorbing their humiliating laughter, wishing I was far away, out of their reach. I gazed up longingly into the rigging.

"I can work aloft," I declared.

"Not prone to the vapors, like most females?" the Englishman needled.

"No more than you!"

He exchanged another look with the captain. "Might as well put her to work," he concluded.

"Aye," Hart sighed. "She's not likely to tempt a planter's purse looking as she does, not in these tightfisted times. And she did lead us to the silver. I suppose I owe the lass a fair trial."

Nada muttered something to the captain about *mala suerte;* I half expected him to start yelling *"Muerte!"* again. Several of the others were nodding in agreement, glaring at me with unvarnished suspicion. Then I remembered something I might yet be able to barter for my life.

"Captain Hart, if it helps to prove my good faith, I . . . I learned something aboard the *New Hope* that might affect every pirate in Cuba."

"What's this, Mistress? Another riddle?"

"A plot, I think. Our Captain Calhoun got such an early start out of Boston because he heard of a fleet of pirate-catchers sailing here to the Indies before him. A naval squadron under . . . Porter."

Hart stared at me. "A squadron? What size?"

"Umm . . . schooners." I shut my eyes to concentrate on the memory of that dank hold and the uncharacteristic purr of Calhoun's voice in the dark, speaking softly to his favorite boy. "Ten or twelve. And barges. And . . . a Connecticut steamer!" I had his full attention, now. "They're to meet up with the English Navy at St. Thomas and sweep all the pirates before them."

"Before them? In what direction?"

"Why . . . I don't know the Indies, Captain." Curse the Worthens for not teaching geography! "But Captain Calhoun meant to sail in by way of Barbados and trail along in their wake."

"Westward with the current," mused the captain. "Sailing for Cuba." He gazed at me again, with less rancor. "How d'ye come to know this, Mistress Lightfoot?"

"The same way I knew about the silver."

"So you're a spy?"

I mustered a weary smile. "By accident, Captain."

"So it takes the combined American and English navies under the fabled Commodore Porter to track us down, eh?"

"In truth, Captain, they're out to catch Diabolito."

At this, Nada actually laughed out loud, a chilling spectacle, and several of the Cubans joined him.

"We're all Diabolito to that lot," Hart chuckled. "Still, it may be best for us to keep to the shelter of the coast for a few days, until we can learn more. Have we stores enough for a short cruise, Mr. Nada?"

"*Si, Capitan.*"

"*Bueno.* Mistress Lightfoot, if what you say is true, it may in fact be an act of Blessed Providence that has brought us together." There were a few more grumblings of "*mala suerte*" among the men, but Hart faced them all down. "A gift from Providence is not to be ill-used," he declared. "If she brings misfortune, there's a sure solution at hand." He glanced over the side and the grumbling trailed away. Nodding in satisfaction, the captain turned again to me. "Are ye sure there's no one waiting for you back home?"

"My people are all dead, Captain."

"Ah. Well. If ye mean to stay aboard, you must swear an oath to defend your brethren and never to betray 'em, neither for profit nor glory nor to save your own neck. Can ye so swear?"

"Aye, Captain." If the choice were pirates or sharks, I would gladly take the pirates.

Captain Hart nodded, and Matty sprang forward to catch my right hand, palm up. Producing a dagger from his belt, he pressed its tip into the underside of my index finger, between the first two joints, and scratched a shallow X.

"It's an oath in blood," Matty explained, eagerly. "Make a fist."

I did, and he wrapped his hand tightly around mine.

"I swear, Captain," I vowed, once I'd caught my breath. Matty looked into my eyes and smiled. Much, much better than the sharks.

"According to the Articles, ye'll get one share of any plunder we don't reserve for the ship or sell in port. Two shares if you're wounded in battle, or more, according to the severity of the wound. Agreed?"

I nodded and tried not to imagine what the more lucrative wounds might be.

"Rudy Herrera!" Captain Hart called, from above. "Go below with Lightfoot and find her some clothes. Then take her into the galley to lay out breakfast." A little olive-skinned pirate with a wide checkerboard grin stepped forward. "We'll see how you fare in the cooking department, Mistress. Afterwards, go with Jack." Hart's eyes searched out the English pirate. "He'll find you something to do, aloft. Mind, I'll keep you aboard as long as ye prove useful. But don't try my patience with any frivolities."

So I went off with Rudy Herrera, an animated little Cuban in a smart, oversized pea-coat weighted down with brass buttons and shod in the scarlet boots I'd noticed before. He kept a large trunk below full of scavenged clothing, as well as the ship's colors and other assorted flags. I found an old canvas shirt to cover me while Rudy tore the rest of my checkered shirt into rags. Then we went into the galley. Rudy's thick curly hair and beard were streaked with brown, black, gold and silver, like a tortoiseshell cat. They hid most of his face but for his merry brown eyes and gap-toothed grin. He spoke Spanish so rapidly I could not distinguish any space at all between the words, but his talk was full of laughter, and I learned from his example how to fry up some mottled bananas over the galley fire to lay out with the salt fish and another round of Captain Calhoun's port.

When the breakfasting was over, I looked for the Englishman, Jack, as the captain had bidden. I'd forgotten the brief sting of my scratched finger, but the rude laughter of the others when the Englishman had jested at my expense still rankled. I stared into every dark face, but I could only recognize him by his long, loping stride as he came toward me. Damn the man, but there was nothing remarkable about him to stick in the mind. He had the same unruly dark hair plaited back in a sticky tail, the same dark beard with subtle glints of silver, and the same earth-brown eyes as any dozen of his mates. He was carrying the red quilt.

"Captain says to put you behind the storeroom. It's

more private."

I moved to take the unwieldy bundle and nearly dropped it; when he reached out to help me, I shook him off with such angry impatience he turned on his heel and stalked down the hatchway without another word. I had to trot after him like a clumsy child to keep up.

"Don't be rude to your elders and betters, boy," Jack muttered, as I drew near.

"You were rude enough to humiliate me in front of the crew!"

"Humiliate? Ah, my apologies. I mistook you for a woman of virtue."

I had some fierce retort ready, but all that came out of my mouth was an errant giggle. It might have been anxiety or fatigue or the mysterious sea air, but all of a sudden, here in the gloomy hold of a Cuban pirate vessel bound for God-knew-where, my improbable situation struck me as hilarious.

"What," I chortled, "would a woman of virtue be doing here?"

Jack gazed back at me. "What, indeed?"

Nothing in New England had prepared me for the still, torpid weather of the Indies. The damp heat was like a living thing crushing me in its sticky, airless embrace. On deck, the occasional cool slap of spray from a breaking swell offered little relief, for the water dried away in the heat and left my skin caked with salt. Aloft, beyond the reach of the spray, the salt baked into a stiff crust on flesh, hair and clothing.

It didn't help matters to find myself trailing after Jack in the top rigging, even closer to the unforgiving sun in the cloudless blue sky. The unfamiliar backward rake of the masts was awkward enough, without my having to witness Jack's careless agility on the ratlines and footropes. Especially since Jack, busy scanning the horizon in all directions, gave all the orders while I did all the work.

"Captain knows what I can do," he told me. "I'm to find out if you know your business."

"I do. But is it always this hot?"

"It gets hot in the summer," Jack replied, his eyes following a speck on the horizon. "This is the temperate season."

I clawed a wet strand of hair off my face and sighed, loudly.

"You didn't have to come aboard," he reminded me over his shoulder. "You might have kept your mouth shut about the silver."

"I'm not sorry about that. It was worth it, to see Calhoun's face. Besides, Captain Hart would have murdered Jem."

"Who?"

"Our cabin boy."

Jack shot me a brief, pitying glance. "You've been very badly duped, Mistress, if you think our captain would ever harm a boy." But before I could even respond, I felt a tremor of alarm in the lines and Jack lunged out over the deck, shouting, "Sail ho, Captain! *Vela a estribor!*" He continued to shout in Spanish until Captain Hart barked a command to the helmsman below and the schooner came about so sharply, I was almost pitched out of the shrouds.

"She's flying Danish colors," Jack sang out from above as I scuttled down for the safety of the deck. "Looks like a supply ship out of the Virgins."

"Rudy! Raise the stars and stripes," the captain commanded. "Mateo! You're in command, lad. Arne!" A thin, weathered pirate hove into view with eyes of such pale blue, they were nearly colorless. "You're the mate, in case we need a translator. The rest of you, lay low. And *no armas!* All I want is information, and I don't intend to waste any blood getting it."

Over the grumbling of Bustamante, the gunner, the captain ordered the helmsman to keep the schooner pointed southeasterly, toward the Dane, and instructed Matty to say we were a Yankee trader out of New Orleans. Having hoisted American colors, Rudy produced a military-style coat that the captain helped Matty ease on over his sore arm.

"Very dashing. Now we'll see what sort of diplomat ye make."

Then Hart's eyes fell on me. And narrowed. "Jack!"

"Here, captain." He'd come down from the top and was helping Hector, the African, give the *Providence* a shipshape merchantman look by heaving empty bottles, discarded scraps of clothing and other miscellaneous junk down the nearest hatchway.

"When we close, Jack, take Lightfoot below."

"I didn't sign on for a nursemaid," Jack barked.

Captain Calhoun had flogged men for far less, but Hart was too intent on his business to take offense. "I need someone fluent in English to stay with her," he explained. "And to keep her quiet, *comprende?*" He finished out the rest of his orders in Spanish.

"*Si, Capitan.*" Jack nodded. There was no further argument.

I was not sorry to go below; whatever deviltry the pirates were planning could be done without me, at least until I had my bearings. From where we stood at the foot of the companion ladder, I could command a decent view up the hatchway of Matty at the rail, making ready to hail the Dane. He looked splendid in his fine coat, and I suppose I'd opened my mouth to say so when Jack hissed, "Hold your tongue, Mistress, or I'll have to gag you."

"But . . . why?" I was mystified.

"It's not unknown for pirate hostages to cry for help."

"I'm not a hostage!" I spluttered, and Jack's hand clamped across my mouth with such force, I was pinned backwards to his chest.

"My orders are to slit your throat if you make a sound. Now you could save us both a great deal of bother."

I could feel the point of a blade at my throat, and when I glanced up into his face, I read nothing at all in his dark eyes, impassive as stone. The eyes of a stranger. There was no reason to suppose he would not carry out such an order. I nodded slowly, his hand relaxed a fraction. I clamped my teeth tight shut and prayed no untimely hiccough would cost me my life.

Above, Matty was singing out pleasantries to the Danish captain, who replied in respectable English that he was Knudsen, master of the *Margarethe.*

"What news out of the sugar islands?" Matty sallied.

"Much news! Your war hero, Porter, many days in St. Thomas with a small navy!"

"What, are we at war?"

"At war with the pirates! Make the sea lanes safe for business!"

"Has he caught any yet?"

"We pass him three days back off Puerto Rico." Knudsen laughed. "Porter say the Spanish fire on him, and now he waits for an apology. He may be there, still!"

"*Bueno, Mateo!*" Captain Hart cried, when the *Margarethe* had sailed out of range, clapping Matty on his good shoulder as he signaled the rest of the men to come up out of hiding. I was just following Jack up out of the hatchway when the captain spied me.

"So, Mistress, it appears you were telling the truth after all. And as you are still in possession of your life, it seems you also know how to hold your tongue. Rare traits, indeed, for a female. But essential for the pirate trade."

"*Si, Capitan.*" I beamed, which at least drew another grin from Rudy.

"*Hombres,*" Hart went on, with a glance toward the lowering sun. "We'll lay to out here, tonight. At first light, we'll make for the coast."

This brought noises of approval from the others.

"But there's no time for a run back to Cabo Cruz—not unless we want to meet Porter's squadron head-on on our way back to the Windward. We'll keep to the north coast for now to learn what we can and fit out for a longer cruise."

This was greeted with much less enthusiasm.

"*Si,*" Hart continued, raising his voice just enough to meet the rising protests. "Commodore Porter could grow old, *muy viejo y gris,* waiting for a Spanish apology. But sooner or later he'll come to Cuba looking for pirates. And when he does, we'd best be gone."

What's called dusk in Boston happens in a moment in the Indies. Daylight gives way to darkness in the brief time it takes the sun to sink below the horizon, a bright gold watch tucked suddenly into a black pocket. There were more stars in the West Indian sky than I had ever seen in Boston, brighter stars more full of promise. It was possible to imagine that each star was a dream I might yet achieve, now that I was free of my old life. However precarious my new one.

We'd had a supper of boiled fish spiced with dried hot peppers. But it was still too warm to sleep. As a jug of rum was passed around, the men lounging round the deck cried out for entertainment. Someone called for *malabarismo* from Jack Danzador, and Rudy tried to show me what it meant, pumping his hands up and down in the air as if milking a tall cow. But Jack called out from his perch by the rail that it was too dark, *muy oscuro,* to see. Then a *cancion* was demanded from Hector, who sang a haunting lullaby in a strange tongue.

Then, Matty piped up, "We must have a story. A new one from our new shipmate!"

"But . . . I don't know any stories," I faltered.

"Tell us how you came to be aboard that merchantman, lass." Captain Hart's voice was calm in the dark. "That should make an interesting yarn."

The rum had been so fiery going down that my eyes burned. But now it had settled into a warm little pool of complacency in my stomach, drowning my nerves.

"It's not much of a story. My mother died when I was a child, and I . . . lost my father." It still hurt too much to say more. "I was sent to school in Boston, I had nowhere else to go. And then . . . I ran away."

"They beat you? Starve you?"

"They would have made me a governess." It was no less grim a fate, for me; when Aunt Fiona stopped paying my boarding fees, the Worthen Sisters lost no time arranging to sell me to a family in the church with a large, petulant brood.

"A governess!" crowed Captain Hart. "B'God, I've the most educated crew of brigands in all the Indies!"

"But a governess is not so bad," observed Arne, the weathered Dane. "You get meals. A roof. A home."

"But it's not *your* home," I protested. "You've nothing of your own. The gentry treat you like a servant; they can throw you out on a whim and you have nothing to say about it."

"They make slaves of us all," Hector agreed.

"Very bold," said Captain Hart, after the murmuring of the others had died down. "And very foolish. Thought you'd have a career as a merchant seaman, eh? A life of thankless labor and a broken back for less pay than you could drink away in a single night at the grog shop. How did ye mean to disguise your sex in a fo'c'sl crowded with desperate men during endless nights at sea? And what d'ye suppose would happen to you when they found you out? God's blood, lass, had ye no brains at all to consider the consequences?"

"If I had, I would have been paralyzed," I insisted, meeting his gaze. "I had no idea what would happen to me on a merchant ship, that's true. I don't know what will happen to me, now. But I knew exactly what would happen to me in Boston. And I . . . I had a vision."

The captain frowned. "Not another damned Papist, are ye?"

I shook my head.

"*Bruja*," growled Nada, and I saw some of the men crossing themselves in the dark.

"Witch," Matty translated, gazing at me over the arm across his raised knee. "Is that what's kept you alive, Mistress?"

I had stayed alive to find him, didn't he know? "My vision came from Fortune. She showed me there was a better life than the one I had in Boston." I wrenched my eyes away to face the captain again. "I've thrown in my lot with Fortune, and she brought me here. At least I'll be no one's slave."

Hart's laugh was as sharp as a sudden shot in the dark.

"Spoken like a born pirate," he chuckled, taking another swig from the jug as it came his way. Wiping his mouth on the back of his hand, he leaned forward to fix me with his alert black eyes. "But take heed, Mistress. A wee bit more brains and less foolishness will stand ye in good stead aboard the *Providence*."

CHAPTER 4

The Yankee Squadron

"What in the bloody hell . . ."

Jack's mumbling from the foretop fluttered down to where I stood at the foot of the shrouds, but no one else seemed alarmed. Jack was famous for his sharp eye, his balance in the rigging and his ability to stay aloft for hours; perhaps a little brainsickness was only to be expected.

We were making north by west along the windward coast of Cuba, hoping the news of Porter's squadron would travel more quickly through the grog shops and cantinas of the north than the warships themselves could ever sail up the coast. The gray-bearded Cuban helmsman, Salvador Gris, had spent his youth in the smuggling trade, navigating these same treacherous inlets that now sheltered our progress. But as the *Providence* made for a stretch of open sea this morning, Jack had been sent aloft to keep a sharp lookout.

The agitated mumblings suddenly ceased from above. There was an instant of utter silence.

"Good . . . God . . . damn." Jack's voice was low and precise. Then the upper half of his body swung out over the edge of the top, one hand in the shrouds, the other brandishing his spyglass.

"Sails, Captain, off the starboard quarter! Looks like a goddamned convoy! North by west with the current!"

The men rushed to their sailing positions as Jack repeated his alarm in Spanish. We'd been making for the current, but Captain Hart gave the order to come about and ride the trades back to the nearest jagged claw of coastline that might offer protection. He commanded Rudy to stand by with the flags of America, England, Spain and the Republic of Colombia until we could see what the convoy was and what colors she flew.

The intruder fleet had soon drawn near enough to darken the horizon off the starboard quarter. But the *Providence* was fast and sleek, and Hart gambled she could outrun her pursuers—if such they were—before they even realized a chase was on.

There was nothing elegant about our entry into a narrow inlet behind a rise of scrubby hills. But Salvador Gris piloted us into a relatively safe position with only a few superficial bumps and scrapes. And the hill was overgrown enough to shield the ship, once her sails were taken in and her spars sent down. But there could be no sailing away in a hurry, and Captain Hart ordered us ashore to be ready to flee for our lives, for the mere fact that the *Providence* had not been hailed by the convoy did not mean she hadn't been seen. The gunner Bustamante and his men stayed aboard, crouched by their cannons, ready to provide what cover they could, and Hart gave the most difficult command to obey—to lay low and wait—as the mysterious fleet approached.

They made a stately promenade: one impressive naval sloop of war; five fleet little schooners carrying at least two broadside guns and one pivoting "Long Tom" apiece; three flat-bottomed barges, sloop-rigged; and what looked like an ordinary merchant brig. And all of them sailing under the American stars and stripes.

"Commodore Porter, as I live and breathe," murmured Captain Hart.

We'd needed no orders to claw up the rocky hill for a view of the Atlantic out beyond the little bay, praying the scrub thicket that sliced our hands and faces also hid the *Providence* from view. Slowly, the naval squadron began to sail past our hiding place, close enough that sailors were visible in the tops searching the area with their spyglasses. I could hear my breath rattling in my lungs like the Boston mail coach on a rough road, sure that the squadron could hear it, too. What if one of these warships saw us, pursued us, captured us?

Could I claim I was a hostage, forced to sail against my will? I was a female, after all, and an American. No one in the civilized world would ever believe any woman in possession of her wits could choose such a life. Surely, there must be some plausible story I could tell to save my life, and I was no stranger to stories. But was I so ready to abandon the men who had saved my life, fed and clothed me? Had I not sworn an oath?

I felt a pulse of alarm ripple through the men before I heard the low rumble of their curses as we all lay belly-down in the scrub. One of the last of the little schooners had come out of the current, riding the trades for the coastline. She lay to beyond the reefs and put down a boat. We could only watch in an agony of silent inactivity as six oarsmen pulled for the rocky shallows at the foot of the hill on which we were concealed.

"There's no landing," cried one of the oarsman; his voice carried over the water with alarming clarity.

"Farther on, around the point," directed a man crouched in the bows, and my heart froze. Even from here, I recognized the steel in his voice and his tough, wiry frame. "I swear I saw something."

"Fatigue, Mr. Adderly. You've had quite an ordeal—"

"I'm as alert as you are, Lieutenant!" retorted the former mate of the *New Hope*. "We must find 'em before the trail grows too cold!"

"Indeed, we shall, Mr. Adderly. But not by chasing phantoms."

I heard a rustle from behind. Glancing back over my shoulder, I saw a movement halfway down the scrub hill behind us, the arc of Jack's arm lobbing what looked like a large rock into a thicket of leafy bush farther down the narrow beach. A cloud of black crows beat up out of the thicket in a frenzy of cawing and flapping like demons released from Hell, circling in the air above us before swarming off for some safer perch.

"There go your pirate sails," chuckled one of the oarsmen as the irritated birds flew off.

Adderly's low reply was muffled. But the lieutenant's voice was quite distinct as he gave the command to pull back for the schooner.

"Never mind, Mr. Adderly," he went on. "We'll hang every damned pirate in the Indies, by and by. With your help."

Not one of us breathed until the boat was safe aboard the schooner and the schooner back in the current. How foolish I'd been to think for even a panicked moment that I could ever go back to the civilized world. Tom Jones, stowaway and turncoat, was better off dead, and Victoria MacKenzie no longer existed.

"How touching, Mistress," the captain murmured, as the squadron ships receded into the distance. "Your friends have come looking for you."

So he had recognized Adderly, too. There could be no doubt that Adderly would recognize him, as well.

"Are ye sure t'was Fortune sent ye to us?"

"*Bruja*," muttered Nada.

They were staring at me again, all of them, perhaps expecting me to sprout black wings and fly off like the crows.

"She did warn us about the squadron, Captain," Jack pointed out. "If she had some more sinister design, she might've held her tongue and let 'em take us unawares."

"The ways of Providence are ever mysterious," said Hart in grudging agreement. "What can ye tell us about this fellow, lass?"

"He'll stop at nothing, Captain."

"That fond of ye, was he?"

"I doubt if he could loathe me any more. But we've taken everything he had. Revenge is all that's left him."

"Men survive on far less in the Indies. *Hombres,*" Hart went on, turning to the others. "We are delivered again, thanks to Blessed Providence and Jack's good arm. I know there's not a man among you wouldn't relish a fair fight, but I'm damned if I'll hand our lives over to that lot out of foolhardiness. Best to let Porter get to wherever he's going and keep out of the way of any strays who might still be lagging behind."

Hector was telling his mates a story, and low laughter caromed slowly round the deck in the heavy night air. It was a warm, restless evening, and I drifted toward the pirates sprawled on the cabin top. The men were trading two-hour watches aloft on the alert for Porter's ships, and Jack lowered himself down to the deck from the backstay just ahead of me. He had thrown off his shirt in the close heat, and when he paused at the water cask to ladle out a drink, I couldn't stifle a gasp at the grid of pale scars that criss-crossed his back, aglow in the flickering lantern light.

Jack glared at me over his shoulder, but when he saw where I was looking—as quickly as I tried to glance away—he only shrugged. "Just an argument I lost once, with a cat."

"I'm sorry," I faltered.

"You'll find no less on any other man aboard." He hung up the ladle and nodded toward the chuckling men. "Hector, there. He's telling 'em how he first came to the Indies as a boy from the Gold Coast, hunted like an animal and sold to slavers. He landed ashore with his little brother, who was half dead from the passage. They were taken to the barracoons, where the Africans are fattened up for the auction block. One of the guards decided the sickly boy was so far gone, it would be cheaper to let him starve than to waste more provisions feeding him."

I eyed the chortling men. "Sounds hilarious so far."

"That was before. Now he's describing everything he's ever dreamed of doing to that guard."

I watched Hector's hands—the powerful hands that had plucked Adderly off me with such careless ease and saved my life aboard the *New Hope*—as they tore imaginary limbs asunder. The others roared with glee. But even laughter of this ghoulish nature was better than the petty bickering most often heard in the two days we'd spent in this hidden place. Inactivity was proving to be a more formidable enemy than an entire fleet of pivot guns. Between watches, the men had nothing to do but drink and dice away their boredom and curse their fate. No more warships had been spied offshore, but Nada continued to complain of *mala suerte*—bad luck—and always when I was within earshot. And when the pirates grew weary of gaming and arguing, they fell to boasting about the women or boys they'd bedded or the *aguardiente* they had consumed at a single sitting or their degree of "seasoning." Their chief enemy in the islands before the advent of Porter's squadron was the fever; anyone who had survived a bout of the fever was considered seasoned.

Hector ambled off amidships to throw dice with Matty and a dark young pirate with pointed features; the others called him Cuervo. My eyes followed Matty's golden hair, afire from the light of a lantern perched upon the hatch coaming. He was never alone, always with his mates, laughing and jesting in rapid, ribald Spanish that excluded me completely.

Jack had taken himself off to catnap, sitting up in the lee of the cabin top, and I wondered if I might risk bothering him again. Boredom made me stupid, so I edged toward him and sat down.

"Can I ask you a question?"

"When was I elected your maiden uncle?" He didn't open his eyes.

"Will you teach me Spanish?"

"You'll pick it up. We all do."

"But I need to know it, now. What use am I if I can't converse with my shipmates?"

"You're in the pirate trade. Conversational skills are not required."

"I need to know what my captain is ordering me to do. At least if I knew Spanish, I might find some decent company aboard the *Providence*," I persisted. "Think of it, you'd never have to speak to me again."

"That is a point," Jack conceded.

A blistering shriek exploded the quiet, and Matty leapt to his feet beside the hatch with Cuervo at his elbow.

"*Bastardo! Tramposo!*" Matty roared at Hector, his face flushed scarlet. "I'll have a look at the damned dice, I say!"

Hector was rising, too, as ominously silent as a shark, his eyes locked onto Matty's. He murmured something I couldn't hear, and Matty's hand twitched toward his cutlass.

Then Captain Hart came flying off the cabin top and across the deck, catching Matty by the elbow as he shouldered his way between the two men. The captain glared at Hector, who took one grudging step backward, then turned the full force of his fury onto Matty.

"What the goddamned hellfire d'ye think you're doing, boy?" the captain raged, shoving Matty's hand away from his weapon. "Have I brought ye here to do Porter's work for him?"

Matty bit back a protest, then dropped his eyes, his anger turning just as suddenly to shame in the face of the captain's fury.

"But why are we here, Capitan?" demanded Cuervo, in a tense undertone, choosing his English words with care. "To hide like rabbits, like women, from the Yankees?"

Hart glared at the three of them, then swept his gaze all round the deck, at all the rest of us watching the confrontation. Then he barked an order in Spanish to Nada that even I understood. The order to make sail.

Within a week, I had seen enough of backwater island port towns to last the rest of my life. I knew the utilitarian tatters and stolen finery that marked those in the pirate and smuggling trades, the way they herded together ashore to swap songs and stories and throw away their profit on *aguardiente* and spruce beer and women and dice.

This place was no different but that it was even more bustling with every sort of commercial and less savory enterprise. Nuevitas was perched on a little peninsula overlooking a deep bay protected from the Atlantic by a chain of reefy cays the Cubans called *cayos*. The only approach to the bay was long, winding and treacherous, and no one dared attempt it who didn't know the way. The *Providence* had come to Nuevitas to sell her Yankee cargo and purchase supplies and information.

I always went ashore with Rudy, who was teaching me how to haggle for fresh produce, and to test the Spanish I was learning from Jack. And from Nada's grim scrutiny every time we returned, I knew he was hoping I'd get myself lost or murdered ashore so they could all be done with me. But I'd outfoxed him on that point so far.

After today's visit to the market, Rudy and I joined the captain and Hector and Bustamante in a dank village grog shop bustling with custom. For the expenditure of some of Captain Calhoun's silver for drinks all round, we learned the Yankee Squadron had sailed to Thompson's Island, above Havana, off the Florida coast, to set up a naval base. The pirate-catchers were building a permanent home.

"They wanted to set up camp in Havana," the chatty tavern-keeper told us, in Spanish. "But Don Mahy, the Captain-General, wouldn't have it. It was him, after all, sent word to all the Cuban ports that the Yankees were on their way. It's even said," he went on, sizing up Hart and his men with an eye toward future custom, "that Don Mahy has been ordered not to let the Americans pursue pirates on dry land. The safest place for a pirate right now is on Cuban soil."

I couldn't be sure I'd understood what was said. After the barman took himself off, I moved closer to Captain Hart.

"Why does Spain protect pirates?"

"*Tanto para tanto.*" Hart grinned. "This for that. Yankee privateers have bedeviled Spanish shipping in these waters for years. The Dons are delighted that Spanish-American pirates are getting some of their own back, at last. Sadly for them, the Dons entertain a fantasy that the pirates of Cuba are loyalists who only attack the ships of America and England."

Bustamante spat deliberately onto the dirt floor.

"As if *cubanos* had any reason to be loyal to Spain!" he hissed.

But the political turmoil of Spain and her colonies meant little to me, so long as Fortune allowed me to continue aboard the *Providence,* working the ship, breathing the free air of the open sea. Dreaming of Matty. My eyes wandered to the end of the bar, where a large caramel-skinned woman with tightly braided-up black hair was primping before a dim, speckled glass. I sat back a bit to get a better view, some renegade female impulse luring me toward my own reflection. But when the woman moved away, what I saw staring back at me in the glass was like a slap in the face.

I had never been a beauty, tall and awkward with too much wild, rusty-dark hair. But the creature gazing out balefully from the glass looked like nothing human—hair plastered flat and hanging limp in a filthy plait, sun-roughened face layered with sweat and grime above shapeless rags of clothing. If this was all Matty saw when he looked my way, no wonder his eyes passed right over me. Transfixed the way one is by a wretched accident in the road, unable to turn away, I finally noticed Captain Hart's face in the glass. He stood behind me, watching me.

"Sarafina!" he barked, and the hefty woman lumbered over to join us at the bar. Hart spoke to her in Spanish, nodding at me, and tossed a couple of coins onto the bar. Sarafina gazed at me and nodded. "Go with her, lass," the captain said to me. "She'll look after you."

I tried to protest, but Sarafina herded me outside to the open-air cook house behind the tavern and sent for a wooden tub and a basin of water warmed by the cookfire. I confess, I forgot all else in the abandon of scrubbing myself clean and sluicing the grime out of my hair. When I had dried myself, Sarafina brought me a muslin blouse with a deep, flounced neckline and a long calico skirt she fixed tightly at my waist. It was more than an hour later—when she paraded me back into the tavern and set me down again at the bar—that I realized Captain Hart and the other pirates were no longer there.

What if they had sailed without me? They might have left me behind to satisfy Adderly's revenge and free themselves from the *mala suerte* I brought. And my foolish female vanity had made it so easy for them. How could I have been so witless? How would I survive in this strange place all alone?

CHAPTER 5

The Captain's Boy

I don't know how long I sat frozen at the bar, staring down at my hands. The ordinary business of the place continued all around me—mugs and glasses and pottery bottles clanked together, dice rattled in cups, voices rose and fell in fragments of Spanish I could only vaguely comprehend. Much the same things I would have heard aboard ship. But this was not the *Providence*. These people were all strangers, and I was completely alone.

I was afraid to look up or speak, afraid to acknowledge this alien world with any gesture that might trap me here, forever. I tried to shut out the noise, to shrink inside myself and disappear. Was this all Fortune had in store for me, after all?

Then a voice boomed in English behind me, "Here's a fine sight for a hungry man!" And Matty Greenwood came striding up to me, his blue eyes bright and eager. "You must be new here, for I know all of Sarafina's girls. And eager for the work, to be down so early, and in this heat! Dammit, I should have come by earlier, and now it's too late. But you'll wait for me, won't you, my pet?"

Surprise and relief had my heart thundering so fast in my throat, I was unable to speak. Even less so when his hand lightly caressed my cheek as he beamed at me.

"Oh, *perdoneme. Habla ingles?*"

"I *habla ingles* perfectly, Mateo," I managed to bleat, at last. Matty started, and his hand flopped back down against the counter like a mortally wounded grouse.

"Why . . . b'God, it's . . . Mistress Lightfoot," he stammered. "So you really are a wench after all?"

It made me uneasy, the way his blue eyes roved slowly down the front of my person, and even more slowly up again. But I did not feel nearly as discomfited as Matty looked—and that made me feel better.

"You're the one who found me out," I reminded him.

"I'd have known it sooner had you been wearing so fetching a frock." He called for a drink to regain his composure and smiled again—at my face, this time. "Look here, I'm sorry about all that nonsense just now. I didn't mean to sound, ah, familiar . . . ."

"I quite understand. You didn't think I was anyone you knew."

Hot color rose up so suddenly in Matty's tanned cheek that I felt drunk with satisfaction, not only at the way the color intensified his handsome features but at the happy notion that I had caused it.

"You've a female tongue, all right."

"Oh, it's all right, Mateo." I laughed. "It's only me. Your arm looks well."

"Yes," he agreed, no doubt grateful for a neutral topic of conversation. "The bandages are off, at last. A Spanish surgeon I met in a card game saw to it." He flexed his left arm, a bit gingerly, then tested his grip by raising his cup. "And just in time, too. We sail with the tide in another hour."

His eyes closed as he swallowed while I drank in the whole of him. I would never mistrust Fortune again. As my own eyes roved, unchecked, I noticed a brilliant new scarlet sash round his waist; he must have spent some of his silver.

"So many of you men favor that shade of red," I observed. "What does it mean?"

"Heart's blood red. It's the captain's color, sort of a pun on his name. We wear it for loyalty. Of course, you wouldn't know about courtly knights, but they always wore their lord's or lady's colors into battle."

I bristled. Did he think he was the only one who had ever read a book?

"Mateo! *Bienvenido!*" Sarafina boomed, sweeping up to us, saving me the bother of a retort.

"Sarafina! My black-eyed angel!" They conversed in Spanish for a moment as Sarafina waved her plump hand at me. Then she turned to give a short little speech of which I understood very little. Matty, leaning on the counter and watching us with amusement, finally broke in.

"Sarafina would like you to stay on and work for her here," he explained. "She says you look strong enough to make a good living."

I shook my head, puzzled. "It can't take much strength to haul a few mugs of ale around the room."

Matty laughed. "I should think Sarafina's girls make most of their living on their backs upstairs."

"How much of a living?" I frowned. "*Cuanto?*"

Above Sarafina's rising protest, Matty laughed again.

"You don't earn a wage in this trade, Mistress. You get room and board and the clothes on your back."

And when my own few coins ran out, I would be as trapped and helpless as ever I would have been as a governess in Boston. Freedom was only for those who could afford to pay for it.

The last boatload of provisions had been sent out to the *Providence*. When I found them, Captain Hart and Matty and a couple of the others were loitering on the beach, waiting for the boat to return for them. Rudy saw me first, and smiled at my new rig, a man's undyed muslin shirt and moss-green trousers I'd purchased from a second-hand stall outside Sarafina's place. Farther down the beach, I noticed a tall fellow spinning island fruits in the air for a crowd of giggling village children. I stared harder and saw it was Jack. *Malabarismo*. Juggling.

"Come to see us off, have ye, Mistress?"

Hart's voice startled me back to the moment. He, too, must have been hoping I wouldn't return. As if a life at Sarafina's would be as good as any other life, for a female.

"Come to sail with you, Captain."

Hart turned to me, squinting in the sun. "I'm not in the habit of ferrying my hostages from port to port until they find the one that suits 'em."

"I have never been a hostage, Captain. I swore an oath, and I only ask that you allow me to honor it. If I slow you down, you'll have the satisfaction of feeding me to the sharks. That was the bargain, wasn't it?"

I looked out toward the water, long enough for him to notice the new red ribbon that bound my braid. When he did, he barked a short syllable of laughter.

"B'God, lass, you amuse me, and this promises to be a voyage damned short on amusement. Might as well sail into perdition with smiles on our faces, eh?"

"Ahoy, there, Rusty. Shake off this downy sleep."

I blinked up from my daydream. Jack had been teasing me about the rusty tint in my dark hair ever since I'd washed it.

"I don't relish doing the work of two," he warned me. Perched next to a pile of split, junked cordage heaped upon the cabin top, he was using the point of his narrow dagger to separate long, usable strands from the broken pieces. It was my job to knot these odd bits into seizing material that might be used later for emergency repairs to fraying lines. Two could finish in an afternoon, but it was a much drearier task for one alone.

After Salvador Gris piloted the *Providence* to a hidden beach in the *cayos* to spruce her up, Captain Hart ordered all standing and running rigging and all the miscellaneous cordage below tightened and repaired. Bustamante and his men were cleaning the guns and seeing to the shot, bolts and cables. Arne, the Danish carpenter, knocked about the deck inspecting railings, belaying pins, blocks and deadeyes for damage. And Rudy, in a canary yellow shirt and black-and-white striped trousers, led a sailmaking crew in mending canvas spread amidships. I could not see Matty anywhere. He appeared to have no special duties aboard ship, as the others had. And I wondered yet again what he was doing among this crew of searoving devils.

"Jack," I began, attending to my work with more diligence. "I know how I got here. But why do so many men turn pirate?"

"Poverty. Abuse. Ignorance. Survival, mostly." He glanced forward. "Now, Rudy, there, I believe he joined the trade for the wardrobe."

I smiled into my work. "What about you?"

"All of those reasons, I suppose."

Captain Hart came out on deck with a stool, and set it down in a tiny clearing between the sails and the guns, where he could keep an eye on things. He was with his barber, Javier, a coppery Haitian whom, Jack had explained, was *"criollo*—part French, Spanish, black, Caribe and God knows what else, born here in the islands." Javier carried his basin and razor, and when the captain sat down, Javier set to his work.

"What about a man like the captain?" I wondered, aloud.

"Damn few men like the captain."

"But you must know something about him."

"Oh, aye. He was born Edward Cameron Hart in some lowland Scots shire. His mother was deceased soon after, and his father was a wandering country parson devoted to the Bible and the bottle in about equal parts. Reverend Hart's heir and whipping boy finally ran off to Glasgow and the sea. Knocked about the North Atlantic until he found some steady employment in the American war with England in 1812— "

"On which side?" It was out before I could stop it.

"Does it matter?"

I shook my head, trying not to see my brother Josh's face. Kind, dreamy Josh, eighteen years old when he marched off to join the regiment from which he would never return.

"Found a berth on a Yank ship, I believe. He distinguished himself in battle, but he had no interest and couldn't afford a commission. After the war, all the regular seamen were paid off, and he had to sign on with a merchantman to the Indies." He pressed the point of his blade into a stubborn knot of cordage. "You served on a merchantman, Rusty."

"Not for long." I remembered the scars on Jack's back.

"Some berths are better than others, I suppose." Jack kept at his work. "It was just Hart's luck to fetch up in a right hellhole. He put up with that dog's life for three years. When he could bear no more, he killed his captain and led his shipmates to the nearest profitable war, the one the colonies of the Spanish Main were waging against the Dons. Got himself a privateering commission out of Caracas, and his own ship and crew—which he'd never managed to achieve in any honest sea trade. Eventually, he captured this sweet prize. Named her *Blessed Providence*, in memory of his Pa, who always told him that Blessed Providence would provide. As, indeed, she has, since he brought her to Cuba and went into business on his own account."

"The pirate business."

Jack shrugged. "Every white man in the Indies is a pirate. Most of 'em aren't as honest about it as Ed Hart."

"But could he not earn a naval commission? If his service was so distinguished?"

"Not if he can't read. Oh, aye, he can scribble his mark and decipher a sea chart. And he knows every rock in the Indies on sight; the captain could sail round the Horn in a leaky boot and make the voyage pay. But he has no formal education."

"Can no one teach him to read?"

"You're the governess, why don't you volunteer? Anyway, he's past the point now where it makes much difference to him."

I watched Hart jesting in Spanish with his barber, and tried to imagine any man aboard the *New Hope* on such familiar terms with Captain Calhoun. Then, Javier grasped something on a thong around his neck and began to shake it at the captain.

"What's that Javier's got?"

Jack didn't even need to look. "Chicken feet, most likely." He glanced up at my bewildered look. "*Voudon*. Island witchcraft. Some charm against the razor demon or suchlike. For a while, we had a real ship's surgeon aboard the *Providence*, who had some doctoring skills along with the barbering. But he drank up his restoratives and fell overboard. Now all we've got is Javier and his *voudon*."

"I shall remember never to fall ill."

"Oh, there's little difference between Javier's witchcraft and the leeches of a qualified physician. Besides, no one falls ill on a pirate vessel. Not for long." He threw a meaningful glance over the side of the ship.

But this was not entirely true. When Matty had been wounded, Captain Hart wouldn't even allow him to board a prize, let alone fight for it. There had been no talk of heaving him over the side. I shifted a little and gazed intently at my work.

"Is Matty the captain's boy?"

Jack looked at me, one eyebrow arching up into his dark hair.

"No." He kept watching me. "Nada is."

"But . . ." I faltered, "but I thought Matty—"

"That boy doesn't know what his private parts are for," Jack scoffed. "He's all hellfire and glory, our Matty. But Nada and the captain, they're two of a kind. Nada's people were peasant farmers in Havana until the Spanish bought up all the land for sugar. Then poor *criollos* had to work on the plantations or starve." He gathered up a fistful of drawn threads and handed them to me. "It's not a Christian name, Nada. It's an ordinary Spanish word."

"It means *nothing*," I recalled.

"Aye, which is what the Cuban peasants are to the wealthy Spanish planters. Especially after the Spanish found out how much simpler it was to work the land with African *bozales*, who had no rights whatsoever and required no wages. Most of Nada's family had died in poverty by the time he made his way to sea. He met Ed Hart in the privateering trade, and they've sailed together ever since."

"But . . . Nada . . . ." I could scarcely credit such a thing, and not only because Nada was another man. "He looks so . . . ferocious."

"Looks haven't much to do with it. No more than gender. Nada and the captain have been through every kind of hell together. What else do you suppose love is?"

I hadn't any idea. Most of my information on the subject had come from romances the girls smuggled into the Worthen Academy. All I knew first-hand was the way my heart spasmed every time I looked at Matty—not an observation I particularly wished to share with Jack.

"And which one is your boy, Uncle Jack?" I teased instead.

"Some of us must be left with clear enough wits to work the ship."

I busied myself with splicing and knotting for another minute before I piped up again.

"What if Matty is his long-lost son?"

"Whose?"

"Captain Hart's. He seems so fond . . . ."

Jack dropped his work and looked out to sea, muttering a dire expletive, before turning back to me.

"Matty is the captain's greatest prize, can't you see that? An educated gentleman's son who chucked it all to go a-pirating with Ed Hart. I was there when we took that ship.

Matty fought like a lion to defend her and got swept over the side, but when the smoke cleared, he swam aboard the *Providence* to join up with us rather than rejoin his own crew in defeat. Fond? The captain is in goddamned ecstasy! Matty is his victory over every fine gentleman who ever slammed the door of opportunity in his face."

I blinked at him. "I didn't know you were such a philosopher."

"Aye, you bring out the worst in me," Jack muttered, taking up his work again. "Just think of our Mateo as a novelty. Like you."

"Me?"

"Well, you're neither of you exactly the sort of scoundrel the captain's used to. You're a kind of . . . diversion."

"You make me sound like a trained pony. Suppose I run out of tricks?"

"You'll be safe enough here as long as you do your work and keep the captain amused. Only don't let the trouble it takes to keep you exceed what you provide in the way of entertainment."

"A fine way to talk, with your nimble hands." I sighed. "It's not as if I knew how to juggle."

I had returned to my work when I heard Jack cry, "Ho! Rusty!" I looked up in time to see him flip his dagger up by the blade—and let it fly at me. My hand shot up to protect my face, and the dagger's sharp edge nicked my rope-callused palm as my fingers closed awkwardly round it.

"Reflexes all right," Jack observed. "You could learn."

"Damn it, Jack!" I exploded, once the fear caught up with me, along with the sharp sting that made it impossible to close my hand. "I won't be able to make a fist for a week!" I glared at him. "Fortunately for you!"

CHAPTER 6

Trial By Battle

"I almost wish it would rain," Matty declared. "At least a lively squall would break up the boredom."

Matty had paid me little mind since I'd abandoned Sarafina's frock for my trousers. But so desperate was he for novelty this morning, he was even speaking to me. We stood together at the rail amidships, gazing out at the dawning of another crystalline clear and scorching day.

"Or a fresh breeze," I suggested. We had been adrift in listless airs since yesterday afternoon.

Cuban soil was no longer safe for pirates, least of all a marked ship like the *Providence*. When we heard that two of Porter's shoal-draught barges had pursued a pirate vessel to its lair ashore on the coast of Havana and killed all her crew, the men of the *Providence* voted to sail north by east into the Bahamas. But several days of coasting between the *cayos* of the

Great Bahama Bank and the uninhabited southern edge of
Andros Island had yielded up nothing but the dinghies of
spongers and fisher folk, leaving the pirates more restless than
ever.

"If we had a prize, the damned weather wouldn't matter." Matty declared. When he spoke of a prize, his eyes glit-
tered and shone, as if he were speaking of the woman he loved.

Jack was just passing behind us, munching on a hard
biscuit and absently raking his dark hair back from his forehead
as he gazed out at another mercilessly blue tropical sky.

"So foul and fair a day I have not seen," he muttered.
"Right now, I'd even welcome a bank of cold, damp London
fog. That's one thing I never expected to miss."

I turned toward him, forgetting even Matty in my astonishment. "*Macbeth*," said I. "'Fair is foul and foul is fair.' That's
from *Macbeth*. 'So foul and fair a day I have not seen.'"

Jack stared at me, speechless. Then, slowly, he began to
smile. The deep, weather-etched creases at the corners of his
dark eyes suggested that at one time, he had smiled a great deal.
"They never taught you Shakespeare in your fine Boston
school," he exclaimed.

"They did not," I agreed, absurdly proud of myself,
even though Matty's attention had already strayed elsewhere.
"But I learned a little, in spite of my education."

"*Velas! Velas adelante, muchachos!*" Nada's voice, deep
and urgent, boomed out like cannon shot.

"Jack Danzador! Aloft!" roared the captain, and Jack
sprang up into the shrouds as quickly as if he'd never been anywhere else. "Salvador Gris! Heel us around 'til we see what she
is," the captain continued, in Spanish, the official language of
emergency aboard the *Providence*. He went on bellowing
orders, although the men clearly knew their battle positions
and were scurrying into place. Everyone except me, who had
never been in a battle before and had no idea what to do.

The men talked of fighting all the time, but I confess I
was terrified. I had never raised arms before, and supposed I
could postpone it indefinitely. In the weeks I'd been aboard the

Providence, we had avoided confrontations, with Porter so near. But now, my first real trial was at hand, my trial by battle, and I was in no way prepared. I recognized the bitter, metallic taste of fear at the back of my tongue as the ship swept into position behind an overgrown and rocky cay to wait for her prize to sail into range. Jack shouted that the vessel was a Spanish barque riding low in the water, most likely a trader out of Havana heading for the Atlantic and home. By the time she'd worked past our hiding place, a fresh little southeasterly had begun to puff along at our heels. And once the *Blessed Providence* began her pursuit in earnest, I was cold with apprehension.

The *Providence* bore down on her prey like a gnat bedeviling an ox. The Spaniard was unable to outrun us, but she made no move to come into the wind to surrender. Bustamante's first shot across the Spaniard's bows was a warning; the second splintered a gun port, and the men made ready their grappling hooks to attach the *Providence* to her disabled side.

"They want a fight, eh?" Hart muttered, prowling amidships as we closed to board. "*Hombres!* I want her disabled quick and clean. There's no profit in corpses!"

I spotted Jack already in position at the far end of the rail. For an uncanny instant, his eyes met mine across the smoke and commotion, but his dark eyes had gone empty again, giving nothing away. Then I heard the captain bark, "Mateo! Arm the lass and stand by to board!"

Matty caught my arm from behind and hauled me to the cache of weapons under the foredeck. "Don't suppose you know how to use one of these," he muttered, seizing a pistol. "No? Of course, all you know is mending and Shakespeare. Like as not, you'd shoot one of us, or yourself . . . ah! Here's a weapon fit for a girl."

He wrapped my hand snugly around the hilt of a long, thin dagger. Even now, Matty's touch panicked me in a way that was distinct from my terror of the upcoming battle.

"This is for close work," he hurried on. "Go down into the belly and up under the ribs, if it comes to that. The captain doesn't much approve of killing, but sometimes he forgets to tell that to the enemy. If some Spanish Don is close enough for you to use this, you'll only get the one chance, so try to make every strike count."

Rivers of sweat poured down my skin, yet my insides were ice cold. But Matty chose this moment to grin. "Better yet, stay behind me. You'll have the safest berth in the fight. Come on!"

The pirates were now surging across the rails and onto the Spanish ship, shrieking like devils from hell, and I stumbled along in Matty's wake. I landed on the deck of the barque behind a wedge of pirates brandishing swords, pistols, even belaying pins with savage enthusiasm; ahead of them all, Captain Hart was making straight for a Spaniard struggling to load a pistol. Over my shoulder, I saw Nada planted on the *Providence* foredeck, his own pistol ready, never taking his black eyes off the captain. In another direction, I saw Jack vaulting across to the barque's deck at the end of a long pole, kicking one Spaniard aside as he landed, then whirling the pole around sideways to catch another in the stomach.

Directly before me, Matty strode into the melee slicing and parrying with both hands in bold and ruthless precision, a golden icon amid the smoke and dirt and chaos. If he couldn't disarm a man with a single thrust of his cutlass, up came his rapier under the chin, a check no opponent dared to challenge further; a swift elbow in the throat or a bash over the head with the cutlass cleared the way for his next opponent. Others scrabbled ferociously for an inch of advantage, but Matty swept through the enemy ranks like an avenging angel—the angel of Providence.

Men were brawling hand-to-hand; steel was clanging against steel. I saw one dazed Spanish seaman clutching a bleeding head wound, another a blood-soaked arm. I tried to back away, but the battle was now crashing and eddying all around me. I stumbled into something solid and whirled around to find myself staring into the face of a Spanish boy, no older than I and not quite as tall, whose eyes reflected my own terror. His hands were glued to the handle of a cumbersome axe, but I got my dagger up faster. I could only manage a pathetic parody of a feint, but it was enough of a lunge to startle the boy and send him stumbling away. Stricken by his face, I reeled back against a small deckhouse. I tasted salt leaking into the corner of my mouth as my vision began to blur. I scarcely saw the menacing shape that reared up out of the chaos before me, the glint of metal in the sun.

In the next instant, Jack landed on the deck before me to knock the Spaniard sprawling with the end of his staff. Jack kicked the wind out of the fellow, twisted the knife out of his grasp and stuck it in his own belt. Then he spun round and seized my elbow, dragging me behind the momentary shelter of the deckhouse.

"Have you lost your wits?" he hissed, shaking me by the shoulder. "Listen to me! It's far too late for tears. Listen to your Uncle Jack!"

I gulped back my sobs, and Jack forced his staff into both my hands. "Hold this aloft if a blade is coming down, down if a blade is coming up. Straight on, turn it sidewise, like this. Don't let go and don't stop until your back's to the rail. *Comprende?*"

Somehow, I found the wit to nod, tightening my grip on the staff. And Jack lunged away as quickly as he'd appeared. He somersaulted headfirst between Hector and the clumsy but vigorous Spanish swordsman he was holding off with a length of planked wood. Jack kicked the surprised Spaniard's sword out of his grip as he rolled under him, came up in a crouch and dove across the deck for the weapon.

"*Gracias, hermano!*" Hector roared after him, laughing heartily as he smashed his opponent to the deck with his board.

I had to fend off two more weapons, but at last I was able to drag my hide intact back to the rail, where the *Providence* was attached. Then, Captain Hart appeared on the quarterdeck with his knife at the throat of the Spanish captain, who sullenly ordered his men to throw down their arms.

CHAPTER 7

Diabolito's Wrath

I had learned the first lesson of battle—to keep myself alive until the opposing captain called for quarter. But now that the men were herding up the Spanish crew, I had no idea what to do next.

"Lightfoot!" boomed Nada from the foredeck, two syllables like a gale of frost up my backside, despite the heat. He had nothing in particular to command me to do, only that I should make myself useful and be quick about it. By now it must be obvious to every man aboard that I didn't know the butt end of a pistol from a butt of claret. If I could not fight, I might yet end up feeding the sharks.

Casting about for some task to occupy myself, I saw Jack loping toward me with some small arms he'd rounded up from our captives.

"Captain says more line," he hailed me; to further confound the Spanish sailors, we were now conversing mostly in English. "All that can be hauled up. Go tell Nada."

"I'll get it myself." I sighed. "It's time I did something right today,"

"Oh? Still breathing, are you?" said Jack.

"Now and then."

"All appropriate limbs accounted for?"

"The last time I looked."

"Then I should consider the day a resounding success. Line," he repeated, and was off about his business.

Under Nada's disapproving eye, I scrambled across the two rails and dropped onto the *Providence* deck. As I headed below for more line, I wondered what would happen now. These Spaniards had fought back with no little determination, and I tried to steel myself for whatever their punishment might be. Yet, I was not prepared for the dumb show in progress when I rejoined the others on the deck of the captured barque.

The Spanish crewmen were all shut up together in the deckhouse, the deadlights slammed-to over its scuttles to keep them entirely in the dark. Outside, the pirates were tramping about noisily, rattling weapons and laughing and jesting in loud, menacing tones, mostly in English but for a few random cries of *"Muerte!"* or *"Exterminacion!"*

Hector, Bustamante and Julio—one of the heftiest of his gun crew—stood outside the deckhouse door shouting curses and insults at the Spaniards inside. These continued unabated even as Hector grinned at me and beckoned me over with my arms full of rope and cordage. He seemed delighted by the present foolery, roaring blood-curdling threats into the deckhouse while grinning over the lines he set to untangling.

Opposite the deckhouse, Captain Hart lounged against a closed water cask. Piled on its lid were a few confiscated blades, which he was sharpening against a whetstone with great, long, ringing strokes. He nodded for me to come stand behind him. At his side, Matty was loading and priming several pistols. Two of them had already been fastened to either end of a long strap to be worn around the neck, the way the pirates liked to carry their pistols into battle. At the lower fore shrouds, Arne had rigged up some kind of tackle attached to a heavy barrel that Rudy and another man were steadying just outside the rail, on the channel below. On the far side of the shrouds, Jack perched on the rail, looking bored.

"Stay a moment, Mistress, and learn something," the captain grinned. He nodded to Hector, who opened the deckhouse door, dove inside and hauled out a terrified Spanish sailor, while Julio slammed the door shut behind them.

"*Amigo*," Hart addressed the sailor in Spanish. "I know there is money on this ship."

"No, *señor*," stammered the Spaniard. "We are only a trading ship."

"You have one minute to tell me where the money is," Hart continued, sharpening a blade with swift, sure strokes. "Or forfeit your life."

"But . . . we have no money," the sailor cried, with a wild look back toward the deckhouse. "I swear it, *señor!*"

Hart spoke no more, but Matty lifted a pistol and sighted down its barrel as he pointed it at the Spanish sailor's chest.

"*Madre de Dios!* Please, *señor*, no . . .!*"

The pistol exploded too fast for me to look away—so I saw Matty point its barrel out to sea at the last possible instant. In the same moment, Hector forced a rag into the startled sailor's mouth while the others roped his arms behind his back. At the rail, Arne and Rudy pitched their barrel off the channel while Jack cried out, "*Madre de Dios . . . !*" in a failing voice until the barrel splashed into the sea.

Bustamante hauled the now-silenced, wriggling sailor forward and pitched him into the forecastle, where Cuervo and some others stood guard. As soon as Arne signaled to the captain that the weighted barrel had been retrieved and was again standing ready, Hart nodded to Hector to bring out the next "victim."

One Spanish crewman after another was hauled out, questioned and dispatched in the same manner. Most of them were bleeding or limping from the battle, but all were still in possession of their lives; separating them from their weapons had been the primary object of the *Providence* men. By the third or fourth interrogation, I realized how closely Jack was imitating each Spaniard's voice. When a Spanish officer was brought on deck who responded to Hart's questions with a torrent of angry invective, Jack mimicked the man's cursing with imaginative gusto, then turned it into a plea for mercy just before the pistol fired.

Only once did the trick threaten to fail. A frightened crewman fell to his knees the moment he emerged from the deckhouse, clenched hands raised together and head bowed in desperate supplication, too terrified to respond to the captain's questions. Matty was ready with another shot, but Jack caught Hector's eye over the kneeling sailor, touched his own ear and shook his head. Hector obligingly pulled out his own knife and lightly pricked the sailor's shoulder. The Spaniard yelped a few startled syllables, enough for Jack to approximate his voice crying to heaven as the shot rang out. The barrel splashed overboard, and the bewildered sailor was hustled forward to join his fellows.

It was an enjoyable spectacle from my vantage point; less so for the poor crewmen still trapped in the dark, imagining their doom was only moments away. But perhaps there was no specie aboard. Or if there was, it was likely the common seamen knew nothing about it.

Next out of the deckhouse came the Spanish captain, blustering that no baseborn *cubano,* or whatever Hart was, would dare to murder in cold blood the captain of a legitimate trading vessel of the Spanish Empire. There was some chuckling among the men that Spain, ravaged by civil war and colonial revolt, might yet consider herself an empire.

"The world would be well rid of any captain who valued the lives of his men as nothing to a few stores of specie," Hart replied.

"Seamen must do their duty."

"Which is to die for the captain's cashbox?"

"My men are sworn to protect the property of Spain," the Spanish captain responded. "And so am I."

"And you shall be used no differently than your men," Hart agreed, nodding to Matty to fire another shot. Jack let out a cry equal parts outrage and agony as the Spanish captain was gagged and bound and hauled away.

Then Hector dragged out the young Spaniard I had encountered during the battle, and Hart's impatience evaporated. He lowered his knife to gaze at the youth in silence.

"You know where the money is hidden, boy," he said, at last. It was not a question.

The boy looked less frightened than he had in battle. His eyes showed only sadness, now, not fear. "There is no money," he murmured, looking downward.

"Of course there is," Hart continued, very gently, in his fine, persuasive Spanish. "A captain does not embrace certain death with such noble zeal for no reason."

He waited, but the boy did not answer.

"It's no good to him, now," Hart reasoned, in the same confiding voice. "But you can still save the lives of your shipmates. I seek profit, not bloodshed. Tell me what I ask and your mates may go free."

This brought the young Spaniard's wary eyes up.

Hart pressed on. "How many more must die to protect the purse of a dead man?"

The boy's miserable eyes fastened onto Hart's for a long, wordless interval. Then he cast them down again. "Nail kegs," he whispered, so that Hart had to step forward to hear him. "It's in the nail kegs."

Matty and Cuervo raced for the main hatch and descended into the hold. Soon, their whoops of triumph over the discovered specie could be heard all over the ship.

The Spanish youth still stood under Hector's watchful gaze, his face growing more disconsolate. He seemed no less miserable when his captain and mates emerged unharmed from the forecastle, their gags removed, to be marched back into the deckhouse. The boy's face reddened under his captain's furious eyes as the men passed, and the boy turned to follow them. Captain Hart was strapping the brace of pistols round his neck near the deckhouse, and he halted the youth while the Spanish captain and some others were still mustered outside the door.

"They're going to talk a lot of bilge in there about honor and pride and manliness," Hart told the boy, in Spanish. "They'll call you a coward and a woman to prove how brave they are, now the danger's passed. But remember this, boy, you saved their lives." Hart swept his gaze across the last few Spaniards still outside the deckhouse and his voice rose. "It took true courage to put your shipmates' lives above your orders. And something more. Common sense and character, which are in damned short supply in the merchant fleet or any fleet. I would be proud to have you serve with me."

His eyes had swung back to the startled youth, who colored a little, but shook his head.

"*No, Capitan . . . no gracias.*"

Hart frowned, but let him pass. The boy was trudging toward the deckhouse, head down, when the Spanish captain lunged toward him with an upraised hand and a roar of Spanish curses. He could not have had a weapon; we'd taken them all. More likely, he meant to beat the lad like a disobedient cur. But Captain Hart raised one of his pistols with absolute composure and fired. There was an explosion of fabric and blood as the merchant captain's shoulder snapped backward and he was sent sprawling across the deck. Blinking furiously, his mouth still working without sound, the Spanish captain struggled to prop himself half upright on his other arm. But he froze as Hart calmly leveled the second pistol at his head.

"*Señor. . . Capitan . . .* don't kill me! By the blood of Christ, on the souls of my children, I beg of you . . . ."

And on he went, pleading for mercy in language more abject than even Jack could have invented. Captain Hart's mouth twitched in distaste, and he pivoted slowly about to aim his pistol at the Spaniards still massed at the deckhouse door.

"Do not underestimate the value of your lives!" Hart thundered, in Spanish. He nodded toward the Spanish youth.

"Thanks to this fellow's courage, you still possess yours. But I'll take them, as well, if you insist."

The merchant crewmen were petrified into silence. There could be no doubt that this savage Diabolito meant what he said. Hellfire, for one chilling moment I didn't doubt it myself. At a nod from Hart, the boy fled to the others and two of his mates embraced him warmly and bundled him into the deckhouse.

Later, when we'd returned to the *Providence* and cut loose the Spaniards and their crippled ship, I asked Jack about the farce we'd played.

"But how did you know the trick would work?" I demanded.

"It always works." Jack shrugged. "It has never failed."

"But suppose one of these fellows runs into some other you've duped in some Spanish cantina and they swap stories. Would they not warn other merchantmen when they learn how they've been fooled?"

"By the time this story reaches the cantinas of Spain, we'll all have green scales and cloven hooves." Jack laughed. "A few boatloads of hungry *cubanos* struggling to survive in their own islands must become a race of devils, savage *diabolitos*, drooling for innocent blood. How else can any merchant captain explain to his employers and himself the loss of his precious specie without the forfeit of a single life?"

"They put up a spirited fight for a lot of Spanish dogs." Captain Hart waved aloft his bottle in a grudging salute. "They might have held us off a good long while had they been at all prepared."

He perched on a corner of the heavy crate in the *Providence* hold as we made our way back to the shelter of Andros Island. I was logging the day's spoils into the ledger book in Matty's place; he had already proved his value today, and I was desperate to be of use.

"But men are seldom prepared for the intervention of Blessed Providence," the captain observed.

"Amen, Captain!" Matty sang out, from where he and Hector were rolling the last of the Spanish goods into storage, their enmity of a fortnight ago entirely forgotten.

"Remember, Mistress," Hart continued, "ye must never, ever underestimate the element of surprise."

"*Si, Capitan.*" Cuervo's sarcastic voice came from deep in the hold. "No one expects to fight over a load of damned sugar."

This had been the bulk of the Spaniard's cargo, along with a few hundred Spanish dollars and a box of writing paper, quills and ink from the captain's cabin. This modest prize had almost cost my life, and I must have shuddered at the thought.

"Losing your taste for this trade already, are ye, Lightfoot?"

"I lack your gift for riddles, Captain," I replied with mock bravado, "but I don't see how we're to make a profit on sugar in the Indies."

"You can make a profit on anything in the Indies if you know your business. Port towns are always full of enterprising merchant captains looking for a cargo and none too concerned over where it came from. And while nothing much grows in this rock they call soil in the Bahamas, the English gentry hereabouts—what's left of 'em—still require sugar in their tea. Which reminds me, Lightfoot, I'll expect you in the galley. It'll be supper time soon."

"*Si, Capitan.*" I was still fit for the kitchen, if nothing else. The captain had forgiven my cowardice today, but perhaps it made no odds to him whether I lived or died. Perversely, however, it still mattered to me. I remembered how much when I saw Jack again, among the last of the men going above. I called to him, and he ambled over.

"*Gracias.*" I nodded toward his staff, stowed by the crate.

"*De nada.*" He bent to pick it up.

"My life may be nothing to you, but I should be sorry

to lose it."

He paused, then glanced at me sideways. "A word, then, and I'll say no more about it. Leave the fighting to those who know how."

"I'll be shark food if I can't fight."

"Well, if you must plunge into battle, never let the enemy see any weakness. It reminds 'em of their own fear, which a man will do anything to deny. You must . . . well, take a good heart and counterfeit to be a man."

I supposed this was more poetry, but I didn't recognize it. And, as always, my ignorance was plain on my face.

"*As You Like It,*" Jack added helpfully.

I sighed. "I know as much about Shakespeare as I do about fighting."

"All it takes is practice."

"Of which you've had a great deal, it seems. Where did you learn to leap about like that in a fight?"

"Oh, years ago, as a boy. I was brought up among tumblers."

"Can you teach it to me?"

"Teach me Spanish, teach me tumbling," Jack groaned. "I thought you were the one in the governess trade. Well, I suppose if the alternative is to see what few brains you still possess splattered across some deck . . . ." Still muttering, he turned away as Rudy came down behind him. "Mistress Lightfoot is turning the *Providence* into a schoolroom. The next time we take some cut-throat aboard, we'll have to charge tuition . . . ."

Rudy laughed as Jack grumbled his way up the ladder.

"Rudy, why do they call him 'Jack Danzador'?" I asked. "It means *dancer*, doesn't it?"

"*Si! Danzador, bailador.*" Rudy grinned. "Jack, he no fight, eh? He dance."

There was a sharp, sudden cry above that brought feet thundering across the deck over our heads. I had to brace against the sudden pitch of the ship and saw Rudy's face go bright with excitement as he listened to the jumble of shouts and commands from above.

"Man in water!" he cried. "May be a wreck! *Vamonos, amiga!*" And he bolted to the companion ladder with me at his heels.

CHAPTER 8

The Wracker

On deck the men were already hauling aboard the limp figure of a black man, his face bruised and flecked with dried blood, his dark skin blistered by the sun. Over the side, I saw a shallow, open boat without oars or provisions rocking listlessly alongside the *Providence.* The boat was pulled close by grappling hooks, and Arne stood gingerly in her bottom inspecting her, while others got the tackle ready to hoist her aboard. The stranger laid out on deck was a young man, or he had been at the start of his ordeal. Now it looked doubtful if he would ever see old age; Cuervo and Bustmante were making a discreet wager, not over whether the stranger would perish, but how soon.

"Jack, Hector," Hart commanded, "take him below to my cabin. He may be useful to us if he lives. Rudy, fetch some water."

"Runaway?" Matty suggested, at the captain's elbow.

"Not without oars."

"Wrecked on the reefs, then?"

Hart shook his head, his face grim. "Those wounds look man-made."

The *Providence* put into a sheltered beach of a deserted cay during the few days it took to determine the fate of our new passenger. Nada complained that the *Providence* was not a mercy ship, and Cuervo was all in a frenzy to sail for Nassau to sell or spend our Spanish plunder. But the captain was in no hurry. The patient remained aboard with Rudy and Javier trading the watch over him. I sat with Rudy, sometimes, helping to cool the stranger's face with damp rags as his weakness turned to fever. When I asked where Rudy had learned his doctoring, he only shrugged.

"*Yo soy cubano,*" he said. "Everybody know about the fever."

Things were very different when Javier stood watch. He droned on in a low, unearthly jumble of Spanish and a kind of French, prowling round the bunk or rocking back and forth on his knees. Sometimes he called on the protection of the *loas* and the Saints, the benevolent spirits. At other times, he chanted against the sinister influences of the *spectres*, the *fantomes* and especially the *diablesses,* wicked she-demons punished in the next world for the crime of dying as virgins. Since I'd first clapped eyes on Matty, I no longer considered my own chastity any great virtue, but this was the first I'd heard that it was a crime.

Javier was on watch the morning the patient recovered his senses, and the squawking could be heard all over the cay. By the time Captain Hart made his way aboard, Javier was gabbling an indignant explanation.

"I going to call up the *loa,* like I do every day, and suddenly, he sit up, wide-eye, like *le mort!* I think he must be *servi-*

teur, the *loa* going to speak through him. Then he scream, and I think, *Mon Dieu*, he become zombie, the living invisible—"

"*Si, si, bueno*, you've done nothing wrong," Hart assured him, shouldering his way into the cabin, with several of us right behind. The patient was indeed sitting up, pressed into the furthest corner of the captain's bunk, clutching the bed linens. Jack had been aloft when the commotion began, and now perched calmly on the foot of the bunk.

"No need for all this uproar, Captain." Jack grinned. "This fellow doesn't know a word of French or Spanish; no wonder Javier scared the wits out of him. This is Captain Hart," he added, turning to the patient. "The man who saved your hide."

The stranger turned his wary gaze from Jack to the captain and the rest of us crowded in the doorway, and then back to Jack.

"You not from the *William and Mary* out of Portsmouth?" His voice was low and raspy, but there was a distinctive lilt to his English.

"Do we look it?" asked Jack.

"Nor any merchant ship?"

"No, nor the *Flying Dutchman*, either," muttered Hart.

The stranger drew himself up and thrust a hand toward Hart.

"Harry Quick, of Eleut'era Island. At your service, Cap'n."

Harry Quick was given a hot meal, fresh clothing and another day's rest before there was any further questioning. The next evening, he was brought ashore to join us for supper round the cookfire. He looked somewhat refreshed, almost chipper, despite one or two ugly bruises and a still-swollen eye.

"What trade are ye in, Mr. Quick?" the captain asked when the rum was passed round.

"I be a pilot, Cap'n, best in the islands."

"Ah. I expect you tried to pilot the *William and Mary* onto the Great Bahama Bank. That's why they beat you and cast you adrift."

Harry Quick's eyes widened in outrage, then narrowed, but he did not speak.

Hart took another lazy pull from his bottle. "I'm in the pirate trade myself, Harry."

"I go aboard her in Nassau harbor," Harry replied, at last. "I mean her no harm, for true. I take her out past the bar for the channel. Then the mate, he say he seen me talking to wrackers in a grog shop in Bay Street." He lifted his chin a bit. "I be a free man. I may speak to whoevah I please. They have no right to treat me so."

"Oh, aye," Hart agreed, "I've no love for the English merchant fleet, myself. Still, I'll wager you're not unfamiliar with the wrecking trade?"

"It be an honest trade. Why should I trouble to pilot that damn ship aground when they be reefs aplenty to do the job for me?"

"Look here, Harry, I don't care how you make your living. I thought we might strike a bargain."

Harry nodded. "I owe you me own life, Cap'n."

"I don't want it, lad." Hart chuckled. "But I could use a sharp pilot. And a competent spy."

For the first time, Harry broke into a grin.

Despite Nada's grumbling, we tarried a few more days and nights on our lonely *cayo*—with naught but crabs, lizards, shorebirds and each other for company—until our new pilot was fit to travel. Arne used the time to careen and repair Harry's little boat, with Jack and Hector heading up his work crew. Matty went off almost every day with Cuervo to hunt wildfowl or anything else that might pass for game or sport. One morning, the captain sent me with a message to Harry, resting aboard the *Providence*. When I poked my head in at the cabin door and spoke, Harry jumped as if he'd seen one of Javier's *fantomes*.

"It's you!" he cried.

"Me?"

"When I have the fever, I t'ink I hear a woman's voice and feel her hand on me face. When I wake up, I t'ink, Harry, you mistaken, they be no woman here. But now, for true, I hear that voice again."

It had been a long time since I'd bothered to alter my voice, just as I no longer thought of my male clothing as a disguise. From a distance, I supposed I must look like any of the others; what a shock it must be for someone outside the crew to discover a female in their midst. The element of surprise.

"That was me. I didn't mean to frighten you."

"Frighten me? I t'ought you were an angel! Then I wake up and see the little *voudon* man, and I t'ink maybe I be in t'ot'er place." He laughed, and I joined in. "If you be real flesh and blood, you must have a name."

"Tory."

"And you ran away to go a-pirating wit' your lover," he went on, eagerly, "like Mistress Bonny from the old glory days."

"Well, no . . . ." This time, I laughed in dismay. "I joined up on my own account."

"You mean to say no man aboard be your lover?"

I shook my head. Harry's face showed his disappointment, which was nothing to mine. Now that the *Providence* had resumed her piratical trade, my chances of ending up a *diablesse* were improving at an alarming rate. Still, it galled me to think that even a woman in the pirate trade was expected to have an escort.

Harry argued against selling our sugar through the Vendue House in Nassau, where all those officially employed in the wrecking trade were legally obliged to dispose of the goods they'd salvaged.

"For one t'ing, you got to have a wracker's license," he told the captain. "For anot'er, there be a mighty big customs duty and after the gov'ment take its share, there nevah be much profit left. But there be bettah bargains to make."

So, in sheltered, back-door ports from Rum Cay to the Caicos Bank, the *Blessed Providence* traded sugar for food and provisions. Harry, fit at last, guided Salvador Gris through the narrow channels. He took us down the southern coast of Great Inagua island to spy on the trade out of Cuba and the Windward Passage, prompting some fresh grumbling among the men. I had learned that the Windward was a direct artery to the pirates' home base at Cabo Cruz on the southwestern tip of Cuba. It was on the edge of this passage that the *Providence* had captured the *New Hope,* and the men had not been home since. But when Harry went ashore with Jack to a wreckers' tavern, to barter plundered specie for powder and shot salvaged from a naval supply ship, they came back with sobering news—two Yankee Squadron schooners had been spotted sweeping the southern coast of Cuba for pirate lairs. After that, there were no more wistful remarks about Cabo Cruz.

Harry engineered all our business transactions ashore in the out islands. Jack went along to see that no loose talk about the nature or whereabouts of the *Providence* was spread in port, where information was always for sale. Jack was less likely than one of the Cubans to arouse suspicion in the English islands, and he and Harry always came back in the boat at ease and gossiping together like old mates. But it bothered Nada that the fate of the *Providence* lay so often in the hands of a stranger.

Coming on deck for a breath of air one still night, I overheard Nada and the captain talking together quietly at the rail.

"How do we know he won't wreck us on some lonely reef?" Nada was whispering in Spanish.

"How does he know we won't murder him when we're done with him?" Hart countered.

"He knows too much about us for someone who has not taken the oath," Nada insisted. "Who knows what he says about us when he's ashore?"

"Jack knows. And Harry isn't likely to betray us to the English. The English tried to kill him."

"You're far too trusting," Nada muttered.

"*Si, mi corazon*. I trusted you once, and look where it got me."

There was a pause before Nada's softened voice came back. "That was different."

I heard only the captain's low chuckle as I hurried myself away.

"You following a fine old tradition, Cap'n," said Harry, one sultry night, handing the last of the rum bottle back to Hart.

"Old, surely, but there's nothing fine about it." The captain snorted. "I'm in this miserable trade for profit, nothing more."

Most of the men had drifted off to find what refuge they could from the humid air, but I lay under the main shrouds, gazing up at the stars. When I glanced across the deck, I could see the captain and Harry draped over the hatch cover amidships, sharing their bottle.

"The way I see it, Harry, there must be a thousand ways for a man to die," Hart went on. "More if he's young or poor or foolish enough. He can die for his god—which seems to me the mark of a god who's not living up to his end of the bargain. He can die in battle, to enrich the purse of some fat prince. Or he can die a martyr to some glorious bloody cause. But most often, he dies because some incompetent captain or general doesn't know enough to keep him safe—or doesn't give a damn. Dying is easy. What's rare—what's damn near impossible to find in these blighted colonial islands—are ways for a man to live."

"You talk like you been here a long time."

"Aye, too long. I've fought in wars all up and down the Atlantic coast, served in the merchant fleet, campaigned in the revolution against Imperial Spain."

Harry nodded, impressed. "Lots of fellows round here t'ink Bolivar some kind of saint."

"No, but he'll make himself a martyr, and soon, if he keeps driving himself the way he does. But there are hundreds of generals under Bolivar and not a saint among 'em. I served with some of 'em out of Caracas and I can tell you this, the minute they drive out the Dons, they'll be at each others' throats. They're at it already. They all bow to *El Libertador,* but they're damned if they'll give up an ounce of their precious power to one another. Not without a fight."

He offered the bottle to Harry, who shook his head.

"I got tired of all the dying, Harry; there's the truth of it. I thought there must be some way for poor men to make a profit in their own homeland. And b'God, here she is!" He laughed, slapping the deck. "Blessed Providence provides and we make a living. Not a fine living, perhaps. But we live."

Harry Quick left us at Fortune Island, where the principal town was a rallying point for wreckers.

"There'll always be a berth for ye aboard the *Providence,* Harry," Captain Hart told him.

"I t'ank you, Cap'n. But it seem to me a deal more trouble to plunder a ship that be manned and armed than one already broke up and helpless. But you treat me fair, and I won't forget it. If you evah need a pilot in these parts, or a spy, you come see Harry Quick."

"I'll miss him," I said to Jack, as we watched Harry sail off.

"Aye, but he has a life to return to," Jack replied. "Unlike us."

"I liked the musical way he talked. I suppose I thought

he would sound more like Hector."

"But they hale from different sides of the globe. There must be dozens of black races in the Indies, if you figure in all the African tribes along with the *mulattos*, quadroons and all the rest." He smiled at my bewilderment. "Mixed blood," he explained. "Black and white. Black and Indian. Indian and European, for that matter. Mongrels."

I knew what that meant.

"Harry's native tongue is English—well, Bahamian English," Jack went on. "He was born here. Hector came from Africa. He was sold to a Spanish sugar estate in Cuba and then, I believe, an English coffee planter before he ran away, and he's learned a version of both languages. I doubt he remembers much of his African tongue, but for some songs and an oath or two when he's losing at dice."

"The way the captain's Scots burr increases with his rum ration."

"Oh? And what do you know of Scots burrs?"

"My father was a Scot."

"Ah. That accounts for the rust in your hair. And your mother?"

"Mohawk. Indian," I added, with no little defiance.

"Mmm, that accounts for the rest. Mongrel, eh?"

"I had plenty of opportunity to study the benefits of good breeding in Boston," I snapped back.

Jack laughed. "Calm yourself, Rusty. We're all mongrels, here. "

"Well, what are you, then?"

"Dunno. I was an orphan."

"You said your family were tumblers," I reminded him.

"Tumblers reared me. God only knows where they found me."

"A foundling!" I exulted. "Like Tom Jones!"

"Born to be hanged," Jack agreed. "As you can see, finding me here."

CHAPTER 9

The Rebel Doubloons

W hat Jack had called the temperate season gave way to a damp spring now melting into torpid summer as the *Blessed Providence* plied what little trade she could find in the Bahamas. News of Porter's merciless pursuit of pirates along the Cuban coast was the talk of every grog shop. With Adderly still lusting for my blood and eager to identify us to the Yankee Squadron, the men of the *Providence* could have no thought of going home.

But the *Providence* was home enough to me. Jack was teaching me tumbling—landing and falling—whenever we found an empty, powdery stretch of beach. At first I complained I wasn't learning any tricks, to which Jack replied that the trick was to stay alive. After that, I held my tongue.

And as we chased and boarded more ships, I came to appreciate the value of knowing how to land upright on a rolling deck and fall out of the path of an upraised weapon. As I gained the confidence to protect myself, I lost my fear of boarding. In truth, most merchant ships were poorly armed, with no more taste for fighting to the death than Captain Hart. Often, the mere sight of desperate pirates baying at the rail with imagined blood-lust was enough to induce a merchant vessel into surrender.

Still, there was little enough profit in the Bahamas. Occasionally, we were fortunate enough to relieve some stray merchantman of Yankee grain or English cloth. But, cut off from our trading ports in Cuba, we had to parcel out these goods piecemeal for food and provisions at backwater ports in the outer salt islands. The men complained they might as well be serving on an honest merchant vessel, which wounded Hart to the quick. Especially when news of Porter's success lured even more commercial shipping into the trade routes; the passages were full of trading ships eager to finish their business and clear out of the Indies before the hurricane season. At last, Hart gave the order to sail for the Windward Passage to seize some fat trader and make for some richer, friendlier port in the Antilles.

"American trading brig, for certain," Jack confirmed from aloft. Rudy hoisted the stars and stripes, and as the *Providence* closed on her prey, the men stripped off their shirts and cinched their belts for action. "Looks like the Forrester and Clemmons insignia on her foretop banner," Jack added.

"Mr. Bustamante, your men are all ready? Rudy, raise the black flag." The captain glanced around the deck. "Lightfoot, get below 'til you're called."

My head snapped up in surprise, sending a bolt of pain to the back of my eye. I kept forgetting that eye. In our last capture, I had tumbled a big, blustery English sailor backwards over a capstan. Unfortunately, as he went over, his knee had come up and slammed me in the face, blackening my eye. It had swollen and throbbed a little, blurring my vision, but the only remnant now was a purple bruise—and a stab of pain, if I forgot.

"I'm not hurt, Captain," I protested.

"I mean to work fast here, and you'll slow us down."

Hart believed that the wholesale slaughter of enemy sailors only rallied their comrades to foolish acts of heroism, but that speed and confusion cowed them more quickly into surrender. If I could not be fast, I was of no use in a fight.

"Si, Capitan."

"Mateo—take her below and stay there. Stand by in case Nada needs your help holding the ship."

My feeble protest had been nothing compared to the spluttering explosion with which Matty greeted this command.

"Silencio, muchacho!" Hart roared. "That's an order!"

Matty managed to hold his tongue, but there was fury in his eye as he stormed down the hatch. I followed without a word, not daring to express my own astonishment that the captain would enter into battle without his most accomplished warrior. In the dimness below, we felt the ship coming about to bear on her quarry, heard the buckets of shot and rattling langrage being hauled to the guns overhead and the booming and shouting that followed. Matty braced himself at the foot of the companion ladder, riding out the rolling of the hull, straining to see up the hatch, one hand clenched in white-knuckled fury.

He looked so beautiful, so wild and ardent and alive, I forgot all about the battle above. He was my Charioteer made flesh, but I could think of nothing to say to him. I was scarcely an accomplished coquette, and I lacked the boldness to simply claim what I wanted, like Harry's fabled Mistress Anne Bonny of a hundred years ago. Besides, in matters of love, I wanted more than a hostage. Still, I felt I must say something or he would explode with his own suppressed rage.

"Mateo, why won't the captain—"

"It's ridiculous!" he burst out. "He doesn't want me seen. As if I gave a goddamn about that life anymore!"

"That life? On the American?"

"My father owns her. Forrester and Clemmons," he added, venomously. "Forrester is my honored parent."

Of course, the name Greenwood must be another pirate nickname, a pun on Forrester. Then the larger implication sank in.

"Your father owns a trading fleet and you turned pirate?" So they were not all mongrels aboard the *Providence* after all. It was all I could do not to laugh until Matty rounded on me, his sky-blue eyes cold with rage.

"My father is a fool. Made me ship out a common seaman to learn the business before I came into my inheritance. As if I cared about the business! That was no life for me."

I had seen how young men were treated on merchant ships; what a shame if Matty's youthful fire had been crushed in that manner. And yet, his smooth, golden back was unblemished by the lash marks that disfigured Jack and so many others aboard. There must be degradations the owner's son was spared, no matter how "common" his rank.

"Now they'll see what I'm made of," Matty went on. "Or they would, if the captain would let me fight."

"Perhaps he only wants to protect you."

"Do I look like I need protection?" he roared.

Nada's voice called us to come up to receive cargo. But then we heard sudden popping explosions, too rapid for shot, and men roaring and more battle sounds above. Pungent, suffocating smoke choked off the light, but I found the ladder and clawed up toward the hatch, Matty at my heels. But there was nothing to see above but clouds of smoke. Then came the boom of a cannon, the *Providence* shivered, and there was a deafening crack high above the deck. I poked my head out to see an explosion of spars and splinters, then hurled myself back down the hatch, dragging Matty with me, as a riot of twisted timber and tangled lines blotted out the daylight.

At any other time, the pressure of Matty's alert and muscular body against mine would have obliterated all rational thought. But now I was too distracted by smoke, darkness and god-knew-what chaos going on above to savor it.

"The forward hatch," he shouted.

We scrambled out into daylight in time to see the Forrester brig reeling away on an easterly, out of the range of Bustamante's guns. On deck, the pirates struggled to cut loose the tangle of torn rigging that had crashed down, free the men trapped under it and clear the decks for sailing. Matty drew his cutlass and rushed in to assist as Captain Hart bellowed orders from the stern; he and Salvador Gris were grappling with the helm to keep her steady. When the foremast was free of debris, I raced aloft with Cuervo and Hector to spread whatever topsail canvas was still intact; the cannon shot had gone high and wide, severing the upper topsail yard, but the lower topsail and masthead still answered. With some alert hauling on the braces and sheets, the *Providence* was able to beat southeast, away from the escaping brig.

I came down as the others were gathering amidships, their mood weary and angry. Six long, low wooden crates, the only plunder taken from the brig, were stowed in the bulwarks. Bustamante paced nearby, ranting furiously in Spanish, and Jack was limping in from the rail, where he'd helped toss the last of the splintered timber overboard. When he turned to ease himself down onto the top rung of the short ladder leading to the cabin top, I saw a dark, wet stain soaking his ripped trouser leg from hip to knee.

"Lost my balance," he told me, in a disgusted voice.

"Dancing is no substitute for fighting, Danzador," Matty declared.

Rudy came over with a length of cloth and a bottle and knelt below Jack. He yanked the rip in Jack's trousers wider still, but all I could see underneath was blood.

"She gave over meekly enough," Hart was telling us. "We rounded up her crew and started searching the cabins. Came up with that lot right off." He nodded toward the crates.

"We were getting them over the side," Cuervo took up the tale. "Then . . . Boom! Boom! Smoke everywhere, explosions. We thought we were shot."

"Smoke but no fire," Hart added. "Just noise and confusion."

"Firecrackers," said Matty, slowly. "Gunpowder explosives. My father picked them up in the China trade." He scowled, puzzling it out. "He must be carrying them on his ships since they're so small and easy to hide."

"They make a hell of a diversion, all right," muttered Jack. "Damn!" he added, through clenched teeth, as Rudy probed at his leg. He took a pull from the bottle and handed it to Rudy, who downed a healthy swallow before splashing a little of the rum across the gash in Jack's thigh, making Jack grimace again.

"We didn't know what was happening," Hart went on. "Her crew was running around everywhere under cover of the smoke."

"Three of them fell on Julio, guarding their carronade," Bustmante spat out. "It took all three of them to send him to the devil."

"I should've been there," Matty exclaimed. "You should have let me fight!"

Hart gazed at him through narrow eyes but said nothing. I asked about our prize, and Hector and Cuervo went to lift up the top crate and bring it back to us. They pried up the lid to reveal a cache of muskets—grimy with wear and age—nested in straw. Matty gazed down at them shaking his head.

"Old Brown Besses, by the look of 'em," he said. "Left over from the French wars. I wonder what my father's doing with 'em?"

"They were in a passenger cabin, under a bunk," said Hector.

"*Si,* a green-faced *ingles,*" Cuervo snickered.

"Had he any papers on him?" Matty asked, and Hector felt under his belt and extracted a damp, crumpled envelope.

"Holy God, Captain," Matty whistled, as he read the letter inside. "This shipment is bound for the rebels in Puerto Rico. The payment is to be made in gold Spanish doubloons."

"When?"

"Next week," Matty read. "Whoever's transporting

these must've paid the master handsomely to sail so near the hurricane season. The insurance rates double on the first of August."

"Must have anticipated a handsome reward," said Hart. "Where were they to meet?"

"A nighttime rendezvous off San Juan. But they're expecting an Englishman called Doyle. They'll deal with no one else." Matty looked up at Hart again. "The trading Doyles, out of London and New York, that was your green-faced *ingles*. What shall we do?"

"Gold doubloons, eh?" Hart mused. "Well, I think we ought to complete this transaction. Mustn't let a good deal go bad."

Five evenings later, as the *Blessed Providence* lay well off the north coast of Puerto Rico, waiting for nightfall, I was called in to the captain's cabin.

"It's a damned nuisance that my one genuine Englishman has turned up lame, but it can't be helped," Hart was saying.

"Hellfire, Captain, I'm not helpless," Jack fumed.

"We can't have you hobbling about, sowing suspicion. Not with all those doubloons at stake. And you're in no shape to run if it all blows up. So that leaves me."

"You're the captain, not an errand boy," Nada protested in Spanish. "Send Mateo."

Matty looked insulted, but Hart only laughed.

"The minute Matty opens his mouth, they'll know he's no more English than you are, *amigo*," he chuckled to Nada. "Besides, any trader who knows the Doyles might also know the Forresters, and the young Forrester heir is presumed lost at sea."

"Any trader who knows the Doyles is likely to shoot an impostor on sight," Nada muttered.

"How else are we to profit on this prize?" Hart

demanded. "Jack is owed a double share and more shares must be put by for Julio's family on Cabo Cruz. Without the gold, there'll be naught to share."

"Then I'm coming with you," Nada declared. Their eyes locked, and something tender tugged at the corner of the captain's mouth.

"*Si*, all right, *compañero*," he nodded. "Cuervo, I'll want you in the boat for a pilot as we go in, if you know these waters as well as you say you do. Mateo, you stay and hold the ship. Which leaves you, Lightfoot, to complete the shore party." He grinned at my surprise. "Well, lass, this bargain was struck by correspondence. It might be wise to have someone along to read the fine print."

"It would be wise to send me and forget this lunatic charade," Jack protested, but the captain ignored him.

A few lights from the town of San Juan and its Spanish garrison winked across the bay as we rowed in for a hidden inlet, an old smugglers' cove, Cuervo said. He piloted us to the mouth of a small river and around a bend or two, until a silent coasting vessel became visible in the murky shallows, hidden in the riverside foliage.

Rudy had outfitted the captain in a merchant's blue frock coat and me in the clothing and cap of a boy apprentice. Hector and Nada looked like a slave and a servant, so no notice would be taken of them. But as we boarded the coaster under the scrutiny of a dozen fierce-looking men, I was glad to have Hector, and even Nada, at our backs.

In a cramped cabin, by the light of a single lamp, we squinted into the gloom to see a well-dressed *criollo* man seated at a table, flanked by armed men.

"My dear *Señor* Doyle," he cooed, in precise, accented English. "Such a pleasure."

"*Señor* Alfaro," Hart nodded. When there was no immediate response, he added, grumpily, "If indeed, that is you;

one can scarcely see in this confounded dark."

"It is I," Alfaro replied. "Who else would I send on such a delicate business? And how is your dear family?"

I knew Hart had no idea who, let alone how, Doyle's family was, but he betrayed no flicker of hesitation.

"My life on the mainland continues tolerably well, sir, and I am anxious to return to it. Forgive me if I am short," he added, "but sea travel does not agree with me."

"Of course, we shall proceed at once to the business at hand," Alfaro agreed. "You have the merchandise?"

"Six crates, English made. And ammunition," Hart replied.

Alfaro frowned. "We bargained for much more."

The hiss of drawn weapons snickered in the darkness.

"And you shall have them," Hart agreed. "Due to unforeseen delays, these were all I could lay hands on in time to honor our agreement. Arrangements are being made even now for a second shipment, which only require my safe return to be completed. I thought you would appreciate this partial delivery as an act of good faith."

Alfaro nodded. "Show me the guns."

"Show me the doubloons."

Glancing at his own comrades, Alfaro set a box on the table and lifted the lid. I recognized a dull glint of gold even in this dim light. With a bored, businesslike "May I?" Hart stepped forward and sifted his fingers through the coins to the bottom of the box, to see that no layers of tin or lead were hidden underneath.

"And now, *Señor* Doyle—"

"First, *Señor* Alfaro, indulge me by asking your associates to lay down their arms."

"My friend, you insult me."

"Not at all," Hart rejoined. "We are all men of honor, of course. But if I remain here with my clerk while my men fetch your merchandise, there is no need for weapons. It's the boy, more than myself," he added, confidentially, nodding at me. "My sister's son. Mute as a post, but he copies smartly enough.

If anything happened to him, I'd never hear the end of it. You know what women are."

This point was convincing enough for Alfaro. He nodded, and three of his men withdrew pistols from their belts and laid them upon the table, beside the box of gold. When the crates had been brought in and the muskets and the gold counted to everyone's satisfaction, Hart took a step toward the box.

"A moment, please," said Alfaro. He withdrew two half sheets of paper, an inkwell and a shallow tray of writing implements from a drawer in the table and laid them out upon its surface.

"This is hardly the kind of transaction for which one makes out a bill of sale," Hart protested.

Alfaro looked surprised. "But it was your idea, exactly as we agreed. I sign, you sign, each of us keeps a copy and thus ensures cordial relations between our two enterprises in the future."

"Oh, aye." Hart was struggling to regain his slipped composure, and my pulse quickened with dread. "But perhaps it would be wiser to leave no trace."

The quill Alfaro had produced quivered uncertainly in the air.

"No trace? It sounds as if you mean to terminate the business arrangement between us."

I didn't care for the sound of that. If Alfaro perceived he no longer needed Doyle as a business contact for smuggled arms, there was no point in either paying him off or letting him live to tell the tale. Alfaro had only to pick up one of those pistols before him and there would be termination all around.

"Nonsense," said Hart. "I have no wish to lose one of my best customers." He watched Alfaro sign each document, then nodded at me. "Naturally, my clerk is authorized—"

"Really, Doyle, I am in business with you, not your clerk."

". . . to look over the contract," Hart finished. "My eyes are not what they were."

I could feel Nada's tension pulsing behind me. Surely

he had some weapon secreted in his clothing, not that he would need aught but his bare hands if he perceived any danger to Ed Hart. I tried to position myself between Nada and Alfaro to interrupt the invisible fuse burning between them as I seized up the papers. They were accurate receipts of the sale, needing only the one thing Hart was unable to provide to get us out of there—a written signature. Such a trifling thing to die for.

When I dropped one of the receipts in the writing box and clumsily fished it out, Hart muttered a bored reprimand. When I let both papers slip through my fingers to the deck and fell to my knees to retrieve them, Hart fumed, "Clumsy ass!" and aimed a swift but not very hard kick at my backside. But his ranting gave me the moment I needed to lightly scrawl the name *Doyle* on both documents with the nub of a leaded pencil I'd liberated from the writing box. I struggled to my feet and nodded vigorously to Hart, holding both out to him.

The captain took the papers and glanced down at what I'd written. In truth, he had the eyes of a hawk; even in this dim light, he could tell the difference between Alfaro's name, in ink, and my pencil scrawl. He laid the papers down on the far corner of the table, and I handed him the pen I'd dipped and nudged its point toward the first pencilled "D." The captain studiously covered the rest of the signature with ink, and went on to "sign" the second document with something like a flourish.

"Indeed, this was the best plan." He smiled to Alfaro, as the box of doubloons was handed over to him. *"Viva la revolucion!"*

"So you see, *hombres*," Hart declared to the others as the rum was broken out, back aboard the *Providence*, "it wasn't Nada's brawn nor yet my own bravado, but Lightfoot's wit that saved our hides. I believe the lass must be a born pirate, after all!"

Even Matty was grinning at me in admiration, and

when Rudy left off pounding me on the back, I ducked below
to change into my old outfit and regain my composure. But on
my way back above, I spied a movement in the shadows and
found Jack curled up in a dark corner of the lower deck with a
mostly empty bottle. It took him a long moment to notice me
standing there, longer still to focus, and then his startled look
told me that, for once, I'd taken him by surprise.

"I never thought to see your sorry carcass again," he
mumbled, at last, his voice thick with alcohol. "Not in this
world."

"Yes, I see I've interrupted your celebration," I
snapped, in a hurry now to get above. I don't know why it disturbed me so to find Jack in this state. Perhaps because I had
never seen him surrender his wits before. But I forgot about it
as soon as I gained the deck, where Matty thrust a cup of spiced
rum into my hand, slipped an arm round my waist and proposed to the others a toast to their pirate queen.

CHAPTER 10

Fiesta

The *Blessed Providence* had been too long at sea. Her chains were rusted, barnacles fed on her hull, and salt was corroding everything else. Captain Hart had brought her down the Puerto Rican coast to the uninhabited islet of Culebra to careen her on this hidden beach, where we'd been scraping, cleaning, caulking, tarring and mending ever since. Today, Arne was finishing up the carpentry with a small work detail while the others spent their shares of Spanish gold across the channel in the port town of Fajardo. Cuervo had been born there, and the captain said the man had more relations there than a beach has sand flies.

The chief amusements in Fajardo were cockfighting, thievery, horse-racing, brawling and whoring. We couldn't stay on the ship while she was hull-over on the beach, so I'd been adopted into the home of Cuervo's sister, Maria Elena. Her family lived in a thatched bamboo cabin attached to the coop where Maria Elena's husband, Miguel, kept his prize gamecock. It was largely up to this dyspeptic fowl to maintain the family. In addition, the women harvested mangos and cashews and wove palm leaf hats to trade for supplies from smugglers who put into the hidden coves of Fajardo to avoid the steep tariffs imposed in San Juan. Miguel's flint-eyed brother, Rafael, also went out nights to the Fajardo cantinas in search of unwary sailors to separate from their pay over dice or drink. By day, it amused him to teach the children petty thievery toward the time when the burden of family maintenance would be theirs.

Myself, I preferred the calm and quiet here on Culebra, the perfect peace of the powdery beach, turquoise sky and the pale green water, scarcely rippling. Since Arne had stilled his hammer, the only sound now was the idle rustling of the palm fronds in the mild breeze overhead, like the lazy shuffling of a deck of cards.

"I've been learning the cutpurse trade," I ventured, as Arne lit his pipe in the shade of a traveler's palm. I produced the dagger Miguel had given me. "If Porter ever does drive us off the sea, at least I'll be able to make a living on dry land."

"Aye, the only trade open to poor *criollos*," Arne chuckled, his pale blue eyes disappearing in a mirthful squint. "Some future in revolution, so they say, but crime is not so dangerous and pays better."

"How long have you been in these islands?"

"All my life. I was born on St. Thomas. Aye, a poor *criollo*, just like these *cubanos* eh? But I never wanted to live anywhere else."

"Not even Denmark?"

Arne pretended to shiver. "I hear it's very cold there. No, with good fortune, I'll die here. At sea, I hope."

We turned at the sound of shouting and saw a little fishing boat out on the water, sailing in for our hidden cove. The occupants scrambled over the side and dragged the boat up the beach, and I recognized Cuervo and Miguel. The lookout on the point had seen them, too, and was calling for the captain, who emerged with Nada from the canvas shelter they'd rigged up ashore.

"It's all over the cantinas!" Miguel crowed. "Porter has the fever!"

Speculation that the Yankee Squadron was besieged by fever had been circulating for weeks. Apparently, Miguel had found confirmation.

"Dead?" Hart asked, hopefully.

"The next best thing," Miguel exulted. "He's taken a ship for home. The Yankees are leaving the Indies!"

The men of the *Blessed Providence* were all afire to sail home to Cuba. But the blustery tail end of a hurricane drove us all into the shelter of Fajardo's shuttered houses for a night and a day. After that, nothing would do for Maria Elena but that she be allowed to hold a fiesta for her kinsman and his friends to celebrate our deliverance. Tables were moved outside the house and laden with jugs of ale and platters of fruit. Chickens roasted over an open fire pit, and the ground was cleared for dancing. A trio of guitarists strolled among the revelers playing the *danza*.

Maria Elena decreed that I must wear one of her frocks for the occasion—a filmy, ivory-colored gown that exposed my shoulders and bosom. I felt like a sausage stuffed into a skin, the bodice was so tight. But I recalled the effect on Matty the last time I'd worn a gown and so gritted my teeth and even suffered Maria Elena to pin a wild orchid behind my ear, letting my rusty-dark hair spill free around it.

Once outside, however, I was so embarrassed that I merged with all haste into the crowd. I searched automatically for Matty's luminous hair, but when I spied him in the center of a festive group at the rum cask, I dared not approach him. For weeks, he had worked beside me on the ship, stripped to the waist and gleaming like a bust carved on a golden coin, yet now I felt too undressed to be seen by him. But someone saw me, for I felt the wolfish black eyes of Miguel's brother Rafael

boring into me from across the yard. I was on the point of flee-
ing back into the house when I turned to find Hector bowing
low before me.

"You the prettiest *señorita* here, Mistress," he told me.
"You dance with me, now, eh?"

"Oh, Hector, I'm not very good."

"Nor me either." Hector shrugged. "But nobody ever
laugh at this African when he dance."

He steered me along in time to the lively music with his
usual solemn confidence, his powerful arms keeping me afloat
or twirling me before him, so that I was actually sorry when the
tune ended.

"*Gracias*, Hector. You're the best partner I've ever had."

"Then I think you don't have many partners," he
chuckled. "You try some of these *jibaros*, here, see what you
think."

Then he bowed again and veered off to where two
mulatta girls—one fair and one dark—were waiting to claim
him. I turned to find Miguel offering to lead me into the next
danza; indeed, I had no shortage of dancing partners as the sun
sank behind the hills and lanterns were lit in the trees. I scarcely had time for a cup of spruce beer before I was dragged back
into the melee, nor any time for surprise when I found myself
handed off to Matty in the middle of some rollicking tune. I
tossed back my hair and beamed at him furiously like some witless coquette all through our last frantic paces, and his eyes
shone like seasplashed turquoise. But when the music ended, he
only murmured something in Spanish and reeled off, giving no
indication that he had recognized me, or that it mattered to him
if he had.

The night air felt suddenly chilly and the festivities
turned shrill and grotesque and pointless. I slunk off into the
shadows beyond the blazing lanterns of the fiesta, as deflated as
if I'd received a blow, and angry at myself for feeling that way.
What did I expect of the fellow? But I expected him to be my
Charioteer. I had been promised him, dreamed for so long of
his love. I needed him to make all my other dreams complete.

"*Buenos noches, señorita.*"

I spun around, but saw only shadows. The lights were far behind me.

"I've been waiting for you," came the voice again, in Spanish, and I recognized Rafael's unctuous purr. "The next dance I think is mine."

"All right, *si*." I was struggling to disguise my alarm and remember my Spanish. "Let's go back—"

But he caught my shoulders with both hands, and his grip hurt. His body gave off heat like a bonfire reeking of stale wine.

"Here," he commanded. "Now." He started to lean into me, and I stumbled backward. He stumbled, too, and swore, but he did not loosen his grip.

"Stop it, Rafael! *Basta!*"

"*Puta!*" he hissed back. "You dance with the big black *bozale* and the pretty *norteamericano*, but no time for me, eh? You're a guest in my brother's house!" His hand slid down my spine to my backside, and he pulled me against him and bent me backward, as if we really were going to perform the *danza*. He drove me farther into the darkness until my shoulder slammed against the wall of the chicken coop, to an outcry of agitated clucking, within.

"Only one little dance," he grunted, pinning back my arms and sinking his face into my bosom, scraping my flesh with the bristly stubble of his beard. My frock might as well have been made of morning dew for all the protection it offered from Rafael's body, thudding against mine with enough force to send us both through the unstable coop wall. The chickens gabbled furiously from the other side, and all I knew for one instant was raw, blind, white panic when I couldn't think, couldn't feel, couldn't move.

But then I felt entirely too much. Revulsion burned at every point where Rafael's body or his breath or his hair touched me, and resistance surged up inside me, clenching my body like an angry fist. He released one of my arms to paw at his trousers; when I sensed him shifting his balance, I threw my coiled strength against his other hand, breaking his grip, then dove to the ground and rolled aside. Rafael spun around and hurled himself at me, but I had drawn back my knees and launched a hard kick up square into his belly. He reeled backwards, soggy air gushing out of him as he fell, and I sprang to my feet and darted around the chicken coop. I could hear him wailing and cursing in the darkness, but it didn't sound as if he had breath enough to pursue me. Still, I didn't wait to find out, racing farther into the shadows around the back of Maria Elena's house and up along the far side toward the lights of the fiesta.

I suppose I was half out of my ripped dress, covered with dirt and scratches, my face flushed with fear and rage and relief, but there was no time to compose myself. As I came round the corner into the flickering light of a lantern hung above the front porch, I almost careened into Matty, strolling away from the merrymaking. I brought myself up short, but it was all I could do not to throw myself into his arms on a sudden, cresting wave of emotion. It was too late to hide my shame; I was as vulnerable as I'd ever been, and in the greatest need of comfort.

But Matty merely fixed me with a dazzling smile and raised his mug of rum.

"Why, hello, Lightfoot. Having a good time, eh?"

He clapped me on the shoulder, as if I were a sport, and ambled off to join a dice game in the shadows. For an instant, my limbs trembled, and I sensed blackness swelling to engulf me—which must be what happened to silly females who gave in to the luxury of fainting. I shook myself free of it and stormed into the house, angry now, and alert. I had no patience to clean myself up, only peeled off the ruined gown and pulled on my own clothes. I found my new dagger and strapped that on, too, resolving never again to go out among men without it, whatever the occasion.

Outside, again, I kept to the shadows with a sharp eye out for Rafael. Safely past the last stand of trees, I broke and ran for the beach. I tossed a coin to the two lads in the fishing boat hired to take strays back across to Culebra, and as they rowed, my thoughts fumed along in time to their strokes. What did it matter who I gave myself to—Rafael or one of Sarafina's customers—if Matty was so indifferent? Why long for a man who cared nothing for me? I should never have put my faith in Fortune, ought to have ignored the warning in my head and my body, and let Rafael finish the job, freed myself for good and all of this addled yearning—

"Who's there?" from the watch, above, as I clawed up the chains to the *Providence* rail. I knew Jack's voice.

"Anne Bonny, the goddamn pirate queen."

"What's the matter with you?"

"Men," I snapped, swinging down to the deck. "Men are the matter with me, and the world."

"Aye, you'll get no argument from me, there." Jack was backing off, but I followed him, too agitated to be left alone and unsure what to do with myself.

"Will we never be away from here?" I fumed. "What's the time?"

"Past midnight, which makes this the seventeenth," Jack offered, stopping under the lantern to get a better look at me and frowning at what he saw. "We'll sail when the tide turns, in a few hours."

"The seventeenth?"

"Of September, yes."

Had we been at sea so long, already? So many months? I sighed at the rail and made a sound that might have been a chuckle or a sob.

"It's my birthday," I reflected. "I'm seventeen."

"I doubt if many happy returns of the day are in order," Jack observed. He pulled out a cloth from his shirt, the kind he used to tie back his hair aloft, and went to dip it in the water cask. "Here," he said, putting the wet rag in my hand. "Go and clean up. We'll have Rudy see to your clothes when he comes aboard. For now . . . ." He shrugged out of his shirt and handed it to me. "Call it a birthday present."

When I awoke before dawn, still wrapped in Jack's shirt, I was sorry I'd snapped at him the night before. Safe in my own berth, I'd used his rag to scrub away the stench of Rafael, and then sleep had come more easily. Rudy brought my freshened clothes, and I went above to help cast off. Most of the men were fighting down the effects of too much rum and *bonhommie* the night before, and it was a while before I could seek out Jack to make peace. I found him winding up spare cordage at the fore halliards.

"Can I help?" I tried my most conciliatory smile.

Jack nodded, apology accepted, and I set to coiling up the last loose line dangling down to the deck.

"I didn't see you in town, Uncle Jack."

"Towns don't interest me, much. Arne can always use another hand around the ship."

"So you're a carpenter, too?"

"Arne is a carpenter. But I've done some building."

"Ships?" He did not respond. "Houses? Prisons? Cathedrals?"

"Playhouses." He didn't look up.

"Playhouses?" I echoed. "I thought tumblers performed in the road."

"After the tumblers. I was an actor, once. It was a long time ago."

"An actor!" I exulted, recalling the glee with which Bet had once told me that playhouses were no better than brothels. "On the stage! But aren't actors terribly wicked?"

"As opposed to the noble profession of pirate, you mean?"

"One of the most cherished illusions of my girlhood was that actors are monstrously wicked. You're not going to disappoint me, I hope."

I saw the effort it cost him not to smile, but he managed it.

"I was the personification of sin," he promised.

"But how does an actor end up on a Cuban pirate ship in the mid . . . ."

"I'm here because I'm here, and there's an end to it." And Jack turned and marched away across the deck before I could plague him with any more questions.

CHAPTER 11

Laguna Escondida

We stood at the edge of a broad clearing carved out of a thicket of thorny chaparral, cacti and gnarled mangrove. The dense scrub concealed the clearing from the beach below. Buildings of some size had stood here, once; there were vague outlines of charred rectangles in the dirt where walls had burned to the ground. But it was a gray, desolate place now, marked by deep drifts of cold ash and planks of blackened timber that disintegrated at the touch of a boot.

Captain Hart frowned. "Not all gone, surely."

"Every house, every storeroom burned," *Señor* Garcia confirmed. "All the goods stolen from the caves. They wrecked what boats they could find and took away our cannons."

"And our people?"

"Safe." Garcia was obviously glad of some good news to report. "Chased and frightened, but none killed or taken. They fled into the hills when they saw the Yankees in the bay."

The Yankee Squadron. While we'd been idling away the long summer months plundering small trade in the Bahamas and refitting in Puerto Rico, Porter's ships had sniffed out the pirates' only refuge here at Cabo Cruz and burned it to cinders.

"We did not know, *Capitan*, if you would ever return."

"Aye, nor did we, *amigo.*" Hart's busy eyes returned again to Garcia. "But we are here, now, and the *norteamericanos* are gone."

I could not help but share the dismay of the men at the devastation the *norteamericanos* had wrought. Cabo Cruz was an isolated, overgrown point at the foot of the Sierra Maestras. Its inhabitants were poor fisherfolk and turtlers living up on the bluff. The men of the *Providence* had established their base camp below, within the natural fortress of chaparral, mangrove, limestone caverns and shallow, hidden lagoons. All of the people of Cabo Cruz made their living from the sea.

Señor Garcia, a merchant from the nearby trading port of Santiago, acted as agent and auctioneer for the captain's prize goods. The men had been anxious when he alone appeared to greet them. But now, as we returned to our boats on the beach, others were beginning to emerge from the undergrowth that hid the pathways leading up to the bluff. Excited children, at first, then weathered old fishermen and strong-featured island women. One dark, sloe-eyed young Fury came shrieking down the beach to launch herself at Hector, raining kisses and curses down on his bald head as he caught her up in his arms and swung her aloft. Two naked little black boys toddled along in their mama's wake, and I found myself backing away as the men were engulfed by those with a right to call the pirates husband, lover, father or son.

Hector's woman Jasmine planted herself in the doorway. "I'm going down to the camp," she called to me.

I'd been given a little cupboard here in the Garcias'

storeroom on the bluff while the community in the hills waited for the threat of fever to drift out of the marshland below.
"Come along with me, Tory," Jasmine continued.

As usual, she issued a command, not a request, but I
was glad to obey. I thought I'd had my fill of females at
Worthen, but I liked Jasmine, with her languid brown eyes, full
mouth, loose-limbed gait and the pert rump she carried high in
the air, as if she were walking on tiptoe. A Negress from
Havana, she spoke in the exuberant mix of Spanish, English and
French she'd learned in that cosmopolitan port. She said whatever came into her head, raged when she was angry, laughed
when she was pleased and told everyone what they ought to do
to improve their lives. She never left off trying to convince me
how foolish it was to sail with the pirates in dangerous waters
when I might better become the mistress of one and stay home
in safety in Laguna Escondida, the name the pirates gave to
their sheltered camp.

"Let the fool men go off to get drowned or shot, if
that's what they want," Jasmine had advised me. "Women have
more important things to do. You find yourself a good buckra
man, a white man. Woman of color, she need a white man to
protect her and give her light-colored babies."

I had watched the life drain out of my mother's face in
her struggle to give birth, the face I had loved above all others.
I was not eager for babies. Yet, according Jasmine, a woman of
color was fit for little else. And I realized I was as much a
woman of color here as I had ever been in Boston. The only
place I'd ever really been free was on the open sea.

The men had moved down to their burned-out lair
under the bluff to begin clearing away the bramble and ash and
debris as soon as the days grew clear and dry. What supplies
Garcia could not find for them in Santiago, we plundered off
the trading ships that began to appear in the passages again after
the first of October, the end of the hurricane season. The cannon from an unwary American brig was now mounted on a
hidden promontory overlooking the lagoon where the
Providence lay. A huge cistern for rainwater had been erected,

and the new storehouses and cabins were almost complete. Today, I supposed, Jasmine was on some errand to Hector. There was a parcel wrapped in cloth in the shallow basket she carried on her hip.

"The babies sleeping so we go spy on the men," Jasmine announced. "And I want to talk to you."

I knew which lecture I was about to receive. Even in this outlaw community, there were rules for female behavior.

"Have you found one of these men to keep you?"

"I get on well with Rudy." I teased.

"*Sí*, you and Rudy and his muchachos. You no get much sleep, there. Now, no more jokes. What about Cuervo?"

I scarcely relished the idea of Rafael as a kinsman. "Don't I have a right to choose a man I'm fond of? You did."

Jasmine had met Hector when he was a slave in Havana on the estate of an English coffee planter Jasmine called a *gran blanc*, the wealthiest class in white *habanero* society. When Hector escaped and dared Jasmine to come away with him, it never occurred to her to hesitate. The choice between outlaw mistress and respectable drudge like her "free colored" laundress mother was an easy one.

"What about our *leon dorado*?" she suggested.

That was what the villagers called Matty: the golden lion. I kept my head down, rounding a thorny outcropping of cactus, so Jasmine wouldn't see my discomposure. How often I had imagined a life with Matty like the one Jasmine shared with Hector—keeping his house, cooking his meals, sharing his bed, here in this sunny tropical dreamscape so far away from the world. I imagined his homecomings, me flying down the beach and into his embrace as he folded me in his arms. But then I imagined his departures, and I could not bear it. How could I ever let him leave for the sea without me, not knowing if he would ever return?

"How can you bear it when Hector sails away?" I wondered aloud. "Would you not rather go with him and share his fate, whatever happens?"

Jasmine stared at me. "And who look after my babies if

anything happen to me, eh?" She continued on, again, muttering at my perversity.

We came down into the clearing. Past the new storehouses, we headed for the sleeping cabins—long, low, timbered buildings under thatched palm roofs built up on short poles to keep out the legions of sand crabs that clacked and scrabbled their way through the scrub. We saw men at work layering palm thatch, fastening hinges, stowing their belongings in plundered chests or hampers; we heard ringing hammers and joking and cursing. As we passed Matty's cabin, I saw a straw pallet carelessly tossed in a corner under a rack of well-oiled and polished weapons.

"Perhaps Mateo not such a good choice for you," said Jasmine.

"Why not?"

"One day he no come back. Either some Spaniard gut him or he go home to America. He never live to be an old man, here."

We'd come to a spartan little shack that stood apart from the rest. The door stood open and Jasmine stepped up on the crate beneath it and climbed in over the sill, with me in tow.

"Jack Danzador! You at home?"

"As you see." Jack smiled from the corner, where he was stringing up a hammock. "Hector isn't here," he added.

"My business is with you."

Jack's smile broadened. "You come for no innocent purpose, I hope?"

Jasmine withdrew her parcel and handed it to him. He looked at her, puzzled, and unwrapped it, his dark eyes growing wide and astonished. Inside the cloth was an old, well-worn book on whose binding I spied the gilded name of Shakespeare. The complete works, from the heft of the thing, although it was compact enough in size for Jack to pass from one hand to the other, inspecting it front and back, staring in wonder. He had apparently lost the power of speech, and Jasmine was delighted to have produced this effect.

"The *norteamericanos* no get everything. I remember

the foolishness in this book important to you, so I snatch it away. Now I bring it back. Is *buena suerte* to have something old in a new house."

Jack grinned. "It's good luck to have such a true friend, *encantadora*." He shifted the book to the crook of his elbow and reached for Jasmine with his free hand, drawing her face to his in a gesture that was evidently familiar to both of them. I confess myself discomfited when they kissed, a long kiss that flustered me even more; I scarcely knew where to look. But Jasmine appeared to enjoy it, playfully slapping Jack's hand away only when he was quite finished.

Then she swept a hand at me and demanded, "What about Tory?"

"What about her?" Jack echoed.

"She must have some place to live."

"Do you think the captain would let me take some corner in one of these cabins?" I ventured.

"Sleeping in a kennel like a dog!" Jasmine fumed, waving a hand to the heavens.

"The captain will let you do whatever you like," Jack said, with a quick, amused glance at Jasmine. "But perhaps you'd be better off in your own place."

My own place. Jack's room was scarcely more than an outbuilding, but the idea of four walls all to myself was irresistible. And utterly impossible. "Aye, but I know nothing about building," I sighed.

"I can do it." Jack took up his hammock again.

I narrowed my eyes. "In return for what?"

"For some peace in my own home." Jack let go of the hammock with an exasperated sigh. "I'm not often generous, so you'd better make haste while the mood is on me. Now, if you ladies will excuse me, I've work to do. Jasmine . . . ." He had ushered us to the door, but his hand lingered on her arm, and a long look passed between them. "Thank you," he said to her at last. "Rusty, go ask Arne to set aside some spare timber. Come back in a day or two, and we'll see what we can rig up."

Jasmine was unusually silent as we came away, gazing at

me with a long speculative look. Then she abruptly shook her head.

"No. Jack never take a woman."

"Certainly not me!" I laughed out loud. "Besides, I don't need a buckra man to protect me."

"But Jack, he need a woman," Jasmine replied. "Only he too stubborn to say so."

"Then why is he here?" I protested.

Jasmine shrugged. "Some bad thing happen to him once, I think. Make him close up into himself."

"Does no one know what it was?"

She glanced at me, sideways. "You ever ask Jack to talk about himself, eh? Easier to pry the teeth out of a shark, Hector say."

"A guilty secret, then?" I enthused.

"*Si,*" Jasmine agreed with a dismissive wave of her hand as we began to climb the steep, stony path up to the bluff. "But if you mix together all the guilty secrets in Laguna Escondida, you make a tangle more dense than this chaparral."

CHAPTER 12

The Wager

In the last week of the year, Captain Hart collected a party of Christmas merrymakers from Laguna Escondida and ferried us aboard the *Blessed Providence* to Santiago for the Negro parades. All over the sugar islands, landowners released their slaves in the week between Christmas and the New Year to celebrate. Negro men, women and children thronged the streets for days in colorful costumes stitched together from a year's worth of hoarded scraps or in their Sunday finest, chanting and dancing to the fluting of cane pipes and the deep-throated drums.

When we arrived in the heat of the day, the celebrations were already feverish—leaping, twirling bodies, a thousand voices raised in laughter and catcalls and song, the restless, pounding drumbeat and the caroling of vendors on every corner crying their sweetmeats and liquor. The slave parades always drew a multitude of curious onlookers and the town was a whirlpool of careening color, heady scents and hypnotic music swallowing all in its path until everyone was a part of the revels.

Javier and his wife were carried off by a wave of chanting dancers, and Matty and Cuervo waylaid a pretty rum-seller. Captain Hart drifted off with the Garcias. I stayed close to Jasmine and Hector and Rudy, who remained with us until he was swirled away by a group of masked dancers. With nightfall, fresh stores of rum and potent *aguardiente* were broken out, and the dancing grew more frenzied. Time lost its meaning, and everything seemed to be happening in simultaneous vignettes. Now Jasmine was teaching me to move in time to the drumming. Now she and I were swaying together, each with a sleepy child on one hip. Now I was dancing in a circle with Rudy and a young *mulatto* stranger with startling blue eyes. I could not say how I came at last to find myself leaning on Hector's broad shoulder like one of his own children, listening to his low chuckle as he led me away from the feverish crowds into the night.

"Can you see it, Mistress?" He was steadying me with a steely arm round my waist as he pointed down a dark road toward a distant circle of light. "Just down there, at the sign of the red cock. Tell them you with the Garcias. I walk with you, but I got to see to Jasmine and the boys."

"Of course, *hombre*, I'm quite all right." I had to reach deep into my memory to produce a voice far more sensible and sober than I felt. I stretched up to kiss Hector's black cheek in thanks, then set off down the road for the Gallo Rojo inn, where the Garcias had reserved us rooms. But as I tasted a fresh, salty breeze up from the bay, another in a day and a night of seductive sensations, I wondered if sleep in a lonely bed was what I truly craved. Rum had made my thoughts fluid; I knew that what I wanted was an answer to this restless ache inside that tightened like the strings on a guitar late at night, when I found myself all alone.

I passed the entrance to the cantina on the ground floor of the Gallo Rojo and strolled instead into a little byway beyond it, nearer the bay and the sea breeze. I paused to fill my lungs and gazed back up at the terraced hills of Santiago looming up behind the town. Ghostly, torchlit shadows were flickering in the street that I'd just left, accompanied by distant drumming and laughter. Then a sound much nearer, a skittering of gravel on the rocky path behind me, startled me into sobriety. My dagger was in my hand, and my body braced to lunge or run just as a figure stepped out of the shadows and halted.

"Mateo." A part of me relaxed, but the guitar strings tightened another peg.

"Oh, it's you, Mistress." Matty smiled, glancing at my dagger, which I quickly stuck back inside my belt. "Sorry, I didn't mean to come charging through the bushes like a mad boar. I'm afraid I'm a little drunk"

I smiled back. "I'm afraid I am, too."

"Are you coming in or going out?"

"Neither." I shrugged. "I don't think I can sleep."

"Nor I," Matty agreed, shaking back his loosened hair, almost white in the moonlight. "Do you mind if I walk with you?" He fell into step beside me, along the path that overlooked the harbor. "Do you ever miss your home in Boston?" he asked.

"Boston was never my home. I was a stranger there."

"I miss New York sometimes. I miss the harbor and the great ships from all over the world. I miss the grand buildings and the elections and the scandals . . . everything." He grinned. "In New York, you feel that everything happening is so . . . important."

"Not like Cuba," I suggested, and Matty laughed and shook his head. "Why don't you go back?" I hated myself for even suggesting it. "The captain has protected your identity all this time. You could say you'd been washed ashore on some deserted island, like Robinson Crusoe."

"You're very sharp," he said, in genuine surprise. "Aye, that's what I will do someday. But not yet. Not while my father . . . until I . . . ." He stopped, gave a self-mocking chuckle and shook his head. "Forgive me, Mistress, I'm not much good with words. My father runs his life like his empire. He planned on three sons, the first to take over the business, the second for the clergy and the third to go into the law. But he only had me, and I don't fit into the plan. Oh, I'll be his heir one day, family is everything to him. But the less he sees of me in the meantime, the better."

Matty, too, was more cunning than he looked. I stole another glance at his handsome face, more relaxed in this moment than I had ever seen him. We'd reached the end of the path before it wound down the slope to the harbor.

"Have you a plan of your own?" I asked him.

"The captain thinks I ought to go into the diplomatic trade. Says I'm good with languages and have the sort of face everybody wants to trust."

I laughed. "That's true enough."

"Is it?" He gazed at me for a moment, then looked away. "For now, I suppose I'll stay on the *Providence*. Captain Hart will make a man of me yet, if anyone can."

I was disarmed into speechlessness by the candor of this remark. Had Matty doubts and longings, too, beneath his brave exterior?

"Forgive me again, Mistress. It's the rum talking, or I wouldn't be boring you with all this bilge."

"Do stop apologizing, Mateo." I laughed as lightly as I could, given the tightening of the strings. "I don't mind."

"No, you never do mind, do you, Tory?" His smile grew a shade more dazzling, as if someone had turned up the wick in an oil lamp. "Tell me, what is it you trust about my face?"

"Nothing! I know you too well!" The string was wound too tight, it would break if it was plucked. "I suppose people want to trust you because you . . . you're . . . ." I stammered to a graceless halt. "You don't need me to tell you how attractive you are, Mateo."

"But I would like your good opinion." He caught my hand and held it so that I had to face him. "You've been very kind to me tonight, Tory."

Without preamble, he leaned over to kiss me. Softly, at first. Then, in the time it took us both to draw breath, he kissed me again with more purpose. I tasted the tip of his tongue, sweet with spiced rum. His hand tightened on mine, and his other arm slid round my neck, pulling me close against him. I pressed myself to him, moving a timid hand around to his back to feel hard muscle beginning to flex beneath his damp shirt. A smoking volcano was going to erupt inside me, and all I wanted in the world was Matty's warm mouth and his arms and his body. Talking so intimately had been difficult for him, but this was easy.

It was too easy. I wanted only to be swept away into insensibility, but even now, I could not stop thinking. Even as I shivered with delight in Matty's embrace, my inner voice began to nag a warning.

"Yes, my pet. That's right," Matty murmured, his mouth moving down my neck. "You're such a good girl." He cupped my breast in his warm hand, kneading and tweaking gently through my shirt, and I could not swallow a surprised little bleat of desire.

"Come upstairs with me, Tory," he whispered, his breath hot in my ear. "Now. Please."

I don't remember climbing the back stairs in the Gallo Rojo. All I knew was heat and light, the damp, warm air in the close little room, the shimmer of a lamp by the door and a candle by the bed, the hot fire pounding in my veins, the suffocating heat of Matty's embrace as he trapped me again in his strong arms and pulled me to him, kicking the door shut behind us. I had to push him away an inch or two to get my bearings, and he took a step back, gaping in astonishment.

"You want me, don't you?"

Confused, breathless, I managed to nod, and was rewarded with his brilliant smile. But why could I not stop thinking? Why was I so aware of my nervous discomfort, the sour smell of the room, the muted cacophony of noise from the cantina below? Why could I not give myself up to Matty, to this moment, with wholehearted abandon?

Then Matty took off his clothes.

And nothing else mattered.

I could never have imagined anything so glorious. His broad chest and back and shoulders tapered down to sturdy, narrow hips and a small, neatly shaped backside above muscular thighs and long, gracefully curved calves. His skin was smooth and golden all over, as he turned himself around for my inspection. Fine red-gold down sparkled all over his body in the firelight, as if he were covered in gold dust, as if he'd been sculpted out of fire. He came about to face me again and grinned as my eyes were drawn to his flushed male member swaying out of its dark golden nest. He was so beautiful. How could this not be what I wanted?

He was standing naked by the bed, now. When he smiled again and held out his hands, I walked to him as if mesmerized.

"Don't be afraid to touch me," he told me, drawing me closer.

"I'm not afraid," I lied, but my hand trembled when I laid it on his chest, my fingers shyly stroking the soft, golden fur. Matty swallowed an impatient sigh, caught my timid hand and guided it down between his legs, closing my fingers snugly around himself as he had once closed my hand around the hilt of a dagger.

"That's what you want, isn't it?" he whispered. "That's what you always want."

Something in me chilled, but I fought it down. Matty's flesh was as thick and stiff as hemp rope in my hand, and I clung to him, my lifeline out of dark, ignorant loneliness and into the world of belonging, of love. It took a moment to realize that his hands were busy with the laces of my trousers. When that garment crumpled to the floor at my feet, Matty's hands were sliding over my naked hips and squeezing my backside.

"So there is a female in here, after all," he teased. With a boyish whoop, he tumbled me backwards onto the bed. "And I know just where she is," he added, sliding his hand up the inside of my thigh. His fingers began to rub insistently between my legs while I struggled to understand what to feel between desire and excitement and unease.

"Mateo . . . wait . . . can we—"

But he shushed me, covering my mouth with another kiss, his tongue pressing hard against mine. He rolled the full weight of his body over on top of me and pushed himself inside me, slowly, at first, then faster. I could only brace my heels and hold on. There was a sharp, tearing pain inside, and I had to bite back a gasp. But Matty's only response was a groan of relief as he pushed deeper, rubbing my insides raw. In the dim candle-light, I saw his eyes close above me, his face pink with exertion. This was a private moment for him; I felt like an intruder, watching him.

Then he grunted and jerked hard inside me and collapsed, panting, on top of me. I snaked one hand gently up his spine and began to stroke his hair, waiting. It would surely happen now, the moment of connection when I would feel beloved.

But all that happened, after another minute, was that Matty rolled off me, swung his legs over the edge of the bed and sat up. Drying himself carelessly with a corner of the bed-sheet, he reached for a fat-bottomed crockery jug on the little table beside the bed, shook it and muttered a curse. He got up, crossed the room, stuck his head out the door and bellowed in Spanish for more rum. Then he sauntered back, perched again on the edge of the bed and finally glanced back down at me, as if he'd just remembered I was there. His smile was brief and vague.

"There's rum coming," he volunteered. "The service is always so damned slow during the parades."

I could only stare back at him, stupidly, as if I'd just woken from a dream. Had I only imagined what we'd just done? There was a tap at the door and a dark-skinned serving girl waltzed in with a full jug. I can remember her vivid yellow skirt, her tight, ruffled bodice and her saucy expression. She didn't seem in the least discomfited to see a white man sitting naked on the bed. She called Matty by name, addressed a teasing remark to the state of his wilting organ and twitched her skirt at him as she set the jug on the table beside him. Matty bantered back in kind and slapped her on the rump as she turned to go out. And all the while, I sank ever deeper into the sour bedclothes, cold with the realization of just how dispensable I was to Matty. I might have been any kitchen wench or shopgirl lying in his bed; indeed, he would likely have found a kitchen wench more to his liking. Matty was no more mine now than he had ever been. I would never mean anything to him. Fortune be damned.

He took a pull from the jug and sat back upon the bed. "Have a drink, Tory. That'll set you up."

But before I could respond, the door was flung open again, and Cuervo strode in, crowing at the top of his voice.

"There you are, *hermano,* I've been looking all over the damned town for you! They're getting up a dice game in the next street with those fellows from . . . ."

He broke off as his eyes adjusted to the dim light and he got a better look at Matty, and me in the shadows behind him. A lurid grin split his dark face as Matty sat more upright in the bed, as if to block Cuervo's view. I was momentarily touched that Matty thought enough of me to protect my modesty. Or perhaps he was merely ashamed to have me discovered in his bed. Even now, when we'd been as close as two people can be, I still had no more idea of what he was thinking than I ever had. And I felt even more alone.

"Why, here I find you with your sword unsheathed," Cuervo cackled, darting suddenly toward the bed. "Let me see the kill!"

Matty did not prevent him tweaking back the rumpled bedclothes as I struggled to sit up and yanked my shirttail across my lap, my bare legs as long and awkward as a newborn colt's. I suddenly thought of my dagger in a heap with my trousers on the other side of the bed, far out of my reach.

"Hellfire, it's Mistress Lightfoot!" Cuervo cried, but Matty stood up abruptly and shouldered his friend back from the bed.

"Let's talk outside, *amigo*. . . ." Matty began, but by then, my brain had reconnected with the rest of my body. I lunged across the bed for my things and dragged on my trousers under my shirt.

"No. Stay. I'm going." Dagger in hand, I slithered past them both. I saw Cuervo's crafty leer as his black eyes followed me and only a bland smile from Matty as I gained the open door and slipped out.

In the corridor, I had to lean against the wall to get hold of myself. A hot, sticky trail of Matty's seed and my own blood was leaking down the inside of my thigh. I felt as if my insides were draining away, all that was vital inside me, leaving me empty, hollow. Certainly not loved. Through the open door, I heard Cuervo still chuckling while Matty's voice, softer, tried to shush him.

"You win, you rutting hound," Cuervo wheezed.

"That's twenty Spanish dollars you owe me."

"*Si*, Mateo, tonight, after dice—"

"Now," Matty retorted. "That was the wager. I've earned it."

The rest was lost in laughter and mumbled epithets and the clinking of coin as I fled blindly down the corridor.

CHAPTER 13

Neither Fish Nor Fowl

"Of course I remembered the witches," I said to Jack. I turned another page in his volume of Shakespeare, open on my lap as I sat on the floor of his cabin. "The witches in *Macbeth* and the fairies in *Midsummer Night's Dream* are what children like best in Shakespeare."

"I'd have thought little girls liked the *Dream* for the lovers."

"That shows what you know about little girls, Uncle Jack."

Little girls were fools to waste their dreams on lovers; I'd learned that much in the Gallo Rojo. Jack stretched out in his hammock, paging idly through some other book. But it was far too hot to concentrate at this hour of the afternoon, and the heat made me prickly.

"Besides, there aren't any lovers," I added sourly.

"We're speaking of the *Dream* by Shakespeare?"

"There are only foolish young couples bewitched by a potion."

"Ah, but are we not all bewitched in love?" I heard the sarcasm in his voice.

"You told me love was going through hell," I reminded him.

"That shows what you know about lovers, if you think they never go through hell."

I knew more than Jack suspected about that particular subject—not that it was possible to qualify Matty as my lover. Still, I cast down my eyes before Jack could read my humiliation in them. I didn't want him to know what a fool I'd been. I'd been ashamed to show my face for days after the Gallo Rojo, for fear the others would all know of Matty's triumph. But I'd found myself attracting no more than the usual snickers. Apparently, I had not even been worth boasting about.

"It doesn't mean they love any less," Jack went on. "Look at Oberon and Titania. It's because they love so fiercely that their quarrels are so explosive.

> *"The spring, the summer,*
> *The childing autumn, angry winter, change*
> *Their wonted liveries, and the mazed world*
> *By their increase, now knows not which is which."*

"When their love is out of joint," he concluded, drawing breath, "the whole damned universe is in upheaval."

"Why do you never recite aboard the *Providence*?" I asked. "It would certainly pass the time."

"Pirates do not care overmuch for poetry."

"That may change, when we next go out." Gazing out the open doorway, I saw Rudy lounging in the shade behind the cabins with his arm around Esteban, the young, blue-eyed *mulatto* from Santiago. They had been inseparable since Christmas. I sighed. "If we ever do go out again."

Porter and the Yankee Squadron had returned to the

Indies, a most unwelcome Christmas present, and for weeks since, the *Providence* had lain idle in the brush at Laguna Escondida.

"Why can't he die of the fever, like everyone else?" Captain Hart had grumbled. "Like all those green boys he leads down here to perish in these damned swamps."

It was said Porter's squadron was now hunting illegal slave ships as well as pirates. While the trading of slaves from Africa had been outlawed, the actual practice of slavery was still perfectly legal in the sugar islands—which meant twice the profits for enterprising slave smugglers. No wonder Calhoun of the *New Hope* had risked his life savings to enter the business. No wonder Adderly was so dogged in pursuing us.

"Witches and fairies excited your girlish mind," Jack was saying, now. "What else? Rosalind, I suppose. *As You Like It*," he added, when he saw my baffled look.

"I don't know that one."

"No? Rosalind, a lass 'uncommon tall' who's banished from her homeland and dresses like a boy to go have adventures among the outlaw men? You don't know it?"

I frowned. "You're not inventing this?"

"'All the world's a stage,'" Jack prompted, "'And all the men and women merely players . . . .'"

"Oh, yes, I've copied that out." Twice a week, we Worthen girls had been marched to the writing master to improve our hand.

"Copied out?" Jack echoed, appalled. "No wonder the world is in such chaos when Shakespeare is copied out, but not read." He grumbled on in this vein and returned to his book.

"Jack, tell me."

"What?"

"About Rosalind. What becomes of her?"

"She ends happily. They always do, in the comedies."

I paged eagerly through the book to find the play and mark it for future study. It would be so comforting to think of my own life as a tidy and benevolent comedy that would end happily—not this endlessly confounding farce.

"But isn't it odd? Shakespeare writing about a girl dressed as a boy?"

"It was a very common device. He used it all the time."

"You mean there are others?"

"Of course." Jack laughed. "Rosalind, Viola, Imogen, Portia. In those days, acting was forbidden to women—"

"Why?"

"Because women are so pure and actors are so damnably wicked, as you once took such pains to remind me. But plays were still written with women characters, of course, so female parts were played by young boys. It made sense to dress 'em up as boys part of the time; put less of a strain on the wardrobe and the audience's imagination. There's hardly a major female character in Shakespeare who doesn't spend at least a scene or two disguised as a page."

I gazed at him for a long moment. "As an actor, then, you must have seen lots of women dressed as boys. That's why you saw through my disguise that first night aboard the *Providence*."

Jack hitched up one shoulder. "It wasn't much of a disguise."

"But you didn't give me away."

"I thought you probably had your reasons. And I didn't imagine it would take too long to find you out."

Still, had my sex been discovered that night, with the battered *New Hope* and her crew still in sight, my fate might have been very different. I wondered if Jack would accept my tardy thanks, but his eyes were already fastened back down upon his own book, closing the matter.

"And what is Rosalind's fate?"

"Oh, she weds Orlando, the duke's son. Rather a tedious young lout, but handsome enough."

"That's all?" I protested. "That's considered happy?"

"Aye, to be properly wed is all that matters in the romances." He glanced up, again. "I'm surprised you don't know the play. It's a much more suitable production for a young lady than *Macbeth*."

"Oh, I've never actually seen a production."

"No? Had they no theaters in Boston?"

"Yes, but the Worthen sisters would sooner embrace Satanism than attend a public performance in a theater." I laughed. "No doubt they thought they were one and the same thing."

"They may have been right, at that." Jack smiled. "But you can't claim to know Shakespeare if you've never heard his language spoken."

"I've heard it," I declared. But where? Certainly not at the Worthen Academy, only the Bible had ever been read aloud there. But I could hear it in my memory, all the same—the comic braying of the man in the donkey's head, Puck's brittle, piping falsetto, Macbeth railing against the witches and his fate. Macbeth, the Scot.

"My father." My voice was scarcely audible, even to me. "He read to us all the time, when I was a child. My brothers and me." I was surprised by the memory. For so long, all I had remembered about my father was the cold eye of his madness. But now I saw a different face, kind gray eyes crinkled with laughter, cheeks pinkened by the heat of the kitchen fire. "He read all the parts, each in a different voice: fairies, Scotsmen, witches . . . I suppose that's why he never read us the romances, he knew the boys would never sit still for them. We got King Arthur and Roderick Random and fairies and ghosts and witches and murder!"

Memories I had put away long ago with my lost girlhood came flooding back. "My father was determined the boys would lose nothing in the way of education by leaving Boston for our farm in the country. And he educated me, as well, even though I was only a girl. He taught me sums. He took me swimming in the river. He taught me to read, and . . . ."

"And?" Jack prompted, very gently.

I blinked at him. I suppose I'd forgotten he was there. "My father loved me, once," I whispered.

"Not uncommon, in fathers," said Jack.

"But I'd forgotten. How could I forget my father loved

me?" The last living person who ever had. Or was ever likely to.

"Forgetting can be a blessing, sometimes."

"You think so?"

Jack nodded. "Tell me about your mother."

"Oh, she was wonderful! She was beautiful and delicate and small, nothing like me. And so full of life! My papa adored her."

"What became of her?"

"She died. In childbirth."

"Then . . . she died giving life?"

"No, the baby died, too." I was amazed at how calm I sounded, that I could speak of it without tears.

"And that's when you ran away to sea?"

"No, I was only a child. That's when they sent me to Boston."

"Had your father nothing to say about it?"

"My father went out of his mind." It had been too much, losing Josh, his eldest, in the war. And then losing my mother when she tried to give him another child. What could he do but retreat into the refuge of madness? That was when my brother Andy ran off to sea. That was when my life ended.

"I'm sorry."

"Me too. It was a sorry business."

"You don't have to tell me."

"But I don't mind. I think he loved my mother so much that when she died, he lost his reason. Otherwise, it would have hurt too much. It was . . . ." I drew a wavering breath, "unbearable at the time. But now I feel almost proud of him. That he could love so much." The facts of the matter had never occurred to me so clearly before. I had spent so many years resenting my papa for abandoning me, making an orphan of me after Mama died. Leaving me so alone. But things looked different to me, now.

"Had he loved a little less, he might have preserved his wits," said Jack.

I glared at him; my father's love for my mother had been fierce and genuine, not something manufactured for a

twenty-dollar wager in the Gallo Rojo, and I would not have
Jack snickering at it. But how could I say Jack was wrong? Had
my father borne his grief, I might still have a home on the farm
and the security of his love. How had my life improved since
then? I had the freedom I'd fought for, true, but at the expense
of the love I craved. I knew now I could never have both.
Fortune had been playing with me all this time.

"He might have, at that," was all I could say.

"You'll need your wits aboard the *Providence*," Jack
reminded me. "Feeling is a liability in this trade."

How fortunate Jack was to feel nothing, care for nothing. That was the only way to survive.

"Is that why so few women go to sea?" Asked to
choose between love and freedom, I supposed most females
could be counted upon to make the wrong choice.

"You know why, Rusty. *Mala suerte*."

"I haven't brought any bad luck!"

"Aye, but you're neither fish nor fowl in your 'masculine usurp'd attire.' Dame Fortune hasn't figured out what to
make of you, so for now, she's left you alone."

Intermittent stars winked down from a cloudy night
sky as I leaned in the doorway of my little cabin, gazing out
across the sleeping camp. Once, the thousand stars had stood
for all my hopes and dreams, and the nights were full of promise. But night-fogs had been creeping in off the water of late,
swallowing up one dream here, another there. My more foolish
dreams.

I rubbed my hand again, trying to ease the cramp. The
lamp still burned low on the little table behind me, where I'd
been filling up the pages of my logbook. As I did most nights,
now, in the long, dark hours between nightfall and sleep. I had
plundered this new volume bound in mahogany-colored
Spanish leather from a prize ship we'd taken back in the
Bahamas. I'd found it in the captain's cabin while Jack was raid-

ing the captain's library. My writing in it had begun idly enough, as a way to pass the weary time ashore during these months in Laguna Escondida. I began with all that had happened to me since leaving Boston, attempting to account for myself, to make sense of my dreams. I could give up a few old, shopworn dreams for the sake of this life of freedom I'd chosen. I would never be a man's beloved and knew I must find some other way of belonging in the world. Working in my book helped to establish some measure of peace in my life. A peace worth maintaining. Even Jasmine had stopped pestering me about a lover. She knew when a cause was lost.

I crossed back to the table and turned down the lamp until the flame sputtered out. Blind for an instant in the all-consuming dark, my other senses grew more acute—I might have sworn I heard a rustling outside the cabin that was distinct from the usual whirring and clacking of the night insects. Bats? But the sound was too low, too near. Rats? Lizards? It might have been anything. Or nothing.

I realized I had frozen in place, straining my ears. Waiting. Listening. But I heard nothing more.

CHAPTER 14

Mala Suerte

It was the last hour of daylight on an early spring evening at Laguna Escondida. We'd eaten the last of the turtle meat, and the men had broken out the pipes and rum when Captain Hart mentioned the pestilential nature of this year's mosquitos.

"Early rain and early mosquitos are always a bad sign for the fever," he said. Indeed, the clammy weather, pregnant with soon-to-be-shed spring rain, made us all irritable. "Perhaps we ought to clear up to the bluff."

"But why not clear out to sea, like always?" asked Bustamante. He stilled the dice cup he'd been rattling with some of his gunners.

"We've been fortunate, with Porter occupied in the north," said the captain, thoughtfully tapping tobacco into his pipe. "But we never know where or when the Yankees will strike next."

"All the more reason for us to be gone the next time they come," Bustamante argued.

"And then who will defend us?" Jasmine cried out. She had shared our meal and now sat between Hector and me while their children slept in my cabin. Jack lounged nearby. "Must we watch helpless again, while all our stores and boats are burned?"

"Some of us would rather be here when the *norteamericanos* come back," Hector agreed.

"To defend a few stores and a few women?" Cuervo sneered, from the far side of the fire where he and Matty were sharing a bottle. "Why sit idle here when the richest ships in the Indies are waiting out there for anyone bold enough to take them?"

"And the biggest military fleet," Hart pointed out.

"Have we become so old and feeble that a few guns frighten us? Are we women, afraid to fight?"

It irritated me that Cuervo always invoked women as the ultimate insult when he wanted to goad the men to action. And that it so often worked.

"Any man who isn't afraid of a gun is a fool," Hart replied. He dipped a long twist of dried thatch into the dying cookfire until the end flamed up and brought the burning end to the bowl of his pipe. "But no man under my command has ever run from a fight." He sucked at his pipe stem in short, rapid tugs until the bowl smoked, shook out the thatch, and tossed it into the dirt. "What I object to is handing ourselves over to Porter on a spit when there's no need. Especially if that rabid dog off the *New Hope* is still sailing with 'em, thirsting for our blood."

He glanced at me, and I lowered my eyes, ashamed to be the lightning rod for Adderly's implacable wrath, ashamed of the *mala suerte* I had brought them.

"It will be just as easy to clear out of his way until the mosquitos eat him alive or he goes home," Hart concluded.

"But that could take forever," Matty protested. "Porter has already survived the fever once, and come back. Now that the squadron is harrying the north, why can't we steal south to the Windward?"

Jasmine snorted with impatience. "Like last summer, when we did not know where you were, if fever or the Yankees had got you first, if you were alive or dead?" she fumed. "Now you abandon us by choice?"

"Does your woman always speak for you?" Cuervo muttered to Hector.

"Only when she talk sense."

"But is not a bad plan, Captain," Bustamante urged. "We leave Cuba to the *norteamericanos* and beat down to the Mona and Puerto Rico."

"We'll use Fajardo as a base," Cuervo chimed in. "When we get too full of plunder, we can sail back to Santiago—"

"And get shot out of the water like a pregnant whale by the Yankee patrol," Jack finished.

"We know you have no belly for a fight, Danzador," Cuervo retorted.

"The *Providence* is not a warship," Hart reminded him. "We're in this trade for profit."

"And for glory," Matty added, stubbornly.

Jasmine's bitter laugh startled us all. "Is it so glorious to get killed?"

"B'God, can't somebody silence the bitch?" Matty snapped.

Jack's head came up fast, his dark eyes so full of rage that I jumped. But Hector remained unperturbed, even smiling, as Jasmine rounded on Matty.

"There be plenty of silence when you fool men lie at the bottom of the sea and we women run things in peace!"

"No woman runs my life!" Cuervo shouted. "I say we sail!"

"Could be a profitable voyage," Bustamante agreed.

"But how much of the profit would we have to spend on provisions and repairs, so far from home?" Hart reasoned. "How much profit did we bring home last summer?"

There was some muttering among the men over this point. We all remembered those dreary months of long days and small trade in the Bahamas.

"How much profit do we earn sitting here?" Matty countered.

"I say we sail!" Cuervo barked, again, leaping to his feet. "The *Providence* belongs to all of us, not just one man. You can stay here with the women, if you like," he said to Hart, "and anyone else who's afraid."

Nada, crouching at Hart's elbow, was on his feet in an instant, fists knotted, black eyes livid with rage; several of the others scrambled to get out of the way. Even Cuervo blanched and stumbled backward into a protective knot of men—Matty and Bustamante among them—who were on their feet, shouting in favor of sailing. I was stunned by the volatility of the scene, how suddenly their anger and enmity had flared up; in a moment, their weapons would be drawn. Then a voice as clean and sharp as a new blade sliced through the confusion.

"*Hombres*, there is no need for a brawl." Hart still sat upon the outcropping of limestone where he had been all the time, sucking at his pipe. "I won't stop your sailing, if that's what you decide. We'll put it to a vote tomorrow, when we're all here."

The Articles stated that no decisions could be made unless every hand had a say in the matter, and tonight Javier was up on the bluff with his family, Arne was out on the *Providence* polishing her woodwork, and Rudy and Esteban had taken themselves off, somewhere. Ed Hart held his command only by consent of the men, but it likewise needed the consent of all the men to revoke it. The pirates put a great deal of stock in their Articles, so while there was still some grumbling, the tension in the moment slackened off. I no longer feared murder. Mutiny had been averted, for now.

"Stupid men!" Jasmine fumed, as we went to fetch her boys. "They even have to fight about if they will fight."

"They get restless if they stay in one place too long." I knew how I would feel without the solace of my logbook and nothing to do week after sweltering week but drink and dice and stew with inactivity. "Perhaps it wouldn't be such a bad idea for some of them to leave for a while."

"If they vote to sail, they all go, even *Capitan*," Jasmine sighed. "They always do."

And I knew I would, too. The life of a landlocked female was not for me. Now that I had sacrificed everything for my freedom, I would enjoy it on the open sea, like the men. Besides, the long, listless months ashore had only taught me how much I missed the *Providence*. The mournfully creaking wood and sighing lines and the slack, sticky ratlines were more like home to me than any place since my papa's farm.

"Captain want to see you," Nada grunted, a few mornings later, as I came off lookout duty on the promontory above the lagoon. Down below, Laguna Escondida was a hive of activity, now that the men had voted to sail. We kept watch at all hours, to prevent Porter's squadron swooping down on us unawares before we could clear out to sea.

"Well, Lightfoot, what news from the beach?" Captain Hart smiled as I entered the modest cabin overlooking the bay he shared with Nada. "No invasions this morning?"

"Not so far, Captain."

"But it's like the damned rain, eh? Sooner or later, you know it's coming." He nodded for me to sit down and gazed out his window for another moment. "Nada tells me there's a light in your cabin late at night, when the camp is asleep. He says you labor over a book."

I glared at Nada, crouching near the door. So he was the rat I'd heard in the brush outside my window. "That's true, Captain. I'm writing a history of my life since I came aboard the *Providence*."

"A factual history?"

"Names? Dates?" Nada muttered. "Positions . . . ?"

"I'm not ripping out the pages and hurling them out to sea in bottles, if that's what you mean!" I barked. "It's only for me, Captain, no one else will ever read it." My hands had come up from the armrests of my chair, and I saw the small, white x-shaped scar inside my finger. "I would never do anything to betray the ship or the crew, Captain. I swore an oath."

"Of course ye did, Mistress." Hart smiled. "I think your history-keeping is a splendid idea." I was too surprised to reply; so, apparently, was Nada. "I'm unlettered, myself," Hart went on, "but I respect history. A man who knows no history knows nothing. I've learned most of mine in grog shops or under fire. But an odd thing seems to happen to history once those who live it are done with it and it falls to the lot of the scribblers. It becomes fiction."

He gazed seaward again.

"In years to come, they'll say we were nothing but a band of murdering cut-throats who cared only for blood and torture. Aye, they say it now. A few boatloads of hungry Cubans with damn little else in the way of recourse have become a vast navy of bloodthirsty monsters, ripe for conquest. I would like there to be one dissenting voice."

"Yours?" I ventured.

"No, indeed, Mistress. Yours. When the *Blessed Providence* sails again, I would like you to keep a ship's log. The rations, the weather. What ships we encounter and how we treat with them and they with us. It needn't be at all fancy; I've no taste for literature. I only ask that there be some record of the truth. Can ye do that, lass?"

"*Si, Capitan.* I'm . . . honored."

More than that, I was profoundly grateful. Captain Hart could never know what a prize he'd bestowed on me. He had given me a purpose.

"The *norteamericanos* sniffed this place out once before," Hart went on, his gaze shifting once again to the window and the sea, beyond. "Sooner or later, like the rains, like the damned fever, they'll come back. And when they do, we'd best be gone."

I nodded again. I should have known that nothing escaped the captain, and no skill was so useless he could not find a way to exploit it. Not even mine.

CHAPTER 15

The Ghost Ship

The *Providence* was becalmed in the Windward Passage, south of Punta de Masai, when Jack spotted the American trading brig. Rumor had the Yankee Squadron foundering in the grip of another outbreak of deadly fever, but the fever had ravaged commercial shipping as well, and trade in the passages was slow. And now that there was a likely prize in view, the tradewinds had died away to nothing; Captain Hart and Nada had been tediously working the gaff mainsail for what felt like hours, hoping to stir up a breeze.

The American seemed to have a little momentum from the current nudging her into the passage from the Haitian side. But there was no way for us to get near enough to board her—short of breaking out the oars and sweeping halfway across the passage, hardly the way to mount a surprise attack. But there might be other ways. I had signalled to Rudy to meet me below, and now we were climbing back up the main hatchway, eager to show the others what we'd been up to.

"So near but so far out of reach," grumbled Bustamante, with a longing glance at his swivel gun.

"As long as we're trapped here like a ghost ship, so will she be," Hart noted. "At least we can keep an eye on her."

"A beggar may see cake in a shop window," Jack tossed down from the fore shrouds, "but it doesn't feed him."

"We'll be fed, by and by." Hart laughed. "We've nothing but time."

"I'd sooner have a fresh breeze," Nada muttered.

"Any breeze that springs up will be to her advantage," Hart pointed out. The brig had been advancing on the north-easterlies, when there had still been some. "In the time it took us to tack to her windward, all she'd have to do is spread her magnificent canvas and run away."

"We could run straight across from here and block her path," Matty suggested. "Or wait here until she passes, then chase her."

"If there was a breeze and if we were waiting in some hidden cove instead of out here in the middle of the damned passage." Hart sighed. "By now, she's seen us as surely as we've spotted her. Any move we make to either approach her or hide ourselves will put her on her guard."

They were too preoccupied to notice me, loosely wrapped in an old oilskin, emerging with Rudy out of the hatch. "She might come to us, Captain," I said.

"So might Armageddon."

"But she might come sooner. If she thought we were in distress. You said it yourself—a ghost ship."

Hart shook his head. "That only works in storybooks. The crew with blackened faces sprawled across the deck as if dead. Or done up like ladies, adrift . . . ."

He stopped and looked at me again. I shrugged the oilskin off my shoulders to reveal the short puffed sleeves and low neckline of a cotton chemise taken from our last prize, a cargo of English linens. The others fell so silent, I was embarrassed to go further, but Rudy tugged at the oilskin until it fell at my feet. There was no mistaking the female outline of my body beneath the soft, translucent folds of the white gown.

"*La dama en peligro,*" Rudy declared, beaming happily. The lady in distress.

"Better than any of this lot could do," the captain agreed, looking me up and down.

"If we seem crippled and helpless, she might chance a closer look once the breeze picks up, and do our work for us," I reasoned. "And even if she passes us by, we'll be to her windward and still have time to make sail and chase her."

Hart grinned. "Aye, but what gallant Yankee captain could resist such tender bait?"

While the others were engaged in a lively debate over whether I ought to be lashed to the mainmast as if tortured or allowed to pace amidships, wringing my hands in provocative despair, Jack came down from aloft.

"It's no good, Captain. It will never work."

"On the contrary, *hombre,* I believe it will work very well." Hart glanced over at me as I unfastened my braid and shook my hair out across my shoulders. "Ahoy, there, Mistress, don't cover up your bosom. We want 'em to be able to see you're the genuine article."

"It's an ignorant child's trick," Jack protested.

I was close enough to overhear, and I glared up at him, stung. Here at last was one thing that I could do better than any man aboard, but now for some unfathomable reason, Jack wanted to take my triumph away.

"I thought you were the one so eager for cake!" I chided.

"I wouldn't dish myself up on a gilded platter to get it," Jack retorted. "Suppose they send an armed party to board us and there's a fight," he went on, turning again to Hart. "She can't maneuver in that outfit, Captain. She'll be of no use to anyone."

Hart's keen gaze bounced from Jack to me and back to Jack. "Don't forget, we'll all be waiting in the bulwarks," he told Jack, at last. "No one can get to her without going through us, first. She'll be quite safe."

Jack suddenly found something fascinating to look at among the blistered planks of the deck at his feet.

"But, Mistress," Hart called to me, "just to be prudent, if we are boarded, I expect you to dive down he hatch." He raised an eyebrow at me. "We'll want to preserve that lovely frock for the next time we need this clever ruse."

And I nodded in agreement, beaming under his praise.

The first little sigh of air came just after noon. As it began to freshen, Arne slid a small kedge anchor on a towline over the port rail astern, to cause a little drag. Our mysterious bare-masted schooner seemed to flounder about without making any headway while the American gradually bellied her sails before the rising easterlies and began to advance at a stately pace.

I draped myself across the forward edge of the cabin top, my white gown surely visible to anyone with a spyglass aboard the brig. Even with the breeze, the air was heavy and humid; sweat was pooling in the deep creases beneath my breasts and spilling down my ribs. The crew formed a row of brown backs tensed in readiness, crouched beneath the starboard rail. It took an eternity for the blasted *norteamericano* to come within hailing distance, and then the American seemed to halt in her progress; she might yet veer away south, leaving the *Providence* to scramble and catch up.

I rose up on one arm and tossed my hair back behind a shoulder so they could get the full effect of my soaked gown. I raised an arm above my head, partly in a wave and partly in what I hoped was a suitably imploring gesture. The brig moved closer, and when I could hear voices shouting at me, I pretended to swoon again.

The splash of oars in the water told us the American was sending over a boat to investigate. I eased myself to the deck, as if trying to greet my rescuers, but making ready to dive for the hatch as soon as the fighting began; my clothes were just below, at the foot of the ladder. Then the first face appeared above the rail as the boarders climbed the schooner's chains. And I forgot to run. It was a dark face, under a thatch of black hair with a knife clenched in its teeth. Another brown face under long hair tied back with a filthy bandana popped up beside the first, and then a bearded, bare-chested fellow in patched trousers hurled himself over the rail, almost on top of Hector, who caught him by the middle and knocked his head against the deck.

Now the *Providence* men sprang up to grapple with what was surely the most dubious merchant crew ever to sail under the stars and stripes. Men were wrestling, punching and kicking each other, weapons whistled in the air, and only a pistol shot reminded me to hit the deck and crawl toward cover. Then, above the clamor of battle and the yelling and cursing— all of it in Spanish—Hart's roar carried above all else.

"Villalobos, ye goddamned son of a whore, is that you?"

"Edouardo?"

This from a compact, powerfully built man dressed all in black, his silvered black curls tied back behind his ears, his upraised hand clutching the barrel of a pistol he was about to crack across the head of Rudy, who was fending him off at knifepoint.

"Edouardo, you Scotch devil! This is a joke, no?"

Unexpectedly, Hart burst out laughing.

"The joke's on me, *amigo!* Since when do you captain an American merchant brig?"

"Since I capture her in the Mona when I lose my own *Lobo del Mar*. I take this one home to Trinidad to fit her out for the trade." Villalobos's fierce visage split in two with a huge grin, showing all that remained of his stained teeth, and his guffaw rattled the ship's timbers. "Who would think I be waylaid by *los piratas*, eh?"

Both he and Captain Hart found this a great joke; they shouldered their way through the knots of confused men and draped their arms around each other, laughing fit to burst. Nobody else knew quite what to do. Jack had moved between me and the boarders, staff upraised, while Nada hovered near-by with his pistol drawn. Matty had both his cutlass and his rapier out, itching for a target, but Hart called us off, announcing that he and Villalobos had shipped out of Caracas together. Villalobos signalled his own men to stand at ease, limbs were disentangled and weapons recovered while the two captains bantered on over old times.

"I never thought to see you employ women, Edouardo. Are times so hard?"

I climbed back up on the cabin top to get a better view and saw Hart grin up at me. "I employ one woman, and she's very handy, indeed," he told Villalobos. Had you been genuine *norteamericanos*, you would be in our possession, now."

"*Norteamericanos!*" Villalobos spat. "They are killing off the trade. I wait weeks for that prize! My men, we almost starve, we no go home for over a month. Now they say the *norteamericanos* have the fever again, so we make a little profit, maybe. But the sons of dogs keep coming back— like mosquitos, like the hurricanes, eh? Hunt us down, steal our food, burn our villages. How are we to live?"

"With our swords," Hart muttered, "as men have always lived, if they would not be slaves."

"Is another war, Edouardo," Villalobos agreed, shaking his curly head. "Like Caracas."

"It's a plague. They all spread the same damn contagion of blood and ruin in the Indies, whether they be *norteamericanos* or Europeans," seethed the Scotch devil. "I'd hoped to escape that kind of lunacy in this honest trade."

"*Y yo, hombre.*" Villalobos nodded. "But these little Yankee toy soldiers must come down and kill a few *cubanos* over cargos of dry goods to prove what heroes they are. They go home and become admirals, commodores, and our people are left here to starve."

"You haven't starved yet, *amigo.*" Hart laughed, patting his friend's solid middle. "Nor shall ye thirst, not aboard my ship. Rudy, fetch the rum!"

But Villalobos declined. His crew was anxious to get

home to Trinidad, several days' sail away on the leeward coast of Cuba. They took themselves off in their plundered brig, and Hart ordered the *Providence* crew to make sail for the Atlantic.

The men fell in to work the ship, and I backed up along the cabin top to get out of the way. I knew every plank in the deck, of course, but when I sprang back behind the davits where the ship's boat was secured, I didn't reckon on the long hem of my chemise getting fouled in the tackle. My heel caught in the snagged gown and my other foot crashed down behind me in two more awkward hops as momentum propelled me backward. Then I ran out of deck.

There was no railing, here; I could only make one futile grab for the curved iron davit as I twisted in the air and saw green water rushing up to meet me. But something caught my arm, jerking me upright again with a force that rattled my eyeballs in their sockets. I found myself blinking into Matty's flushed face as he threw his other arm around me and hauled me inboard.

"Hellfire, Mistress, this is no time to feed the sharks! There's work to be done!"

He was grinning with all his might; the thrill of his impromptu heroism had temporarily erased his disappointment over our lost prize. He pulled me to his chest, swung me up off my feet and carried me across the cabin top, to a chorus of sarcastic cheers from the men. I could not have sworn I was in complete control of my limbs, but I felt awkward hauled aloft like a child, like some sort of prize.

"I'm all right," I protested. "I can stand."

"Oh, I think not!" Matty cried, playing to his audience; the men had not had much to amuse them, of late. From astern, Hart eyed us for a moment, noted the chuckling of the men and returned his attention to the binnacle with Nada and Salvador Gris. "Why, Mistress, you're shaking like a leaf," Matty went on, with a smug grin. "I can feel it."

I was shaking, all right, with fury. I knew how close to naked I was in Matty's arms; what right had he to brandish me about as if he owned me, to make sport of me? Because I was a helpless female. Because I had once shared his bed.

"Put me down, Mateo!" But because I was outraged, my voice came out with a light tremor, as if I were laughing, and Matty laughed too. I refused to kick and squirm like a half-wit female; I knew how strong he was. Instead, I worked my hand round his waist and all the way up his broad back, surreptitiously closing my fist tight around a handful of his long golden hair.

"Put me down or I'll break your neck," I hissed.

"Ah, what sweet nothings the wench whispers to me," Matty crowed, gripping me more tightly and bracing his neck muscles as something malicious crept into his dazzling smile. "You're quite right, my pet, that's an outfit better suited to the boudoir than a working ship. I'd best see you belowdecks where we can make better use of—"

"Sail ho!"

It was Jack's voice from the foretop, booming and urgent. "Port quarter!" he roared again, and chaos erupted as the men raced across the deck to the port rail to strain their eyes against the rising breeze and glinting water. Matty let go of me so quickly, I scarcely got my feet under me before he leaped off the cabin top to join the others. I clambered down after him, yanked the hem of my damned useless gown up round my knees and leaped up to the rail securing the water cask at the foot of the mainmast to see over the heads of the others. But nowhere on what I could see of the surface of the water was anything moving but swells and sunlight. The atmosphere aboard the *Providence* had again become tense—and uneasily quiet.

"Damn it, Jack, where away?" the captain hissed, at last.

"*Lo siento, Capitan,*" Jack sang out, wonderfully calm. "Sorry, *amigos*, my mistake. Must've been a dolphin."

The response to this was explosive as the pirates gave roaring voice to all the frustrations of a long, wasted day of anxious plotting, tedious waiting and no payoff. Some of them hugged the rail, certain they *had* glimpsed a sail, even if Jack had not, or could will one into existence on the spot. Hart ordered another man aloft to scan the horizon, just to be sure, while the others grumbled about ghost ships, Jack's eyesight and the damnable whims of Fate. The momentary diversion of Matty's dramatic rescue of me had now been completely forgotten— especially by Matty, who was stalking the deck in a fury.

I was just as glad to be forgotten, but still seething. I stepped down to the deck to go below when Jack came down the backstay and landed a couple of paces away.

"Fine tumbler you are, falling overboard," he muttered, as he headed for the water cask.

"Fine lookout you are, mistaking a dolphin for a sail!"

"If that's how you want to be treated, you ought to have stayed at Sarafina's."

I whirled on him, but he was too quick, catching my upraised arm. For a split instant, we both stared up at my trapped hand, not flat open but knotted into a fist.

"Save your blows for someone who deserves 'em," said Jack, flinging down my arm and turning away.

Before I could retort, another sudden, startled shout directed everyone's attention up to the sky. A grey seabird was careening awkwardly toward the masts on the headwind. But instead of gliding over or around the foretop rigging, the bird collided with it. Its single, sharp cry lengthened painfully, then dwindled down to a mournful tumble of falling notes as the creature floundered about, caught, head and one wing tangled in the lines, flat feet paddling uselessly in the air.

I could not make myself look away from this ghastly vision. There was no human sound anywhere on the ship until Hart finally found his voice—or a dry, grim semblance of it.

"Diego!" he called to the man aloft. "Go finish off the poor damned brute and cut him down. The rest of you, back to work."

But his false briskness did little to reassure anyone. There were mumbles of *"Mala suerte"* and *"Brujeria."* Witchcraft. Some of the men crossed themselves.

"What an awful omen," I murmured.

Jack was still near enough to hear me. "That's no barnacle goose," he said. "Only some misguided gull, likely injured already. Or addled."

The creature hung suspended above us as Diego made his way out along the footropes. Every now and again, a foot or a wing would spasm grotesquely in the air, to no avail.

"Nothing that gruesome can bode any good," I whispered.

"It bodes nothing," Jack insisted. "It's an accident, nothing more."

Diego finally reached the creature and snapped its neck. And when I cast my eyes downward, I saw the outline of my body beneath the thin chemise. Never before had I worn such an outfit aboard the *Providence*.

"But it is more, Jack. These *hombres* know *mala suerte* when they see it. It's me. I'm . . . 'out of suits with fortune.' Like Rosalind."

"Meaning what?" Jack frowned.

"Meaning your Dame Fortune has found me out at last for the impostor I am. And now she means to make up for lost time."

CHAPTER 16

The Slaver

Spring continued languid and fretful in the waters off Cuba. But with the constant news of Porter's renewed raids along the coast, life ashore in Laguna Escondida was intolerable. To keep the *Providence* out of his hands, the men elected to sail eastward for Puerto Rico to search for prizes in the Mona Passage.

I finished recording another uneventful day in my logbook, sitting cross-legged in my corner behind the storeroom. Closing the book with a sigh, I put it on top of Jack's Shakespeare in the wide, shallow basket Jasmine had brought me on the day we sailed.

"I can no be running up and down these cliffs this time, if the *norteamericanos* come back, eh?" she'd told me. And I tried to mask the alarm I always felt whenever Jasmine made mention of her thickening belly, swelling now with her third child. She nodded at the book as she handed the basket to me.

"You keep this for Jack."

Now I stroked the intricately woven contours of the basket. It was certainly the finest object I possessed, all the more cherished because it was a gift from Jasmine. I hoped some of her energy and good sense came with it to guide me through this voyage. At last, I slid the basket back into place under my straw-stuffed pallet. Then a shadow fell across the light streaming in from above, and I looked up. It was Nada.

I got to my feet, keeping an eye on Nada's square brown face and deep-set black eyes. I was no longer physically afraid of him; there was nothing malevolent about him, unless he suspected some danger to Ed Hart. He was more like a force of nature, like a high wind or a heavy sea, inexorable but unemotional. A thing to be skirted if at all possible, not to be tackled head-on.

"Am I called above?" I prompted, carefully.

Nada lifted his heavy shoulders. "Nothing to do. Nothing to see. Same *mala suerte*. We have bad luck, you put it in your book," he went on, in English, as if he didn't credit me to understand his Spanish. "Is trapped here, in your book. *Brujeria*. It grows."

"If I knew any witchcraft, I'd use it against Porter," I declared. "Why would I curse my own ship? I'm as loyal to the *Providence* as any man aboard." But how could I argue that bad luck was not a physical thing, like water shipped in through the hatch to fester below? How could I even be sure it wasn't true? "I'm only following the captain's order. You were there."

"Was foolish order," Nada muttered.

"But I must obey it. Unless he orders me to stop."

Nada looked grim, but said no more. He turned to take himself off up the hatch as silently as he had appeared. But I had not long to savor my relief before there was a thundering of feet above, mingled with excited cries of "Sail, ho!" By the time I hauled myself up the companion ladder to the deck, however, the tension had gone out of the moment. Matty was slouching aft, toward me; surely, he'd be off howling in the bows if anything exciting were going on.

"What is she?" I hailed him.

"Only a slaver," Matty replied, irritably. "No good for plunder. Not that her cargo wouldn't bring a handsome profit in any Spanish port—if the captain would go after her."

I could just see the full sails of the slave ship off the port bow, heading for the *Providence* on the trades.

"What does he say?"

"He says we can't spare a prize crew," Matty huffed. "He says she's too fast, as if any craft with her lading could outrun us. The captain says a lot of damn fool things. We're in this trade for profit, but he won't chase her. Somebody's going to profit on her. Why not us?"

He shouldered past me as the stench coming off the slave ship slapped me in the face; a heavy, sour, animal smell that stung my throat and nostrils and made my stomach turn over. I caught my breath, then spit it out again, suffocated.

Captain Hart had moved to the port rail with Nada and Bustamante. "No doubt, she watered at Puerto Rico on her way to Cuba," Hart was saying, as I drew near.

"The *norteamericanos* no catch this one," Nada observed.

"Aye, not a damned squadron ship in sight when they might do some good in these waters," Hart muttered.

I turned away from another gust of foul air on the trades. Rudy was disappearing down into the galley, Arne worked astern, his face wreathed in pipe smoke, and Hector leaned absolutely still at the opposite rail, watching the slaver without expression. Jack was just coming down from the top.

"Well, we'll have no part of her," Hart concluded. "Nada, all hands to braces and sheets. Jack, take the lads aloft to make sail. Lets get upwind of her."

Nada sprang forward to bark his orders, but Jack spun away and lurched astern. Hart gazed after him for a moment, then repeated his order to me.

With a grateful *"Si, Capitan,"* I called for Diego and Esteban. I had never felt so glad to get aloft, although there was no escaping the overpowering reek off the slaver, however high we climbed. Up on the yards, we trimmed the topsails to maneuver the *Providence* onto a new course, across the slaver's bow and out to windward, clearing a wide path for her. But I couldn't see Jack among the others working the ship below. When I did finally spot him, far astern, wedged against the starboard rail behind the cabin top, he was heaving his breakfast over the side. When I came down he was still there, staring after the slaver, some distance to starboard. He was absently wiping at his mouth with the back of one hand; the knuckles of the other were white as he gripped the rail.

"Unusual time to get seasick, Uncle Jack, with the day so fair."

"It's not the sea sickens me." He wouldn't look at me, but neither did he bark at me or send me away. Another minute passed.

"I shipped out on a slaver, once," he said at last, his voice low. "I was on a merchantman that broke up in a gale in the Atlantic. Those of us who didn't drown were picked up by a slaver out of Liverpool bound for the African coast. She was short-handed and I had no money. I had no choice but to sign on for the middle passage back to the Indies or starve on the Gold Coast."

His words came out so stiffly, I knew they'd never been spoken aloud before.

"Most of the common seamen were spared the sight of the cargo, packed end-to-end like crated fish in the hold." He still did not look at me. "We called 'em cargo or blackbirds, anything to disguise what they really were. But there was no escape from the sound they made. Or the smell. I stayed aloft as much as I could, as far away as I could get.

"When we finally got within sight of the Antilles, a British frigate came out of nowhere and pursued us. Our captain knew a few maneuvers, but he couldn't outrun that damn frigate. He swore every oath and tried every trick, but in the end he did what any sensible smuggler must do, in like circumstances." His words stopped as he stared aft at some vision I couldn't see.

"What?" I prompted.

"He . . . jettisoned the cargo." Jack paused for a single, shallow breath, then plunged on. "They used a cargo port out of sight of the frigate and ran 'em out chained together to weigh 'em down. Even those more dead than alive had the wit to scream as they were dragged under the surface. You could hear every syllable of their screaming, even from high aloft. You could see the writhing black trail in our wake. It was . . . it looked . . . . "

This time, he did not go on.

"What did you do?"

"Do?" Jack echoed, his eyes swinging back to me. "I leaped into the sea and dragged them all to safety a thousand leagues away. I fomented a mutiny. I challenged the captain to a goddamned duel." He drew a furious breath. "I didn't *do* anything."

He stared back out to sea.

"We put in to Nuevitas, but there was no payoff, since we'd lost our cargo. I stumbled into some dingy waterfront *aguardiente* shop and found Ed Hart and Nada recruiting for the *Providence*. I knew what kind of a ship she was, but I also knew it could be no worse than the hell of a slaver."

I forced myself to breathe. "Vile things . . . horrible things happen sometimes," I offered. "It's not always anybody's fault . . . . "

"I promise you, this was somebody's fault."

"But not yours."

He didn't say anything, staring hard at nothing out over the rail. But after another moment passed in silence, he turned to me again, this time with neither anger nor sarcasm to mask his troubled eyes.

"It's just . . . I can't forget." His voice was almost a whisper.

"What sort of a man would you be if you could?" I had his full attention, now. "You couldn't stop it, Jack," I reasoned. "But you must never forget it. That's the one thing you can do."

The foul mood from the passing slave ship enveloped the *Blessed Providence* for a few more irritable days at sea. But at last, at the mouth of the Mona Passage, we surprised an English merchantman with some private specie aboard. Bustamante's guns splintered her bow and left her floundering in the doldrums between the land breezes off Santo Domingo and the trades. The *Providence* ran eastward along the north coast of Puerto Rico until we reached Fajardo, where the men were eager to spend their shares of the plunder.

But I remembered all too clearly my last visit to Fajardo and chose to remain aboard with the watch. It was stifling below tonight, and I finally tore myself away from my logbook and went above to find Rudy and Esteban sitting on the foredeck, throwing dice. They both smiled up at me, and Rudy offered me a pull from his jug.

"Who's winning?"

Rudy let out a ribald yelp of laughter as he shook the dice out of his cup. "Me! Game of chance, I always win." He glanced fondly at his partner. "Game of skill, Esteban win every time."

Esteban gazed up with his guileless blue eyes. "You play cards?"

Rudy laughed again. "Is a trick, *amiga!* He never lose."

Esteban looked wounded. He picked up a worn deck of playing cards stacked beside him and fanned them out to me.

"No game, then. Choose a card, I read your Fortune. Is no trick, Tory," he added, with a reproachful glance at Rudy.

I plucked out a card. It was a masculine face card with a Spanish suit pip, round, like a gold coin.

"*Sota de oros,*" said Esteban.

"The Jack of . . . coins?"

"Or gold. Is like, ah, Jack of Diamonds," explained Rudy, who had played cards in every language with men of all nations. "The suit of money. You be rich!"

"Maybe not money, maybe hidden treasure, like gold or diamonds hidden in the earth," Esteban explained, in Spanish. "The Jack must labor for whatever good comes in life. Is a card of hard work."

"How do you know, this?" I asked.

"My sister. She tells sailors their fortunes in Santiago."

"She'd better tell them they'll have passionate lovers and prosperous voyages or she'll starve!" I laughed. "Not that they must work hard all their lives."

Esteban shrugged. "This is your fortune, not theirs. Hard work rewarded. If you never give up."

I looked at the card, a foursquare male figure in black and white and red. Nothing fancy, like Madame Romano's cards. It was a plain card for a plain life of hard work. A life that I had chosen, that suited me. I started to hand the card back, but Esteban shook his head.

"No, you keep it. Is your Fortune." When I still hesitated, Esteban produced a second, cleaner-looking pack of cards from the pouch hung over his shoulder, and smiled. "It's all right. It's not my lucky deck."

We all looked up as Jack came sliding down from his watch aloft. He dipped a drink from the water cask and came over to us, muttering, "*Mal tiempo.*"

"Esteban says there's a hurricane in the south."

"*Si.*" Jack nodded, rubbing the back of his neck. In the light from the lamp Rudy and Esteban had between them, Jack's face looked weary. I'd scarcely seen him with his feet on the deck and not in the rigging since the day we passed the slaver.

"Let me go aloft for a while," I said. "I'll keep an eye on the weather. It's stifling below, and I'd be glad of something to do." As I moved toward the shrouds, Esteban fanned his newer deck of cards at Jack.

"*Naipes, Danzador?*"

Jack laughed. "Hellfire, Esteban, haven't you won enough of my money?"

It was a still, silent night; we might have been the only vessel on the sea. Even the usual cacophony from Fajardo, a mile inland, sounded far off and muted. I settled myself in the top, back against the rail and knees drawn up, gazing out at the vast shimmering beadwork of stars in the black night. After a while, Jack's head appeared over the rim of the top as he hauled himself up the futtock shrouds. We sat for a time in companionable silence, while muttering and occasional halfhearted cursing among the few men still aboard wafted up from below.

"Do you ever wonder what would have happened had you stayed in Boston?" Jack ventured, after awhile.

I shook my head. I rarely gave Boston a second thought.

"It would soon be time for your coming-out ball, would it not?" Jack went on. "When a young lady turns eighteen?"

"I'm hardly the kind of girl they allow to come out in Boston." I laughed. "What I remember most about the place is the way everybody tried to keep me shut in."

"Do you ever think of going back?"

"Never."

"Perhaps you should."

"Perhaps you should return to England."

There was just enough starlight to see Jack smile. "A palpable hit," he acknowledged.

"Are you so anxious to be rid of me, Jack?"

He didn't answer right away. "These are anxious times," he said at last, his voice more serious. "There are far bigger risks in this life now than there were even a year ago. The captain forces no one to sail against his will—"

"Then I'm sure he'll let you go, if you ask." I knew what he was going to suggest, and I didn't want to hear it. Where else would I go?

"Me?" Jack echoed. "I'm not going anywhere."

"Neither am I. Life is full of risks, wherever you are."

Jack looked as if he would argue the point, but he only sighed and raked back his hair and swallowed the rest of his speech. And I was relieved that I wouldn't have to hear in words my own unspoken fear, that this life I'd chosen, the only life I knew, might be coming to an end.

CHAPTER 17

The Spanish Ring

But all fears were forgotten a few mornings later when Captain Hart discovered what his Blessed Providence had planned for us. We'd been cruising for days along the currents above the island of San Domingo, heading for the Inagua Islands in the tail end of the Bahamas. At first light this morning, Jack reported a smudge in the west making for the Caicos Passage. As the sun rose and the *Providence* lay to in her reefy hiding place, the indistinct spot grew into the majestic sails of a merchant brig, low in the water, tacking complacently toward us under the red and gold colors of Spain.

"A cargo of sugar from the Ever Faithful Isle to sweeten the discord of civil war back home," mused Captain Hart. The ship was drawing near enough now to see the sun sparkling off her polished woodwork and chains. "But something more fine than the usual Spanish trader," the captain went on. "Fine enough to show us a profit, I should think. Nada, get us to windward; we'll meet her head-on. And when she tacks, keep us clear of that blunderbuss she carries amidships. Mr. Bustamante, run out your guns. A shot or two across her bows should do it. Rudy, fetch the black flag. We'll show the Dons what they have to fear from faithful *cubanos!*"

Our black schooner coming suddenly out of the sun with the easterlies at her back seemed to take the Spaniard completely by surprise. She could not position herself to fire, yet it was almost a disappointment that the Spanish captain surrendered so swiftly. Disappointing and suspicious. As we tied up alongside our prize, gunners on the alert, our crew armed and ready at the rail, Nada had a presentiment of something *muy malo*. I heard him hiss a warning to the captain.

"Don't go aboard, Edouardo. Is a trap."

Hart cast a shrewd glance across the faces of the Spanish crewmen and the nervous countenance of the Spanish captain, making extravagant gestures of accommodation toward the pirates.

"*Si, hombre*, I feel something," Hart agreed. "But not treachery, I think. Secrets. And we shall know what they are."

It didn't take long to discover the secret harbored by the Spanish brig *San Pedro*. Hart ordered the Spanish crew locked away in the deckhouse, except for Captain Reyes, who was all but dragging him into the hold to show him where the valuables were. But, perversely, Hart decided to take a turn round the deck, chatting amiably all the while in his fine Spanish, but always with an eye toward the face of Captain Reyes. When the complexion of that worthy person faded and his clumsy replies became a faltering stammer, Hart found himself abreast of the door to the captain's private cabin.

Ignoring the Spanish captain's pitiful cries, Hart ordered Hector and Cuervo to shoulder open the locked cabin door. There was a breathless pause on deck as they vanished inside, then a muted crash from within followed by Cuervo's caw of triumph.

"See what finery he keeps in his cupboard, Captain!"

Cuervo came out through the cabin door dragging his prize—a slim, pale young man in handsomely cut clothing—whom Cuervo hauled along ignobly by an ear. The youth could not have been any older than Matty, with skin as pale and fine-grained as a tropical beach, silky black hair and eyes as dark and rich as chocolate. His coat and modestly ruffled shirt and neck-cloth were impeccable and expensive; impeccable, too, was his air of quiet resolve at being hauled before the pirate captain in this undignified manner.

"Hiding in the cupboard like a woman!" Cuervo jeered.

"That's enough, *amigo*," Hart said, mildly, in English. "Let him go."

Cuervo turned the boy loose, but sulkily, having caught the low warning in the captain's voice. *"Hijo de puta,"* he muttered into the ear of his captive. The youth spun around and boxed him so soundly across the jaw that Cuervo sprawled backwards on the deck. As the others roared with laughter, Hector stepped in front of his fallen and now furious *compañero* and gazed calmly at the youth, without making any move to touch him. But the boy's anger was spent, and he turned back to face the captain.

"Quite right, laddie." Hart grinned, and continued on in English. "No gentleman allows a man to insult his mother. And you're quite the young gentleman, I've no doubt. The son of some wealthy *habanero* planter off to Castile for a proper education, eh? I'm sure *su madre* would pay a great deal to see your face again."

"Mi madre esta muerta," the young man replied with an admirable show of cool indifference, perhaps responding to the only words he had understood.

"But somebody is buying you such handsome cloth-ing," Hart pointed out. "This one is our prize, *hombres*," he told us. Across the deck, Captain Reyes shivered with agitation, stuffing fingers into his mouth as if to keep from screaming.

"Somebody important will miss you, my lad," Hart went on. "Hector, take him aboard the *Providence* and stay with him. He's no good to us damaged. Cuervo, Mateo and the rest of you, search the cabins. It's not likely any Havana planter would cast his son into the great world without the means to pay his way."

Certainly Spanish, I decided, as Hector paraded the youth past me at the *Providence* rail; an impressive swarm of bodies had not been required to subdue the *San Pedro* crew, so I'd been ordered to stay behind to tally up such plunder as the others might find. Our hostage displayed not a trace of *mulatto* or *mestizo* or any of the other arcane gradations of race and color that so preoccupied everybody here in the islands. This handsome boy descended from a pure bloodline that still prided itself on the whiteness of its complexion. He had the bearing of a young aristocrat, aloof and very calm—even under Nada's brief, withering stare.

As a formality, our men hauled up as much sugar out of the *San Pedro* hold as the *Providence* could carry. Here in the passages, we were sure to find some trader or other willing to purchase a profitable cargo for the voyage home. But our men were far more interested in the plunder Jack, Arne, Diego and Bustamante were hauling up from belowdecks—trunks of exquisite clothing, linens, boots, belts and silver-worked riding gear. All of these items would bring good prices among the smugglers of Fortune Island. Other men scavenged the storeroom for liquor and other delicacies. They brought over smoked pork salted down in barrels, tins of dark cake soaked in molasses and a tall rumpot of preserved and sugared island fruits.

"What can be keeping the captain?" Jack asked, materializing at my elbow. "This lot'll keep us in cakes and ale in the Bahamas 'til Christmas. What's he looking for?"

Hart was still aboard the *San Pedro* with the last of his scavengers when more raucous crowing told us he'd found what he was after. Matty and Cuervo reappeared on the deck of the *San Pedro* with a small iron strongbox, which they laid at Captain Hart's feet. Matty drew his cutlass and hammered at the lock until it broke and Cuervo flicked the lid back on its hinges and gave the box to the captain. Hart rooted out a sheaf of papers, which he handed over to Matty, who confirmed that they were bank draughts and letters of introduction worthless to our purposes. Hart tossed them aside, then produced from within the box a claret-colored velvet pouch. He gave the box back to Cuervo, drew open the pouch, and peeped inside.

"Your mother's most elegant jewels." Hart nodded, approvingly. "Just the thing to establish a young gentleman in Castilian society."

Cuervo was sifting through the rest of the strongbox. "A gold pocket watch and chain!" he sang out to those of us watching from the *Providence* rail. "Gold buttons inlaid with pearl. One ebony snuff-box. And a silver cameo brooch of some ill-favored female engraved '*To my loving son Ernesto.*'" Cuervo paused to leer at the company before planting a lewd kiss upon the brooch and tossing it back into the box.

The back of the Spanish youth stiffened, but he uttered no sound. Hart tossed the velvet pouch back into the strong-box and nodded at Cuervo to snap the box shut and make for the *Providence* with Matty. Directing the two men who'd been holding Captain Reyes to lock him in the deckhouse with the rest of his crew, Hart then herded the last of the pirates to the side where the two ships were fastened together. When he hoisted himself up to the Spaniard's rail, he paused to address us all.

"*Hombres*, we've taken a prize more valuable where we're going than a troublesome hostage. Hostages require feeding, watering and guarding. So I think we'll let this little *gran blanco* go back to his nursemaids."

Hart leaped across to the *Providence* rail and down to her deck, the last of the pirates scrambling along behind him. Cuervo jumped across to the *Providence* cabin top with his box held aloft in triumph and Matty followed, brandishing his cutlass. He was still planted at the main shrouds when Hart motioned Hector to bring the young captive forward.

"Back to your own ship, boy," Hart addressed Ernesto, in Spanish, jerking his head back toward the *San Pedro*.

"*Mi caja, Capitan?*" The boy nodded toward his strongbox, still clutched in Cuervo's greedy claws.

"I am giving you your life, *muchacho*." Turning away abruptly, Hart called out, "Mateo! Cuervo! See the lad safely across."

Hector loomed up behind the boy, who climbed up to the cabin top where Matty and Cuervo were waiting and glared at them both with all his injured, youthful nobility. He put a hand on the shrouds to steady himself for his leap between the two ships and Matty suddenly feinted round behind him and brought the curved blade of his cutlass up under the boy's outstretched arm, its sharp point tucked under Ernesto's chin.

"*Momento, por favor,*" Matty purred. He nodded at a golden ring glinting on Ernesto's hand and raised the point of his blade a little higher. Unable to stare Matty down, Ernesto slowly withdrew his upraised hand from the shrouds. Matty cocked his head and raised his cutlass point another fraction, and the boy twisted off his ring with trembling fingers, passing it to Matty over the blade.

"*Muy bonita, si?*" Matty withdrew his cutlass and stepped back, holding the ring aloft for Cuervo to see, over the head of the boy standing between them. He then slid it onto his own little finger on the hand that held the cutlass. The other pirates on deck chuckled and hooted. Cuervo was cackling with the sport when Ernesto, without a single warning sound, turned to knock the strongbox out of his hands and into the narrow passage between the two ships and into the water, below.

Before we even heard the splash, Matty's cutlass drove through the air after the boy. Ernesto was off-balance, spinning back around to grab for the shrouds, when the point of the blade caught him in the throat, with all of Matty's strength behind it. There was a stark impression of red against white, a garish red river flooding a snow bank as blood poured out of the boy's throat and down shirtfront and pumped out of his gaping mouth. For the horrible moment he was held there, skewered on Matty's blade, it was possible to watch the life draining out of his pale, startled face. Then Cuervo thrust him furiously aside and the limp body plunged between the rails and into the sea, with a louder and much more ominous splash.

There was an instant of awful, absolute clarity, the kind that only occurs when things are happening very fast. I saw Matty motionless at the edge of the cabin top, clinging to the shrouds with one hand, his cutlass still aloft in the other. Blood sparkled on its blade, as he stared stupidly into the air where the Spanish boy had just been. Cuervo grasped at the davits, struggling to regain his footing. The instant of silence aboard the *Providence* gave way to a low wail that rose to a blistering crescendo as the men of the *San Pedro* exploded out of their deckhouse. Some of them ran to the rail, cursing us or crying after their passenger; some ran to their stations on deck. I saw two men hauling powder and shot to the carronade amidships.

Matty had turned to stone, the sun glinting indulgently on his coppery golden hair. No pair of Spanish eyes that beheld him in that instant would ever forget him. Only Cuervo had the presence of mind to grab the cutlass and shove Matty forward to the *Providence* deck. He hacked at the grappling line that still fastened the two ships together until a swell of the disturbed sea, reddened with Spanish blood, floated us apart.

Then all was noise and confusion. Instinct drove us to braces and sheets, bringing the *Blessed Providence* sharply around to attempt a tack into the breeze that was driving the *San Pedro* astern. I dove aft to take a hand at the main sheet, spitting out a mouthful of bitter smoke as Bustamante, his swivel gun already primed, made the only parting shot he could, off the starboard quarter. But the shot went high into the *San Pedro* rigging, carrying off a spar, at best. Ordered aloft, I was racing forward when the taffrail exploded behind me with a force that hammered me to the deck; the report of the Spaniard's answering volley reached my ears as an afterthought. No hot splinters were driven into my flesh, but shrieking from the stern told me others had not been so lucky. I scrambled to help catch at the runaway sheet, and heard cursing from the men aloft as they struggled with the slackening shrouds. The ship began to labor in the stern, and Salvador Gris roared that the helm would not answer, but our very desperation kept her going. Sweeps were stuck out the stern ports for a rudder, and the *Providence* moved close-hauled into the wind that drove the *San Pedro* farther astern. We beat down for the anonymous cays of the Caicos Bank until darkness, at last, covered our tracks.

In the middle of a tense, sleepless night, I came down from my watch to find Matty crouched on a crate below decks, under a dim lamp, turning the Spanish ring over and over in his fingers.

"The Dons are such proud fools," he muttered.

I thought he meant the ostentation of the ring, elaborately carved with a family crest featuring two entwined *Rs*. But Matty's expression was searching as he looked up at me; he lacked Jack's gift for masking the emotion in his eyes.

"Why would he do such a foolish thing?" Matty demanded. "There was no profit in it. I had no quarrel with him."

Even Matty must be able to sense the difference between his awful engagement on the rail with the Spanish boy and a legitimate fight with an armed enemy. He did not seem to understand what had happened.

"Spite," I suggested. "Better Neptune should have the family fortune than a gang of thieving pirates. He no doubt thought he was defending the family honor."

"Honor!" Matty spat back.

"And glory, of course," I mocked.

"Aye, and he got himself killed for his trouble, the fool."

"You might have let him keep the damned ring."

But I struck the wrong nerve. "Don't you lecture me, *puta!* If you're so concerned about it, you keep it!" Matty flung the tiny spark of gold at my feet and stomped off for the hatch.

I dropped to my knees and mustered up the will to close my fingers round that cursed ring. But Cuervo must be lurking somewhere in the shadows, he was never very far out of Matty's brilliant orbit. And I couldn't stomach the thought of Cuervo swooping down upon this ring in final, gleeful triumph. So I snatched it up. Had I been above, I'd have thrown the ring overboard and been done with it. But now, I hurried off to the corner where my things were stowed, hunted up a rag and knotted the ring inside, quickly, as if the touch of the metal might burn my fingers. I slipped the knotted rag into the pocket tied inside my trousers, where it could not be tampered with. Sitting back on my heels, I saw the corner of my logbook sticking out of Jasmine's basket, under my sleeping pallet. But I knew for once I would find no solace there. The *Blessed Providence* was on the run.

CHAPTER 18

Bewitched

W aiting was the hardest thing to do. In those endless, sleepless hours melting into night and back again into day, we lay hidden among the cays. All ears strained to hear any hint of pursuit while all hands worked. Arne and his crew constructed a false sternpost and makeshift rudder to replace the gear shot away by the Spaniards while the rest of us knotted and spliced the damaged rigging and patched the sails. A dozen times a day, all fell silent, anxious and waiting, if any vessel strayed too close to our hiding place.

Now darkness protected the *Blessed Providence* again. But grumbles of ghostly talk or laughter wafting down from some dockside taproom or the splash of small craft pulling in or out of the little bay confused the ears and shredded our nerves. We strained together in silence to identify the particular slap of oars on water that would tell us Hector and Arne were coming back. The *Providence* was seaworthy again, but we still hid among these cays waiting for news of the British naval cruiser Jack had sighted today in the passage. Captain Hart would not make a run for the open sea until he knew exactly where she was.

Some of the men wanted to return to Cuba, but Hart said he was damned if he'd endanger the inhabitants of Laguna Escondida in such a manner. Yet it was clear from the presence of the cruiser, wherever she was, that we could not remain here much longer. Tonight, we'd worked in along the craggy coast of this salt island, keeping to the most overgrown inlets, out of sight. There was a tavern in its tiny port village popular with wreckers and smugglers. Because Arne looked the least Spanish—save for Matty, who dared not show his face—he went ashore in the boat. Hector, who would be taken for his slave, went with him. Their mission was to learn what they could about the warship and its purpose. That had been hours ago, but it felt like weeks, months. When there was nothing to do but wait, time itself grew becalmed.

At last, we heard Hector's signal from the blackness below—a gull's sad cry, three times, then three times more. The tackle was thrown down and the little boat hauled up, but only Hector's massive silhouette rose up over the rail.

"Where's Arne?" Hart demanded.

"English navy seize him," Hector reported. "Marched out of the grog shop by dragoons off that warship. She right across the bay, Captain, laying off the west end of this rock."

"Seized?" the captain echoed. "By what authority? The French wars are over, men are no longer pressed into service."

"They take him prisoner. For a pirate." Hector's expression was stormy. "I wait outside with the boat on the beach, like the other Negroes, and two fellows come out talking about it. Warships sweeping for pirates in every port in these islands, because of the *San Pedro*. Any fellow look like a seaman and can no say where he be two days ago, with a witness to speak for him . . . ." Hector shook his head. "He taken up for questioning. Is no matter what kind or color, Spanish or no. If he be a stranger, the English carry him off. I should have gone in with him, Captain, but he think it look too odd, a fellow going into a grog shop with his slave."

Hart sighed. "It would be no help to us to lose you both, *amigo.* Where did they take him? Some government house?"

"To the warship, Captain."

"Damn! You're sure?"

"Had to row him right by me. Four of them in the boat with Arne. He never even look my way."

"He'll tell them nothing," Hart agreed. "Even if he'd never sworn an oath to us, he would never betray the *Providence.*"

This was greeted by a heavy silence in which I sensed a kind of dull, collective acceptance. Would they give up Arne so easily?

"But if they only question him . . . ." I began.

"With the barbed end of a rope, that's how they'll question him!" Jack flared up.

"But if he tells them nothing, perhaps they'll let him go!"

"There's been murder done, lass," Hart growled. "It's bad for business. If they've decided to round up any poor sod who might be a pirate, or can be passed off as one, it amounts to the same thing. There's nothing like hanging a few pirates to prove the sea lanes are safe for commerce."

"Then . . . we've got to rescue him!"

Hart stared at me. "From a British warship?"

"But Arne had nothing to do with murder!"

"We all did, lass." The captain's black eyes were warning me to say no more. But there must have been something so desperate in my face that he tried to soften the blow of his decision, for my sake or his own. "It's true they have no proof against him," he conceded. "It may be he won't hang straightaway. Perhaps they mean to ferry him back to the *San Pedro* first and parade him in front of witnesses. He doesn't look Cuban, he may yet brazen it out. Or he may be able to claim his Danish birthright and get himself transported to St. Thomas—

for whatever awaits him there. In any event," and here, his eyes fixed upon mine, "he's lost to us. He might as well be dead already, or carried off to the moon. We are in no condition to harry a British warship."

Captain Hart was being sensible, thinking of the rest of us, but I could not bear it. Why did it have to be Arne and not . . . Cuervo? But this was no time for female feeling; my very thoughts were bad luck. Fortune had made this decision for all of us.

She was an ordinary-looking merchantman, American by her colors, low in the water and slow enough to make an easy mark. She would have to be easy; we were in no condition to chase her very far. Plunder was no longer the issue. The false rudder was laboring, and there were no longer supplies enough on board to make a new one. We'd gotten this far keeping well inside the current and coasting along the northern edge of Santo Domingo. But a fresh store of seasoned timber and a replenished food supply would ensure a safer journey back to Fajardo, where our fine Spanish goods would buy the repairs we needed.

"It's risky," Hart told us. "We'll have to terrify her into submission and be gone, before she notices how lame we are."

We were still capable of terrorism. The grim faces around me were ready and eager for some action to dispel the sense of helplessness that had settled over the ship since Arne's capture. And the riskier, the better. I suspected this, more than the need to repair the ship, had motivated the captain's proposition, for with care, the *Providence* might yet coast all the way to Fajardo just as she was.

We took shelter behind a rocky point jutting out from the mainland, waiting for the current and the trades to deliver our prize. But this time, there was no false bravado, no jesting, no boasting, no chatter of any kind as the men prepared their weapons and took their places, faces set, eyes cold. Instead, a current of silent purpose ran through all the men—one will, one mind. And I confess I was afraid of the single-mindedness taking over the ship, afraid of its power. I had skirmished for profit and sport on dozens of prize ships with these men, but had never felt the weight of righteousness that bore down upon them now. As if they had something to prove that had nothing to do with the enemy they were about to face; indeed, that no enemy could hope to satisfy.

Common sense had departed the *Providence* in favor of something more abstract. I did not fear for my own life, that paltry thing of which I had made so little; I'd lived as freely as I could in the brief time allotted me. But I could not relish fighting for its own sake, out of spite, to settle a score. I searched in vain for a spark of dissent in any other eye, but saw only fierce resolution. It was a kind of *brujeria*—the men were all bewitched with their savage purpose.

Jack was still aloft with the spyglass, and when my eye fell upon Matty, he was the most bewitched of all. He stood beside the captain, his fair hair greased and tied back, ready to lead the charge. Since the *San Pedro*, Matty had given up arguing and complaining; he did everything he was told and defended Captain Hart's every decision with a zealous loyalty that rivaled Nada's. I might have believed the tragedy of the *San Pedro* had shocked some sense into him. But it was not sense I read now in Matty's face; it was a kind of ecstasy. This battle would be his penance for the *San Pedro*, for Arne, for all the *mala suerte* that had befallen us. His trial by blood. His vindication.

And then the *Blessed Providence* was running into the open sea to cut out her prize. The American did not even try to run when we closed behind her; indeed, she appeared to slow down, to wait. Unable to stifle my shameful thoughts, I found myself pleading silently with the merchantman to keep running. *Flee, don't stop, you can outrun us! Don't stand and fight!* And yet, the American came placidly about, showing her broadside to the *Providence* like a strumpet begging to be mounted. Almost as if she were a warship making ready to fire instead of an unarmed trader, as if that rumbling activity along the white stripe above her waterline were—

"Gunports!" I breathed the word in the same instant Jack shouted it from aloft and Bustamante bellowed it in Spanish from behind the swivel gun. Captain Hart roared at Salvador Gris to starboard the helm, drawing the ship off the wind to port, and as she paid off, the first of her starboard guns went off, then the next.

The answering explosions from the American—three in rapid succession, churning up blazing geysers of seawater just beyond the starboard rail—restored common sense with a vengeance. We all raced to work the ship toward the protection of the coast, out of range of the American's guns. But the other vessel was wearing ship to pursue us—confirming to all that she was some species of warship employed by the squadron to decoy unwary pirates into a battle they could not win.

The decoy ship was better armed but also heavier and square-rigged, and it took time to work her way out of the current. But we could scarcely turn this to our advantage, lame as we were. Captain Hart ordered as much Spanish sugar jettisoned as could be hauled up, all hands working like demons, but at last we were able to work the ship around the bends in the coastline, praying to lose ourselves in the gathering nightfall.

Hart, Salvador Gris and Nada—and apparently the *Providence* herself—knew every swell and eddy of the sea route to Fajardo. We cracked on throughout the long, anxious night, aided by land breezes and the tropical night fog that oozed out of the water to engulf and conceal us. When the fog evaporated at dawn, Jack could still see a tiny smudge of pursuing sails far astern, but darkness and fog had provided the advantage we needed. There was no more looking backward as we beat across the Mona Passage for Puerto Rico.

CHAPTER 19

La Bruja del Mar

"There she is."

"*Si*, but is she the decoy?" I whispered.

"Hard to tell." Jack held the oars still and squinted against the sun's brassy glare off the water. "From down here, they all look alike, bold as paint and showing off their colors."

"But this one's making no effort to hide her guns," I pointed out. I could see them even from here, winking in the new sun from the deck of the American schooner laying to off the beach.

"She's a squadron ship, too, make no mistake," Jack agreed.

We observed her in silence a moment longer before Jack suddenly hissed, "Damn!" and slapped away yet another fat mosquito. "A true *compañera* would at least pretend the damn things were biting her," he added resentfully. "It's inhuman that you can just sit there."

"I can't help it, *hombre*. It's not something I do on purpose to annoy you."

"It's unholy. Like a pact with the devil."

"You think I'd sell myself to Satan to keep mosquitos off me?"

"I would, right this minute, if given half a chance," Jack declared.

We'd sailed the little boat across the channel from Culebra Island before dawn, and the wretched little vermin had bedeviled Jack the entire time. There were greedy stragglers around even now, despite the rising sun. We'd found a sheltered cove and struck down our mast before pulling out again for a closer look at the Yankee schooner. I was hardly looking forward to another day in Fajardo, but at least this time, I would have Jack with me.

"Your sex, my dear, is your best disguise," Captain Hart had counseled me, when he sent me ashore in a flower-printed frock borrowed from Cuervo's sister, Maria Elena. He sent me in with Jack; we both looked Spanish enough to blend in with the local population, yet would understand even the most furtive English that might be spoken carelessly in our presence. And since the American decoy ship—and now, this new one— kept appearing in these waters, English would likely be the official language of intrigue in Fajardo.

For weeks now, the *Providence* had been careened for repairs across the channel from Fajardo on Culebra Island. Hidden by high, scrubby hills, she was protected by a circle of her guns set up on the beach, her boats ready in the underbrush in case of discovery. Cuervo's brother-in-law Miguel brought out food in his fishing smack, and sold what remained of our Spanish plunder to *contrabandistas* in town for enough cash to buy what we needed for repairs. His frequent visits kept us informed on the activities of the decoy ship, which had followed the *Providence* to Fajardo like a bloodhound, but now seemed to have lost the scent. Yet she would not leave. Twice, she'd departed these waters, only to return within days, still sniffing about. Afloat again at last, the *Providence* might have chanced a flight from Culebra this very night, but for the appearance of this second Yankee ship.

"I have seen nothing." The fellow behind the bar didn't even look up from his bottles and tankards when he spoke.

"But perhaps, *señor,* you have heard talk . . . ." the young American tried again. Learned his Spanish out of a book, I was certain, as I lingered indolently at the other end of the bar.

"I hear nothing!" snapped the barman. "I already told the other *norteamericanos*—nothing!"

He grabbed a bottle from beneath the counter and slammed it onto the bar in front of me, next to the reales I had tossed there. Still, I lingered; no one moved in haste at noontime in the cantinas of Fajardo. No one but the young American who hurried off to join his fellows at a wobbly table across the room. There were three of them: another young man with a blue frock coat, a sword, and an air of authority and two burly youths I took for guards. They wore no brass or braid, as if to move about unnoticed in the town, but it was no secret they had come in off the Yankee ship this morning, rowing ashore with another party of men left on the beach to watch the boat while this group hiked the mile into town. They had inquired at other cantinas, stirring up ribald jesting among the market women about the strange *blanco* fish washed ashore and the state of their *dagas*—a Spanish word for both a sword and the male organ. I didn't suppose the young officer had read that in his Spanish book.

I grasped my bottle and sauntered past the Americans' table to a smaller table in the shadows behind it. A man sat slumped over the tabletop, head heavy on his arms, in the loose white clothing and broad straw hat of the locals. I nudged his arm with my bottle.

"*Por fin,*" Jack muttered, glaring up at me.

I tried not to grin, he looked so like every other *jibaro*

in the room, sullen with the heat. There was more to acting than quoting Shakespeare, I was finding out. Jack sat up, took a pull from the bottle and wiped his mouth. Then he caught my waist and yanked me down onto his lap. My body stiffened as I struggled not to show my surprise.

"They only let women in here for one purpose, Rusty," he whispered, mouth close to my ear. "You don't have to enjoy it, but don't fight me."

I felt heavy and awkward as he arranged me on his lap, wondering what to do with my elbows. But then the Americans began to converse in English.

"You're sure that's what he said, 'the other Americans?'" quizzed the man in blue, the senior officer.

"Yes, sir."

"What other Americans?"

"He wouldn't say, sir."

"*Pardon, señors,*" a voice wheezed, nearby. "Perhaps I know these *norteamericanos.*"

Over Jack's shoulder, I saw another face in the shadows—the wizened, toothless face of a breed of wharf rat I'd seen in every port town from Boston to San Juan. The Yankee officer recognized the breed, too, and showed his distaste.

"Speak up, then, sir!" he commanded.

"*Cuantos, señors?* Is worth something, no?"

When the first reale or two offered up to the grizzled little man met with no response, the blue officer authorized the ante to be raised. At length, the informer began his tale in broken English augmented by the junior officer's awkward Spanish. He told of the party of Yankee mariners he'd seen in this very room, and described in detail the American ship I remembered all too well.

"She sounds like the *Decoy,* sir," said the junior officer.

The informer related the story he'd heard of how the *Decoy* had been fired upon off Santo Domingo by *malditos piratas,* who had fled into these waters and disappeared.

"When did they say they engaged these pirates?"

"Two weeks, perhaps three," translated the junior offi-

cer, growing excited. "Sir, they might be the vermin we're looking for."

"Aye, the trail from the *San Pedro* may not be so cold,
after all," the blue officer agreed. So there were at least two
Yankee warships searching for us.

"Ask him where the *Decoy* is now," the officer continued.

The Fajardan's black eyes glinted with malicious glee,
enjoying the tale he told.

"He says St. Thomas," the junior officer explained.

Jack's body tensed beneath me. An American ship poking around St. Thomas just now was not good news.

"Apparently . . . ," the junior officer continued, "er, the
Captain of the Port here refused to cooperate with their inves-
tigation."

"Refused to cooperate?" echoed the other officer,
indignantly. "I think it's time we paid a call on this Captain of
the Port."

"Aye, sir!"

But this brought an attack of wheezing hilarity from
their informer.

"*Señors*, you go to *el calabozo* for sure if you call on *el
capitan* dressed like that!"

"Of all the impertinence, sir!"

But the junior officer murmured that, indeed, the
Puerto Ricans, like all the Dons, were known to be impressed
with formal majesty, and perhaps they would be wise to pay
their official call in uniform.

"But the time lost returning to the ship," the officer
protested. "Particularly if there has already been some insult to
the *Decoy* in the line of duty. We represent the United States of
America, sir. We shall waste no more time in taprooms!"

"St. Thomas," Jack sighed into my ear as they marched
out. "Just our luck."

It was Cuervo's idea to raid the warehouse in St.
Thomas. Captain Hart appreciated the irony of it at once, req-
uisitioning the supplies we needed from a warehouse owned by

an American merchant company on Arne's home island. We'd made off with thousands of dollars' worth of goods. A convoy of small boats had done the job, working silently in the hours before dawn to carry off grain, water, cordage, canvas, arms, hardware, powder and shot. Stores the *Providence* would need for a long voyage across the Caribbean for our next destination—the revolutionary colonies of the Spanish Main. In the Republic of Colombia, or perhaps Mexico, a ship and crew in fighting trim would surely find employment. It was a grim decision, for a man so weary of warfare. But Captain Hart declared that if we must fight for our lives like dogs, we would damn well be paid for it.

"Tell the captain it must be tonight," Jack whispered to Miguel as they bent their heads together over the dice. "The *Decoy* may be coming back from St. Thomas this very night, with news of the raid, and when she does, the *Providence* must be gone."

Miguel nodded, sang out the lay of the dice and scooped them up into his wooden cup. In the general din of clattering dice and clamorous drinking, nobody took any notice of us. Dusk was falling, and Fajardo was shaking off its midday doldrums. Miguel threw the dice, swore, tugged at his drooping black mustache and pushed a reale across the table at Jack.

"It's safe?" Miguel muttered. "This American will not patrol the bay tonight?"

"Her officers are still in the Government House," said I, reaching for the bottle on the table.

It was all over town. The Captain of the Port had had the party of American seamen marched under armed guard to the *alcalde's* residence on suspicion that the out-of-uniform mariners were "Yankee privateers." So far, they had not re-emerged. No orders had been sent to the boat crew still waiting on the beach. And now there was gossip that officials in San

Juan were being sent for to arbitrate the matter, which could add days to the Americans' detention.

"If the Americans are held overnight," I murmured in Spanish, "Or if they are allowed to send to their ship for their papers, or even if their shipmates storm the beach to free them, it will suit us."

"The point is," Jack explained to Miguel, "whatever happens tonight will happen here, in Fajardo. No one will be paying any mind to Culebra. We'll give you time to get out in the channel. As soon as it's dark, you must signal the *Providence* to proceed south for Vieques Island. She knows the place. If they send a boat to meet you, tell them if they see the *Decoy* or any other suspicious ship, they must keep going. If they haven't heard from us by dawn, they must not wait."

Jack had been rattling the dice noisily in the cup all this time while Miguel, gazing off in another direction, drank from the bottle. Jack tossed the dice, and Miguel laughed like a devil, seizing a couple of coins from the table.

"I'll go, then." Miguel nodded and pocketed the coins as he reached for his hat. "It will soon be dark."

"There is one more thing, *amigo*," Jack murmured. "Take Tory with you. I want her back aboard the *Providence*."

"I'm not going back to the ship! Don't be an idiot, Jack."

"There's no point in both of us—"

"The plan calls for two. There's work for two."

"And if we fail, there's two of us dead."

"We won't fail. But you will if you try to do the thing all by yourself. And then where will the *Providence* be?"

Jack had no ready answer to this, and in the instant he hesitated, I hissed to Miguel, "Go, now. It's late and we're wasting time."

The edgy American sailors were still waiting with their boat on the beach while the rest of their party was incarcerated in the town. Above them loomed the dark, squat shape of the two-gun battery overlooking the beach, manned with Spanish officers keeping an eye on the *norteamericanos*. Jack and I had to cross this beach to get to the scrubby cove where we'd hidden our little boat. A lantern in the bows of the Yankee boat marked their whereabouts in the dark, and we veered well away from it, keeping to the edge of the beach for some distance before daring to strike off into the sand. It was laborious work in the soft sand, Jack steering me ahead of him while keeping an eye over his shoulder on the Yankee light.

When the figure stepped in front of me, I reared back like a spooked horse, even before the stranger cried out, "Halt!" in English. We had not thought about stray Americans patrolling the beach apart from their fellows in the boat. But, of course, they were here to hunt pirates, and where better to find them than skulking across the beach in the black of night? In the same instant, Jack plowed into me from behind, sinking into the sand on one buckled knee and swearing loudly in Spanish.

"Who are you?" demanded the Yankee sailor.

"What's the matter with you," I lashed out in Spanish, hoping my pretense of anger would mask my fear. "Sneaking around in he dark, frightening people to death! What are you doing, eh?"

The sailor hesitated, staring at me, bewildered. I made an impatient gesture with my hands and turned to help Jack up, felt him crouched in the dark beside me, ready to spring or to run. As if running were possible in this infernal sand.

"Who are you?" the sailor tried again, craning forward to get a better look at Jack. It was too dark to see what kind of firearm he cradled in his arms, but it didn't matter. Even the clumsiest musket would find its target at this range. "What are you doing out here?"

I shoved Jack with my knee, making him stumble again, but I caught at his arm and hauled him upright, pulling his arm across my shoulders. *"Mi esposo,"* I told the sailor, rolling my eyes with a sigh of irritation. *"Borracho, eh?"* I pantomimed hoisting a bottle to my lips. Jack took the cue at once; sagging against me, head down, he began muttering in wonderfully colorful and disconnected Spanish.

"Oh, aye. Drunkard, is he?"

"If you're not going to help me, let us pass," I hurried on, in rapid Spanish.

"Yes, I can see he's drunk, *señora*, but where are you off to? There's nothing out here. The town is back that way. *A donde?*"

How fluent was his Spanish? Had we slipped up?

"My husband, he drinks, he gets crazy. He wants to find his mother who drowned in the sea when he was a boy —"

"*Mama*," Jack whimpered, utterly forlorn. "*Mi madre . . . .*"

"Sometimes he wants to save her, sometimes he wants to throw himself in after her." I kept my eye on the sailor's befuddled face to see how far I could go. "He drinks to forget. Then he sees the sea and he's off again. He is stronger than he looks, *señor*, it would take a team of oxen to keep him on the road."

The sailor's eyes darted from my face to Jack, then back again. I tried to keep my eyes off his weapon, to look impatient and not guilty, to will him to stand aside. Then Jack lifted his head and lurched forward, his eyes glazed with grief, glistening tears rolling down into his beard.

"*Mi madre, señor?*" he implored, pitifully, his voice breaking into a sob. "*Donde esta mi madre?*"

The sailor loosened his grip on the gun to fend Jack off with his forearm, shoving him back toward me, shaking his head with disgust.

"Oh, get him out of here, go home!" he ordered, affronted and a little shaken by this unseemliness. "Go!"

We stumbled back up to the roadway above the sand and continued along in the opposite direction from the Yankee boat. At last, under the protection of the darkness, we stepped into the sand again and rounded back to our cove without further interference.

"All right, Rusty, I've learned my lesson," Jack grinned, when we had gained the shelter of the cove. "Partners we are and partners we shall stay. *Contra todo el mundo.*" Against the world.

It was slow, cautious work getting our boat out of the shallows with only the stars and a pale sliver of waxing moon for illumination in the black night. Rudy had scavenged black-colored clothing for us to put on, as well, two more shadows in the dark night. But now I perceived different gradations of black—the solid shape of the coast against the dimmer black of the sky, the starlit water rippling below, and the hull of the American schooner looming up just ahead. She lay with one side facing the beach and the other toward the channel, ready to defend herself from either direction. There might be another dozen men or more aboard. We would be overwhelmed in a fight. Our only chance was the element of surprise.

Dipping our oars, we circled stealthily up under the schooner's bows, holding our boat still, straining to see and hear. There was only one other vessel out in the bay—a little coaster, indifferent and unarmed. Lazy fragments of talk wafted down from the deck of the schooner above, and we sat still, listening, trying to gauge the movements of the watch. I fingered the little metal tinderbox on a cord round my neck, under my black shirt. Jack wore one just like it. Under the thwarts in our boat were two canvas sacks packed with bottles, wrapped in muslin so they wouldn't clank together. Each bottle was partially filled with rum and stuffed with fabric knotted to a length of braided mangrove slowmatch corked inside. Flaming *granados*, Bustamante called them.

When we heard the watch above marching away toward the stern, we drew our oars inboard, warped in tight under the stem and tied up, out of sight of the deck above. We strapped on our canvas sacks, and Jack leaped for the chains and began to climb. I followed. When we suddenly had to freeze, upside-down in the shrouds, because of an unexpected footfall above, I noticed even our breathing was synchronized.

The tread moved off, and Jack reached for my arm and pulled me up to his perch, then swung himself under the bowsprit. After a moment, his head peeped up above the bulwarks on the starboard side of the bow. He glanced across and nodded to me, and I pulled myself up to the rail and peeked inboard. The men on watch strolled toward their rendezvous in the stern and two other men talked together at the foot of the mainmast, under the lantern. I might have three, maybe four minutes before the watch reached the bows again.

Jack had already slithered over the bulwarks and down onto the foredeck on the starboard side. I hauled myself over the rail to land in a heap on the other side, hugging the deck, waiting to hear some murmur of alarm from the Americans on board. When there were none, I crept along the raised foredeck until a small deckhouse at its foot blocked me from the idling sailors' line of sight. I chanced a grope in the dark nearby and felt coiled line stowed out of the way. Still crouched behind the deckhouse, I moved my canvas sack around to my front, drew out the first bottle and eased out the cork.

For a panicked instant, I feared I'd not be able to reach the slowmatch in the neck; my fingers were trembling too badly. One of the sailors coughed suddenly and swore, and the bottle all but shook out of my grasp. But at last I pulled a short length of slowmatch out of the mouth of the bottle and set the bottle upright into the coil. Four flaming *granados* dashed into the most flammable material we could find—that was the plan. Jack had been a juggler all his life and could throw anything anywhere; he would aim high, for the tarred rigging and spars and furled sails. I must aim for something I might actually hit. And I peered out at the tackle of coiled lines and wooden belaying pins at the foot of the foremast, a few yards away.

Just within reach behind me, I felt a portion of the furled staysail. It was lashed to the length of the bowsprit, lapping inboard onto the deck. I eased the end of the slowmatch out of the neck of my second bottle and settled it into the thick folds of canvas. I popped open my tinder box and went to work with steel and flint, using my body to shield the spark I finally struck on the third fumbling try. I lit the slowmatch in the first bottle and stuck it back into the coiled line, deep enough so the glow would not be seen for the minute or more we would need to get away. I reached behind me for the second bottle, hoping to get it lit before my tiny flame went out.

But my clumsy fingers knocked the bottle out of its perch. It clunked to the deck like a death knell and began to roll noisily across the bows to the starboard side—where Jack still crouched at his work.

"What's that?" and "Who goes there?" came the cries. Footsteps were galloping from amidships toward the starboard bow, and I heard a gasp of withdrawn steel. I flattened myself to the deck to smother my pounding heart when I heard a hiss and saw a small flame sizzling in the dark on the far side of the bows. Jack's eerie shape reared up, clutching an ignited bottle high over his head, his figure etched in firelight from the ship's lantern. I heard a pistol shot, but the smooth arc of Jack's body continued as he hurled the bottle onto the deck at the feet of the approaching sailors. A halestorm of shattered glass sent the men reeling backwards and a tongue of liquid flame sparked up across their path. I lunged forward to grab my lighted bottle out of the coil and thrust it deep into the folds of the furled staysail, where it might yet do some good. As I slithered over the side, I saw Jack rise a second time and hurl a second lighted bottle high up toward the foretop—and heard a satisfying burst of glass—before I dropped into the cold water, below.

Blackness closed over me, swallowing up every other shape and sound in the black night, robbing me of my senses. There was no time to think about our boat. I could only stroke through the absolute blackness beneath the surface, disoriented, until my lungs were straining for air. A tiny light like a winking star wavered far away. I strove toward it, the blackness swirled and roared around my head, and then I broke the surface. Gulping for air, I saw I was treading deep water out in the channel well off the schooner's port side.

The tiny light was, in fact, a great orange fan of flame fluttering all the way across the schooner's topsail yard; sparks and burning splinters and debris rained onto the deck below. Comical little black stick figures like clumsy marionettes capered at the rail. When the water splashed a few yards away, I realized they must be more pistol shot, but they were nothing to the roar of the fire and the explosive popping of old timber in the flames. Another splash warned me to duck under the surface, diving deeper and clawing my way farther out. I came up again, spluttering, and saw Jack's dark head break the surface nearby.

"Let's get away from here," he gasped, "the fire's lighting up the whole bay."

I paddled in place a moment longer, until I saw a new sheet of flame dance out suddenly along the schooner's bowsprit. At least one of my charges had gone off as planned. Then we began to swim in earnest. We had no clear idea where we were in the bay; I only knew to keep slicing through the chilly water, to keep kicking, to keep searching . . . .

Then the hull of a little coaster loomed up ahead, a faint flicker of light dancing across her faded paintwork where she faced the flaming schooner. A lone figure stood illuminated at the starboard rail near the stem, watching the inferno. Surely, if anyone else were on board, they would be standing there, too.

Jack's head came out of the water. I pointed to the coaster and held up one finger and he nodded.

"Give me ten minutes," he whispered, between laborious breaths. "You get his attention."

He dove under the surface for the coaster's starboard side. I followed, coming up under the stem, and waited. When I thought Jack had had time enough, I paddled around to the port side of the bow and grabbed a cable. Several long, damp, curling snakes of hair had come loose from my plait and I dragged them forward, over my shoulders. My dark clothing was plastered to my body like skin, but I tore open the yoke of my shirt, peeling the wet fabric away from my breasts. There must be no mistaking what I was. I climbed the cable as noisily as I could, clawed my way over the rail and landed with a cry and a loud thump on the deck. The watchman stood across from me, gaping, his back to the opposite rail. He carried no firearm, but his hand clutched at the hilt of a knife in his belt as his eyes widened in amazement.

"*Señor!*" I cried. "*Ayudame, señor! Salvame, por favor!*"

I ran toward him, hands raised, long hair flying, breasts bouncing, mouth begging, my eyes never leaving his knife. If he pulled it out suddenly, could I fight him off? Had I the strength left to feint, roll away, kick him off his feet? I brought myself up short, out of his reach, and collapsed to my knees with my hands clasped aloft.

"Please, *señor*, help me," I wailed, in Spanish. "They tried to drown me! They'll come looking for me! Hide me, save me, I beg you!"

The watchman threw a nervous glance over his shoulder at the burning ship in the bay, then stepped closer. He caught my wrists in his hands, and his grip was strong, but at least he could not now draw his knife.

"Who are you?" he demanded, in Spanish. "Where do you come from, like a witch out of the sea?"

I let him pull me to my feet, fighting down the impulse to resist, keeping my knees bent so I could still look up at him.

"I'm not a witch, *señor.* Can't you see I'm flesh? Hide me, *señor*, keep me. I'll do anything you want."

His eyes were still uncertain, but his mouth was curling into a crafty grin when I heard a soft thud. His eyes popped a little before he sank to the deck at my feet without another word. Jack hopped on one foot behind him to catch his balance, brandishing something heavy wrapped in his own wet black shirt. I stumbled backward, staring down at the crumpled figure.

"Let's go, Rusty," Jack panted. But the frantic energy that had brought me this far was draining away. I stared down at the fallen seaman as if dazed, too exhausted to remember what to do next. "He'll wake up with a hell of a headache and his mates will all say he was drunk," Jack urged me on. "There's

a boat in back we can manage. Rusty, come on!" He grabbed my
hand and dragged me into the stern.

It was only a flat-bottomed, deep-sided jolly boat miss-
ing its middle thwart with an old, blackened canvas tarp fastened to the stern for cover. But it looked seaworthy and carried two sets of oars. It was up on chocks on the port quarter,
lashed to the rail, without davits. We would never be able to
hoist it over the side, but Jack thought if we cut her loose, we
could drag her to the break in the rail and heave her over.

"Are you all right, Rusty?" he asked, as we worked, and
I nodded, dumbly. I no longer knew what I was thinking or
feeling; knew only that we had to keep moving. "If it's any con-
solation, *compañera*," he added, stopping to get his breath once
we'd dragged the boat to the side, "the captain will probably
give you your own ship for this. You can call her *La Bruja del
Mar*." The witch from the sea.

We shoved the little boat over the side, and Jack dove in
after to keep her from capsizing. I hesitated; with the burning
ship behind me, I was nightblind again. But I made out Jack
scrambling into the boat, below. He stood up, grabbing hold of
a cable running down the coaster's hull.

"Jump, Rusty! Hit me—I'll catch you. Now!"

Then I was airborne, the wind in my face, my nostrils
full of salt and ash. It was a short jump, and I hit my mark, but
the impact hurled us both into the bottom. The boat rocked
crazily, and Jack rolled on top of me to steady us, yanking the
tarp across the wales above us so it wouldn't drag in the water.
We dared not sit up and row, afraid to draw the Yankees' attention in the garishly lit bay, afraid to draw their fire. We could
only lay pinned together as the little boat rocked, praying we
would not capsize, straining together to urge the boat out on
the tide while the coaster still stood between us and the blazing
schooner.

In the close blackness, I was suddenly aware of the
tense urgency of Jack's body against mine. I surprised myself
by arching upwards, pressing myself into him. It must have surprised Jack, too, but his arms closed around me. We were both

soaked and shivering, but Jack's mouth was a sunburst of sudden warmth on my cheek, my lips, my chin, racing like fire down my throat, moving hungrily across my breast, closing around a nipple with a shock of paralyzing sweetness.

I was vaguely aware of hands—his, but possibly mine—clawing at the wet clothing still between us. Jack's naked skin was cold and abrasive with salt, but I needed to feel him against me. Something wild inside me lurched forward to keep pace with the steady rhythm of his body. My hands slid down the long, taut curve of his back, holding him tight as he worked himself inside me. The deeper he went, the more tender I was, and when the tenderness made me gasp, Jack froze above me, waiting. But I pulled him back down, needing to hold on to him, needing his strength in the midst of this chaos. It was like being aloft in a squall, plastered to the mast, and I wrapped my arms and legs around him to get a better grip, clinging to him for dear life, and nothing was more important than getting to the top, nothing. And then, the same dizzy urge to let go, to abandon myself, to fly. And I did, soaring and falling, because Jack was here, he would catch me. He always caught me, always.

Jack gave a low, fierce, sudden cry, and the storm burst inside me. Then all the breath exploded out of my lungs like one of Bustamante's slowmatch bombs.

"Jack," I gasped. It was the only thing either of us said.

Our hearts hammered together, stubborn life in the close, dark, damp little womb of the boat. For a moment, there was nothing in the world but Jack's ragged breathing against my ear and his strong arms holding me so close. I belonged in this moment. Here, with Jack.

I no longer cared if the boat capsized. I half hoped it would. I'd welcome a plunge into sweet, black oblivion, cradled forever in Jack's arms. Jack felt it, too; his hold on me tightened, and he pressed his cheek against mine. I pulled him as close as I could. *Contra todo el mundo.*

But the moment passed. Slowly, I grew aware of the hard, uneven wooden planking digging into my back, the see-

sawing motion of our masterless boat. I could glimpse the dim
pink glow in the sky over Jack's shoulder, under the black edge
of the tarp, and hear the distant crackle of flames. Jack was
heavy on top of me, and far-off voices cried alarms.

Jack's mouth found my ear. "We've got to get out of
here."

"*Si, hombre.*"

He crept off me and pulled at his trousers in the dark.
I tried to right my own clothing, my movements slow and dull,
my fingers clumsy. Yet, I felt oddly calm, liberated from any
further need to think or speak. Jack moved forward and peered
out under the tarp. I stayed crouched in silence behind him, and
when it seemed safe, we peeled back the tarp and got out the
oars.

We rowed mechanically for hours, beyond ordinary
fatigue, for a rendezvous we would surely miss with a ship that
must be long gone by now. I don't remember seeing the
Providence that night, only the ship's boat with six brawny men
pulling toward us, silhouetted against the graying sky, and
Hector's deep, thunderous laugh and huge arms pulling me
aboard. And at last, the ecstasy of sinking into my own bedding
belowdecks, with no other thought in my mind but to sleep.

CHAPTER 20

Fever

"*Amiga!*"

It was so dark when I finally unglued my eyes, I thought they were still closed. But even in darkness, I could see Rudy's gap-toothed grin above me as he pressed a cup of rum into my hand. I couldn't quite see the bowl of fish stew he'd set down beside me, but I could smell it and hunger flared up so volcanically in my belly, I was afraid I would drool. When had I last eaten?

"Have I slept through to supper?" I sat up and poured down a draught of rum.

"Almost to breakfast." Rudy grinned again. "You get yours first. *Capitan* want you aloft in a few minutes."

I set to gobbling the spicy stew, hot pepper and lime exploding on my tongue. "Where's Jack?"

"Aloft. *Capitan* send him down when you come up."

"You don't mean he's been up all this time while I've been idling down here!"

"No, no!" Rudy laughed. "Jack, he sleep too, like *los muertos*, all that morning after we pick you up. It was dawn already, but *Capitan* send the boat, tell them no come back until they find you. But by then, is too light to run away. We coast along Vieques Island all morning, like fishermen. When is safe, we head south for open sea. Then we see the *Decoy*."

I nearly choked on a peppery mouthful of fish as my heart sank.

"Merchant brig." Rudy nodded. "Yankee colors. Jack say she may be the *Decoy*, when he come up. Standing between us and the sea. *Capitan* set a new course, east for the Atlantic. He say more than one way to sail to South America."

"Did she chase us?"

"She never get close to us, but she never go away. She still off the stern when we lose her in the dark. *Capitan* want a sharp lookout. Jack and Diego trading the watch all night."

"I should have helped," I protested, gulping down the last of the stew. "You should have called me."

"Jack say no. And when he say what you do, *Capitan*, he agree. Say you deserve to sleep."

Apparently, Jack had not mentioned how my clumsiness had nearly scuttled the plan and gotten us both killed. What had he told them? Well, I must brazen it out, come what may. My trousers were so stiff with brine, I could scarcely peel them off, my skin so crusty, I felt like a piece of salt fish. I washed as best I could from a bucket of water Rudy brought from the galley. Then I pulled on my old clothes, eager to get above and find Jack. I scarcely knew what to think about what had happened between us, but I knew this much—I had not been afraid.

"Damn me eyes, *hombres*, the dead walk!" Captain Hart sang out with a jovial laugh as I emerged on deck. He was squinting at me through the predawn dark from his station at the binnacle with Nada and Salvador Gris. "We were ready to ship you overboard in a canvas shroud, Mistress."

But I was busy searching the rigging. Jack was just descending by the foreshrouds, his figure black against the fading stars. Somewhere above the rail, he stumbled in the ratlines and lost his footing, only just managing to right himself and drop to the deck with an inelegant thump.

"Dammit, Jack, ye look like a green-gilled landsman!" shouted the captain. "Go below and get some sleep!"

I took an eager step forward to catch Jack's eye before he hurried away. But in the instant our eyes did meet, all I read in his was a bleak, wordless misery. He said nothing and lurched away, clearly ashamed, and dove down the forward hatch.

I just stood there, stunned. It had never occurred to me to feel ashamed. Perhaps I should. Perhaps I'd done a shameful thing. Then a hearty hand clapped my shoulder, and I turned to find Matty standing beside me, beaming with eyes and teeth that outshone the stars.

"Why, Mistress Bonny, the queen of the Indies," he sallied. "I hear you had the devil's own time in Fajardo!"

But I had only one, mute, astonished glance to spare for him as I looked again after Jack.

"Look here, Tory," he went on, his voice dropping to a more intimate pitch as his hand slid lightly down to my elbow. "I'm so sorry we quarreled that day. I had no right to be angry with you. Can you forgive me?"

"It doesn't matter, Mateo. We've all been on edge."

"It matters to me. Please?"

I stood there, utterly confounded. I'd awoken into an upside-down world where Matty was pleading for my friendship and Jack wanted nothing to do with me.

"Please," Matty repeated. His blue eyes turned mischievous. "It's the least you can do for the man who saved your life."

"What?"

"Who do you think commanded the boat that found you? I was determined to bring you back, safe. I . . . I realized I didn't want to lose you, Tory."

Somehow, his hands were holding both of mine, very

lightly, his ardent eyes searching my face. What was this, another wager?

"I bear you no grudges, Mateo," I fenced, withdrawing my hands. "I swore an oath. We're shipmates. We're sworn to look out for each other."

"At the very least." He smiled. "Especially now. If I save your life, it belongs to me. Every sailor knows that."

I had to laugh at this. "I hope you can make something more of it than I have."

"How curious that you should say that." Matty's voice grew softer and more serious again. "I'll be two and twenty next summer. High time to make something of my life. Of both our lives." He smiled again. "Since yours now belongs to me."

"Lightfoot!" boomed the captain's voice, no longer jovial, and I took the opportunity to flee up into the shrouds.

Dawn blossomed into a crystalline morning without much wind or commerce. A flock of gulls wheeled in the air, flashing snow white in the blue sky as the sun struck their bellies. When I spied a thumbprint of sail bearing up from the southeast, Captain Hart corrected our course to north by east to keep well above her. There was a tense hour or two when the *Providence* could not shake her off, struggling to make speed in flukey airs. But the other ship made no better progress and finally fell off astern, veering to westward on the rising easterlies. Past midday, Nada called me down again. But when the captain bellowed for Jack, the only response was from Hector rising up out of the forward hatch.

"Jack can't come up, *Capitan*."

"I was not issuing a social invitation."

"He's sick. Bad sick. You best come take a look."

I huddled below the main shrouds, hugging my knees to my chest. Jack had the fever. There was not a man aboard who didn't recognize the symptoms, and I didn't have to go below to know it. I could feel it in the air. In my bones. In my heart. It had been different with Arne. One minute, he was with us on the ship and the next, he was gone. But Jack was like a handful of sand, slipping through our fingers by degrees. Soon there would be nothing left to hold on to.

Captain Hart called for a new course, due north, straight for the eastern tail of the Virgin Islands.

"What? I suppose we're going back to St. Thomas to give the *norteamericanos* another chance?" Cuervo brayed. But Hart ignored him.

"Keep us well to the east," he instructed Salvador Gris. "Head for those little unpopulated cays the smugglers use. Find me one with a strip of beach and some shelter. Nada! Prepare to lower the boat. Rudy, bring up whatever you can spare from the galley."

I knew what these preparations meant. The captain scowled when he saw me coming.

"Captain, you can't do this."

"Can't protect my own crew from yellow fever? Of course I can."

"But you can't just maroon him!" I pleaded.

"Would ye rather I set him adrift in an open boat, like our friend Harry Quick? We are being pursued by the warships of two, possibly three nations. There's no time to argue. Jack has been at sea a long time. He knows the Articles."

"But he'll die!"

"He's going to die anyway, lass, can't you see that?" Hart's voice frayed with exasperation. "But we're all like to die if I keep a sick man aboard. Is that what you want? Hell, I'm as fond of Jack as I'll ever be of any goddamned Englishman, but I can't risk the lives of every other man aboard for his sake. I'm taking too damned big a risk as it is."

Even if Jack's fever didn't spread to the rest of the crew—and the danger of contagion to others within the close confines of a ship was legendary—we would lose precious time having to detail someone to keep watch over him every hour of the day and night. Time we could ill afford if we were pursued by fleet Yankee schooners or merciless British warships. I thought of Jasmine waiting in Laguna Escondida with her two babies and a third on the way, waiting for a Hector who might never come home, who might be feeding the rats on an English prison ship or decorating a scaffold on Gallow's Point. That was too much of a sacrifice.

But the alternative was to let Jack die.

"Let me go, too, Captain." My voice was scarcely a whisper, but Hart's head and Nada's jerked up as if I had screamed.

"Are ye so tired of living, Mistress?"

"Two of us might survive." It was so clear what I must do, the confusion had drained out of my voice. "You don't need me aboard. Any green hand can do what I do and you're better off without the extra mouth to feed. But Jack will die alone."

Captain Hart glanced at Nada, whose black eyes had become slits of ferocious attention. "You're a useful hand on the yards and in the top," Hart noted. "I should be sorry to lose you."

"I'll be sorry to go. But that won't change my mind."

When such provisions as the *Providence* could spare had been packed in the boat, Hector brought Jack up on deck. I hadn't realized how abstract my thoughts about the fever had been until I actually saw him. Pale and shivering, he swayed against Hector like a marionette with his strings cut, head lolling, feet shuffling. When Hector eased him down to the foot of the mainmast, Jack slumped across the low rail that secured the water casks as if he hadn't a muscle left in his body. His head drooped onto his folded arms as if the effort of holding it up were insurmountable.

I tried to fight down my panic. There was nothing left of my Jack in this limp, lamed hull; I was letting myself be marooned with a corpse. But I had made a bargain. I would not quit it, now, like some whimpering female. I broke out of the ranks of nervous onlookers and strode to the mainmast, arriving at the same moment as the captain. He crouched down and touched Jack's shoulder.

"Listen to me, Jack . . . ," he began.

"Cut me loose, Captain," Jack interrupted, his voice dry and hoarse, but distinct. He raised his head a little, although his eyes could not quite focus. "I'll only slow you down."

Then his head rolled onto his arms again. Hart stood up, slowly, but I knelt at Jack's other side, where one of his hands hung open over the rail. I slipped my hand into his and was astonished at how fiercely he gripped mine in response. In that instant, my heart broke, I lost my fear and gained my resolve.

"It's all right, *hombre*," I murmured, bending my head low over his, stroking his tangled hair, still holding his hand. "We're partners, remember? Everything will be all right."

His hand tightened on mine again.

Jack was shaking when Hector and Captain Hart laid him in the bottom of the boat. I reminded them I had a quilt belowdecks, and Nada disappeared down the hatch to fetch it. I was about to climb into the boat when Rudy hurried up and pressed several cloth pouches of herbs into my hands.

"This for headache, this for backache, this for fever," he instructed me. "And lots of rags in cool water, don't forget." When he looked up into my face, tears were streaking down his cheeks, but he still had on his huge, broken grin. Then he was gone.

Hector came out of the boat and put his arms around me, with as little ceremony as if I were one of his own children.

"My woman be proud to hear what a brave thing you do," he told me. I made myself step away, afraid if I lingered too long in his comforting embrace, I would never have the courage to leave.

A hand brushed my elbow, and I turned to see Matty beside me.

"This is madness, Tory. You can't think of leaving like this, not when we've meant so much to each other."

I stared at him. "I believe I meant twenty dollars to you, once, nothing more."

He looked startled, but only for an instant. "I know

I've been a fool, but I can change—"

"What?" I could only gape at him.

"If I knew I had you here, by my side—"

"Save it for your more gullible *putas*, Mateo." I was out of all patience. "I don't know what you're after, but I haven't got—"

"Jack is a dead man," Matty broke in. "All right, it's a damned pity, I suppose, but we all die sometime. This is his. But it's not your time, Tory. Jack has no claim on you. Stay here with me and live!"

I suppose the Boston schoolgirl who had fallen desperately in love with Matty on sight would have accepted in an instant. If possible, he was even more attractive now. Lines of maturity were beginning to tell at the corners of his mouth, his youthful fire giving way to a deeper sensibility— diplomacy, perhaps. Or cunning. But I was not the ignorant chit I had been, with so little self-regard that a Matty was all I aspired to.

"I'd sooner share Jack's grave for eternity than spend another hour in your bed, Mateo."

That silenced him; his mouth fell open but no more words tumbled out. I lunged past him and made my way to the boat. Captain Hart still stood inside, and he reached down to help me in. After we changed places, he leaned back in to point out the stores packed under the after thwart—food, biscuit, a lamp and tinder. There wasn't any plunder; we'd spent all our shares repairing the ship. Not that we'd need any, where we were going. Finally, the captain showed me a flask of brandy and a jar of rum stowed in the bows.

"For you, Mistress. To save on the water." Then, in a lower voice, he added, "I suppose you've already had the fever?"

I frowned at him. But he read my expression and shook his head and gave out with an unexpected bark of laughter.

"Hellfire, Mistress Lightfoot, you're the damnedest thing I've ever seen in all my years in the trade!"

Nada came thundering up from below, my red quilt squashed into a thick bundle in his hands. He stuffed it into the

boat and climbed in after it, stepping around Jack to settle himself onto the middle thwart, nodding me to a seat in the bows.
Then he told the others to lower away.

It was a stubby green finger of a cay on the southeast-
ern edge of the chain. Scrub hills seemed to slant right down to
the waterline on both sides, but there was a little beach dead
ahead, separated from the hills behind it by a stand of wind-bat-
tered coconut palms. At the back of the beach gaped the mouth
of a little cave in a grey outcropping of rock mostly hidden by
scrub and drooping palm fronds.

While Nada was unloading the stores, I went to cut
down as many of the fan-shaped palm fronds as I could reach
and took them inside the cave. The sandy floor was cold and
damp, and I arranged the fronds into a mat and tossed a blanket over it for Jack to lie on. I saw Nada outside go down on
one knee to sling Jack's limp body over his shoulder. He hauled
Jack into the cave like a sack of grain and we both lowered him
onto the mat. I was still fussing with the bedding when Nada
came to crouch beside me, shaking out the red quilt. What
shook out of it was Jasmine's finely-woven basket with Jack's
volume of Shakespeare and my logbook inside. I looked into
his face, astonished.

"*Buena suerte, muchacha,*" he grunted. Then he rose and
strode out of the cave.

I stared after his broad, cinnamon-colored back, at the
thick, tarred rope of black hair hanging down between his powerful shoulders. Nada had never before shown me any kindness,
and the surprise of it now came closer to triggering my tears
than anything else that had happened. Or it was possible that
Nada was simply taking advantage of the opportunity to rid the
ship of my unlucky presence and my cursed logbook in one
clean shot. I bent over Jack again, not wanting to think that my
world, once as wide as the seas and as full of promise as the
stars, had shrunk to the size of this small, dark cave. That

Nada's retreating back was the last of my crewmates I would ever see. Alive.

I raced back to the mouth of the cave. Nada's boat was already being hoisted aboard the *Providence.* As I leaned against the rocky cave wall, something hard pressed into my hip. When I fished inside my pocket, I found the scrap of cloth with the Spanish ring knotted inside.

No wonder Matty had been so eager to keep me near-by. He knew I still had the Spanish ring, hard evidence that connected him to a murder. To what extravagant lengths might he go to keep me and this ring under his power?

The sun was slanting sideways across the bay as the black schooner began to work to eastward. I stood at the mouth of the cave and watched the *Blessed Providence* sail out of my life, forever.

It was a long, exhausting night with Jack muttering in his discomfort and writhing away from my efforts to calm him. I had to wrestle with him to ease a water-soaked rag between his swollen lips. He wore himself out, eventually, but it was daylight before he rested quietly again.

The screech of a gull diving in the bay made me jump, but Jack was undisturbed. I was the one who had been asleep. My logbook was open in my lap, the playing card Esteban had given me, the *sota de oros,* stuck in its pages. Where was Fortune, now? Where was my witchcraft? It was so hard to sit and wait. If only I could fight or bargain for Jack's life. I even thought of praying, but to whom? Surely not the God of Wrath who kept such excellent accounts. Mine must be long past due by now, but I was damned if I would let Jack pay with his life. I thought of my mother's gods, Sky Woman, Creator. The only prayers I could remember were for planting and harvest and a condoling prayer Mama said after Josh died, to ease the spirit into the next world. But I didn't want to make it easy for Jack to leave me. I would have settled for Javier's *loas* and jumbies if

I'd known how to invoke them. The plain fact was I was all alone here, waiting for Fortune to play her next card. But Jack deserved a better hand. I would defy them all.

Jack tossed a little, mumbling, and I touched his hot cheek.

"You had a hell of a nerve, sailing around the Indies unseasoned." The sound of a human voice, even my own, made me feel less alone. "How long did you think you could get away with it? And you were supposed to be so smart."

I reached for another damp rag, and he grabbed my arm so suddenly, I all but sprawled across him. "Tell him!" he hissed, eyes bright.

"What?"

"Tell the captain to cut me loose."

"Oh, fine." I sat back on my heels, exasperated. "Play the great hero, get yourself marooned. What makes you think you can just throw your life away? It may surprise you to know that I care what happens to you. Aye, well, it surprised me, too, I don't pretend to understand it, but—Jack?"

His hand slid off my arm, he stopped muttering and his breathing slowed. I seized his hand in both of mine, squeezing as hard as I could.

"Damn it, Jack! If you die on me now, by all the gods, I'll find a way to make you pay!"

There was the faintest trace of response in Jack's hand. He drew a slow, shaky breath. "I don't . . . doubt it for a minute . . . Rusty."

I was so startled I dropped his hand, but when I leaned over him again, he had already slipped back into a feverish sleep.

It was difficult when Jack was agitated, twisting in discomfort, but much worse when he was too quiet, sprawled across the mat like a corpse. At other times, words came tumbling out of him as if he'd sprung a leak. He spoke softly of Old

John and Missus John. He spoke at times of Emma, and once he called out quite wretchedly for Madeleine. He spoke of the rest of the *Providence* crew, murmuring in a drowsy singsong of English and Spanish. I was surprised at the frequency and intimacy with which he addressed Jasmine, mostly in Spanish. The words were often slurred, and what I could make out was often so private, I was almost ashamed to listen. Almost. Jack called Jasmine *encantadora*, enchantress, and if I held his hand and spoke to him in Spanish, he was comforted.

The sun was up outside, although I'd forgotten if it was morning or afternoon. But the thickening air threatened a squall. Our water was running low, and I feared being holed up for days in a storm. Jack had been quiet for a while, and I took stock of our supplies. I swallowed the last of the rum from the crock jar, found a tin basin and carried them both outside. I tucked the flat basin in the sand beneath a palm trunk growing sideways across the beach; the jar I propped up in an outcropping of grey volcanic rock, hoping to catch enough rainwater in the coming storm to buy us another day or two. I found a fallen coconut out on the strip of beach and brought it back to the cave, but had no appetite for its milky water. I was too knotted up with fear, afraid to lose Jack, afraid I would not be strong enough to save him. Afraid to be left alone. Again.

When he cried out suddenly behind me, I almost leaped out of my skin. He was tossing on his mat, gripped by some nightmare; from the fragments of his words and cries, I guessed he was dreaming of the slave ship—trying to climb, to get away. His sudden strength was frightening; it took all of mine to hold him down. The episode passed, but there were others. Sometimes it was the slaver nightmare, but most often it was sheer physical distress. The fever raged through him, burning him up alive or wracking him with chills, and nothing could ease him. It was all I could do to pin him down bodily to keep him still.

I don't know how long it was before I realized it was pouring rain outside. Jack lay still at last, exhausted, and I cradled his head in my lap. With the squall blowing, I could not even tell if it was night or day, could not remember how many nights or days we had passed in this place. I stroked Jack's dark hair back from his face.

"You're still here, aren't you, Jack? " I gripped his hand and held it tight. "I'm doing everything I can for you, but I can't do it alone. You've got to help me. You must stay here and help me. I know it's asking a lot; I always ask too much of you."

I closed my eyes and pressed his hand to my cheek. "You're my best friend, Jack. Don't leave me here all alone."

Jack began to tremble a little, then rolled over on his side, shaking violently. I lay down beside him and wrapped my arms around him, holding him close as he shivered against me, protecting his life with my will, alone—all I had left. Even if Death came, I would never let him go. It would have to take us both.

I saw daylight again when I awoke. It was quiet outside and inside the cave. I had no feeling in either arm, the one twisted underneath me or the one still thrown across Jack's chest. But I felt the rest of my body all too well; every muscle ached and complained.

Jack lay very still. I sat up too fast, painfully, on my unsteady arm, afraid to look into his face. But I forced myself at last. And what I saw left me all but undone. Jack was sleeping. His cheeks had lost their flush; I touched them and felt cool skin, slick with sweat. The fever had broken. His heartbeat, when I felt for it, was not strong. But it beat. He was alive.

I'd never felt so dull and stupid in all my life. This was the time to cry, to chant my thanks to every god I'd ever heard of for this miracle, Jack's life. But I was too numb, too weary. I only came back to myself when I dragged my eyes away from Jack's sleeping face and saw that the little water cask beside the mat had been kicked over on its side, spilling the last of its contents into the sand. It was all we had left to drink. Jack seemed calm enough. I gently touched his cheek, and he murmured very softly, but didn't wake up. I thought he would be all right.

The sand was wet and spongy outside, but the passing squall had refreshed the air. I found the basin I'd wedged under the horizontal palm tree half-buried in sand churned up in the storm, the water inside turned to mud. My crock jar, too, had been scuttled, lying empty among the rocks.

I grabbed the jar and began a frantic search of the beach and all its crannies for some crevice of rock or a puddle or anything in which water might have collected. I foraged back among the palms and up the scrub hills, clawing from one slanting plateau to the next. I crossed trackless, ashy cliff faces that would have stymied a mountain goat, the prickly vegetation slicing into my hands and legs. Scrabbling like a crab across one low peak and down the other side, I could not see even so much as a strip of beach below, on the backside of the cay, let alone any kind of running or standing water. Just more sheer rock sparsely decorated with slick moss and lacy green fern and spikes of stubborn cactus.

Before I tumbled head-first down this forbidding hill, I managed to find a foothold and a ledge in the scrub to sit on. I must have sat there a long time, too tired to move, waiting for inspiration, waiting for my strength to return. But all that happened was the morning sun climbed higher in the brilliant blue sky, washed clean by the storm. Finally, more slowly this time, I crept back over the summit and made my way carefully down the hill toward the stand of palms. How long could we exist without water? Should I light a signal fire? There were other green islands all around. But who would see it? Suppose I attracted the attention of another squadron ship or a British cruiser? Even if some harmless fisherman came to our aid, I'd seen the tempting rewards posted in every port town for the capture of pirates.

And so I stumbled back into the dimness of the cave and blinked into the gloom. And stopped.

Jack was gone.

The palm mat was still spread on the ground with the scuttled water cask beside it. But Jack was not there.

I stared stupidly around the cave. My eyes were not adjusting as well to the dark, now, and my brain was growing sluggish. How far could Jack go? He must have left tracks in the wet sand. Or perhaps there was some other living thing on this rock after all. I turned around slowly, toward the mouth of the cave, facing the light. But the light seemed to be moving farther away, like the opening at the end of a long, dark tunnel beginning to vibrate with the unsteady racket of my own blood pounding in my ears. Then the light went out altogether.

CHAPTER 21

Runaways

The first sound I heard in the dark was a high, fanciful piping, like tinkling bells. Or giggling children. I opened sticky eyes and was blinded by bright daylight that swallowed up whatever else there was to see. But I tried again, more slowly, and saw that the light poured from a corner doorway into what was otherwise a rather dark little room.

I found myself in a shadowy corner, sprawled across a thin pallet that offered scant padding over the wooden slats of an unsteady cot. Blinking away the gloom, I saw the children I'd heard before tumbled all over another bedstead against the opposite wall. There was a man tucked under the bedcovers in their midst, propped up on one elbow and telling some sort of tale. His words were too soft for me to understand at first. But I knew the timbre of his voice, its teasing tone. It was Jack.

I lay on my side, watching them for several minutes.

Four or five dark-skinned children perched on the bed all around him, prattling away in musical island English as Jack spun his yarn.

"But wasn' she pow'ful mad when she wake up an' see that donkey?" demanded the biggest girl.

"No. The king was sorry afterwards, so he made her think she only dreamed it all," Jack explained.

"Me like the donkey bettah, anyway," declared a very small boy. As the others all snickered, Jack's gaze rose up over their heads, and he saw me watching them.

"Go get your mama," he told the eldest girl, in a low voice, and she scrambled down from the bed. To the others, he added, "All right, that's enough for now. Go with Lucy and I'll tell you the rest tonight."

There was an outcry of disappointment, but Lucy and the eldest boy mustered the three smaller children down from Jack's cot. As they all squeezed out through the sunlit door, Jack pushed himself upright and looked over at me again, his dark eyes anxious.

"Rusty," he began, and stopped, and tried again. "Are you all right?"

"Funny. I was going to ask you the same thing." My voice sounded hoarse to my own ears, but the vision of Jack did not dissolve. He tried out a tentative smile.

"I'm on the mend, they tell me. For which I believe I have you to thank."

I shifted a little, sending the bedstead into creaking complaint. My hip was sore, as if I'd been lying on it for a long time, and there was a fearful ache in the small of my back.

"I suppose this isn't Heaven, or I'd feel better."

"You'd never find me here if it was," Jack agreed, tucking up one leg where he sat. The clothes he wore were too big for him, made of some worn, faded blue stuff.

"Too sunny for Hell," I continued, glancing toward the open door. "Where are we?"

"Safe. You've been asleep a long time."

"Did I have the fever?" I felt cramped, but not ill.

"Worn out, I think." Jack's glance shifted away. "Looking after me."

I fished in the well of oblivion for my last memory and suddenly sat all the way up. "Where the hell did you go, Jack?"

"Ah, I see you're feeling better already." He grinned.

"I thought you were going to die!"

His smile evaporated. "I'm sorry, Rusty. I've caused you so much trouble."

"But what happened to you?"

A shadow loomed in the doorway, blocking out the light. A roundly proportioned black woman strode into the room, dressed in a plain cotton skirt and shift with a boldly colored bandana wrapped round her head.

"Don't you even t'ink about gettin' off that bed or I tie you down!" she warned Jack, before turning to smile at me. "Gal, we t'ink you nevah goin' to wake up. You sit quiet, now, 'til Asia get you somet'ing to eat."

As Asia bustled about, I saw the child, Lucy, leaning against the doorframe. Looking in over her head with a grin that rivaled the midday sun stood Harry Quick.

"I be wracking in the Caicos when I hear tell of that Spanish ship taken by pirates who kill that planter's son." Harry sat straddling a chair with a cup of Asia's fruit mawby in his hand. "From what they say, it sound like the *Blessed Providence*, although I can scarcely believe such a t'ing"

"It was an accident, Harry," I volunteered.

"For true, I t'ink it don't sound like Cap'n Hart, 'less you be in some powerful trouble." Harry nodded. "I owe the cap'n me own life, and I got me a fast little sloop, now, so I decide to follow the story down the islands. See if I can be any use. Pretty soon, I hear about the black schooner chased by that decoy ship, but when I get down to San Juan, I lose the trail. Until I hear tell of the Yankee ship afire in Fajardo." He took another sip and glanced at me with dancing eyes. "Down in Fajardo, I hear me a wild yarn about how the fire set by black demons who fly off in the night. All these fellows be laughin' and hollerin' they heads off at the one tellin' the story, and I get one of 'em to translate for me. He say one of 'em come aboard his ship when he be alone on the watch. A she-demon, he say, eight feet tall with seaweed hair and a black, shiny fishtail and breasts like a woman. He call her the witch from the sea. T'ot'er boys, they all fit to bust, but I believe this poor little fellow, he see somet'ing. And only one ship I know of count a female among her crew. That's how I know I pick up the trail again."

"I ought to be insulted." I laughed. "It's not a very flattering description."

"You lucky it not more true. This way, nobody believe him."

I wondered what sorts of tales were circulating about the *San Pedro*. If they described a golden warrior with eyes like the sky and hair spun from rays of the sun, they might be discredited and forgotten. Like the witch from the sea.

"I still be poking about Fajardo when a Yankee merchantman from St. Croix come in one day," Harry continued. "Say they spend a morning becalmed in sight of a black schooner beating nort'east for t'outer Virgins. I go out that way, and find a fisherman who seen a black schooner off one of those little smuggler's rocks south of Drake's Channel. He say two folk go ashore in a boat but only one come back. So, I t'ink I go 'long and see if anybody be needin' me help."

"I got to hang back the day that squall come in, but the next day, I find one wit' a cave, and damn if I don't find Jack inside. He don't look any too spruce, but he know me. Well, we 'bout halfway across the channel when he come round again and start moanin' and cryin' that we got to go back for Tory. So I say, boy, you dreamin' or you still feverish, ain't nobody on that rock but you. But he start to make such a ruckus, I t'ink as weak as he is, he goin' to jump out of my sloop and swim back if I don't turn round."

"But how could you know?" I demanded of Jack. "You were feverish the whole time."

"Most of the time. I do remember one threat that promised to follow me to the grave. That could only have been you." His expression grew more thoughtful. "But it's not like the captain to maroon an able-bodied hand for no reason. You didn't quarrel with him, did you, Rusty?"

I didn't know how to explain how I'd pleaded for Jack's life, demanded to stay with him. It would only embarrass him and mark me for the foolish female I was, after all.

"The captain thought you picked up the fever in Fajardo," I improvised, "and that I was too big a risk for getting it, too. I didn't blame him," I added, hastily, seeing Jack's frown. "He had to protect the rest of the men."

"For true, when I get back to the cave, there you be," Harry took up his tale again. "First, I t'ink you dead, and I don't know what I goin' to say to Jack. But then I see you alive, all right, just in a swoon, and you don't give me no trouble when I get you in the boat. I bring you here to me good friends, Sam and Asia, on Tortola."

"In the British Virgins," Jack explained.

"But how do you know people way down here, Harry?"

"Sam and me grow up toget'er, back on Eleut'era. And I do him a good turn, once."

I waited for Harry to take another drink.

"Sam is free colored, like me, and a fisherman. Asia was a kitchen slave. Slaves forbidden to marry and Sam too poor to buy her, but on market days, sometimes, Sam spirit her off to his boat for an hour."

Harry smiled, and I promised myself I would not look at Jack.

"Well, Asia, she start gettin' big and pretty soon she have her little Lucy an' mistress say she goin' to sell her off. So Asia take the baby and run off to Sam. If they catch her, she get the lash or they chop off her foot. If they catch her wit' Sam, even tho' he be a free man, they can sell him for a slave and flog him besides."

I felt myself blanch. "What happened?"

"Why, I put the t'ree of 'em in me boat, and we haul

down across the current for these little islands." Harry shrugged, as if he were discussing a cargo of pineapples. "Folk all talk English, here, and this village full of Africans off a captured slaver. Nobody pay no mind to one more poor African family."

"Asia and Sam will do anything in the world for Harry." Jack smiled at me. And I understood. They were not likely to turn away two more runaways on their doorstep.

"There's a lot I still don't understand." Jack sighed, and risked Asia's wrath to come sit beside me in the storeroom doorway. Harry had sailed with the tide, and we were enjoying the first cool stirring of the evening breeze. Out beyond the little planked veranda, a steep hill sheered away to reveal a recess of the bay, its placid waters purple with hidden reefs. Its passages were guarded in the distance by other islands in the chain, the green rumps of impudent Virgins dipping in and out of the water like eels. "How did we even get to the Virgins from Puerto Rico?" Jack continued, "I thought we were heading south."

"We were, until we saw the *Decoy* . . . ." But my words trailed off into a weary little laugh of realization. "But it probably wasn't the *Decoy* at all, more likely Harry's Yankee merchantman from St. Croix. By then we were all in such a state, we were seeing Porter's men in every bumboat and smack."

"Who said it was the *Decoy?*"

"Rudy said you did. Don't you remember?"

Jack shook his head.

"Off St. Croix?" I prompted. "Vieques Island? Fajardo?"

We looked at each other for a long moment.

"I remember rowing out to the squadron ship and swimming for our lives," Jack said, at last. "After that . . . I can't be sure what happened and what was only a dream."

Our tryst in the boat off Fajardo was feeling more like

a dream every moment, even to me. Whether Jack had truly forgotten it—or chosen to—it was no use dredging it up now.

"I had so many dreams," Jack added, his voice softened, as he gazed out at the water. His dark eyes caught mine for an instant, but darted away again. "I suppose I talked a lot of nonsense when I was ill."

"No more than usual."

"Still, it must have been . . . difficult. For you. A sensible person would have left me to my fate."

"Suppose you were fated to survive, did you never think of that?" I didn't mean to snap at him, but it infuriated me that he thought so little of the life I had struggled through so much to save. I didn't expect his gratitude, but he might at least pretend to be happy about it. "You don't owe me anything, if that's what's worrying you."

"Christ, Rusty, I owe you everything," he muttered, eyes downcast.

"You'd do the same for me. We swore an oath."

Now it was my turn to gaze out into the bay. The evening would be cool; already the palms were beginning to flutter their lazy fingers in the rising breeze. The sun was descending in the west, somewhere behind us, sending golden shafts skittering across the smoky purple water. It seemed odd to be looking at the sea from this distance and not to feel it rolling and swelling under a deck beneath my feet, not to hear the creaking and muttering of the lines and boisterous arguments and sporadic laughter of the men.

"I'm so sorry, *compañera*." Jack's voice was low and urgent, as if he read my thoughts. "It's my fault you're stranded out here alone in the middle of nowhere. I'd make it up to you if I could."

"By stranded, you mean in this quiet place with these kind people?"

His wary dark eyes met mine again.

"And I'm not entirely alone. Or have you forgotten we're partners?"

Jack permitted himself a slow, wry smile. "*Contra todo

el mundo."

At least he remembered that much.

I never wrote a word in my logbook all the time Jack was ill with the fever, as afraid as Nada of the power of words, afraid that writing about Jack's suffering might prolong it, somehow—make it more vital, more deadly. But now he's growing stronger, I've found solace in these pages, again. It has been far more comforting to write about past events whose outcome is known, however painful they might have been at the time, than to face my uncertain future.

Sam and Asia risk much to harbor us; we cannot stay here forever. Yet, how are we to live in these islands without a ship? My dreams, my freedom, my livelihood, all sailed away with the *Providence,* lost to me forever. But if that's what Fortune demands in return for Jack's life, I give them up, and gladly. We have no claim on each other, only a quarter of an hour together in a stolen boat expecting every breath to be our last. Jack doesn't even remember it, and I must try to forget. Whatever comes next, Fortune has dealt her cards, and we must play her game.

BOOK II

JACK

You would play upon me.
You would pluck out the heart of my mystery.

Hamlet, Act III, Scene ii.

CHAPTER 22

The Foundling

"**I**f you don't hold still, I'm liable to cut something far more critical than your hair." I pulled up the scissors in exasperation and got a firmer grip on Jack's thick, sticky pigtail, lifting it again off the back of his neck.

"I'd welcome a clean, merciful cut, but you're hacking away as if it were a joint of old beef."

"There's enough tar in here to caulk the *HMS Victory*, Jack. The blades won't go through it clean."

"So you mean—ow!—to saw it off one strand at a time?"

"I'll take an axe to it in a minute, if you don't keep still. Just be glad I'm not shaving you, too."

"There'll be blizzards in Hell the day I let you near me with a razor."

Still, the shaving would have to be done. Any ordinary

mariner might sport a tarred pigtail; it was a common enough sight in the Indies. But in these English islands, only a confirmed blackguard wore a beard. And there were rewards posted everywhere for the capture of pirates.

"Done," I announced, wiping the scissor blades on a rag tucked into my apron; with diligence, I was remembering how to wear female clothing. Snapping the scissors aloft, I added, "Now the beard!"

"I'll have those, thank you." Jack's hand shot out to pluck the scissors from my grasp. "You hold the glass."

I sat on a crate in front of his stool, steadying the glass on my knees, watching him over the rim. He trimmed at his beard until the rough shape of a jawline emerged, laid the scissors aside and wet his face from a mug of steaming water heated over Asia's cookfire. Then he unfolded the razor and set to work. The face that emerged was all angles and planes, raw bones above weathered cheeks still gaunt from the fever. His newly exposed chin was sickly white, but his wide mouth with one crooked corner gave him a humorous expression. And he looked much younger, even vulnerable, without his ragged beard and its few glints of silver; the rest of his hair was quite dark. I was still gaping at the transformation as his dark eyes shifted up to meet mine.

"What?" he demanded.

"I've never seen your face before."

"Well, you couldn't expect your luck to hold out forever."

It was like a reprieve from the gallows, finding ourselves at liberty on this brisk and balmy morning. I knew Jack would go out of his mind if he had to spend another day locked in the storeroom, and it was too dangerous for him to be seen laboring over the fish pots in the bay with Sam and the African fishermen. Such abnormal behavior in a white man might provoke the kind of scrutiny the household could ill afford. At

least I could pass for a colored island lady, although my association with a Negro family might also arouse suspicion, if it
were noticed. But Asia had come up with the idea of sending us
to the quayside market in Road Town, where a white buckra
man and his colored "housekeeper" were a common enough
sight.

I had Jasmine's fine basket full of Asia's yams on my
head, perched on a *cotta*—a thick vine I'd learned to wrap round
the crown of my headscarf as the island women did. As we
walked along, Jack sounded out tentative notes on a cane-stalk
pipe that he'd borrowed from the children. In his dark trousers
and an enormous old shirt and disreputable palmetto hat of
Sam's, he would never pass for a member of the planter class.
But he looked more like a harmless shopkeeper's huckster than
a pirate. He would certainly never pass for a musician; at one
particularly harsh bleat of his pipe, a crow foraging in the roadside scrub let out a squawk and flapped away.

"You're scaring off the wildlife, Jack."

"Just let me know if I start attracting rats."

I was glad to see him in such high spirits after being so
long shut up in the storeroom with only Shakespeare to amuse
him. Most recently, we'd started in on *Hamlet*—long and complicated enough to distract us from the sameness of our days,
but hardly the ideal play to soothe a man chafed by his own
enforced inactivity. I could scarcely recall when we'd last had
time to read Shakespeare together. It must have been in Laguna
Escondida, before that last, fateful cruise.

"I suppose you think often of the *Providence*," Jack
said, suddenly. It was unnerving, the way he sometimes read my
mind.

"Of course. Don't you? I mean," I amended, when the
familiar shadow of guilt passed over his face, "don't you wonder what Dame Fortune had in mind when she sent the
Providence to Colombia and landed us here?"

"Dame Fortune has never seen fit to take me into her
confidence." Jack strolled on, then turned to face me again,
waving his cane-pipe aloft.

> *"Blest are those*
> *Whose blood and judgement are so well commingled*
> *That they are not a pipe for Fortune's finger*
> *To sound what stops she pleases."*

He finished with a flourish of mismatched notes.

"I'll never understand why you went to sea, *hombre*." I smiled. "You must have been a very good actor."

"This from a woman who has never seen a play performed."

"Did you never want to return to England, and—"

"I can never go back to England."

"Why not? You could play in London. You could be famous."

"Oh, I was famous once. In your precious London, too. I was the most celebrated Romeo who ever trod the boards there. The local wags, I'm sure, are laughing still."

"It was . . . not a success?"

"It was a bloody travesty. I can never go back."

I was speechless for a full minute, struggling to suppress a laugh. "A bad performance?" I spluttered, at last. "You can't go home to England because of a bad performance?"

Jack glared at me, but it was too late.

"Hellfire, Jack! Jasmine and I thought you must have killed someone, at the very least!"

"You didn't see young Montague when I got done with him."

I had to pluck the basket off my head to keep from scuttling its contents, I was laughing so hard, stumbling blindly into the scrub. The sight of Jack scowling at me, his arms folded across his chest, only made it worse. But I thought I detected a renegade twitch at the crooked corner of his mouth, and when I gave out with a fresh cackle, his scowl dissolved, and he laughed out loud.

"B'God, Rusty, I was awful!" he roared, almost choking with laughter. "What a disaster! You could hear poor old Will

Shakespeare rattling his bones from Westminster Abbey to the Tower!"

"I had been in the provinces for four years," Jack recalled, as we collapsed under the meager shade of a scrubby tree. "I joined any company that would have me—sharers, boothers, anybody. I would play the First Soldier, the Second Gentleman, anything. Of course, the smaller the company, the more leading roles I got to play, mostly in barns or rustic inn-yards unchanged since the time of Elizabeth. One summer, a great lady of the stage joined our company. It was the off season in London—"

"The what?"

"Summer, when the patent theaters in London are closed. That's when celebrated players from London perform in the provinces to dazzle the yokels and get themselves through the lean summer months. Our manager contracted with Mrs. Emma Standish, the great tragedienne, to play Lady Macbeth. It was one of her most celebrated roles, so we took it on, even though it's considered an unlucky piece—"

"Is it? Why?"

"Oh, you know—witches, ghosts, evil, murder. Tampering with nature. Players are a superstitious lot."

"And was your production unlucky?"

"Not for me. I played Malcolm. Thanks to Emma."

"Emma?"

"Well, we all called her Mrs. Standish, although if there was a Mr. Standish anywhere in the picture, she kept him well hidden. Especially from me."

"Why, you infamous rogue!" I could not hide my delight.

"She cast me as Malcolm, first," Jack protested. "The other came after."

"Seduced and abandoned, I suppose?"

"Well, no. She had an engagement at Drury Lane in the fall to play Juliet. It had been her first success in London, and she wanted it to be her farewell performance before she retired from the stage." He paused and shook his head, as if he still could not believe it. "She took me along for her Romeo. I was nineteen years old."

"She must have been very fond of you." I knew all too well the mementos of Jack's seafaring career before the *Providence*—a whip-scarred back and recurring nightmares. I was glad to think that someone, somewhere, had once been kind to him.

"I don't believe she loved me. But she flattered me. And I must have flattered her, as well." He smiled a little, thinking back, and I saw a trace of the lad he must have been in his dark, thoughtful eyes and the wistful curve of his mouth. "She had a voice like thunder and honey," he went on, softly. "She'd been in the theater forever. And I was in awe of the theater. She must have been forty or more at that time, and still a small, neat figure onstage. It was only her presence that was enormous, the way she filled the house. And physically, I suppose I was just what she wanted, a raw young bullock full of clumsy ardor who didn't know enough to upstage her. Which is just what she got."

"Well, at least you were the right age for Romeo."

"But I understood nothing about the role. I was far too grand for any kind of comic business, and that's a mistake because Romeo is actually quite a ribald fellow, roistering about with his mates. But I had to play him on a single note of grand passion—the ardent, tragic lover."

"Still, that must have been effective," I reasoned. "Given the circumstances. You and . . . Emma."

"But that wasn't love!" Jack laughed. "I mean, I fancied it was, then. I fancied I knew everything there is to know at nineteen about pleasure and lust. I knew about the favors of a great lady. But Romeo's kind of love, that nurtures you while it tears at your gut, that you could die from or die without . . . no, I knew nothing of it," he finished quickly, glancing away.

I could only stare at him, bewildered. Never in this life had I thought to hear such impassioned words from Jack.

"What happened? After?"

"Well, if you must know. We had a good, long run because Emma was so popular. On our last night, I collected my pay and went off to have a good sulk. I was expected to escort Emma to the company supper, but instead, I slunk off to some noisy Thameside grog shop where I thought no one would have seen my disgraceful performance—which had become the butt of jokes all over London. I kept ordering round after round of whatever they had—gin, porter, whisky, I don't know what all. I was going to drown my humiliation. As it happened, I didn't yet know the meaning of the word."

He paused, but I stared him down, waiting.

"I woke up on a hard bunk in the reeking hold of a merchant brig in the middle of the Atlantic, with a head the size of St. Paul's Cathedral and ringing just as loud. My money was gone, of course, and I spent God knows how many days choking and retching and praying to die. And that, dear lady, is how I came to be in the seafaring trade."

"Oh, Jack, how awful." My reckless hand started toward him, but I jerked it back; this was not the cave, and Jack awake was too brittle to be touched in that familiar way.

Jack shrugged. "Serves me right for being such an arrogant young fool." He got to his feet, reaching out to help me up. He handed me my basket and plucked out two small, rosy yams. "Let's go, Rusty, or Asia will wonder what's become of us."

We didn't speak for awhile, but Jack began to juggle the yams and his pipe as we strolled along.

"You never told me about the tumblers who reared you," I ventured. "Or is that a trick you learned from the great Lady Emma?"

"What I learned from Emma can only be discussed among grown-ups," he needled back. "This I learned from the finest juggler and acrobat in the West Country of England. And the kindest man."

"The man who found you?"

"Aye. John Chester. Everybody called him Old John,

and his wife, Missus John. Past their prime by the time I knew
'em, but in their heyday, they were featured in a troupe called
the Tumbling Jacks and performed all over Britain. They were
already middle-aged when they found me in a box at the May
Fair, so I was told. They had no business harboring a squalling
infant of unknown origin. But they'd never had a child of their
own and . . . I don't know. They decided to keep me."

"And this from the man who claims to be abused by
Fortune."

Jack smiled at the objects he was still spinning before
him, as if the scene he recalled were playing there. "A lady on
the same fair circuit, a strongman's wife, had just given birth,
herself. She came in as a wet nurse, and off we all went. No one
was ever fool enough to claim me, of course, so I grew up with
the Chesters. They taught me everything. Tumbling, first,
although I was the wrong build. The best acrobats are compact
and muscular, and I was all arms and legs. But Old John was a
master teacher. And then the juggling—balls, knives, torch-
es . . . . " He grinned again at my horrified expression. "They
used to tell people I was a born performer, that I must have
tumbled in the womb."

"They must have been very proud of you."

His face darkened so suddenly, I glanced at the sky,
expecting to see a passing cloud. He turned away.

"I suppose so," he mumbled.

I tried to scramble for safer ground. "And they taught
you Shakespeare?"

"No. They couldn't read. It was the strolling players we
met at the fairs. I was always making a pest of myself around
their wagons, and one of the players once told Old John I had
a good memory for lines. After that, whenever we went to our
winter lodgings when the fairs were closed, Old John packed
me off to the parish school. During the fair season, he let me
spend all my free time among the strollers. I fetched water,
groomed horses, helped build flats and repair the booth —anything they would let me do. In return I got to see all their
shows for free, and I got to know the parts so well that I was

sometimes indulged with a tiny role. When I got older, I was often put on for some ailing player. And my foster parents loved it, all the attention I got. As long as I was never late for one of our performances and I did all my chores, they were never jealous of the time I spent away from them. They only wanted me to be happy . . . . "

Jack stopped, abruptly, staring down at the yams now clenched in one of his hands, the pipe in the other, his expression unreadable under his hat.

"What became of them?"

When he looked up, it was as if a door had slammed shut behind his eyes, making his face a perfect mask of impassivity.

"It's getting late," was all he said. "We ought to hurry."

I bit back a protest and quickened my steps. He'd told me more about himself this morning than he had in nearly two years aboard the *Providence*. But that was Jack—a book with the pages ripped out just when the story got interesting.

By an hour past noon, all the freshness had gone out of the day. Sunlight glinted off the water like a barrage of grapeshot, stinging my eyes, but we had to prowl the docks and the beach to sell our wares. The only market activity midweek was quayside, along White Wharf, off the market square. Trading ships putting into the wide, deepwater bay off Road Town stopped here to reprovision on their way to someplace else.

Because of its splendid bay, Road Town was a tiny replica of a respectable English port town, not the sort of smugglers' watering hole we'd been accustomed to in the Spanish islands. The activity of sailors and hucksters and vendors along the wharf was exhilarating; even Jack lost his melancholy. But I didn't much care for the peddling trade, sidling up to strangers to offer my basket of goods. I felt dependent, like the dark-skinned women leaning in their doorways in a row of tumble-down shacks at the least prosperous end of the docks. They, too, were waiting to sell or to trade, waiting without anticipation or enthusiasm. Such was the fate of poor island women without employment or protection, and I returned to my own project with renewed energy.

At last I found a Negro cook off a trading sloop to purchase the rest of Asia's yams. Jack kept the two he'd been juggling and started up again as we continued along the wharf. I suppose I was gazing out into the bay when I heard a muttered oath behind me and something hard struck my shoulder. I spun around to see Jack lurching sideways to catch his pipe in one outstretched hand and a falling yam in the other. The yam that had struck me was rolling in the dust at my feet.

"It was an accident, I swear it!" Jack laughed, as I scooped up the errant yam. Glaring at him, I tossed it from hand to hand as he trotted a few steps backward, then danced toward me again, provoking me, his cane-pipe and yam spinning all the while. "Had I meant it, I would have taken better aim."

"Oh, aye, then aim for this!" I feinted sharply with my empty hand and hurled my yam with the other. Jack hopped and stretched to catch it, using a knee here, an elbow there, to tuck both yams and the pipe back into a manageable pattern while he regained his balance. He plucked off his hat at last to catch the yams as they fell, seized the pipe out of the air and made an ironic bow.

"Bravo!" A young Englishman stood in the lane above us, sweating in his high clerk's collar and sober frock coat. His arm linked through that of a young *mulatta* woman in a neat, striped English morning dress. Jack broadened his smile and made a more formal bow.

"Well done," crowed the young gent. With a sidelong glance at his lady, he tossed a coin into Jack's hat, then steered his mistress back toward the square. Jack's eyes were dancing as I came up beside him and he showed me the silver Spanish dollar inside his straw hat.

"Honest coin," he marveled. "And at my time of life."

I smiled back. "They buy as much as the other kind, I'm told."

In the bustle of the square, *mulatta* maids from the townhouses shopped for provisions, gentlemen of business argued outside the Government House and busy slaves, sailors at liberty and packs of footloose boys jostled about everywhere. Jack and I kept to the margins, but there was some commotion across the square, and we were caught up in the tide of onlookers surging over to have a look.

Two white men, followed by a silent black man, were mustering along a frightened young black woman in torn plantation linens. Her bare arms and lower legs were scratched and bleeding, her wrists roped behind her back.

"What ye got there?" came a sally from the crowd.

"Runaway," grunted one of the white men, shoving the girl before him. "Found her hiding in the scrub. It's her second time."

"We had 'er up to the gallows at Burt Point," piped up the other white captor. "But her master sent word he wants her back."

"Wouldn't you?" leered his companion.

They dragged the poor woman over the rocky ground toward the heavy wooden stocks that decorated the middle of the square. Two more Englishmen approached from the direction of the whitewashed Government House, one inspecting a paper. The captors shoved the woman to her knees before the stocks. The heavy wooden bar was lifted, her wrists unbound and pressed into the half-moon holes, and the bar crashed down again, pinning her in place as the iron bolts were shot. One of the men ripped open her torn blouse in back, exposing her shoulders. Immobilized by the crowd, I reached blindly for Jack, my hand closing on his forearm.

"Somebody must get a magistrate," I whispered.

"That *is* a magistrate," Jack replied, his voice low and terse, nodding toward the man with the paper.

"Yes, yes, it's all very clear," that worthy gentleman was muttering testily, as he handed back the paper. "The girl's an incorrigible runaway, and the law allows fit and meet punishment to be determined by the owner. Get on with it, Mr. Rich." And he turned and marched back toward the refuge of the Government House.

"Is he the owner?"

"The overseer, no doubt," Jack muttered back. Nodding toward the black man, he added, "That fellow must be the driver."

Mr. Rich produced a rolled-up cartwhip from his belt, shook it out and handed it to the driver. "Do your duty, Mose," he said.

Mose set to it, applying ten rapid strokes to the back of the tethered woman, who struggled to swallow her sobs. Hemmed in by the onlookers, I could only lower my eyes. Jack's arm had gone as hard as a length of chain cable under my hand; in another second, the tensed muscles would burst through the flesh.

"Christ, let her scream," he breathed.

When the miserable woman could no longer suppress a wail of agony, Mr. Rich brightened.

"That'll do, Mose." Bending down to face the captive, he went on, "Now, Belle, that was for your first offense. You know what master said if he ever caught you trying to run off again."

The terror was gone from Belle's eyes as she faced her tormentor. Only contempt and fury remained.

"Don't care none. I glad to be gone from this wicked place."

The flash of anger across the overseer's face was followed by an odious mask of goodwill.

"Why, Belle, you ain't leaving us." There was acid in his smile. Straightening up, he turned again to Mose. "Fetch me the brand."

I must have pushed myself forward, enraged, the impulse exploding from somewhere deep inside me, certainly not my brain. But Jack was quick enough to catch my arm, and I snapped round to face him in wild desperation.

"Jack, we can't . . . they can't . . . ."

"Stop it," he hissed.

"But . . . she could be Asia!"

"That's right. She could." His face was only inches away from mine, his grip like iron. "Stop and think."

Of course. I dare not cause any kind of commotion that might bring attention to us. Or to Sam. Or to Asia. We were all runaways.

I smelled the acrid smoke and heard a sizzle and Belle's scream, but I didn't watch the branding. Jack's long fingers twined through mine, and I saw his eyes close briefly under the brim of his hat. But everyone else seemed to be taking in the spectacle as if it were a political address or a pantomime or some other entertainment. No one shouted encouragement, but neither did anyone try to interfere. And when it was over, all of them—factors and ladies' maids, tradesmen, sailors, errand boys and dockhands—went off about their own business, leaving Belle forlorn in the stocks under the watchful eyes of her captors.

"Is there nothing we can do?" I whispered to Jack. "Can we bring her water? Something for her back . . . ?"

"She wouldn't feel it," Jack muttered, and I knew he spoke from experience. "Leave her in peace and let's go."

CHAPTER 23

Honorable Men

"I've got to leave here, Rusty."

I looked up, startled. I'd not even heard Jack come in.

"Every day that I stay here endangers Asia and Sam and the children," he hurried on. "And I can't spend the rest of my life in a storeroom."

I followed his uneasy glance all around the low-ceilinged rectangle of a room—scarcely more than a shed, built onto the back of the one-room house the family shared. I was trying to find beams and shelves and pegs enough to hang up bunches of Asia's thyme for drying; they were usually hung from the slatted racks we were using as beds.

Of course, we could not stay here forever. Sam and Asia had been kind to us, out of the debt they owed to Harry. But they were deferential to Jack; they called him "sir," and he hated it. He'd all but stopped telling stories to the children because it made Sam uneasy. Too dangerous for black children to grow too trusting of a white man. More often, now, Asia found excuses to take the children off; today they were sitting with a sick woman in some other part of the village.

"What will you do?" I had to fight to keep my voice calm. "Take another ship?"

"I don't fancy returning to the merchant seaman's life. In fact, I thought I might take up the juggler's trade again."

"But you have skills, Jack." Unlike me. "Might you not make a better living as a carpenter?"

"I'm a bit old for an apprentice. And no craftsman will engage a white laborer for wages when he can buy Negro slaves to do his work and hire 'em out for profit, as well."

"Then start your own shop."

"Using what for capital?" He laughed. "My good name? No, I don't want my own shop. I don't want to be a part of this society, tipping my hat, keeping my place, standing idly by every time some rebellious Negro is dragged into the stocks. If I can't go back to sea, I can try to find some honest trade that doesn't depend on their rules. Street performers have no sort of standing, whatsoever. Nobody takes the slightest notice of 'em, which is fine with me." He paused and raked a hand through his hair. "For some reason and against all natural laws, Fortune has spared my sorry life. Perhaps I'm meant to begin again, in the first trade I ever knew."

How tidily he had it all worked out. Men were so accustomed to doing whatever they liked.

"Where will you go?" I asked in a reasonable voice, as if this were a reasonable conversation, this announcement that he was leaving me.

"I think I'd better steer clear of the Spanish islands and the Bahamas. I might hop down to the Leewards, where no one has ever heard of the *Providence*. St. Kitts is said to be a green, fertile place. I've heard of players performing there."

"And what about me?" I had no power to stop it blurting out, and Jack cast me a sharp, searching look before he put on his mask of impassivity.

"Why—no one will take you for a pirate, Rusty; there's no need for you to go traipsing all over the Caribbees. Tortola is a nice, quiet place—you said it yourself."

"Still, perhaps it would be safer—for Asia—if I went along to the Leewards—"

"We have no money," Jack interrupted. "Alone, I can earn my passage on any coaster or smack for a couple of hours of hauling sheets and setting yards."

"I can work a ship!"

"Aye, but you must never let anyone know that. Not in the civilized world. It would be more than conspicuous, Rusty, it would be a scandal. A female mariner in Road Town bay? Every vessel for miles would crowd in to have a look. The magistrate would have to know what all the fuss was about, and you would be obliged to give a strict accounting of how you came to learn the trade—which I, for one, would be most interested to hear. No, you're far better off here. I'm sure you can find some shop or taproom in Road Town—"

"Do I look like a serving wench?"

"Ah, you have something loftier in mind? I hear there's a shortage of brides among the planter class, since Englishwomen are so loath to come out to the tropics."

"So you mean to sell me for some planter's bed after all."

"There'll be no profit in it for me. I'm thinking of you."

"You would have me sell myself into this same damnable society for which you are entirely too grand! I'm not fit for the housekeeper trade, Jack. I lack the skills."

"Then what do you want?"

"I want a life, just like you. Why is that so difficult to understand?"

"Fair enough. And what sort of life would that be?"

He had me, there, and my defiance melted away.

"You must have had some plan when you left Boston," he reasoned, more gently. "You didn't set out to turn pirate."

"Getting out of Boston was my plan. I had no other."

"Well, you'd better come up with one. I can't afford to

dally here much longer."

"I'm not your problem." I sighed gloomily.

"No, but I am the reason you're here, so I feel responsible—"

"Well, don't! If you want to do something for me, teach me to juggle," I hurried on, reining in feelings too chaotic to confront. "Then at least I'll have the means of earning my own way when you decide to abandon me."

Something so raw flickered in Jack's expression that he turned his face away. Studying the floor beneath him, he finally muttered, "All right. I owe you that much."

Was I only a bargain to be paid off, after all? Was that all I meant to him?

"I thought we were partners." My voice came out a forlorn whisper.

Jack turned toward me again with an assumed heartiness; he even managed the ghost of a smile. "Yes, for now. Until you find some handsome young creole who suits your fancy. And your Uncle Jack will be glad to see you settled."

He would be glad to be rid of me; I could well believe that. And why not, if all I could do was whine and complain like a helpless female? I had saved his life, but I didn't own him. I was behaving like a child, not like a woman who had crossed half a continent to be free.

"I know better than to depend upon a man for my living," I declared, with no little asperity. "Teach me juggling, Jack. You said I could learn."

"A female juggler, showing off her ankles," he mused. "It might draw an audience, the novelty of it . . . still . . . it's a bitter, footsore, melancholy life in many ways. I'm certain you'll be much better off if you—"

"You must stop telling me what to do! It was one thing aboard the *Providence* when I was an ignorant green hand and you were the damned Ancient Mariner. But things are different, now."

"Aye, so I see." Jack smiled. A genuine smile, this time.

Jack enjoyed teaching me to juggle, I knew it. The lessons gave purpose to our days, eased his restlessness and restored some of his humor. As long as we were practicing together, I could almost forget that Jack wanted to leave me.

The sun was not yet up on the morning I woke to the light touch of Jack's hand on my arm.

"Throw on a wrap and come outside, Rusty. We're going exploring."

"It's the middle of the night!"

"Not for much longer. Hurry, we'll be off before anyone sees us."

We took along the stunted yams and dried gourds we'd been juggling and fruit to eat on the way. I had no idea where we were headed. As the sky lightened to grey, then pink, Jack led me off the footpath to follow a trail through low, scrubby foothills rising above the water. At a stand of three raggedlooking palms, we turned off the trail. Jack helped me scramble down a short, rocky slope to a sandy strip of scrubland and tidal pools that passed for coastline. This gave way to a dense thicket of seagrape wedged between the cliff and the water. It was almost twice as tall as Jack and looked impassable, but he found a place where the trunks grew farther apart and some of the lower branches were broken away. Hunching down, he crept into the thicket, and I followed into a narrow passage carved through to the other side. The dense, murmuring foliage of flat, round leaves in every shade of green and gold hid us from view. A carpet of dry brown seagrape leaves, as stiff and starched as ladies' fans, crunched beneath our feet.

When I caught up to him, Jack was standing upright under a high canopy of seagrape. Before him stretched a crescent of white sand beach as soft and fine as flour, lapped by a foamy tide whispering like silk along the shore. It was only a small beach at the mouth of a hidden lagoon whose inland shore disappeared into a dark and forbidding mangrove swamp, but it looked as wild and unspoiled as it must have looked on the first morning of the world.

"It's beautiful," I breathed.

Jack smiled. "Runaway Bay."

"You knew this was here?"

"I wasn't exactly sure where. The cove is hidden from the road by all this foliage and those cliffs, and the bay is protected by reefs. Runaway slaves sometimes hide here on their way to wherever they're going."

"But how did you hear of it?"

"Sam's boy, Young Harry, told me about it." He shrugged his sack of juggling props off his shoulder down to the sand. "If you ever want to know something really useful about a place, ask a child."

It might have been the tranquil isolation of Runaway Bay, or the mangrove lagoon that reminded us so much of Laguna Escondida, or the progress I made in my juggling lessons on the days we managed to take ourselves off there. But for a while, Jack spoke no more about leaving Tortola. We sat together in the shade of the seagrape canopy one balmy afternoon—tired but content with our day's work, feeling the first cool caress of the trades. It was almost possible to believe we were still *compañeros*, that at any moment, Captain Hart would signal us and we would row back out to the *Blessed Providence*.

"The first day I ever saw Ed Hart was in a grog shop on the Cuban coast," Jack mused, as if he shared my thoughts. "I was less than two hours off that wretched slaver, and when he and Nada offered me a berth on the *Providence*, I leaped at it. They gave me a tumbler of rum to seal the oath, and I was promptly sick all over the dirt floor. The captain helped clean me up, and then he said, 'Fetched off the slaver, have ye, lad?'"

Jack cast me a wry glance. "I could still be taken for a lad, then. Well, it was noon, and they were already several tankards ahead of me, so the captain's burr was thick as porridge. 'Laddie,' he says, 'the world's a perishin' damn evil place, especially this corner you've fetched up in. Ye canna change the world. But ye can try to live with honor.'"

Jack's imitation of Captain Hart's accent was faultless.

"Then he said, 'Aboard the *Providence,* we owe allegiance to no nation, prince or god. We fight our own battles. And each man is responsible for his own honor.'"

"I miss them too," I ventured. "Even Nada."

Jack smiled. He stretched his arms over his head to work a kink out of his back, resettled himself and gazed out toward the bay. "I saw them together, once. Hart and Nada. It was a hot spell, and we were laying off the passages one night, stripped down to rags and sleeping on deck. When I came down from the watch, I found the two of 'em tumbled together in a mess of cordage and canvas under the cabin top. Both of 'em naked as eggs and snoring like the mother of all gales. Nada was built like a tree trunk, you'll recall, just as knotted and about the same color, flat on his belly with that long tangle of black hair down his back. And Ed Hart was sprawled across him with an arm round his back and their faces very close together. Dead to the world. Joined." He paused, and I confess I was oddly comforted by the image of the captain and Nada eternally locked together. *Contra todo el mundo.* "No matter what's become of 'em," Jack went on, very softly. "I know they're still together."

I nodded, not wanting to give voice to all my fears about the fate of the *Providence* and her crew. "I wonder you weren't more . . . shocked at the sight," I teased, instead. "If you were such a tender young lad."

"Oh, my precious backside was safe enough on the *Providence*, if that's what you mean. The captain didn't allow coercion, unless there was prize money involved, of course. The men could do what they liked to each other if they were willing, but his standing order was that any man who forced himself on another would lose his berth on the *Providence*. Why do you suppose you were treated with such chastity?"

"Me? Because I was female. And I suppose I . . . wasn't desirable."

"Forgive my being blunt, but a hole in the ground is desirable to a male in rut. No, Ed Hart felt that men who raped and assaulted each other might not make the jolliest possible shipmates when lives were at stake."

"I notice his principles did not extend to women in port."

"He had no interest in women in port. He didn't sail with 'em. You fell under his protection because you were a member of the crew."

Had the captain's protection accounted for Matty's indifference to me? As if Matty needed to be ordered to ignore me. No, the captain's order must have upped the ante at the Gallo Rojo, nothing more; it meant that Matty could not win his wager by force. He'd had to use guile.

"Although it must've made things difficult for you," Jack observed, "the way you lusted after our Matty."

Appalled to have my thoughts thrown back in my face, I blurted out, "You were in love with Jasmine!"

"Oh, God, yes!" Jack laughed. "What a woman! I could scarcely keep my hands off her."

"You couldn't, as I recall!" I wasn't sure why his euphoric response needled me so.

"No. No, in plain fact, I could not." Jack's expression sobered. His gaze held mine for a moment, then dropped away. "So much for honor," he muttered.

I gaped at him. "You and Jasmine . . . ?"

He nodded, eyes fixed on the sand.

"Well, it's not as if she were under the captain's protection." Surprise made my voice more harsh than intended. Jack did not reply, but I saw a small, silent muscle working at the corner of his mouth. "Did Hector know?"

Jack scooped up a dry, brown seagrape leaf and began to pick at its brittle edge. "I don't know."

"How could you not know? You were like brothers!"

"Thank you very much for reminding me! I was in danger of forgetting who I'd betrayed." But his anger burned out just as quickly, leaving him even more glum. "I never told him, if that's what you mean. And Jasmine was sensible. She only . . . dallied with me when she was already carrying a child.

But . . . I doubt if they kept many secrets from each other."

Jasmine still cared for Jack; I knew that much. It was unlikely he'd ever mistreated her.

"Well, I don't imagine Jasmine could be dragged into anything against her will."

"No." Jack shook his head, fiddling again with the starchy leaf. "But that's not the point."

"What *is* the point?"

"Hector. What I did to him."

"What you did to Hector? It sounds to me like you did everything to Jasmine."

"Don't act like a simpleton, Rusty. You know what I mean."

"I know that Jasmine had the wit to make a choice," I told him. I had to lean over a little to distract his eye away from that damned leaf. "Just as you did. And I know that Hector sometimes bedded women in port."

"That was different."

"Oh? How?"

"Because Hector is a man . . . ." He stopped, abruptly, but it was too late.

"And Jasmine is only a possession to be owned and used," I finished for him. "I hope you didn't tell her that in bed."

"I never thought that!" he protested. "It wasn't like that."

"I know it wasn't," I agreed, more gently. "She was very fond of you."

Jack offered up one half of a sarcastic smile. "But she didn't need me. She had Hector. He was the one she loved. I was only recreation. No, less than that. I was charity."

"I was not even that much to Matty." I could laugh about it, now. "He didn't love me, he didn't want me and he cared nothing at all about me—"

"But he was such a damned handsome fellow," Jack suggested. And he hurled the brittle leaf some distance across the sand.

"Talk about acting the simpleton," I agreed.

Jack peered at me for a long moment. "I couldn't bear the way he treated you sometimes," he said, at length.

"Aye, well, there's two of us."

"I used to wish you would stand up to him once in awhile," he went on softly. "You're worth a thousand Matty Forresters, Rusty. I only wish you knew it."

If he thought so, why did he want to leave me? I could scarcely recall Matty's handsome face, and had managed without him quite well. But if I tried to look ahead into the future, to a life without Jack, I could see nothing—a bleak, empty, airless nothing, a slow suffocation that would last forever. I could not lose Jack. He was a part of me. It would be like tearing out my heart.

CHAPTER 24

Give Sorrow Words

A low reverberation—a swallowed cry—roused me from a light, troubled slumber. All was still in the dark storeroom, but for Jack's restless mumbling in the opposite corner.

"Madeleine!" he cried out, in a pitiful voice. It fell away to a moan as he rolled over in his sleep, shivering the cot beneath him.

A silver grin of a moon was just rising into the wide airspace between the top of the bamboo wall and the roof thatch, flooding Jack's corner with cold white light. I gathered up my skirt, slid off my bed and crept across to his.

"Jack." I gingerly touched his shoulder.

His entire body started. His eyes flew open, but there was a long, tense moment before he seemed to see me.

"Rusty? What . . . ?"

"Shh-h-h. It's all right. You were having a bad dream."

He blinked, looked away. "I'm sorry." His eyes flitted all around the room, unable to rest. "Did I . . . ?"

"No, nobody heard." I wished I knew how to say more.

He propped himself up on one elbow and raked a hand through his damp hair. "Sorry," he mumbled again.

"Are you all right?"

He nodded, not looking up, his body tense as a bowstring.

"Who is Madeleine?" I tried to sound casual. "The name you call out in your dreams."

He stared at me, then looked away again. "My dreams are not about Madeleine. She was just the beginning of it all."

"You may say it's none of my affair," I said, when he did not go on. "And you may be right. But it doesn't look as if either one of us will get much more sleep tonight."

He sighed and sat all the way up, crossing his legs under him. I sat on the bed beside him.

"Miss Madeleine Butler was the ingenue in a company of players we met at the fair one summer She . . . oh, Rusty, you can't possibly care about any of this . . . . "

I stopped him with a look. He huffed an exasperated sigh, but he went on.

"We met them at Bartholomew Fair, the summer I was fifteen. I was still tumbling with the Chesters, then. Their joints were starting to creak, but they never complained . . . . " He paused, his mouth a thin, tight line, proof against any wayward emotion. In a moment, he continued.

"I had known dozens of players, but I'd never seen the like of Madeleine. Curls of fine, spun gold, eyes of cornflower blue, cheeks and lips as pale and delicate as moonbeams kissed with roses. Fairy bells tinkled in the air when she spoke and flowers bloomed wherever she trod the ground." There was no mirth in Jack's eyes to match the sarcasm in his voice. "She was sixteen and a full-blown woman of the world to my eyes. Of course, I said I was eighteen, and I was tall enough, no one disputed me. I was utterly besotted, but the lady played her cards close to her chest. She never actually discouraged me, and I suppose she was just as glad to have an escort. Toward the close of the fair, she told me her troupe would be leaving on a tour of the north and suggested I come along. Her parents ran the company, so I suppose she could bring along whomever she fancied. At that moment, she fancied me.

"It was very hard to think of leaving Old John and Missus John, who had been more than parents to me. But otherwise, I would never see Madeleine again—which was not to be borne. I told myself I'd make my reputation and a fat purse in the theater and return to my foster parents in triumph, with Madeleine an adoring bride on my arm. I'd see to it they could give up the fairs and live out their days in comfort and ease. I might as well have dreamed up a cure for consumption and the capitulation of Napoleon into the bargain." His mouth twisted in self-mockery. "No fancies are as grandiose nor as useless as those dreamed up by a fifteen-year-old boy in love."

"What did your parents say about it?"

"I never told them," Jack replied, eyes downcast. "I didn't know how. I ran away with Madeleine's company on the last night of St. Bart's, like the proverbial thief in the night. My parents would soon be off to their winter lodgings, I reasoned. I expected it would only take me until Christmas—Easter at the latest—to get rich in the theatrical trade and then I'd come back and all would be well. I wrote as much in a note I left for them. Not that they could read it."

"There must have been people about who could read it to them."

"It doesn't matter. It was a load of rubbish, anyway."

"So you went north with Madeleine?"

"We went north, but we were not long together. I carried a few spears, fleshed out a few crowd scenes in York and Newcastle. Madeleine soon grew bored with me and turned over her affections to a young fellow with a private income in coal. 'There has been no understanding between us, sir,' she told me, when I went to plead with her. 'And you have been greatly deceived if you ever thought otherwise.' Implying that I'd deceived myself. Which of course, I had. I might have borne her rejection. There's a certain amount of tragical romance attached to the role of spurned suitor. But without Madeleine's interest, I was promptly dismissed from the company. By Martinmas, I was stranded and freezing in Newcastle without money or employment."

"Did you go home, then? To Old John?"

"I did not. I had far too much manly pride. Besides, I hadn't a farthing to my name, and it would have been a long, cold walk. I contrived to stay on at the theater after Madeleine's company moved on. I swept out, polished the woodwork and saw to the hinges and traps, all for my keep. Every time a new company of players came along to make use of the place, I auditioned, and eventually a troupe took me on. We went on to Hull and Leeds and Dublin and Edinburgh. I changed companies many times, and I was on the road all the time, in every season of the year. But I never got rich by it. And every time I thought about my parents and how I'd left them . . . well, I was determined not to go back until I had something to show for myself."

"Did you never meet up again with Madeleine?"

"Oh, aye, in every female I took a fancy to in every troupe I joined. And I was determined to make 'em all pay for her crimes. I went in for duplicity and deceit and heartless flirtation—all the black arts I thought had been practiced on me." Here, he almost smiled. "As if any such wiles were needed to make a fool out of me. But once I found out where flirtations lead to, I forgot all about my broken heart. Forgot all about Madeleine, too, or so I thought."

I frowned. How did this explain the ferocity with which Madeleine still haunted his dreams?

"After about four years of that life, I met Mrs. Emma Standish," Jack went on. "I was a bit more stable and a lot more experienced by then. Anyway, you know that part of the story."

"Yes. Romeo." I nodded. "But how can you say you knew nothing about love when you played Romeo after all that business with Madeleine?"

"I did not love Madeleine. Hellfire, I didn't even know

the girl, and once I got to know her, I didn't much care for her. But I was bedazzled by the idea of love. Madeleine was just the face and form I chose to complete the package."

It was difficult to imagine Jack ever being young and silly enough to make as big a fool of himself over a girl as I had made of myself over Matty. But comforting, too.

"I suppose Old John and Missus John came to see you in London," I ventured. "They would not have missed that!"

Jack was quiet for a long time. "I never sent them word. It was such a travesty, especially after the notices came out, and I couldn't bear for them to see me fail. I just . . . I thought . . . I don't know. I always thought there would be more time. I told myself my next play, my next performance would be brilliant. And then—"

"And then there was no next play," I finished for him. "You were on a ship in the middle of the Atlantic."

It seemed he would not go on, this time. I could feel the tension in his silence, lacerating if it were unleashed, and forced myself not to prompt him further; there was something too fragile in his expression. But he finally did speak again, describing without anger or any other emotion the kind of brutal shipboard life I remembered from my own experience out of Boston.

"I was fool enough to try to resist at first," he told me. "After all, it's not as if I'd signed up of my own free will. But I soon had all that foolishness flogged out of me. And once I learned not to try to fight back, it didn't matter so much what they did to me. It was easier to become anonymous, a part of the great machine. No one had a past. No one had a future. Nothing mattered. I started calling myself Jack; you can't spit aboard a merchantman and not hit eight fellows called Jack. I learned a new trade and turned out to be rather handy at it. There's nothing like acrobatics to teach you to be sure-footed in the rigging."

But seafaring lined his purse no better than the acting profession had. Voyages out took months, and unskilled or unsavory merchant captains unable to make an honest living often turned to smuggling, to which they were no better suited. Cargoes were jettisoned or lost; hands were often paid off or left stranded in strange ports, and Jack had no way of getting home to England and nothing to show for it if he could.

"By that time, there was not much left of young Johnny, the tumblers' boy, or even John Young, the name I'd taken for the stage. There was only nameless Jack, the man with no past and no expectations. And I suppose I was . . . content."

Until one day in a waterfront grog shop in Kingston, Jamaica, when he happened across a Londoner named Clarke, a carpenter who used to work at Bartholomew Fair before coming out to the Indies to make his fortune. Over a round or two of rum, they spoke of showfolk and fair gossip, as strangers often do who discover they are in the same trade.

"At last," Jack recalled, in the same low, toneless voice, "Clarke called to mind Old John, once the leader of the Tumbling Jacks, who'd gone so lame, he'd had to retire from the circuit. But inactivity didn't seem to suit him; he died soon after, up country somewhere; no one knew where. His goodwife nursed him to the last, but she was carried off by a fever that same winter.

"'That's the way of it with old people, sometimes,' says Clarke, with a snap of his fingers. 'They go just like that, with no family to look after 'em.'"

Jack's voice stopped, and he sat gazing into the empty air. He lowered his eyes and hung his head a little, staring at his hands in his lap. Then his head dipped lower still, and he put up one hand to cover his face. I touched his shoulder, but he shrugged me off and turned his face away, now buried in both hands. His shoulders heaved with a sob, and I got to my knees, put my arms around him and pulled him close, and this time he did not resist. I could only hold on to him while he shook with the misery that had been building inside him for God knew how many years.

"It's all right, *hombre*." I could scarcely trust myself to speak. "Let go. You have to let them go."

"I was . . . so far away."

"It wasn't your fault."

"Yes, it was." His voice was stark with grief, between ragged catches of air. "Mine. And Madeleine's. What must they have thought of me?"

"I'm sure they loved you. Nothing changed that."

"But . . . I ran away like a child."

"You were a child."

"But how could I hurt them like that? After all they'd done for me?" He was whispering, now, shaking in my arms. "I never even said goodbye. They were all alone when . . . . " His voice broke again.

I closed my eyes and rocked him in silence, struggling with my own feelings.

"My poor Jack," I murmured, when he had grown quieter. "It's not like a play when people die. They don't expire with a pretty speech and a benediction. You don't get to exchange elegant couplets that make everything all right. Everybody leaves things unsaid."

"But I should have been with them."

"It wouldn't have made any difference."

"It would to me. If I had been there—"

"I was there when my mother died, and I couldn't stop it. And when my father lost his reason. It made no odds in either case."

Jack sat up as if he'd been slapped, dark eyes stung with shame. "Forgive me, Rusty. As if I'm the only one who's ever known grief."

"No, I didn't mean it like that." I kept my hand on his arm, to reassure him. "But we all have painful memories of things that can't be changed. And you must talk about what hurts you sometimes, or you'll never be free of it. 'Give sorrow words,' as Malcolm says, or you'll break your heart. I learned that at Laguna Escondida, that day you let me talk about my father."

"I've never . . . told this to anyone before," he admitted.

"I know. I bring out the worst in you, remember?"

"Did I say that?" There was a wry twist at the corner of

his mouth for an instant as he raised a hand to swipe at his eyes and rake back his hair. He took a deep, steadying breath that only shook a little. "For whatever it's worth," he added, "I would not have put you through this, Rusty, if . . . if I could have helped it."

"No, it's my fault, *hombre*." Malcolm be damned, I had ripped open a wound that might never heal, only to satisfy my own curiosity. Hadn't Jack enough scars to bear? How could I have been so thoughtless? "The Mohawk say a prayer for the dead," I offered up, desperate to help put things right. "My mother told it to us when my brother was killed in the war. I think I can remember most of it."

"What good are prayers if they're already dead?"

"It's only partly for the dead. It's mostly for the survivors." He nodded, so I went on. "They say to the dead: 'We release you on your journey. Let nothing of this world hinder you, let no friends or relations trouble you. Forget the sadness of this world and go in peace.'"

Jack nodded again, waiting. I took his hands in mine.

"This is what they say to the survivors: 'The journey of the dead will be yours, one day. If you love them, let them go in peace. Do not trouble them with your sadness. Do not be idle with grief. Do not lose hope.' Then—you're supposed to abstain from wickedness for a year."

"It's a little late for that."

"The Mohawk say if you cannot be good for a year for the sake of ceremony, you must take time to mourn, out of respect."

"I never did mourn," he said, at last.

"You have now, *compañero*."

The late moon had risen above the roof line. Jack's face was in shadow when he spoke again. "I don't suppose any part of the dead survives to hear prayers."

"I think they do. I used to speak to my mama all the time when I was alone in Boston. She was so much more comforting than the terrible God of Wrath. I still do talk to her, sometimes, and to my Papa, too. It's as if they're watching over me."

"But that doesn't mean you commune with spirits," Jack reasoned. "Those are only memories you carry in your heart."

"But that's where the dead survive." I realized I was still holding his hands. "Your parents forgave you a long time ago, Jack. Can't you feel it? They'd tell you themselves, if you'd let them."

Jack looked at me for a long time, but he said nothing more.

CHAPTER 25

Runaway Bay

I scarcely remembered crawling back to my own cot, but the morning sun was already bright in the doorway when I woke again. I rolled away from it with a groan and my toes struck something solid at the foot of my bed. Unable to nudge it away, I leaned up on one elbow for a better look. It was Jack's volume of Shakespeare, carefully placed on the end of my cot, propped up against the wall. When I glanced over my shoulder to ask him about it, he wasn't there. The pallet and sheet lay rumpled together on his cot. But there was no sign of his few things— the old straw hat of Sam's, the razor, the three juggling gourds, my old red quilt from the *Providence*. All that was left was his Shakespeare, left for me on my bed. A token of farewell.

I was up and washed and outside in a heartbeat, hastily tweaking my old cotton shirt and linen skirt into place. Asia was working in her vegetable garden with her children, but I scarcely saw them. I ran two steps toward the road into town, then stopped and dashed off in the other direction for Runaway Bay.

I couldn't let Jack run away all alone like this; he had been alone for so long. And I was tired of letting him do my thinking for me. I loved him, I knew that now. My love might be a poor, fledgling, untested thing, but it was all I had to give him, after he had given me so much. He might not even want it; he'd had plenty of time to tell me if he did. But we'd been through every kind of hell together, and I was damned if I would lose him this way. Not without a fight.

When I got to the seagrape thicket, I could see him on the other side, sitting under the shady canopy on the quilt he'd thrown over the leaves and sand. He sat with his bare back toward me, facing the blue water out beyond the little beach, his knees drawn up and his arms folded across them; his crumpled shirt and a little bundle of his things sat beside him. I crept cat-footed into the thicket, but it was hardly silent work, and when Jack turned and saw me, his only greeting was a frosty stare.

"Go back to the village, Rusty," he said, at last. "Don't do this."

"Don't you even want to say goodbye?"

"It doesn't matter what I want," he snapped, turning his face back toward the sea. "I don't even know what I want."

"Yes, you do." I crept onto the quilt and sank down to my knees behind him. I stretched out one hand to his scarred back and felt every muscle in his body tense. One of my fingers brushed the ridged flesh of one of his scars. He started again, then bent his head onto his folded arms.

"Don't," he whispered.

I stared at the white, ragged scar. He had so many scars. I stroked this one with tender fingers and then pressed my mouth to it. The narrow stripe of ruined flesh stretched from below his shoulder across his backbone to the middle of the opposite ribcage. And I kissed every inch of its vicious length, tasting the warmth of his skin and the faint tang of salt. He was shaking when I finished, his heart racing; I could feel it pounding. Jack's body was speaking to me, even if he was not.

"Don't make me do all the work, Jack," I whispered, stroking the scar and lifting my face to nuzzle the curve of his neck. "I don't know how."

"Yes, you do," he mocked me, but his voice was very soft. Then he twisted round on his knees to face me, catching my shoulders with both hands. "And I do know what I want. I want you to go back to the village. I don't want this to be a terrible mistake. If you—"

But I lurched forward to kiss him and stop his words. I kissed him a second time, and it was no mistake. His mouth opened under mine, and I wanted to dive in and drown, but something restrained me—Jack's hands, like iron clamps fastened round my upper arms, pushing me away from him.

"Stop this, Rusty!" he cried, shoving me back to arm's length.

"Don't you care for me at all?"

"How can you even ask me that?"

"Then show me."

Jack's dark eyes were pleading, but his mouth flattened into a stubborn line.

"You would if I were white!" I cried.

"What?" He let go of my arms. His eyes were furious.

"You think of me as the poor helpless colored girl you have to be responsible for, who lacks the wit to make her own choice."

"Someone must protect you if you won't."

"Protect me from what? From you, the evil buckra?"

"You ought to know." He turned away as if to rise, but I grabbed his arm to stop him.

"Look at me, Jack. I'm not a slave who needs protection. I wasn't dragged here in chains. I'm here with you because I choose to be. I keep choosing to stay with you, no matter how hard you try to get rid of me, and it must be for some reason. It's not because you're some powerful buckra man who will keep me in style."

I hoped he would laugh, but his expression was bitter.

"No. It's because you need another lesson from your Uncle Jack. And when I have nothing more to teach you—"

"Is that what you think I want from you?"

"What else am I to think?"

"That I love you."

He did laugh this time, and it was etched in acid. "You can't possibly—"

"Hellfire," I exploded, "all my life people have been telling me what I can and cannot do, and I'm sick to death of it! Do you think I want to keep humiliating myself this way? If you're so damned honorable, why can't you be honest with me? Tell me honestly that you don't want me, and I promise that will be the end of it."

Jack stared at me, his eyes wary and utterly miserable. With a shake of his head, he finally whispered, "You know I can't say it."

Something much hotter than anger pulsed through me. "I'm a free woman," I told him in a more rational voice, as my hand stole across the quilt to cover his. He did not pull away. "You can't tell me what to do. You can't stop me loving you."

He sighed. "I can try to talk you out of it."

"But why?"

"Because you deserve better."

"I could never find any better, not if I searched for the rest of my life. You're my best friend, Jack. You're all I want. Don't leave me." I lifted my other hand to stroke his cheek, as gently as I could, and saw his eyes close. "Let someone love you, *hombre*," I whispered. "Even if it's only me."

"Only?" Jack caught my hand and pressed it to his cheek. "Hellfire, Rusty, you're everything I've ever dreamed of, more than I ever dared hope for, don't you know that? Don't you know what a sorceress you are?"

I snaked my arms around his neck, and he pulled me into his lap, lifted my face very gently and kissed me as if he would steal the life out of me. It took a long time. Then we were tumbling across the quilt together in a tangle of arms and legs and kisses and laughter. I was on fire to kiss him, to touch him, to feel the play of his long, supple muscles under my roving hands, to make him moan in my arms. I found myself underneath him, breathless with giggles and nerves, shuddering as Jack's warm, searching mouth explored my lips and my face and my throat. His fingers traced the curve of my breast beneath my shirt, and he began twisting open the buttons and kissing everything he found underneath. His hand slid up under my skirt, drifting lazily up the inside of my thigh, stroking with slow, gentle urgency. I could not seem to bear it when he touched me, and I could not bear it when he stopped. At last, I twisted away to wrestle my shirt off over my head. I let Jack peel away my skirt, but my heart almost stopped beating when he did not come back again into my arms. I opened my eyes and saw him kneeling beside me, staring down at me.

"Holy . . . mother of God," he breathed, raking me more provocatively with his eyes than he had yet with his hands or his mouth. "How can you be so beautiful?"

"Don't tease me," I pleaded.

"I have never been more in earnest in my life. Although I soon will be." His fingertips slowly traced the fullness of my breast, the soft swell of my belly and the curve of my hip with a caress that scarcely touched me, yet left me feeling flayed. "I was so accustomed to seeing you in boy's clothes and Asia's shapeless things," he murmured, bending down to me again. "I never . . . ."

Then, too, it had been as black as pitch under the tarp in that little boat in Fajardo Bay. We'd navigated each other by dead reckoning that night, and it had been enough. But now . . . .

I reached up to trace the long curve of Jack's throat, letting my fingers drift down his chest, through soft, dark hair, across one puckered nipple, past the subtle rungs of his ribs and down into the waistband of his trousers. I tugged, and he scrambled out of them, and I touched him again, exploring him as tenderly as he had handled me until he sank into my embrace again. I knew his body so well, had trusted myself to him so often. I trusted him now and wanted him more than life or breath, but my body did not seem big enough to contain so much feeling; I was sure to explode with it. I was already shaking so violently, my teeth all but chattered. Jack felt it, too, and his arms closed underneath me as he cradled me beneath him.

"Don't be afraid of me, Rusty. You know I would never, ever hurt you."

"I know, *hombre*. I'm not afraid. I just . . . can't help it." I closed my eyes and caught my breath as he began to move inside me. Slowly, this time, as if we had all the time in the world.

"It's all right," he murmured, his mouth close to my ear. "Hold on to me. Tell me what you like. Tell me what you want."

I wanted nothing. Only Jack. Only everything.

We lay entwined like twin yarns in a rope amid the wreckage of our quilt and clothing. Prey to any enterprising beetle or stinging ant we had not already crushed beneath the seagrape leaves, but I didn't care. I was too fascinated by the dark hair that branded Jack's chest like a long, ragged cross. There was a small mole near its center; when I touched it, I could feel his heart beating underneath. The long tail of the cross melted into the small crater of his navel, where the hair was soft and fine. I tickled it with the tip of one lazy finger until Jack caught my hand and flattened it gently against his stomach. Smiling, I rolled up to kiss the mole over his heart, and he sighed and his arm tightened around me, and we lay still together awhile longer.

"You're very quiet," he said, at last. "are you all right?"

"I'm speechless. It's so different from—"

"From Fajardo," he finished.

"So you do remember."

"Hellfire, Rusty, I'm not made of iron. I'm not Saint John, the bloody Divine. Of course I remember."

"You never said so."

"Neither did you."

"I . . . I thought you had forgotten," I faltered. "I thought it must have been . . . forgettable."

Jack sighed and stroked my cheek. "I wished to God I could forget. I'd have given anything to forget what a bastard I'd been."

"It's not as if I ever told you to stop," I pointed out.

"You didn't know any better."

"Of course I did. I'd stopped others. But you're my *compañero*. Some part of me must've known you loved me, even then."

"If you only knew how much," Jack murmured. "Or for how long."

I could not suppress a giddy smile. "I do know. If you didn't, you would have sent me away, today."

"Christ Almighty, Rusty, I did everything but take a stick to you!" Jack laughed. "How much discouragement do you need?"

"You would not have run away to the one place on this island where I would be sure to find you."

"I thought you would have the sense not to follow me," he said, at last. "And I didn't know where else to go. I wanted to keep out of Road Town until nightfall; you never know what ships will be in the bay. But I couldn't trust myself to spend another day with you. Not after last night. When you held me . . . ." He ran out of words, shaking his head.

"I held you often when you had the fever," I whispered.

"I know. I've . . . missed it."

"So have I. Why couldn't you tell me how you felt?"

"Because it's hopeless." He sighed again. "I have nothing at all to offer you—"

"Oh, I wouldn't say that."

"No home," he went on, stoically. "No fortune. No family. No name. No prospects—"

"As if I cared about your prospects," I snorted. "You can't talk your way out of this, Jack. I'm not a child . . . ."

His entire body tensed under me, and he rolled up on

one elbow to look into my face. His was full of dread. "A child," he echoed. "Christ, Rusty, I never even thought . . . you took me by surprise, and . . . ."

"What?"

"A child," he repeated again. "Suppose I've got you with child."

"It's all right."

"No, it's not," he protested. "Your mother . . . if anything were to happen to you . . . ."

"It won't. I was lucky, once." Twice, if I counted the Gallo Rojo, far more luck than any one person deserved. "But one cannot depend on luck. I have something to take, if I need to. To make the blood come."

He frowned at me. "Is it dangerous?"

"Not as dangerous as the alternative." I was smiling, but he looked so apprehensive, I began to lose my nerve. "Asia gets it from the old African medicine woman," I hurried on. "It's not witchcraft. The Africans say every child is a blessing from God, but Asia says she has all the blessings she can feed now."

"You mean . . . you planned the whole thing out?" Jack faltered.

I nodded. "The old woman made me up a packet. I traded her Jasmine's basket."

Jack's expression was astonished. "For me?"

I nodded again and he lifted my face in his hand and kissed me, very slowly.

"It's been a long time since anybody . . . wanted me . . . that much," he whispered.

My heart somersaulted once, plunged through my belly and began to beat wildly in my loins. I leaned up on one arm and rolled Jack onto his back.

"Well, you'd better get used to it," I grinned, crawling astride him.

Stark, white, blue-shaded clouds were scudding across the sky when I next awoke, and for a moment I did not know where I was. But I felt Jack's warm, naked body beneath me, and I smiled with satisfaction over what I'd accomplished. Jack was all right; he was safe. He was mine. I might have lain there in his arms forever with my tangled hair spread out across his shoulder, my arm draped across his middle, and one of my legs snugged between his. I could not resist peering up to look at him, and I only started a little to find his dark eyes open, gazing down at me.

When he noticed me gazing back, he smiled a little sheepishly.

"I was afraid you were a dream." He smoothed back a strand of my hair. "This is exactly the sort of trick Fortune would play on me, to torture me with a dream that would vanish the minute I awoke."

"I can pinch you," I volunteered. "Or something." I settled for a soft kiss in the hollow of his throat. I saw his eyes close as he lifted his chin and bit back a soft groan.

"Christ, don't let this be a dream," he murmured.

I saw the sun well past its zenith overhead. Midafternoon. Jack saw it, too. He stretched himself a bit, but seemed to have no desire whatever to move. It was even possible that he couldn't move, that we would never move again, and the thought made me smile.

" I suppose it's late," he sighed, still stroking my hair. "They'll be wondering where we are."

I raised my head to look at him, propping my chin on the back of my hand. "Are you sorry?"

Jack laughed. "Do I look sorry?" His eye strayed to something he saw beyond me; I turned and noticed a smudge of sails far out in the channel, another merchant vessel making for the deepwater bay at Road Town. "But, Rusty . . . I still have to go. I can't bide here forever."

"I know." I held my breath.

"Will you come with me?"

Relief flooded me with such ferocity, I could barely

form a smile. "What do you think?"

"I think you're going to make a very foolish mistake."
He was smiling, too, but his heart was pounding very fast. I
could feel it. "At least, I hope so."

"You're wrong. I'm going to say yes." I kissed him again
to seal the bargain. "I hope you're sure," I added, softly. "You
know how difficult it is to get rid of me."

Jack grinned, full of the devil. "I'll risk it."

CHAPTER 26

Witchcraft

Loving Jack was like learning to read, or sail, or fly. He was a new language whose every nuance must be understood, and I was eager to study him, to know him by heart if it took the rest of my life. I noticed little of what happened during the day, so long as I could crawl into his arms at night, in the corner of the storeroom where we'd pushed our cots together. Jack's body radiated heat like a sun on even the chilliest nights. I could not imagine how I'd ever slept anywhere else.

We had few opportunities for lovemaking. Our cots would not bear much activity and Jack worried about endangering me, in spite of the old woman's herbs. But we could not always help ourselves. On one occasion when I pitched myself at him like a Fury, he had to hold me back a little, as I panted beneath him. "Easy, easy, Rusty," he murmured with a soft laugh. "It's not a race. You don't win a prize for being first."

As we grew more accustomed to each other, Jack taught me the virtue of waiting. I learned to trust myself to his strong, callused hands and his slow, searching mouth all over my body, even when I thought I could bear it no longer. The first night he stroked me to satisfaction with only his long, gentle fingers, I was surprised, but pleased. When, after much coaxing and reassurance, he loved me with only his mouth, I thought I would drown in a flood of pleasure that left me drunk and shaken; he had to rock me in his arms for a long time, after, to calm me.

I was discovering how much Jack liked to be held and stroked and touched after so many years alone. I learned to rouse him slowly, the way he liked best, no matter what sort of pandemonium came later. I was learning what pleased him and what irritated him and what irritated him just enough to cause pleasure, to make him groan softly under my hands and mouth, to make him shudder.

This was certainly witchcraft, but it needed two to make the charm work. It shamed me to think of the whining little chit I'd been, begging Fortune to reward me with love when I had nothing to give in return. Bodies might be bargained for on such selfish terms, but never love—I knew that, now. Loving Jack was its own reward, made all the sweeter in the way I lost myself in his arms. Every day I earned more of Jack's trust, learned the secrets of his heart, explored the vast, resounding ocean of his love—in addition to the astonishing pleasures of his body.

Jack was not as broad-shouldered nor as heavily muscled as Matty, whose every sculpted contour had screamed for attention. Jack's muscles—for all their power—were long and ropey, discreet beneath firm, scarred flesh. Raw-boned and rough-hewn, battered by life, Jack's body was an unchartered treasure map full of mystery and power and secrets, and I would have them all. I learned him by touch in the dark of the long October nights in that tiny room scented with sea salt and thyme.

Late one night, I curled myself behind Jack on our

shared bedstead, not yet ready for sleep. The only sounds were the whirring and clacking of the night insects outside and the deep, contented thumping of the surf. My fingers roved up and down the contours of Jack's body, from his shoulder to the diagonal scar across his thigh suffered on the Forrester and Clemmons ship. Then I felt the rough scar that crossed his spine, the one I had kissed at Runaway Bay.

"You never told me what this was," I said. "It doesn't feel like the other flogging stripes."

"It's not."

When he said no more, I leaned forward to kiss the little hollow between his shoulder blades. "I'm sorry, *hombre*. It doesn't matter."

"It was on one of my first merchantmen," Jack answered me, softly. "There was a great ox of a fellow, about one grade above me, came upon me in the hold one day and had me face down over a cask before I even knew he was there. He had a knife. Swore he'd cut me if I fought him."

I went very still, my fingers resting on the scar.

"I was scared, so I tried to fight, and he kept his word. Then he had me, anyway. Didn't seem to mind about the blood."

"Oh, my sweet heart." I flattened my hand tenderly over the scar, as if I might yet staunch this old wound.

"Well, it wasn't so unusual, in the merchant fleet," Jack murmured. "Or any fleet. It was another kind of seasoning. After that, I learned to be a damnsight quicker on my feet and keep my back to the wall, both very useful things to know."

I could not make myself smile. "Did he never bother you again?"

"No. It wasn't . . . personal. He had no interest in me. It was the fight the fellow wanted, the victory."

I closed my eyes against angry, useless tears, thinking of the night Rafael had assaulted me in Fajardo, when Jack gave me his shirt. I slipped my arm around him and held him tight and his hand closed over mine.

"It's all right, Rusty," he whispered. "It was a long time

ago. I was . . . I don't know, twenty or less when it happened. I thought I'd left behind everything good in my life when I was fifteen and this was the sort of thing I had to look forward to. After that, I lost the trick of being . . . close . . . to anyone." There was a long pause in the dark. "Until now."

This time I did smile and kissed the curve of his shoulder and the nape of his neck. "Except Jasmine?" I felt the laughter in his back.

"Aye, she was a careless flirt, Jasmine. But at least she made me feel I was not entirely repulsive."

"She told me you needed a woman."

"Did she? Well, she ought to know."

"I wish I'd had the wit to act on her advice, back then." I murmured.

"We were neither one of us ready. And you were very young."

I swallowed an impatient sigh. "And how old are you, exactly, Uncle Jack? As old as Time—or merely as old as the hills?"

"I don't know . . . seven or eight and twenty? Far too aged for you."

True, the difference between our ages was half of my own life. Still, aboard the *Providence*, he had seemed much older.

"It's the trade turns your hair grey," Jack went on, as if I had spoken aloud. "The first place it shows is your beard. But I'm still a lifetime older than you."

"Not for long."

A little hill of scrub and brush rose up behind Asia's back garden, affording a view of the shipping in Road Bay, the sea passage into Road Town. Jack liked to climb to a knoll some little way up the hill at night, when he wouldn't be seen, and watch the traffic in the bay. There was no moon tonight, but the stars were bright, mocking the faint winking lights of the vessels far out on the water.

He'd left me alone to labor over my logbook in peace. But I found my eyes straying away toward the little back door, where he'd gone, until I could bear it no longer and got up to go find him. I'd gotten as far as the doorway when I saw something stir in the yard and recognized Sam's square, solid figure emerging from the shadows. Sam was generally aloof, but now he crossed the yard and climbed to the knoll where Jack sat. He must have some serious purpose in mind. So I stayed in the doorway, where I could hear their conversation.

"Fine evenin', sir," Sam drawled around the pipe in his mouth.

"Aye, it is that." Jack nodded, and Sam sat himself down.

"I nevah met no Englishman who wasn't afeared of the night dew," Sam observed.

"I like the night. It's more private than the day."

"For true." Sam sucked again on his pipe. "You keepin' well?"

"Your hospitality agrees with me. You've been very kind."

Sam waved a careless hand in the air. "Harry do us a kindness, one time. We do one for you."

They were both quiet for another minute.

"Sunday, tomorrow," Sam spoke again. "Plenty of strangers at Road Town market. Coming and going."

Jack glanced sideways at the fisherman in the dark. He heard what Sam was saying. So did I.

"Tory and I will be going into town, then. As soon as we can find a ship and earn our passage, it will be time for us to leave."

Sam nodded. "But you must stay until you well."

And no longer. We both heard that, too.

BOOK III

COMPAÑEROS

We work by wit and not by witchcraft.

Othello, Act II, Scene iii.

CHAPTER 27

Strange Fish

The trick was not to pay too much attention to the three gourds spinning above my hands. If I thought too hard about what I was doing, I might overthrow and upset our rhythm. I must also try to engage the crowd. Jack said I had such a ravishing smile, my lack of skill wouldn't matter, and I smiled, now, at the memory. I stole a covert glance at him, his dark hair falling loose to his collar, his sleeves rolled back to the elbows, his capable hands manipulating four odd-sized papayas. He moved with the careless ease of someone at home in his own body after a lifetime of acrobatics and hard work. I glimpsed the thrust of his hip and the strong outline of his thigh under his dark trousers, and I smiled again.

After another glance up at my gourds, my gaze swept across our little audience of boys, slaves and seamen off the trading ships. Sunday was the principal market day in Road

Town, when armies of slaves came into town from the sur-
rounding plantations with fresh produce they'd grown on their
own account or chickens or hogs they'd raised to sell in the
market square. After which they turned over most of their
profits to the grog shops and gaming rooms, so Asia said.

The wharves and beaches of the wide, horseshoe-
shaped bay were busy today, and the mariners and dockhands
down here by the water were the ideal audience for a female
juggler. I enjoyed confounding their expectations of how a
woman of color ought to behave in public, and my audacity and
Jack's skill were rewarded with the occasional clink of coin into
Jack's upturned straw hat. Most of them were the two-penny
pieces the locals called "dogs," but I'd glimpsed a silver bit or
two, as well.

My gaze flicked across our small audience, again, and
snagged briefly on a figure standing a little way off, watching us
intently. I could not place his face, but there was something
fleetingly familiar about the way he stood—feet planted, like a
seaman—and his broad forehead and watchful gaze. But then
he moved off into the crowd.

Checking my gourds again, I darted a glance down to a
strip of beach just below the path where we stood. Two slaves
in coarse white cotton had been offloading barrels from a ship's
boat. The taller, heftier one straightened up to a remarkable
height and arched his back. He plucked off his straw hat and
wiped the sweat off his bald head as he gazed around. For an
instant, he faced me.

It was Hector.

I almost dropped my gourds, but managed to catch
them quickly and made a curtsy, surprising Jack, who had to
scramble to conclude with me. The barrels were being loaded
onto a mule cart, and by the time Jack collected his hat and our
things and turned toward me, his expression stormy, the cart
was climbing the little rise that led past us and up to the main
street. Beside the carter on the board sat an Englishman with
windblown wisps of graying hair, a ruddy nose and a weary
expression.

"Rusty, what the devil . . . ?" Jack began, but his protest died on his lips when he followed my eyes and recognized Hector on foot, placidly following the cart up the hill.

Without another word, we made our way up to the main street and the square. We hung back when we saw Hector carrying the barrels out of the cart and into the back entrance of a mercantile shop. When the work was done and the carter drove off, Hector came outside again. Then the windblown Englishman appeared in the doorway.

"I've a great deal of business inside, Samson," he said to Hector. "Wait for me out here."

"Yassir."

"Pardon me, sir," cried Jack, scooping the coins out of his pocket as he hurried toward them. The Englishman looked up, annoyed. "Forgive this intrusion, sir, but I have some heavy work that needs doing not far from here, and I wonder if I might hire your fellow for . . . an hour? If you'll not need him."

Jack smiled, and the Englishman frowned back. Hector took no notice of either of them, nor they of him.

"Half an hour, no more," said the Englishman. "I'm a busy man."

"Of course." Jack smiled again. He counted out three coins into the other's upturned hand. Then two more. When the Englishman went back inside, Jack led Hector away from the shop and into a little side-road. Neither spoke until I emerged from the shade of a sheltered doorway, and Hector broke into a grin.

"Is true what they say," he chuckled, in his deep, Spanish-accented English. "You never know what strange fish wash up in the Caribbees."

"Puerto Cabello," Hector answered, when we asked where the *Blessed Providence* was. "The Colombian rebels have a naval base there. That where she be heading last time I see her."

We'd taken refuge behind a gnarled old tamarind tree at the end of a forgotten byway far off the main street, away from curious eyes.

"But why aren't you with her?" I asked.

"Captain Hart sold me."

He took another pull of the watered-down rum and lime we carried in a stoppered gourd, then grinned at our stricken faces.

"Was my idea. Jasmine near her time. I got to get back to her. In Trinidad, we meet an *ingles* trader—Murdock, of the brig *Determined*— heading north with a cargo of cocoa. North for Cuba." Hector shrugged, as if the sense of the arrangement was beyond even mentioning. "*Capitan* make a little profit on the bargain, and Murdock, he get an experienced hand. And I get home. I be there now, but for Murdock's investors here."

"But . . . you're a slave!" I protested.

"Only until we raise Cuba. First landfall we make, I run off to Cabo Cruz."

"It may not be so easy as that." Jack frowned. "Your Murdock may want to protect his investment."

"As if I never run off before," Hector scoffed. "And Murdock, he like his bottle, eh? Is why he never make a fortune in the Indies and all his hands desert him."

"Does he treat you well?" Jack's expression was tight.

"Well enough, for a slave." Hector shrugged, again.

"Is there anything we can do for you, get for you?"

"I have what I need when I get to Cuba."

"And the others?" I prompted. "The rest of the crew made it safely as far as Trinidad?"

"*Si*. All but Mateo."

I could not swallow a gasp of surprise and felt Jack's eyes fasten onto me. "What happened?"

"We ship him over in a boat off Barbados. Yankee trader come up on the trades, carry him right into Bridgetown."

"You mean he just abandoned the captain?" Jack demanded.

"Well, he take some persuading," Hector reflected,

cradling his fist in his hand. "But we get him in the boat and send him off to the Yankee brig. Make it look like a shipwreck. The *Providence* long gone before he wake up again."

"So . . . he didn't want to go?"

"Why, Mistress, is hard to know. Ever since we leave Culebra, Mateo sweet as cane to everybody, follow every order, never pick a fight. Is like a different fellow. And all the time, he swear he never desert *Capitan*, that he be proud to die by his side."

I could just imagine the effect such declarations must have had on Captain Hart, the constant reminder that he was leading his golden boy into the mouth of chaos. Yes, Matty was far more cunning than he looked.

"Outfitting for the diplomatic trade," I speculated, aloud. "He told me he'd take it up, one day, when the time came to leave the *Providence*."

Jack was watching me in inscrutable silence, but Hector nodded.

"*Capitan* believe his time come," Hector agreed. "He say the *revolucion* is no Mateo's war. Is no my war, either." He swallowed another mouthful. "Is nothing to me if the Dons in these islands or no. Is not even my fault I be here. But Jasmine, she where she is because of me. Our boys and the babe she carry depend on me. Is my business to take care of them. And so I tell *Capitan*."

Jack was staring at the ground, but I touched Hector's arm and smiled. "Wish her well from us."

"I be glad to carry back good news of you." Hector smiled back. "She take it hard if I tell her Jack die of the fever."

Jack met Hector's eyes and mustered a wry grin. "Tell her Tory wouldn't let me."

When Hector asked how we came to be on Tortola, we told him about Harry Quick, mentioning his friends in the African village as briefly as possible; I should have felt uneasy speaking their names aloud, even to Hector. Then he asked what trade we found ourselves in, now.

"Vagabonding" Jack confessed.

"Any money in it?"

"There might be. On a wealthier island. But we must leave here soon, in any case. We're a danger to the people looking after us."

"Where will you go?" Hector asked.

"The Leewards. If we can earn our passage."

"How much you got?"

We could only share a feeble laugh over the scant handful of dogs we had left.

"Less than when you hire me, eh?" Hector noted.

"And worth every penny, *hombre*," said I. "To see you again."

Jack couldn't see any way out of our dilemma. As former pirates, we ought to lay low and pass unnoticed, but as performers we were obliged to make a spectacle of ourselves. To earn our passage off this island, we must follow the commerce into Road Town, but we must still return to the secret hospitality of Sam's storeroom every night because we could afford no other.

Seeing Hector yesterday, enslaved to that petty merchant trader, made us even more determined that our trail should not lead back to the African town. We could not look at Asia now without seeing Belle, branded and moaning in the stocks. This morning we were up and out in the hour before sunup, heading for Runaway Bay with a breakfast of cassava bread and mangoes. It was a roundabout way to get to Road Town, but safe from prying eyes until the day's commerce began on the wharf.

Jack said I was still our best insurance against a charge of piracy, in my female rig with my hair bound up under a modest headscarf. In my company, he would be seen as nothing more sinister than a poor buckra with his mistress. I glanced over at him, now, as we trudged along and saw him gazing at me.

I smiled, stifling a yawn. "What?"

"I was just thinking how fetching you look in that frock."

"You don't have to wear the infernal thing," I muttered, pausing to disengage the hem of my long skirt from a thorny patch of scrub.

We came to the seagrape thicket, and I hiked up my skirt, crouched down and entered into the hidden passage to the beach, with Jack right behind me. The sky was at the colorless stage between dark and light, and the land breeze was beginning to freshen along the shore. I'd just emerged out onto the sheltered carpet of dry, crunchy leaves when a massive shape rose up suddenly out of the foliage before me. I had no time at all to react before Jack's hand clamped down on my arm from behind and jerked me backwards, pulling me off my feet, as he leaped in front of me with his knife drawn. I rolled back up onto my feet in an instant, ready to launch myself at anyone, anything, that might hurt Jack. But he was already on the man, shoving him off balance and twisting his arm behind his back, knife at his throat, as he dragged him out beyond the seagrape into the light.

"Hellfire, Danzador, this no way to treat an old friend!"

"Hector?" Jack dropped his knife and took an awkward step backward, shaking as if he still had the fever. "Christ, you scared the life out of me!"

"What about me," Hector protested, "I be asleep!" He straightened up, working his arm in its shoulder socket. "What must I think, eh? You roaring through the bush in the middle of the night—"

"Hector, what in hell are you doing here?" I demanded.

He turned toward me and beamed. "I run off." We couldn't think what to say to this, and Hector's grin broadened. "Easier than I think, Murdock snoring over his rum all night. A child could do it."

"But . . . why?"

"To find you. And here you are! Who say there be no Blessed Providence, eh?"

I got out our flat round cakes of cassava bread and the fruit, and we resettled ourselves under the canopy.

"I run off last night," he elaborated. "Everybody know where the African village is."

"But how did you find this beach?"

"Is plain you never been a slave. Plenty slaves in Road Town know where the runaways go. I knew three such hidden places in Havana; I used one when I run off there." He accepted half a cake. "So I think I hide me here tonight and find you in the morning. I don't believe it take long to find a white man in the African village."

"We'll do whatever we can for you, *amigo*," said Jack. "But we can't take you in. We have no right to be there, ourselves—"

"Take me in? What for? I'm going to Cuba." When we looked no less bewildered, Hector heaved an impatient sigh. "You must take me back to Murdock," he explained.

"But you just ran away," I protested.

"*Si*, and Murdock, he post a reward for me today, once he find me gone. The man short-handed, and he got a schedule to keep. You take me back and claim the reward." We still looked confused. "I thought you say you need money."

"I can't sell you for a reward!" Jack exclaimed.

"Then you the sorriest pirate I ever heard of."

"But they'll flog you," I cried. "Or worse."

Hector made a derisive click of his tongue. "He no hurt me much. He short-handed, he need me fit enough to work the ship." His eyes narrowed at us, perplexed, even angry, that we might balk. "You still touched with the fever? The man offer thirty dollars for me, easy, and don't you take a penny less—"

"I won't trade in slaves."

"Don't you scruple on me, Jack, there be no time. I got to get to Cuba, and you got to get off this island. Murdock the answer for both of us. Is my business you got no money. I got nothing of value but my black hide, and I can't profit on myself. But you can. You a white man."

"He's already run away," I reasoned, as the enormity of

Hector's action struck me. "Anyone might pick him up, now. Look at the risk he's taking for us."

"It was a foolish risk to take," Jack muttered. "And a stroke of bloody genius."

"*Si,*" Hector agreed. "No white man ever think of it."

The red sun had turned to gold an hour later, climbing in a cloudy sky. But it was still cool down by the waterline. The white foam murmured along the shore, and Jack and I sat gazing out at the blue water in the reefy little bay. Hector was snoring softly up the beach under the seagrape. We planned to wait until noon before returning to Road Town, to give Murdock plenty of time to post his reward; in the meantime, Hector was catching up on the sleep he'd lost when his *compañeros* had come crashing through the underbrush. We'd tried to practice juggling, but Jack could not pay attention. It didn't take long to discover what was troubling him.

"I've got to tell him," he declared.

"Tell him what?"

"About Jasmine and me. Look at the risk he's taking for our sakes. How can I sell him into slavery knowing how I've deceived him all this time? Fortune must have washed him up on this island for some reason. I must admit it, like a man, come what may."

"Men and their idiotic notions!" I somehow managed to keep my voice down to a fierce whisper. "You have no right to say anything to Hector, don't you see? If he knows, and he's doing this for us anyway, it would be unforgivably cruel of you to fling it in his face. If he doesn't know, think of the wound you'd be giving him. And why?"

"To take responsibility. For once . . . ."

"To ease your own conscience. And at Hector's expense."

"But if he does know," Jack reasoned, "and I say nothing . . . ."

"Perhaps he's depending on your silence. You've never been known for your loose talk. And whether he knows or not, if you tell him to his face, he's probably obliged to kill you. That would be the manly thing to do."

Jack's mouth twitched, in spite of himself.

"You don't care overmuch for the male species, do you? Not that we give you cause."

"I care very much about you, *hombre*. And Hector. I don't want to see you hurt each other when there's no need." I slipped my hand over his and twined our fingers together. "It's too late to ask his pardon, Jack."

"I know," he agreed. "I suppose I must . . . bear it."

"Like a man," I smiled, gently squeezing his hand. "And we must get him back to Jasmine. That's the only way to make amends."

CHAPTER 28

Ophelia

Hector insisted we bind his hands, or no one would ever believe he was our captive.

"I thought I was supposed to dominate you with my masterful white presence," said Jack.

"*Si*, if you had any. Stop looking so shamefaced about it and start looking like a fellow greedy for profit."

Jack put on a leer worthy of King Midas as he knotted our fishnet sling, pulled taut, around Hector's thick wrists; I'd dumped out our juggling props and stowed them under the seagrape for later.

"You get thirty dollars, Spanish gold," Hector was instructing Jack. "Don't sell me back for less."

"It's a reward, not a fish market. Haggling isn't allowed."

"I do the work of three men on that damn brig, so don't

insult me by taking less."

I could only bear the attention we drew on the way into town by thinking of it as a kind of performance. It swept me past the smug approval on the few white faces we met on the road—a planter's attorney, a merchant, a parson on muleback from an outlying parish. And past the covert glances of the slaves closer to town, wondering at these strangers so anxious to meddle in the business of a runaway Negro.

But somewhere along the east end of Road Bay, we slipped into the brush off the road. Jack was damned if he would continue this charade if there was no profit in it, and I was delegated to go ahead into town to make sure a reward had been posted. I ambled down the main street for the wharves with what I hoped was the unobtrusive dignity of the poorer caste of free colored women. In a dockside chop house window, I found the posted public notices, some on paper already yellowed and curling, others still damp from the printer. I scanned the listings of slaves and merchandise for sale, Negroes confined as runaways and vagrants in need of identification. Then I found the item I sought:

> Ran away the 20th instant, a Negro Man, over six feet tall, heavy build, baldheaded, very black, 30 years of age. Answers to the name of Samson. Very knowledgable in all shipboard skills. Property of Captain Chas. Murdock at the Prince William. Reward offered.

I memorized the particulars and was about to hurry off when another notice caught my eye:

> Substantial Reward Offered for information leading to the capture of Pirates in the waters of Cuba and the Bahamas. Descriptions and whereabouts of said Pirates most particularly desired. Reply to office of the Deputy Provost Marshal, Court House.

I kept my expression unchanged, but my heart was

pounding. I took one cautious step back, away from the notices, then stopped, aware that someone was standing very near behind me. Expecting at any moment the iron grip of a magistrate's hand on my arm, I fought down the guilty urge to flee and instead glanced surreptitiously around. But it was only some shabbily dressed fellow, compact and wiry, bent slightly forward, reading the notices. His short, cropped hair was receding from a broad, bony forehead, and as he read, his hand came up unconsciously to rub the right side of his jaw. I could not look away. There was a tattoo below the knuckles. A small blue snake.

Adderly.

I hadn't recognized him without the brutal confidence of rank with which he'd paraded around the *New Hope*. He seemed physically smaller without it, or perhaps it was the way he was stooping to read the notices. Nor was he puffed up with rage, as he'd been the last time we met. But I knew how dangerous he was, and I was already moving sideways, like a crab, to slip away when his gray eyes rose to meet mine. He straightened up as I turned away.

"I know you."

I froze, afraid to turn back around. Of all the damned strange fish to wash up in Tortola now. He'd known me only as Tom Jones, seaman, had never seen me in female dress. Would he know my face?

"I don't think so, sir."

"Wait. I think I do!" In one swift stride, he was standing before me, eyes sharp. He was not much taller than I, and not big, but he was quick and sinewy. Strong. I knew to my cost how strong he was, could feel his arm round my throat, even now. I dared not let him gain any advantage, but neither could I tumble him over on his backside and run in the middle of a busy public street at noon.

"Sir, I'm afraid—"

"You're the acrobatic wench. I saw you yesterday by the docks."

I'd seen him, too, of course, when I was juggling with

Jack. How could I not have placed him? And he'd seen Jack,
too. Had he recognized him from the pirate crew? Had he lingered long enough to spot Hector? Jack had shaved his beard,
at least, but Hector looked exactly as he had on the day he'd
nearly choked off Adderly's life on the deck of the *New Hope*.
Adderly was not likely to ever forget him. As a runaway slave,
Hector would be flogged, but pirates were hanged. From the
look of him, now, with his torn jacket and dirty linen, I guessed
Adderly was no longer sailing with the Yankee Squadron. But
he looked very much in need of a reward. How easily it might
be Jack as well as Hector paraded through the streets in captiv-
ity, betrayed for profit. All our fates rested with this man.

"Why, yes, sir." I forced a smile. "How kind of you to
notice me."

"Don't see many wenches in that line. Where's that fellow you were with?"

My heartbeat faltered. I tried not to imagine Jack's long
neck with a rope around it.

"He's gone. Off-island to some wealthier port."

"And left you here all alone? With no man to protect
you?" He took a tentative step closer, his fingers starting to rub
his jaw again, but his smile was sympathetic. "Then we've
something in common, you and I. I know what it is to be cast
off in an unfriendly port. Pity, though, a fine, handsome girl
like you."

I did not know how to color on command, but I lowered my eyes and squeezed out another weak smile. Buckra or
not, with no ship and no money, he could never hope to attract
a respectable colored mistress or buy a dockside whore.
Perhaps a friendly female might distract him, for a while. Had I
only been quick enough, I might have warned Jack and Hector
not to come into town together; if Adderly remembered no one
else from the *Providence*, he would remember Hector. But now
that he had seen me, spoken to me, I dared not leave him alone.
He might not yet recognize me as Tom Jones, but I couldn't
allow him a single free moment to reflect upon the matter. I
must give him no opportunity to take himself off to the

Deputy Provost Marshal.

"For true, sir, I don't know what will become of me." I sighed. "I'm all alone, now."

"Why, it can't be as bad as all that," he responded gently, and I struggled to master the strangeness of it. The Adderly I'd known had never been gentle. "He didn't damage you, did he? Your fellow? Leave you with no means to live?"

"I can earn a good living," I said, glancing at my hands. "But . . . as a woman, I'm not allowed to practice my trade without a man to employ me." I entirely fabricated this, but it seemed as plausible as any other rule for public female behavior. It must look as if I had some reason to offer myself to him so brazenly.

"Like that, is it?" He was smiling, now, intrigued. "Aye, a seaport's a wretched place to be without a friend. I know." Then he stuck out his hand. "Name's Adderly, Miss. Tom Adderly."

I dipped my head and put my hand in his, hoping my calluses would seem to be from juggling and not ship's ropes.

"I'm called . . . Ophelia." It was surely madness to attempt this. But I had no choice.

"Will you come inside and take a drink with me, Ophelia?"

"Is there some place more private we can go . . . Tom?"

That took him by surprise, but I needed to get him alone, by whatever means. I wanted no witnesses about, should he suddenly recover his memory.

"I've a room nearby," he volunteered. I nodded, and he threaded my hand through the crook of his elbow, patting it in place like a gallant. "Come with me. It's not far."

The walls of Tom Adderly's room were of raw, splintered wood, and a stench of sour wine and old urine hung in the air from the grog shop below. Near the door, a piece of a cracked glass was nailed to the wall above a washstand—a little table on which a chipped crockery jug stood in a tin basin. In the opposite corner, about four feet away, a sagging, straw-filled mattress dressed in dingy linens lay rumpled upon a wooden bed. The only other furnishing was a small chair drawn up to the bed, on which sat a single naked candle in a saucer. There was no chest or wardrobe in the room; Adderly was apparently wearing the only clothing he possessed. How far Fortune must have tumbled him from his lofty perch as first mate aboard the *New Hope*—with no little help from me. But for me, he might be a man of some prosperity, now.

I was glad when he produced a bottle of cheap, acrid wine. But while it might poison us, it wouldn't get Adderly drunk enough unless I made sure he drank it all; seamen were accustomed to much stronger stuff. We sat side-by-side on the edge of the bed, and I kept talking while he sipped from his glass. I watched him down one full glass while I embroidered a fanciful tale of my life as a strolling performer on islands as far removed from Cuba as I could think of. But at last, he interrupted my flow of words with a tattooed hand laid gently on my knee.

"Why have we come here, Ophelia?" His smile was kind, but his expression said he would not be put off forever.

My entire body clenched at his touch, but I stayed still, letting his eager hand knead my leg through the worn linen skirt. There were so many secret places in my body that only Jack knew of, that I could not bear to let this stranger touch. But I must submit, for all our sakes. Jack would be frantic; how long before he and Hector came looking for me? I must not allow Adderly back out into the streets. I could trade my body for Jack's life, and Hector's, if it would keep Tom Adderly in this room long enough to fall asleep or drink himself into a stupor.

"Because . . . I need a friend."

He shifted closer and put his hand over mine.

"I'm your friend," he murmured.

"Yes . . . ." I made myself smile. "Tom."

He turned my hand palm up and lifted it toward his

mouth, but paused when his thumb grazed the tiny cross scratched into the underside of my index finger. My pirate mark. Could he know what it was? The Yankee Squadron had apprehended many pirates in Cuba. I saw his brows knit slightly together, puzzled, saw his eyes lower.

My free hand dove into the split seam of my skirt and grasped the dagger I kept strapped to my thigh; in an instant, its sharp point was pressed into the soft flesh under Tom Adderly's jaw. Reading the fear and anger in his frozen-open eyes, I yanked my other hand away—and wondered what to do next.

"Take off your clothes," I commanded, in a husky whisper. Then I smiled.

He didn't move. I played the tip of my blade very gently, very slowly, along the underside of his jaw. He swallowed once, carefully, and I saw the confusion of unease and arousal in his eyes.

"Or aren't you ready for me?" I got to my feet to stand above him, dagger still at his throat, and drew the hem of my skirt up above my knees. A tentative grin began to tug at his mouth.

"Little hellion, are ye?"

"I like to see what I'm getting."

He stood, too, slowly. He backed away from my dagger, and I let him. He unwrapped the single length of his ragged cravat, unbuttoned his collar and hauled off his shirt. He was all lean, hardened flesh and sinew underneath; I could almost count the ribs below his smooth, hairless chest. He unfastened his trousers and stepped out of them, then stood before me, touchingly naked in his wrinkled stockings and scuffed shoes, his ruddy organ standing out from a thicket of coarse brown fuzz. And I felt a pang of something almost sympathetic, looking at him—he seemed so vulnerable. So different from the arrogant merchant seaman who'd taken such pleasure in harassing me aboard the *New Hope*, who'd tried to throw me senseless into the sea. Yet, I knew the stringy, snake-like power in those sinewy arms and legs should I suddenly find myself grap-

pling against them for my life. There was a better way to subdue him, but I would need more fortification.

"Ready enough for you, now, am I?" He grinned.

"All but the shoes," I teased. He lowered himself onto
the edge of the bed and bent over his feet, and I turned round
to the washstand, where the half-empty wine bottle stood. I
reached for it, pausing for a silent moment to warn my stomach what was coming.

A movement in the looking-glass before me caught my
eye. Tom Adderly rose up suddenly from the bed behind me,
white limbs spreading toward me like a spider out of the gloom,
lunging across the narrow space between us. My dagger was in
the wrong hand, but I felt the neck of the bottle under my
grasping fingers and raised it aloft. I spun around, liquid pouring down my upraised arm, and as he reached me, I cracked the
bottle down against the side of his head. His whole body
swerved with the impact, and he crumpled to the floor.

The sudden silence was thunderous in the wake of the
bursting glass. I slumped back against the washstand, shaking,
staring down at the naked body sprawled at my feet. Some remnant of wit made me utter a high, kittenish laugh, as if nothing
were amiss in the room, but it sounded ghoulish. The broken
bottle neck slipped out of my right hand, and I seized back the
dagger and raised it aloft, staring down at Tom Adderly's back,
corded with sinew and pale flogging scars. A seaman's back. I
ought to finish the job, now I'd begun. Nada would do it. Any
of the men would do it. Lives were at stake—mine, Jack's and
Hector's, and I was running out of time.

But as often as my hand reared up, clutching the dagger, I could not plunge it home. Adderly had bullied me and
harried me aboard the *New Hope*—even tried to murder me.
He could identify the pirates of the *Blessed Providence* to the
authorities; his testimony could get them all hanged. If ever it
was necessary to take a life, I had reason to take his.

But his only crime today had been taking in a woman
he thought had been abandoned. Taken her in for his own grat-
ification, of course, with an eye to his own living, perhaps, but

at her request. Hellfire, at her insistence. He'd said or done nothing to indicate he recognized me, made no threats. He was a poor fellow, now, thanks to me, far from home, obviously out of employment without a friend in the world. Abandoned by Fortune. As Jack had been, once. As I had been, myself. And I lowered my dagger for the last time, muttered a curse, and stuck it back into its sheath under my skirt.

I knew how much harm he could cause if he talked. Would anyone believe what he said? I withdrew my hand from my skirt and answered myself. The tiny white cross on my finger. Jack's finger bore the same mark. So did Hector's. Perhaps other pirates Porter's men captured or killed were marked in the same way. Adderly would be able to name the merchant ship from which he had been taken, whose encounter with Cuban pirates would be a matter of public record by now. He could claim his association with the squadron ship that had picked him up in the open sea. Whatever had happened to him, since, the records would prove him an eyewitness to piracy.

No, he must not talk.

He must not leave this room. Not until Jack and Hector and I could get off this island.

I was glad to feel the slow, slight respiration in his lungs as I hooked my arms under his and dragged him back to the bed. The slackness of his limbs made him heavy. Bracing one foot on the bedstead, I had to heft his limp torso up onto the mattress, then hoist up his legs. I peeled back the bedding and rolled him into the middle of the bare mattress. Fishing out my dagger again, I cut the sheet into long strips and used them to bind his hands and feet, tying the loose ends of both knots together. Then I found his cravat, doused it in the water in the jug and wrung it out, finally stuffing it into Adderly's mouth, as gently as I could. I shook out the blanket and threw it over his naked body, leaving only his head exposed, turned away from the door. With a broken wine bottle so nearby, he might be seen to be sleeping off a drunken carouse. Should anyone trouble to look.

Still, I would have to hurry. I could only pray I'd

bought myself enough time.

CHAPTER 29

Refuge

Jack would be out of his mind. It was nearly two hours since I'd marched into the town and disappeared; he would think me murdered, robbed, taken up for a runaway. Or a pirate. There were no end of calamities that might befall our fragile existence in this place, and Jack would imagine them all. What if he and Hector had come looking for me? What if someone else had captured Hector for a runaway and Jack . . . but I could not let myself consider all the possibilities. I must press forward, think only of what was yet to do, certainly not about what I'd left behind. And I turned off the road and headed for the outcropping of rock and short, scrubby trees on a rise above the town.

As I drew closer, Jack's head rose up to peer over a rock, and he saw me. He bolted over the rock and raced down to meet me, catching me by the waist and crushing me against him and all my bravery and resolve began to drain away. I dared only let him hold me for an instant, or I should have wept like an infant, like a female, and there was so little time. My hands were trembling on his chest as I pushed him back.

"Rusty, where in the bloody hell . . . ." His anger was automatic, but I knew from his embrace how frightened he'd been.

"There's no time!"

Jack swallowed the rest of his words, but his eyes searched my face. "Tell me you're all right."

"*Si, hombre*. The reward is posted. We have to hurry!"

He released me and turned toward the rocks where Hector was waiting, holding out the fishnet sling.

"Let's go, then."

The Prince William was another waterfront tavern with a couple of damp rooms upstairs to let to mariners putting into Road Bay. Captain Charles Murdock, seated alone in a back corner of the taproom, disliked having his dinner chop interrupted by the three of us—his escaped slave accompanied by a couple of beggarly jugglers.

"Why, the ink is scarcely dry on the notice," barked Murdock. "Devilish eager for your reward, hey?"

"Reward, sir?" Jack echoed, with a guileless smile. "We stumbled upon this fellow by the roadside this morning. I knew him from yesterday, when he did a job of work for me. I knew he belonged to you, so I thought there must be something amiss."

"Something may indeed be amiss," repeated Murdock, narrowing his eyes, "if you took it into your head to spirit off my property last night to claim a reward today."

"Do you doubt my word as an Englishman, sir?" Jack regarded Murdock with cool authority, reminding him, perhaps, that this was a public room, and he was not a slave to be abused. Reminding him that it was color and not pedigree that counted in the Indies. Jack's color was as good as Murdock's,

his bearing far more assured in this moment, despite his tattered clothing.

"I should be very sorry, if that is what you thought."

What a performer Jack was, standing there with ice in
his veins, demanding respect without even raising his voice,
when I was ready to collapse if given half a chance. But I'd not
given myself half a chance; had Jack held or comforted me one
moment longer, I'd have come apart. This was all that mattered
now, this interview. Murdock blinked several times, then his
gaze dropped to his plate.

"Samson has never run off before," he muttered.

"Naw, sir," Hector interrupted, immobile, eyes downcast, absolutely calm. "I be lost."

"Lost?" cried Murdock, rising to his feet, grateful for a
target upon whom he could freely vent his irritation. "Lost,
from here to the wharf? No, sir, you were never lost!"

"I be lost," Hector repeated, and I heard in his calm
passivity a self-possession more challenging than outright inso-
lence. Murdock perceived it too, and his cheeks flamed to the
same hue as his nose.

"Then I shall escort you myself to the ship, where you
shall answer to the cat for causing me this vexation. And
expense," he added, with a resentful glance at Jack. But he
fished in a pocket inside his coat and withdrew two coins,
which he laid on the edge of the little table, in front of Jack.
Two gold Spanish doubloons. A little more than fifteen English
pounds. Thirty-two dollars. "I, too, am a man of my word,"
Murdock declared. Then he led Hector toward the door.

Passing us, Hector threw a swift glance over his shoulder from me to Jack to the doubloons, nodding once with satisfaction when Jack scooped them up off the table.

But I could not look at Jack as we emerged out of the
Prince William into the heat of the afternoon. I felt as if every
pair of eyes we passed in the street was staring at us—Judases
who sold human flesh for profit. Despite his bold words,
Hector was now back in the possession of Murdock, who was
likely flogging him at this very moment. And it was our fault.

We could do nothing to help him. We would scarcely be able to
help ourselves, should Adderly somehow get free to accuse us
of one or more of our various crimes. But I had no anxiety to
spare for that. We headed for the road out of town and followed
it eastward all the way to Runaway Bay to collect our gourds as
the sun dipped toward the water.

It was long after dark when we returned to the African
village. Asia had left us a dish of stewed vegetables in a covered pot in the storeroom, but we could not eat . . . could not
speak . . . couldn't bear to touch each other. We climbed into
our shared bed and lay apart in the darkness, cocooned in our
separate melancholies.

How long had we lain in the silent dark, our thoughts
in turmoil? I heard Jack stir, behind me. How long had it been
since we'd spoken? The ghost of Hector in chains seemed to
stand between us in the bed, his stoic silence a kind of reproach.
Would he always be between us now, keeping us apart? Would
we hate each other for what we had done? I felt Jack's tentative
touch on my shoulder at last, but I could not respond.

"Rusty . . . ?"

Then, I could not stop myself. "Jack," I rasped, "hold
me. Please . . . ."

His breath came out in a rush, and he reached for me,
gathering me close in his arms. His hands moved up and down
my spine, sculpting me to him like a second skin. My arms
locked around him, and my hands slithered up his back, fingers
curling like claws into his shoulders. I buried my face in his
chest, but did not stay there long. I began kissing his chest and
his throat and his neck, my mouth searching upwards for his.
Devoured by my desperate mouth, cradled between my legs,
Jack rolled onto his back beneath me, holding me close, giving
himself up to me to use as gently or as fiercely as I needed.
When I was almost spent, he rolled us both over again and bur-
rowed deeper inside me. This was all we had, our bodies, the
refuge of our love. Our only refuge.

"He won't be badly hurt," Jack murmured, some time
later, as if we'd been conversing all this time. "Not if he's need-

ed to hoist yards and heave up the anchor all the way to Cuba."

"I know." My head was tucked under his chin, one of my fingers gently circling the mole over his heart. "I only wish . . . ." But I didn't know what I wished. I could only inch closer into the comfort of Jack's warm body.

"Oh, *mi vida*," he whispered. "In a few days we'll be away from here. We needn't even stay in these islands, now. If you'd rather, we could sail for South America. Try to find the *Providence*."

For an instant, my heart thrilled to the thought of a wooden deck beneath my feet again, of climbing aloft and tasting the salt and feeling the wind on my face and the lines humming in my hands. Of working side by side with our old *compañeros*. But the *Providence* was a warship for hire now, fighting someone else's war. Fighting for freedom, true enough, but fighting the way men fought, without restraint or reason, driven from their homes with something to prove, slaughtering for glory.

"It would never be the same, *hombre*. Not for me."

"Barbados, then? Track down your handsome diplomat?"

I could not tell if he was jesting, so I bit back a caustic reply and softened my voice. I had learned a little something about acting. "You mean you wouldn't mind?"

"I'd mind." His voice went flat on the instant. "but I wouldn't stop you."

"You had better stop me if I'm ever fool enough to chase off to Barbados for no good reason when everything I want in the world is right here. Everything."

That silenced him for the moment, and I settled my head on his shoulder again.

"What about you, *hombre*?"

"There's nothing I want in Barbados."

"But won't you miss the pirate life?"

Jack thought it over. "I served aboard the *Providence* for nearly five years, and in all that time, I'd have gladly laid down my life for Ed Hart or Nada or Hector—any of 'em—

and considered it a fair bargain. But . . ." He paused to kiss the top of my head. "I have something to lose, now. Something to live for."

"So have I, my sweet heart," I whispered, closing my eyes. "I earned a man's freedom aboard the *Providence*, and I cherished it. I pray to whatever gods there are that I won't lose it. But there are too many things I like about being female." My hand moved down very lightly to his groin with a caress so tender, he shivered with it. "And I'm done with being a counterfeit man. Besides," I added, after a long pause, "I'm not fit for it any more."

Something in my expression sobered him. He was quiet for another long moment before he spoke again.

"What happened today, Rusty?"

And I began to tell him, softly, but without hesitation, about the posted reward for pirates and Tom Adderly and the tiny upstairs room. Jack did not interrupt, letting me sort through all I had seen and reasoned and felt in the telling. Only when I spoke of smashing the wine bottle over Adderly's head did my recitation slow, and then stop.

"I . . . could not kill him," I spoke again, at last. "I knew it was dangerous to let him live, but . . . ." I shook my head in the cradle of Jack's shoulder.

"You're very certain this fellow didn't harm you?" It was the first thing he had said.

"He scarcely touched me. I never even meant to strike him, but he took me by surprise, and then . . . he looked so helpless. He had flogging stripes on his back. I . . . could not do it."

"What did you do?"

I told him about the bedsheet ropes and the cravat gag. "And one other thing. I took his clothes."

"Took them? Where?"

"I don't know, stuffed them in an oxcart outside. I couldn't risk him running out into the street, could I? I thought if anyone found him like that, with nothing to his name, he might be taken up for vagrancy. He's a white man, he won't be sold for a slave. At least he'll be off the streets for a few more days if he's taken for a vagrant."

"After knocking himself on the head, tying himself hand and foot and throwing away his own clothes?" Jack reasoned. "He's far more likely to be taken for a victim of robbery and assault."

"I . . . guess I've made a mess of things."

"Complicated things, perhaps. They may be looking for a female thief next time we go into town. We'll have to be careful."

"I've put you in even more danger, *hombre*," I groaned.

Jack gave a soft laugh. "Do you suppose I'd want you to murder the fellow in cold blood? I'd never again feel safe in your bed."

"But had I only been bold enough to silence him—"

"Aye, that would have been the manly thing to do."

I frowned up at him.

"Any fool can kill, Rusty," Jack went on, softly. "It gets easier every time. Desperate people will do anything to survive in the Indies. But not everyone has the wit to make a choice about how they're going to do it."

"That doesn't mean I made the right choice."

"We can't know that. That's Fortune's business."

I didn't know if I ought to allow myself to feel any better. "We did get Hector back safe to his ship. That was the important thing."

"I got you back safe, *mi vida*. That's all that matters."

I crept a little deeper into his embrace and sighed. "How can everything be so complicated on dry land? Things were so simple aboard the *Providence*."

"Survival is simple." Jack yawned. "It's civilization that's so damned exhausting."

He was quiet for so long, I thought he must have gone to sleep. But I couldn't stop thinking. My fingertips traced the long, relaxed muscle of Jack's thigh, the slight rise and fall of breath in his belly and the slow, steady beating of his heart in his chest. What a wonder it was, a life. What a fragile alchemy of blood and flesh and bone, how easily extinguished. There were a thousand ways for a man to die, that's what Captain Hart said. The trick, the challenge, was to live.

I stroked Jack's hand, very gently. He had such competent hands, callused, flexible, long-fingered, hard-working hands. Hands for building a life. I felt a tiny quarter moon of a scar at the base of his thumb, the relic of some childhood tumbling accident, perhaps, or some piratical engagement. All of Jack's scars, like his life, were precious to me. I drew his hand to my mouth and kissed the scar.

"Mmm?" he murmured, drowsy and pleased.

"You are so beautiful, Jack. Every part of you."

"You're dreaming, *mi vida*." But I could hear the smile in his sleepy voice.

CHAPTER 30

Contra Todo el Mundo

It reminded me of my flight from Boston on that bitter night so long ago. Here I was again, running away in the dark, disguised in male clothing. Running for a ship. But this time, my clothes were my own from the pirate trade, my old moss-green canvas trousers and white shirt with my long braid of hair tucked under the collar. I wore a concealing woollen jacket over all, bought second-hand at the Road Town market. We were taking no chances, in case a *mulatta* woman was being sought on suspicion of assault. And this time, I was not alone. I had Jack, and that made all the difference. And now we had something to run toward. A new life. Together.

Jack had gone into town alone yesterday to convert one doubloon into smaller coins and contract for our passage aboard the English trading barque, *Phoenix.* Her master, a merry little salt called Captain Redmond, had plied his trade for years between the British Leewards and Bristol. But he'd never sailed west of Tortola and knew nothing of the Spanish islands. Before sunup this morning, we'd taken the road into town for the last time, leaving four Spanish dollars in a calabash bowl in the storeroom for Asia to find.

With the end of the gale season, transatlantic shipping had returned to the Indies. There was already a bustle of activity around White Wharf even at this hour, in spite of the thick night fog that still drifted across the water in Road Bay. The dawn had lightened to grey morning when we found shelter on a scrubby hill overlooking the main street and the wharf and beaches below. From here, we could see the blue boat from the *Phoenix* tied up under the wharf, awaiting the last of her stores. The clean lines of the *Phoenix* herself, along with perhaps two or three other vessels, could be glimpsed now and then far out in the roadstead, looming like ghosts out of the fog.

Jack's watchful gaze drifted back over to me, and I smiled at him.

"Frightened?" he asked.

I shook my head. "Eager. To be gone."

"*Y yo, compañera.*" He turned back to the quiet scene below. He wanted to wait until the *Phoenix* boat was ready to pull away before we went aboard, so as not to give her crew too many idle moments to contemplate my disguise. The more quickly we appeared, mustered aboard the *Phoenix* and got ourselves below, the safer we would be.

When the last of the ship's stores were carried down to the blue boat, we left the shelter of the scrub, trotted down the slope and across the main street and made for the foot of the wharf. The boat would be in a hurry to leave so as not to lose the outbound tide. A few more people were milling about the waterfront now, and I had to dodge around a couple of idle fellows standing in my path to the wharf. The little canvas sack of belongings I carried swung awkwardly behind me as I maneuvered round them, thudding into someone's shin, and when I heard a growled oath, I flung a quick smile back over my shoulder with a conciliatory, "Sorry, sir—"

And almost froze.

I was staring back into the face of Tom Adderly.

He looked bulkier, in a suit of too-big borrowed clothing, but there was no mistaking his foot-planted seaman's stance or the angry purple bruise on the side of his bony forehead. Or the puzzled attention in his gray eyes as he peered at my face, then took in the rest of my outfit. His eyes narrowed and his mouth worked, soundlessly for an instant. Then his expression cleared with dumbstruck recognition.

"Jones," he breathed, as I stumbled farther away. He took a step after me, but his companion caught his arm.

"Here, you," the other man warned. "You've new clothing and transportation at the Governor's expense. Wait quiet for the packet now, and don't go accosting lads in the street."

"But, Constable," Adderly spluttered. "He's . . . that's . . . . "

Jack shouldered past them, intent on blocking their view of me until he could bundle me off down the wharf for the boat. But Adderly caught his arm and spun him halfway around. Unable to wrench himself away, Jack hissed at me in Spanish to run for the boat and freed his arm with a fist across the fellow's jaw. But Tom Adderly was a tough character, staggered but not felled by the blow and gasping with rage. The words we heard clearly were "watch" and "pirates," but as Jack wheeled around to follow me, he nearly bowled me over where I stood; two more fellows in short brown cloaks like the constable's were running up the wharf toward us, cutting off our access to the *Phoenix* boat.

Every instinct told us to dive sideways onto the sandy shoulder, run down the beach, perhaps swim out to where the *Phoenix* boat was loading up at the far end of the wharf. But there was no running in sand, not with our pursuers this close. I spun back around in the direction we'd come and Jack pivoted with me. He swung his own canvas satchel in a wide arc before us to clear back Adderly and the constable as we raced up the path for the square and the protection of the few streets, alleys and commercial buildings that Road Town had to offer.

The shouting continued behind us. But there was no one yet abroad in the streets to impede us, only a few slaves, who flattened themselves into the shadows until the commotion passed by. We fled down one street, darted through a narrow alley into a back street and doubled back behind a dry goods shop until Adderly and the others ran past and disappeared around the next corner. Then we raced back through the alley, across a broad street to the main road and the steep, scrubby hills above, finding refuge at last behind an outcropping of ashy black rock and scrub trees and cactus.

"Who . . . ?" I panted, fighting for breath, ". . . those other . . . . "

"Night watch . . . just going off duty . . . but, the constable . . . has the authority . . . . "

Jack couldn't keeping talking and breathing at the same time, but I did not care to know in so many words what the constable of the watch was authorized to do. Sound alarms, I supposed. Catch pirates, certainly.

"We have to get away from here," I began, and Jack nodded, preoccupied with peering through the scrub trees to the wharf, below. I crawled over and looked out over his shoulder. The blue *Phoenix* boat was pulling away from the wharf on the outbound tide, disappearing into the fog. Jack and I exchanged a look.

"I'm getting you off this island, Rusty."

"We're getting off," I corrected him. I sprang around to his other side and shinnied up a rock to get a better look at the beach below. My blood was pumping too high for despair; life was singing too strong in my veins. Jack laid out beside me, and we scanned the beaches that stretched away on either side of the wharf. I spotted them first—two little boats, bumboats or fishing boats, moored in the sand above the waterline a scant half-mile up the beach from the wharf.

"The *Phoenix* is still out there," Jack whispered. "For a while, yet."

"You men, search the hills!" boomed suddenly from below, and we plunged back down into the protection of the scrub, peering downward. At the foot of the hill, off to the right of our hiding place, we saw Adderly, the constable and one watchman waiting in the road. Three others were jogging toward them from the direction of the Court House.

"This had better not be a joke, Mr. Adderly," one of them grumbled.

"Catch the lad, and I'll make him talk!" Adderly retorted. "That damned Spaniard with him must be another one."

"Come, gentlemen, there's a Crown reward for pirates," barked the constable, gesturing toward the slope of the hill.

Jack sat back on his heels, grabbed his satchel and extracted the fishnet sling with our few juggling gourds, yams and hard green fruits. He handed over the canvas satchel with the rest of his things to me, to fold into my own sack with my logbook and my few scraps of female clothing. I drew the straps snugly over my shoulder.

"Cut out one of those boats and get it into the water," Jack whispered nodding toward the left where the boats lay on the beach. "Don't stop. I'll give you as much cover as I can." I suppose I looked as if I might argue, because he added, "I'll be right behind you."

Some of the men below were starting to ascend the hill. Jack plucked out the fattest, hardest yam in his sling and crept up into a crouch. He found a clear shot between the trees and hurled it a great way up the hill to the right, behind them. The watchmen were making such a commotion clomping up the slope that they might not have heard the initial thump of the yam itself. But the sudden noisy skittering of loosened pebbles and gravel as the yam began to roll down the hill caught the attention of all the men below. When a flying gourd made a satisfying clunk against a tree trunk even higher up the hill in the same direction, all the men began swarming up the slope to follow the sound.

Ready with another yam to distract pursuit, Jack nodded to me, and I scampered down the hill to the left, darting first behind this boulder, then to that scrubby patch of brush until I was down in the main road. I sprinted across it and fled down a back street behind a row of residences, cut behind a warehouse and found a cart trail that led down to the shore. I followed the footpath above the shoreline—where there was still an occasional palm or mango tree for cover—until I got to where the boats sat in the sand. Fishing boats, waiting for the fog to lift on the water.

I didn't see anyone around, but there was no time to make sure. I heard distant shouting behind me now, so I plowed out into the powdery sand. I passed the nearer boat with its two oars lying in the sand alongside, and made my way out to the second boat, closer to the water. I checked that its oars were inside, hefted my two satchels inboard, grabbed the painter dangling out of the bow and dragged its head around toward the receding waterline. The sand was damp and firm down here, and I dug in my heels and pulled again, and the boat rocked a little closer to the water. The foam was just lapping at my heels when shouts of "That's him!" and "There he goes!" made me look back up the beach. Jack came racing around a corner, pursued by two watchmen, heading down an incline toward the shoreline footpath and the beach below, his attention focused on me and the boat.

He didn't see the officer on horseback galloping along the footpath to cut him off. But I did, and I dropped the painter and raced up the beach. Jack saw them now too, but he had too much momentum to stop; he could only fly, pushing himself off the higher ground and vaulting across the footpath just in front of the horse, tucking in his head and aiming for the soft sand on the other side. But he landed without so much as a gourd left to defend himself.

I leaped, too, for the discarded oars beside the other boat, shouting to Jack in Spanish so that when he came up out of his roll and gained his feet, he was ready to catch the oar I tossed to him. He grasped it by its paddle end and spun around, sweeping it in a complete arc behind him. The horse, in the midst of being reined about, reared up at this fresh alarm while the cursing officer struggled to stay aboard. One of the watchmen on foot was also obliged to dive aside, which irritation panicked the animal anew, and the horse bolted down the foot-path above the beach, his rider still aboard.

But the other watchman had jumped clear of the commotion and lurched into the sand after Jack—who was already spinning back around the other way with the oar upraised in both his hands. The impact of the oar across the watchman's chest forced all the wind out of him, knocking the fellow to the ground.

I was grabbing for the second oar when a black man in a straw hat sat up in the boat, glaring at me and blinking at all the confusion. A pistol shot was fired, the Negro fisherman disappeared into the bottom of his boat again, and I heard Jack yelling at me to get to the boat. I sprinted down the beach without a backward glance, grabbed the painter and hauled for the water with every ounce of strength I had left. I was thigh-deep in the tide before the water took the bow. Then Jack splashed out beside me and grasped the end of the line, and together we dragged at the boat until the sandy bottom fell away under our feet. There was another pistol pop from the shore, and I scrambled into the boat and got out the oars, crouching low over the thwart, while Jack swam ahead with the painter. He climbed in behind me when the fog cut off our view of the shore.

"Did I not tell you to get the boat in the water?" he panted.

"Aye, and we're in the water. If you also expected me to leave you unarmed on the beach, you chose the wrong partner."

Jack swallowed the rest of his complaint and glanced round the boat. "Damn, I should have kept that oar," he muttered, when he saw our boat carried only two.

"How far out do you think the *Phoenix* is?" I asked, rowing deeper into the perfect muffling whiteness of the fog.

"I don't know. I scarcely even saw her this morning."

"West End or East End?"

Jack shook his head. "Can you tell the difference from here? I can't."

I tried not to shiver in the damp chill. I was soaked,

breathless and exhausted already, and the sun was barely up. Yet I felt vividly, foolishly, alive.

"At least they won't be able to see where we go."

Jack started to nod, then tensed, alert. I stilled the oars and felt it, too. The water was beginning to wash in long swells beneath us, as if lapping against something solid in the gloom. Then we heard the soft, hollow thunking sound of water against the hull of a ship. We waited, silent in the whiteness, until a ragged hole tore in the fog, revealing a dark hull looming ahead. Urging the boat closer, we could just make out her sail plan. Two masts, square-rigged. A merchant brig, not a three-masted barque. Not the *Phoenix*.

Maneuvering into her wake, we drew up under her stern and read the fading paintwork: *Determined*.

"Hector's ship," I breathed.

Jack nodded, staring up at the brig. There were a few fellows up in the rigging, none of them Hector.

"Close as you can for another minute, Rusty."

The *Determined* was starting to pull away, but I kept rowing. Jack stretched up from his seat, cupped his hands round his mouth and made the mournful cry of a gull. He repeated it three times, then stopped, waited. Then he repeated the three cries again. A moment later, Hector's bald black head appeared above the rail on the starboard quarter. When he finally looked back our way, Jack waved. Hector watched us for a moment, then his head disappeared.

The brig was making better time now, pulling for the open roadstead, moving away, and I could not keep pace. Then Hector appeared again at the taffrail, head and thick shoulders and torso stretching beyond the rail for an instant as he bundled something over and let it drop into the water. Jack crept into the bow, urging the boat forward until he could make out what it was—a towline rove through a wooden deadeye to keep it afloat. Jack reached out of the boat to haul in the line. When we had warped in safely under the brig's stern, more or less out of sight of her deck, he slipped off the deadeye and rove the line through the ringbolt that held the painter inboard in our little boat. I folded in the oars and scrambled aft while Jack took my place on the middle thwart.

"We'll get a tow out of the bay, at any rate," he said.

"Do you think they'll come after us?"

"If the Governor keeps a cutter or some other fast vessel to hand, they might. They must be fairly serious if they mustered a horse; I've only seen mules and oxen before. And if Adderly's story is convincing enough. It's clear he told 'em they were chasing pirates and not a thieving female."

"And if they can see anything in this fog," I added.

Jack nodded, looking upwards again. We could no longer see much of the sails of the *Determined*, nor more than ten feet in any direction on the water.

"We're bound to run into some sort of shipping out in the road, Rusty, sooner or later. Even . . . if we miss the *Phoenix*. We can say we were shipwrecked in the fog and someone will pick us up."

We could only pray it would not be someone putting into Road Town.

"Or we could go aboard the *Determined*. Take passage for Cuba," Jack went on. "Murdock would be glad to get what's left of his doubloons back."

"But what about Hector?"

"It was his idea."

I blinked at him, not following his meaning.

"The other day, when you took such an infernal long time about your business in Road Town. Hector proposed we come back to Cabo Cruz with him. Take up the fisherfolk life, ashore."

I gazed up again at the *Determined*. What if this was our only passage out of Road Bay? Could Jack's restless nature ever be content catching fish for a living? Could mine?

"But if we're pursued by a boat from the shore, we can't lead them to the *Determined*," I reasoned. "We mustn't give Adderly a chance to see Hector too."

"Aye," Jack agreed. "We can't risk it."

"Besides," I ventured, "would you not find it awkward?

Going back to live with Hector and Jasmine?"

"Very."

"So would I."

Jack smiled, a little sadly, and noticed me hugging myself against the cold.

"You look like a shipwreck victim, at that. Why don't you wrap up in something for a while."

"Wait. I have a better idea." I fished my canvas sack out from under the thwart, and Jack leaned forward to check the towline. When he turned back again, I was out of my soggy jacket and peeling my damp shirt off over my head.

Jack's mouth twitched toward a grin. "Aye, that is a splendid idea, but this is hardly the moment."

"Idiot." I wiped as much salty brine as I could from my hands and arms and upper body with my shirt. Then bundled it away and pulled out the plain overdress and long linen skirt Asia had given me. "As you said, they'll be looking for pirates, not women." I unlaced my trousers and carried out my meta-morphosis.

Jack sat watching me, his expression melancholy.

"I wish it were so easy to change what we are," he murmured.

I looked up at him, sharply. "I don't want to change what I am." I crouched down before him, my hands on his knees, my eyes searching his face. "If my life ends in this boat here, today, with you, I'll not regret a thing, Jack. Not one thing."

Jack took my face in both his hands, his eyes as fierce as my words.

"Neither will I, *mi vida. Contra todo el mundo.*"

Something splashed in the water alongside the boat and when we looked all around and up, we saw Hector's face peering down from the stern of the *Determined.* He made a nod to port, and we strained to peer through the white gloom. As the mist thinned, we could see one dark shape not far away and another, farther out. The nearer was a coasting sloop. But on the farther ship, we counted three masts, rigged fore-and-aft on the mizzen, like a barque. The davits on her starboard quarter held a blue ship's boat.

The *Phoenix*.

Hector, watching us, gave a questioning shrug, and Jack pointed to the *Phoenix*. When we were as close as we were likely to get before the *Determined* veered to westward out of the bay for Cuba, Jack unfastened the towline and tossed it into the water for Hector to haul in. Braced in the bows, Jack straightened up and gave Hector a ragged salute, which I repeated from the stern, and we saw a brief, wide grin split Hector's dark face before he turned away. Then Jack sat down to the oars and began to pull.

Half an hour later, we stood on the *Phoenix* quarterdeck with short, sturdy Captain Redmond puffing over to greet us. His round face ruddy with interest under cropped, curly red hair, he ordered up toweling and a dry shirt for Jack.

"We despaired of ever seeing you, Mr. Malcolm," the captain exclaimed, addressing Jack by the name he'd given. "It grew so late, and we dared not risk losing the tide."

"My apologies, Captain," Jack smiled back. "We were detained."

"And I must confess, sir, I was not expecting a lady," Redmond went on, with a polite nod at me. "Did you not tell me—"

"Change of plans, I'm afraid," Jack explained. "I expected to travel with my cousin this morning, but at the last minute, my wife decided to make the trip with me. Mrs. Malcolm," he added, nodding at me, "allow me to introduce Captain Redmond."

"I hope we'll not be too great an inconvenience, Captain," I murmured.

"Why, by no means, madame!" the captain cried. "It's my very great pleasure to escort such a charming passenger!"

He made me a gallant little bow, to which I responded

with a demure nod and smile. I'd already endured the indignity of being hoisted aboard in a bosun's chair thrown over the side, instead of climbing up the rope ladder like a sensible person. Despite my plain clothing and the dishevelment of my braided hair—which I'd hastily bound up in the boat—I could continue to play the genteel lady until we were well beyond the reach of any boats from the shore.

"Ought to have a fair passage of it, too, Ma'am," the captain continued, glancing up at the emerging blue of the sky. "Now that this dam . . . er, cursed fog is lifting. I do wish you'd sent us word, Mr. Malcolm, and we'd have held the boat for you."

"As a matter of fact, there was a bit of a dust-up ashore, Captain," Jack replied, with brazen cool. "Someone set the watch upon me."

"The devil, you say! Whatever for?"

"Fellow owes me money." Jack shrugged.

Captain Redmond nodded in sympathy. "Disgraceful, what some folk will do to get out of a debt, eh?"

"And something else that might interest you, Captain," Jack added. "There was talk of pirates in the bay this morning, after your boat hauled away. Flying British colors, as bold as you please. You might want to keep a sharp lookout."

"Thank you, sir, I shall do that." Captain Redmond nodded, a boyish light dawning in his blue eyes. "Pirates, eh?" And he bustled off to order the sails trimmed for faster sailing.

The *Phoenix* stood out of Road Bay for Drake's Channel and the Caribbean Sea beyond. Wind-burned sailors swarmed over the decks and rigging, singing out at the yards and sheets as the sails bellied and shivered in the breeze. Itching with inactivity, Jack and I stood at the port rail, amidships, between the fore and main shrouds. I was wondering how much longer I could master the urge to hike up my skirts and climb into the top to taste the wind. It seemed so odd to be standing here, idle, like a female. A civilized female.

I gazed out toward the green smudges of islets and cays that made up the Virgins. On which one had we been marooned? But the too-vivid memory of Jack—pale and shaking and close to death—made me shudder, even now, and I crept closer to him at the rail, seeking the reassurance of his warmth and strength. He slipped his arm around my shoulders; holding each other had become second nature to us. And I realized how little the destination mattered, as long as I had Jack safe and whole beside me.

"Did you mean it," he asked, after a while, "when you said you had everything you wanted?"

"Of course I did." I thought back to my first ship, when I was a frightened runaway aboard the *New Hope*, sick and freezing in the bottom of the gig. What had I expected to find, back then? "When I ran away from Boston, I thought I wanted so much," I went on softly. "Freedom, adventure, romance, I don't know what all. But when I almost lost you, I realized how little I really need. Someone to love who loves me. It seems so simple, now."

"That's the most idle romantic foolery I have ever heard," Jack declared.

"Aye, isn't it?" I laughed. "But no less true."

"And what about your freedom?"

"Would I be more free if I were alone?" I inched closer. "I don't see how it can compromise my freedom to share life with the man I love."

"I hope we can make a life of it, Rusty," Jack murmured. "I haven't performed for my living since I was a boy, and these islands are not as prosperous as they once were. It might be hard going, at times."

"Then we'll work hard." Hard work rewarded, hadn't that been my fortune? Our fortune. Or was Jack himself my fortune, the *sota de oros*, my Jack of Coins? Hard work had won me Jack, against all odds. Anything was possible. The life that stretched before us now was an ocean of possibilities as wide and varied as the gem-colored Caribbean. And I was glad to be sailing out to meet it, come what may.

"You don't mind a future so . . . unsettled?" Jack wondered.

"I'm glad of any future at all. And I like the element of surprise."

Captain Redmond had just wheeled over to pay his respects when the maintop lookout cried, "Sail, ho! Off the port quarter, sir!"

A boy ran up to the captain with a glass, but our practiced eyes could already discern a dark speck of sails behind us, emerging out of the fog that still hugged the shore. She was making excellent speed on the same breeze that drove the *Phoenix,* and I felt the current of tension crackling through the crew. But Captain Redmond only laughed and ordered more sail.

"She's flying British colors, sir," reported the lookout. "Signalling us to come about."

"As well she might, the vixen," chortled the captain. "Wouldn't expect her to fly the skull and bones so close to shore. But we'll outrun her, yet!" He ordered the men to the braces. "Never was a damned pirate, oh, excuse my language, Ma'am, as could catch the *Phoenix!*"

He leaned over the side, as excited as a boy, calling out commands as the sleek barque began to pull away from the little vessel, now very far back in pursuit. I closed my eyes, enjoying the speed of the ship and the spray in my face, and when I opened them again, the little speck in the distance had all but vanished. When the captain straightened up again, his rosy face was wreathed in radiant good cheer for his passengers.

"Never you fear, now, Ma'am. No blasted pirate has ever set foot upon the *Phoenix,* and none ever shall!"

As he bustled away, I dared to catch Jack's eye, and the bland innocence in his expression triggered a sudden eruption of laughter I could scarcely contain.

"Take that gleam out of your eye, Rusty, or you'll make a liar out of our Captain Redmond," Jack advised, his voice very low, but it was too late. My first giggles were already leaking out, and it was all I could do to hide my face in Jack's shirt and pray my shaking might be taken for a case of female nerves.

"It's a lucky thing no seafaring man would ever take a

woman for a pirate, or we'd be in leg irons by now," Jack observed, his mouth very close to my ear, making me laugh even harder. "Don't be timid, Rusty, I believe there are still two or three fellows off in the stern who haven't yet noticed you cackling like Blackbeard over here . . . ah, yes, there's the mate just gone off down the hatch to fetch the shackles."

With a heroic effort, I managed to get hold of myself. When I dared to raise my face, still flushed with laughter, Jack was grinning at me.

"You are an absolute disgrace, Mistress Lightfoot," he whispered, gently wiping tears of laughter off my cheek with his thumb. Then he kissed me.

I turned to face the sea again, leaning back in Jack's embrace as his arms crept around me. We were quiet for a while as the last of the green Virgins finally fell away astern and a stretch of open sea lay before us.

"We'll soon be in the Leewards, if the wind holds," Jack ventured, after a while. "Where shall we go first?"

I smiled up at him.

"Surprise me."

Historical Note

At the end of the War of 1812 and the Napoleonic wars, international commerce began to thrive again in the waters of the Caribbean Sea. This coincided with the revolt of the South American colonies against Spain, providing lucrative opportunities for seafaring rogues of all nations to sign on as privateers out of rebel ports like Caracas and Buenos Aires. Much of their activity was centered around the island of Cuba, near the principal shipping lanes to and from Europe. Few of these vessels bothered to confine their looting to the merchant shipping of Spain alone, and they were tacitly protected by the authorities in Havana, who earned a tidy commission on plunder sold there at auction.

The trade became so brisk, the privateering ships were joined by growing numbers of runaway slaves, fisherfolk and other dispossessed islanders on their own account, mounting guerrilla attacks from hidden lagoons and shallows along the Cuban coast. Conflicting reports on the death of a notorious pirate captain called Diabolito suggest that more than one pirate adopted this celebrated name for himself, or was so called by his victims.

The United States saw its commercial interests in the West Indies imperiled by the pirates of Cuba at the same time that its fledgling Navy, overstocked with heroes from the late war and facing drastic postwar cutbacks, found itself with nothing much to do. A war on the pirates seemed like the perfect solution to both problems. The first West India Squadron, consisting of three ships, was sent out by President James Monroe in 1819 under the command of the renowned Commodore Oliver Hazard Perry, who succumbed to yellow fever after two months in the service.

Commodore David Porter was another hero in the War of 1812, capturing British warships off the coast of South America aboard the frigate Essex. In February of 1823, he was appointed to command the West India Squadron. Naval ships and officers had continued to skirmish against pirates since 1819, but Porter set out with a most impressive fleet of twelve warships—including one steamship and the armed supply ship *Decoy* and five river barges.

In his twenty-one months in the service, Porter did indeed survive two bouts of the deadly yellow fever that decimated his crews, crippled his fleet and sent him home to the States twice to recuperate. The raid by unknown marauders on an American-owned warehouse on the island of St. Thomas also occurred, and it cost Porter his command. When one of Porter's squadron ships sailed off in pursuit across the channel to Fajardo on Puerto Rico, her captain went ashore in civilian clothing and was detained for an entire day by the Alcalde, who denounced him as a pirate and threatened him with imprisonment before finally ordering him to depart the island. When Porter heard of this outrage against his officer, he sailed to Fajardo himself with three warships; he spiked the guns in the battery overlooking the beach, marched into the town and forced the Alcalde to write a formal apology. But Porter's impulsive action was considered arrogant back home and he was recalled from his command in December of 1824.

The squadron raid on the hidden pirate lagoon near

Cabo Cruz and the burning of the pirate boats and village took place in July of 1823. The incident was recorded in the journal of Lieutenant David G. Farragut, later the renowned Civil War Admiral, who was a junior officer on the expedition and Porter's young protégé.

All other characters and incidents in this book are fictional—as far as I know.